The Last Wayfinder

THE LAST WAYFINDER

BENJAMIN BOEKWEG

Heralds of Life

To request permission, contact the author at
contact@benjaminboekweg.com

Hardcover ISBN-13: 979-8-9861442-2-1
E-Book ISBN-13: 979-8-9861442-3-8

Library of Congress Control Number: 2022915196

First printed edition September 2022

Cover design by: GetCovers
Illustrations by: Adesh Pal
Printed in the United States of America

benjaminboekweg.com

To my Annie, who encouraged me to shoot for the stars.

Acknowledgments

I want to thank my beloved wife, Ann. Thank you for always believing in me and encouraging me. Thank you for giving me the space to write and for reading my early drafts and for offering the necessary criticism. Without you, these stories would still be slumbering away in the recesses of my imagination instead of soaring across the pages.

I want to thank my father-in-law, Jim, for being interested in my stories. Thank you for your insights and suggestions, they have given this story a great flavor.

I also want to thank Apartworks on Fiverr. Your illustrations have added such great character to the scenes. You were excellent to work with. Thank you.

And finally, thank you to Louis L'Amour. Even though you can't read my gratitude in the flesh, I am thankful to you for your novels teaching me the Western genre.

A NOTE TO THE READER

This story was originally written and released in small episodes a couple of weeks apart. Because of this, some repetition of events and concepts was written to remind the readers of what took place two weeks ago, so they wouldn't need to re-read the last episode to fully understand the new one. Much of that repetition has been removed for this publication, but some still remain.

Episode List

Prologue

Chip Hossk paced back and forth across the cold cement floor, his heart pounding in his chest. The dim lamp overhead provided the only light in the warehouse. It was too dangerous to keep a lot of light on. It would attract the wrong kind of attention.

"Shouldn't he be here by now?" he impatiently asked.

"Relax, Mr. Hossk. He still has another two minutes."

The gruff ugly man to his left didn't seem at all concerned with how badly this hand-off could go. More money should have been spent to hire a mercenary of a higher caliber. Hiring a Kuda would have been preferable; at least they took their profession seriously. Too bad the Kuda were too recognizable. This hand-off needed to be as low-key as possible. So, Krem—as unprofessional as he was—would have to do.

"I told you not to address me by name."

"It ain't like we're secret agents or nothin'. You're just scared they'll find out."

"Of course, I am! They have ruined the last three operations."

Krem stood, hearing footsteps in the distance. "This must be Nymm."

Chip stopped pacing. "About time! Where have you—"

The tall figure stepped into the light. It wasn't Nymm. This man's long coat swayed as he walked. His wide-brimmed hat obscured his face with a shadow. The scratches and scuffs on his tall boots attested to rough labor. The low-hanging blast pistol holster at his side meant he was a gunfighter.

The gunfighter raised his head a little higher, allowing the low light to show his face. Chip gasped and backed up a few steps. Krem stood ready to draw. The gunfighter's face was covered by a mask that was devoid of any features except the eyes. A faint white glow emanated from them.

The mask was unmistakable. They were only worn by the Wayfinders. The pesky self-appointed do-gooders refused to turn a blind eye when they needed to. Business meant nothing to them. They knew that opening new business lines was necessary to support the Corporation. They just didn't care. How could they? They didn't understand what was necessary.

"Korr," Chip identified. "What are you doing here?"

Korr turned his masked face toward Chip and spoke with a slightly muffled voice. "You're a long way from the comforts of your plush office, Mr. Hossk. I guess you're getting desperate now."

"How much do you want?"

"I ain't for sale and you know it. I'm here to shut down your little operation for good. This time, I've got you red-handed."

"What makes you think you're gettin' out of here alive?" Krem asked with a snarl, his hand dangling close to his gun.

Korr regarded him with a dismissive glance. "Experience."

Krem drew his blast pistol and Korr's hand flashed to his side. Krem's gun cleared leather in time for an orange bolt of light from Korr's blast pistol to slice into his chest. Krem staggered, dropping his gun and falling to the floor.

Korr turned the barrel of his blast pistol toward Chip. "You can reach for your gun, or you can reach for the sky."

Chip reluctantly raised his hands. "You'll pay for this."

"What makes you think you're in any position to make threats?"

"You think you've won? Well, let me tell you, Korr, this little war between us is just beginning. I have powerful allies. And we're gonna take you down. And I don't just mean you, I'm talking about the entire collapse of the Wayfinders! Do you hear me? Every last one of you!"

"Then, for your sake, you'd better hope you get us all. For if even one Wayfinder remains, you will fall like Goliath of old."

EPISODE 1

I should have said no

1

I SHOULD HAVE SAID NO

Of all the places for a pick-up, why did it have to be Cosstere? Was she trying to get us killed? Let us forget that Cosstere was a dry, rugged rock tumbling through space. Just because it rotated around a star and had a breathable atmosphere did not mean it should be called a planet. To me, it was just another rock on the edge of civilization. But that wasn't what made Cosstere dangerous. It was home to the Davendries.

The Davendries were not much more than a band of thugs. They were too big to fizzle out over time and too small for the thinly-stretched marshals to bother with. In these parts, the only law that people respected was the one that came out of the barrel of a gun. But still, I go where the money takes me. In the end, a job was still a job. And as long as there was work, I could afford to fuel my starship and feed my falcon.

A light blinked on my console followed by an alarm. I leaned forward in my seat. The blasted Davendries were on an intercept course. I'd have to take the *Princess* off autopilot soon. She was a Norgon-class passenger transport. She was still very agile for her age. And in this territory, speed was what mattered most. Her name was *Astral Princess*, but I called her the *Princess.*

I was able to talk my way out of the last encounter, but my luck never did hold out long. The falcon squawked on her perch to my left. She was the other lady in my life. In fact, I named her Lady. She no longer looked like the dying rescue project she was when I found her. Her feathers had grown back and her little body had accepted the cybernetic implants. If you're going to fix something, why not fix it and then some, I always say. I guess you could call them enhancements, but they saved her life.

I turned to Lady. "No need to get excited. I see them."

She squawked again.

"There's only two of them this time and I'm not going to make that mistake again." Even if she couldn't understand me, she was still a better conversationalist than the *Astral Princess.* All I got from the *Princess* was error messages now and again.

I flipped the switch, taking the *Princess* off autopilot, and grabbed the flight controls. I flipped on the communication channel. It was better to be proactive than reactive. "Unidentified crafts, this is Alder one-one-seven. You are trespassing in Cosstere orbital space. You are ordered to cease and desist."

"That's my line, stranger," a gruff voice responded.

It didn't surprise me they didn't fall for my little bravado. Only the inexperienced raiders were intimidated by the authority-sounding chatter. It was time for plan B. "Well, somebody had to say it. You boys sure aren't on your game today."

"Don't get smart with me," he said. "Prepare to be boarded."

"There ain't enough time; they'll be here soon," I said, hoping that would spark their imaginations.

"Who'll be here?"

I smiled. They took the bait. Now to make it sound convincing. "Look, I'll split it with you, but I get a finder's fee."

"How 'bout you tell us who's comin' before we blast you right here."

"Hey hey hey, chill the engines. There are enough high-profile passengers to line everybody's pockets. I just think it's only fair I get a finder's fee."

"Well, in the spirit of fairness," the gruff voice replied. "We'll give you to the count of ten to get outta here before we blast your backside into rubble."

It was almost too easy. But I still needed to sell my performance a little more. "Now wait a minute!"

"Two, four, six..."

"All right! I'm goin'! I'm goin'!" I said. I winked at Lady and accelerated to maximum thrust toward the planet. As entertaining as that was, it also meant they'd be disappointed when they found out it was all a lie. I'd have to remember to make a run for it on the way out. The typical experience for Cosstere. Hence, why I ain't so fond of this place.

The *Princess* passed through the atmosphere and streaked across the light orange sky. The red sun was up, which meant the yellow sun had set. The red sun gave the barren landscape an orange hue. Not dark or cold enough to be called night, but it was the closest Cosstere had to offer. I glanced down at my screen. We were coming right up on the rendezvous coordinates.

Lady squawked.

"You see somethin'?" I asked, looking down at the fast-approaching ground. A large camcam was walking along with two people on its back. I never did like camcams. Those smelly overgrown lizards were too difficult to control. Well, except for Miri. I'd swear she was an animal charmer. It seemed anything you threw reigns on, she could ride. And though she was also handy with a mag-wrench, her difficulty was with starships. Needless to say, she and the *Princess* didn't get along very well.

"That's a good eye, Lady; you spotted them. Looks like we're right on time."

I pulled back on the throttle and engaged the landing thrusters. The *Princess* was fast all right, but she was rather rough on the take-off and landing. I gripped the steering controls as she shuddered during her descent. She set down with a light *thump.* I climbed out of my chair and walked to the door at the side of the cockpit. I turned back to Lady. "Well, are you comin' or what?"

She flew to my arm.

I stroked her feathered head before exiting the ship. Miri was outside waiting for me. She had already dismounted the smelly beast and walked up to the *Princess's* ramp. She wore her curly black hair down—which I hadn't seen in years—and she wore black pants with that long shirt that came down to her knees. It was the kind of outfit that was as close to wearing a dress as one dared in these parts. She looked mighty pretty, which was dangerous on Cosstere.

"On time as usual," she said.

"I aim to make good time in these parts," I replied, putting my hat on. "Okay, what's goin' on?"

"After two years, that's the only hello I'm going to get?"

"Miri, you don't gussy up for casual business. You're wantin' me to be sweet on you because I reckon you got some unfortunate news."

She scowled. "I need to get this girl back to her parents." She motioned to the scrawny beanpole beside her. Her long disheveled blond hair and dirty face made it clear she hadn't bathed for some time. She couldn't have been more than ten years old.

"Well then, climb aboard and we'll get underway," I said, motioning toward the ramp.

"There's just one thing," she said, biting her lower lip.

I sighed. "What is it?"

"Her parents are on this planet."

"Then what did you call me for?" I asked, grumbling. "I'm a transport pilot, not a tour guide."

"You're a Wayfinder," she said, letting her desperation seep into her voice.

I marched a few steps closer and put a finger to my lips. "Lower your voice about that. Those days are long since dead."

Desperation befell her face. "My memory of those days is very much alive, as are your skills."

"If they find out I'm still alive—"

"Nobody has to know. I just need you, Rence. Please."

I always had a tough time sayin' no when she dressed up and pleaded. Lady squawked, perched on my arm. I looked at her. "You too, huh?"

I turned back to Miri. Her pleading eyes and pretty hair were more than a match for me. The problem was that I knew it was trouble. She wouldn't need a Wayfinder if it was as simple a task as she made it sound. She was right about one thing; my skills were very much alive. Being a Wayfinder for twenty years is not something that a person forgets.

I sighed. "Take me to where you found her."

Miri smiled and motioned toward her reeking lizard. "There's room enough on my camcam."

We mounted the camcam and for the next half hour, it lumbered through the rocky barren terrain. The red sun glowed in the cloudless orange sky. The dusk breeze blew across my face. The cool temperature of the wind was refreshing but I had to keep my mouth closed. It kept blowing little bits of gritty sand in my mouth.

"We're almost there," she said over her shoulder.

"Does this kid have a name?" I asked.

"...well, I call her Ryna."

"You call her? What did her parents name her?" I asked.

"I don't think she knows," she said.

That wasn't a very good answer and I wasn't about to let her get away with it. "How about I ask it a different way? What did she tell you when you asked her what her name is?"

She brushed a lock of hair over one ear. "The tall one."

"The tall one?" I said, eyes widening.

She nodded. "Yep."

I shrugged. "Ryna it is."

Miri pulled back on the reigns and the slow-moving camcam halted. Four men in front of us were turning over the wreckage of a hoverwagon, pilfering what they could find. They stopped when they noticed the camcam's approach. Straightening up, they walked toward us side by side.

"I know these men," Miri said. "They're scavengers. I'll go talk to them."

I didn't like that idea one bit. "Why bother? We can go around them."

"This is the wreckage where I found Ryna." She slid over the side of the camcam and landed on her feet. She strolled over to them with an air of indifference about her. She was playing her cards right; indifference meant you were not afraid.

I turned to Lady and stroked her feathery head. "Stay low until you're a ways off, you hear?" I tossed my arm toward the back of the camcam and Lady leaped from my arm and soared low back the way we had come.

I turned back to watch Miri's handiwork. She continued to talk with them, waving her hands as she spoke. Then one of the men stepped forward and touched her hair. She backed up and talked faster. It clearly unnerved her, to say nothing about angering me. I inched my hand toward my blast pistol and unfastened the safety strap. There was no reason for this to turn into a shootout, but I wasn't taking any chances. Something wasn't right about those men; I could smell it.

One of the men laughed out loud and grabbed Miri, dragging her back toward their hoverwagon. The other three drew their blast pistols and shot at me. My gun had barely cleared leather before a hot bolt of green plasma hit me square in the chest. I tumbled backward over the rump of the smelly camcam and slid down the tail. It had been a long time since anyone shot before I did. I was out of practice.

Hearing Miri's scream got my blood pumping hot and fierce. I scrambled to my feet and drew my second blast pistol in less than a heartbeat. I squeezed off a few shots, watching my red bolts streak through the air and tear into one of the men. He dropped his gun, clutching his belly, and fell to the ground. The remaining men hightailed it with Miri to their hoverwagon. They sped off into the distance, shooting as they went.

I kept ducking the green bolts while sending back a few red ones. But it was no use. They were used to quick escapes, by the look of it. The lumbering camcam wasn't about to catch up to a hoverwagon. I turned back to the awful-smelling lizard and found the pistol I dropped.

"Why did they take her?" Ryna asked.

I spun around to find her behind me. She already knew her way on and off a camcam.

Her wide child eyes seemed to plead for an understanding of what had happened. "Did they want her because she is special, too?"

"She is special to me," I replied. "But that ain't why they took her."

"Then...why take her?"

"They took her because she is pretty."

She looked down. "I hope I am never pretty."

If my blood wasn't runnin' hot before it was boiling then. What kind of man creates a world where a young girl wishes never to be pretty? Any place that made beauty something to victimize wasn't worth spittle beneath a man's boot. These men's crimes didn't end with kidnapping or with what they planned to do with Miri. "Now you listen to me, little miss. There ain't nothin' wrong with bein' pretty. You got as much right to bein' pretty as the suns do of shining."

A tear rolled down her cheek. "But then why did they take her?"

How was I to explain? If I was in the right state of mind, I probably would have told her that beauty was rare in these parts. And that some people try to take it without asking. But that wasn't what escaped my lips. I dropped to one knee and looked into her blue eyes. "Because they got a death wish."

She gazed into my eyes, searching for something. Then she glanced down at my shirt and pointed. "You got shot."

I fingered the burn mark on my chest. "Not to worry, little miss. That can be repaired."

"Does it hurt?"

A red flashing light on my wristband distracted me. I smiled. "Good work, Lady."

I lifted Ryna onto the back of the camcam and climbed up the rope ladder. I sat in front of her and she wrapped her arms around me to hold on. I snapped the reigns and kicked my heels. The dumb brute snorted and sniffed the ground for something to munch. I never did like camcams. But desperate times called for desperate measures. So, I drew my blast pistol and shot the end of its tail. The brute reared back. I clung to the reigns and onto Ryna's arms. When its front feet returned to the ground it rushed forward with impressive speed. The wind passed my face and threatened to pull off my hat.

Well, I'll be, I thought. *Who'd have thought all I needed was a blast pistol to ride one of these?* The camcam veered off the road and into the rough mountain rubble. I yanked the reins to the left but the brute ignored me. I tried again but to no avail. My breathing increased and my blood pumped faster. We were on a runaway camcam and it might have been *slightly* my fault.

I pulled back on the reins as hard as I could. The beast shook his head, loosening my grip. It plowed onward through the lifeless wilderness.

"What's happening?" Ryna asked. There was panic in her voice.

"I spooked the camcam and it won't listen to me!" I explained, speaking over the noise of the stampeding lizard.

Ryna removed one hand from around me and touched the camcam. "It's okay," she said. "Everything is fine."

It was a cute gesture, but I didn't think it had a prayer's chance of stopping the brute. The breeze caught the brim of my hat and lifted it into the air. I snatched it with my free hand and planted it atop my head. Then the camcam slowed to a canter and then to a lazy walk.

"That's a good boy," she said, removing her hand.

I looked at her oddly. She couldn't seriously be taking credit for stopping the camcam, could she? Then again, she had been traveling with Miri. I figured I'd let it slide. No sense in telling a young girl she wasn't the cause of stopping the camcam. If thinking like that made her feel like she was contributing, I was fine with that. I tugged the reigns to the left and the dumb brute actually turned left that time. I was grateful, but I still would have preferred a hoverwagon any day of the week.

Ryna tugged on my shirt sleeve. "Hey mister, I don't think he likes it when you shoot his tail."

I glanced back at her. "I reckon we both figured that one out real quick."

I looked at my wristband. The tracking beacon on Lady was still active. We followed her signal for the better part of an hour before we started getting close. And the only way we could have been getting close was if they had stopped. I pulled back on the reigns and the lumbering reptile halted.

"Why did we stop?" she asked.

"We're close," I said. "And I want to sneak in all quiet-like." I reached into the inside pocket of my long coat and pulled out my mask.

"What is that?"

"You sure ask a lot of questions."

She looked up at me. "That was only two questions."

"Well, you got me there. It's my tactical mask. It filters the air I breathe and lets me see things I normally can't see."

"Like what?"

"You remember that falcon of mine? Lady?"

She nodded.

"It can let me see what she sees, among other things." I fastened it on, tightened the straps, and put my hat back on. I turned back to her. "My voice will sound a little strange now, but don't be alarmed."

She nodded again.

I pressed another button on my wristband. My eyesight turned completely black for a split second. Then I saw through Lady's eyes. Her vantage point was high in the air. I saw a rusted metal compound below along with four parked hoverwagons. The parameter seemed vacant. It was an amateur gang that didn't expect anyone to come after them. That would change after tonight. I pressed the button again, switching back to my natural eyesight. I slid off the camcam. "Stay here, little miss. I am going to fetch Miri and bring her back."

"I want to come," she protested.

"Stay with the camcam. I don't want to have to watch out for you, too."

I drew my blast pistols and started up the embankment toward the compound. The terrain was rocky and the breeze was kicking up little patches of dust into the air. With the twin suns, there would be no cover of darkness. Seeing me coming was a guarantee. Speed was all that counted now. Once I poked my head over the rise and saw the compound, I sprinted toward it.

Large green bolts of light streaked through the air at me. They weren't really made of light. They were discharged energy plasma—though that might have been over-simplifying it. It was simpler to call them bolts of light, or blast bolts. One hit the ground in front of me. It kicked up a burst of sand and small pebbles. My mask protected me from the small flying debris. I fired a few shots back, not aiming at anything. It was to keep the other fellers from taking time to aim.

As I got closer to the compound, they stopped shooting. Were they retreating? Not likely. It was too soon for that. A huge green bolt of energy shot out from the compound window and struck the ground a few feet in front of me. The explosion launched me high into the air. It was about then I figured they stopped shooting to watch the blast cannon fire at me. On the way back down, I knew it was going to hurt. I braced for the impact and landed with a dusty *thud.* It took me a few seconds to breathe again. The wind had been completely knocked out of me. My neck ached, and my ears rang. That was too close. A foot or two closer and the concussion wave would have ruptured my internal organs.

For a brief second, I contemplated playing dead. But then again, if I were the cannon operator, I'd want more playtime behind the trigger and shoot again. I scrambled to my feet and dashed off toward the compound wall. I tapped a few buttons on my wristband, running the instant replay of the cannon shot before my left eye. It wasn't smart to run while both eyes were distracted. So, I got into the habit of only playing video replays to one of my eyes. The video playback showed the cannon bolt coming from the second-story window. And judging by the angle, I figured the shooter was about four feet back and off to the right.

As I dashed toward the wall I pointed my blast pistol at the window, aiming, and fired. I didn't have time to look to see if my shot struck the enemy shooter; the other men continued shooting at me. The ringing in my ears started to wear off, giving me some rudimentary sound back. It had been rather disconcerting not to be able to hear the battle. I reached the compound wall and jumped. The robotic implants in my knees gave me a large boost of height. They also softened my landing on the roof.

I heard shouting coming from within the compound. They were scared now. That was good. That meant they wouldn't kill Miri and instead hold her hostage as a bargaining chip. That meant her life was safe for now. But it would not stay that way if they managed to kill me. I still had to be cautious. I scanned the surface of the roof, looking for an easy entrance down. There weren't any. Not even a skylight. *Well,* I thought, *I'll just have to make one.*

I pulled out a small detonator from my coat pocket. It was a number three detonator, only half as strong as a number two, but a whole lot cheaper. I pressed the center button and the red light started blinking. It was a ten-second countdown–at least that was the factory standard timer. I always broke open all mine and readjusted the timer to nine seconds. If anyone stole my detonators, I'd rather it be the last thing they stole.

I dropped the detonator where I stood and bolted to the other end of the roof. The explosion shook the compound and blasted a nice-sized hole. It was large enough for two men to comfortably fit through. I ran back to the hole and hopped down inside. My mask allowed me to see through the smoke that billowed up through the hole. I looked around and saw debris littering the floor. A few chairs toppled over. Even the body of the unfortunate soul that stood beneath the explosion. A colorful scrap of fabric caught my attention. The blue color was charred and spoiled. It was Miri's shirt. The fancy blue one with floral designs which came down almost like a dress. I hadn't even considered that she would be on the upper floor. How careless I had been. I shoved aside fallen debris and broken furniture, searching for her body.

"Miri!"

I pushed aside a fallen roof support beam and saw a charred body. Neither the body nor the clothing was recognizable; it had been too close to the explosion. I froze at the sight. After all the robotic replacements, I was still human; fallible, and imperfect. Why didn't I think before I acted? There would be no time to mourn for her now. Those thugs had climbed the stairs and begun shooting at me.

A cold heaviness tugged at the pit of my stomach. My eyes threatened tears. I ducked behind a pillar, but I had no desire to shoot back. My thought kept returning to Miri. Those were thoughts that would get me killed. But then again, did I deserve to live now? Was my life still worth saving? I didn't get the chance to answer those questions. My combat training took over and I shot back at my opponents. They were maneuvering around hoping to pin me down.

I needed to move and I needed to move now. I looked up at the hole in the ceiling. The thought to retreat was the most logical one, but my heavy emotions got the better of me. Even though it was my fault, I wanted those thugs to pay for Miri's death. After all, I had the right to place some of the blame on them for putting her in the situation in the first place. My heart raced and my breathing accelerated. It was showtime.

I bolted from behind the pillar to the closest side of the room, shouting the only word I had on my mind. "Miri!"

"Rence!" a faint voice shouted from below the stairwell. It was Miri's voice. A feeling of gratitude swelled inside me and a rush of relief coursed through my veins. A deep breath forced its way into my lungs and a lone tear broke free from my eye. My mask hid any traces of the tear, for which

I was grateful. A renewed sense of hope poured into me like a warm cup of tea down my throat.

I unloaded my blast pistols at them, shot after shot. First the left one, then the right one, and so on, taking one step forward after every couple of shots. The men cursed and backed up, ducking behind cover. I laid down enough fire to keep them ducked behind furniture and cabinets. When I got close enough, I leaped over a counter. The man that hid there had a plastered expression of surprise on his face. I promptly swatted him across the face with the barrel of my blast pistol. His head smacked up against the neighboring wall and he fell to the ground.

A few green blast bolts flew past my face. I ducked and backed up a few feet. Then I hopped back over the counter and scurried over to the other wall. I wasn't sure if the other feller saw me or not, so I wasted no time. I dashed forward at full speed down the length of the room. The man popped his head up from behind a fallen support beam and shot at me. I fired back, striking him in the head.

I crashed into the far wall to stop my momentum from the sprint. Both men were down, so I pulled the power cell from each of my blast pistols in turn, inspecting how many shots I had left. I still had a good twenty or so shots remaining. Hopefully, that would be enough. I ran into the stairwell and bounded over the railing, dropping to the ground floor. My enhanced knees absorbed the impact of the fall. I had expected to be met with more enemy fire, but the three men in the other room were not shooting.

I tapped a few settings on my wristband and adjusted my eyesight to infrared. There were only four people in the room. They huddled around Miri, trying to use her as a shield. A part of her pretty shirt was torn away. That was where the burnt scrap of cloth came from. Most likely torn while trying to handle her.

The man in the center, directly behind Miri had brown hair and a scar across his face. The other two had tattoos on their faces. Not the best way to experiment with fashion in my opinion. The scar-faced man spoke. "If you come any closer, she gets it!"

"What makes you think I'm here for the woman?" I said. I *was* there for her but I wanted to throw a little confusion into the mix. Confusion was scary. And fear in the enemy was always a benefit to me.

"What do you want?"

"You boys shot me off the camcam and stole what belongs to me," I explained. Miri didn't really belong to me. I couldn't claim her in any setting. She and I were more or less professional acquaintances, not a married couple. But possession was the language of criminals. Telling them she was a close personal friend wouldn't mean nearly as much as saying she belonged to me.

"That was Bix who shot you," the scar-faced man explained. "And we didn't know she was yours."

"Well, you know it now," I said, with a snarl.

"Bix was upstairs, so you probably already got revenge on him. And we can return your woman," he offered.

It was always important to play the part of negotiation well. I couldn't let on what I really thought, and I had to know what thoughts swirled around in their heads. They couldn't see my facial expression behind my mask. So, I tilted my head to give the impression of consideration.

"I'll accept your offer on one condition," I said. "The woman's clothes have been spoiled. She will need compensation."

The man hastily pulled out a glowing blue bar of metal from his pocket and handed it to Miri. I holstered both of my blast pistols. One could argue it was foolish to be the first to put away a weapon. But I had more than my fair share of practice and experience drawing my pistols with speed. I was confident I could clear leather and take them all down before they could get more than one shot at me.

I beckoned to Miri and she slowly crossed the room toward me. There was terror behind her eyes but an expression of gratitude across her lips. She was in far deeper trouble than she ever expected to get on Cosstere. I could only hope she would avoid this wretched planet in the future. When she came within arm's length I motioned toward the front door. She nodded, walking more confidently, and exited.

I glanced back at the three men and tipped my hat. "Good day, boys. I trust I won't see you again."

"Never again," the scar-faced man promised.

As I crossed the front door's threshold into the red evening light, I kept one hand close to my blast pistol. The confrontation was not over yet. With my back exposed, they would be tempted to try to end our little bargain with a quick and dirty shot. At the same time, I didn't want to give them the sense that I feared them by not turning my back. Bravado and safety were always opposites. But I had a backup plan. I reached over and tapped a button on my wristband. Miri and I walked away from the compound that now looked like a partially bombed-out building.

Lady screeched from behind. I spun around with my blast pistol drawn. Lady snatched a blast pistol from the outstretched hand of one of the tattooed men. His dumbfounded expression gave way to the fear of failing to ambush a superior marksman. I fired a shot and dropped him where he stood. The scar-faced man threw his hands into the air as a silent plea. I holstered my pistol and kept walking with Miri down the embankment to the camcam. Lady circled and landed on my arm.

I stroked her feathered head. "You did real good, Lady."

Ryna scrambled down the rope ladder off the camcam and rushed into an embrace with Miri. I took off my mask and returned it to my inside coat pocket. It ran on battery power and being this far from a charging station, I didn't want to spend all its energy.

Miri turned to me with tears running down her face. She leaned in and kissed me, which took me by surprise. "Thank you," she said in a weak voice.

"Mighty welcome," I replied. I would have come up with something more clever to say if her kiss hadn't caught me off guard. She hadn't ever kissed me before; then again we hadn't ever been in a hostile situation before either. She only knew my work from the stories I told her. It wasn't until today that she had seen what I used to do.

Ryna walked over to me and tugged on my overcoat to get my attention. "Did they get their wish?"

I nodded. "All but two of them."

"I got my wish too," she said. "I wished for you to bring Miss Miri back."

I smiled. "Now if we can get you to your parents, and me off this rock, we'll all have our wishes."

We mounted the lumbering camcam again and set off back to the crash site. I still needed clues to follow. A Wayfinder could track anything as long as there was a clue to start from. And Korr, my trainer, had been the very best tracker. Once we arrived at the site of the wreckage, I slid off the back of the camcam and readjusted my hat. The morning sun peeked over the horizon as the evening sun was setting. The temperature was not far from heating up fast.

"I was right," Miri said.

I turned to her. "About what?"

"About needing a Wayfinder."

I reluctantly grinned. She was right. Any fool with an ounce of book learning could figure out how to track. But assaulting a fortified compound and fighting armed thugs to rescue her was a tall order for anything less than a Wayfinder.

"What's a Wayfinder?" Ryna asked, wrinkling her brow.

Miri pointed to me. "That's a Wayfinder."

I snickered. "Yeah, that description is as clear as mud."

"Well, you know better than I do," she protested. "Why don't you tell her."

I stooped down to get a better look at the charred pieces of metal debris and chaotic footprints. "I'm busy."

Miri sent a glaring look in my direction before addressing Ryna's question. "I don't know a whole lot about them, but they used to be the best trackers and fighters of the outer rim colonies. They were still around when I was a little girl."

"Do they live here?" Ryna asked.

Miri shook her head. "No, they're all gone."

"Where did they go?"

Miri sighed. "Some people convinced the senate to outlaw bein' a Wayfinder."

"It was the Westward Galactic Financial Corporation," I said over my shoulder.

Miri turned to me. "Westward Galactic is a bank that lends to people wanting to settle in the frontier colonies. What makes you think they would want to disband the Wayfinders?"

"The Corporation was led by Chip Hossk. Hossk financed the mercenaries that hunted down the Wayfinders. Any that didn't surrender their badge and seal were killed. The Corporation spent millions of dubblins during the stand-down. That was no financial venture; it was payback for being a thorn in his side for far too long. Trust me, it was Westward Galactic."

Miri turned back to Ryna. "Anyway, they're all gone now except for Rence. He's the last one."

It was true; I was the last one. It was still hard to imagine that twenty years had passed since I was a young seventeen-year-old Wayfinder recruit. Twenty years since I was learning the ways of Aundoon the Great. I shook the memory from my mind. I dearly treasured those moments, but I needed to focus. The tracks were messy but still fresh. I turned over a large half-burned sheet of metal. It was the side paneling of the wrecked hoverwagon. Beneath it, a plastic hospital bracelet lay on the ground. I held it up to the light. "Subject thirty-five," I read aloud.

"Yes?" Ryna answered.

Miri and I looked at her.

I glanced at the plastic bracelet and then back at Ryna. "Is that your name?"

"That's what the doctors call me."

"Doctors?" I asked, my curiosity piqued.

Ryna nodded.

"That's not much of a name," I said. That was more than suspicious, it was downright incriminating. Parents that call their girl by how tall she is and doctors that call her a number were not so mysterious anymore. It was starting to add up. But, I still hoped I was wrong. I didn't want a morality issue to further complicate this mission. "How long have you known your parents?"

"Rence!" Miri said in protest. "What kind of a question is that?"

"A few days," Ryna said matter-of-factly.

Miri stared at her in disbelief.

"You should know by now," I said to Miri, "That I don't ask random questions."

Miri ignored me, still caught by Ryna's admission. "What do you mean you've only known them a few days? They're your parents. Aren't they?"

Ryna returned a confused expression.

"I'll give you a hint, Miri," I offered. "They weren't medical doctors. They were scientist doctors."

Miri looked at me blankly. She needed more time to let that sink in, so I dropped the subject and returned to the tracks in the dirt. There were several sets of tracks. After I weeded out the tracks left by those punk raiders, I determined there were three other sets of tracks. One belonged to Miri, the others didn't.

I stood and walked over to Miri. "Good news and bad. The good news is the parents survived the crash and wandered north through the canyon."

"And the bad news?" Miri asked.

"Five people followed them shortly after."

She shrugged. "More passengers?"

I shook my head. "Only four seats in that hoverwagon. They were followed by someone interested in their misfortune I'd wager."

Miri closed her eyes in exasperation and cursed under her breath.

"Find yourselves some shade," I instructed. I pulled my carbine blast rifle from the camcam saddle. I used the carbine when I needed a distance shot. It packed enough energy to send a blast bolt upwards of 700 meters. I was glad I had sense enough to pack it even though this day had promised to be a quick mission. Old preparation habits were a good thing to keep around.

"Lady, I need a bird's-eye," I said as I tossed her into the air. She fluttered high and soared over toward the horizon.

"Shade?" Miri said in confusion. "But shouldn't we follow the tracks?"

"It's approaching midday's heat, and nobody has had anything to eat for five hours."

"You can't seriously be thinking about food right now?"

"If you think it's hot now, just wait 'til the yellow sun gets directly above us. Not even the beasts of nature do much of anything in that heat," I explained. "Besides, those tracks are looking to be more than eight hours old. Whatever happened to them is long over. I'll be back with something worth eating soon. After midday passes, we'll get a start on those tracks."

With Lady's help, I was able to track down a few game birds. They were too small to snipe with my carbine and too skittish to get in close. So, I had Lady swoop down and grab one for us. I gave some to Lady before cleaning up the rest and cooking it. Miri turned up her nose at my cooking but politely ate it anyhow. The girl was a different story. She wolfed down the meat faster than a snake can bite. I gave her my meal, too. I figured she needed it more and I had survived for longer on much less. I could hold out. When the sun finally started its trek down to the other end of the horizon, we saddled up the camcam. We headed for a waterhole Lady had spotted during the hunt. The camcam needed water.

Five men meandered around the spring at the waterhole. Their hoverwagon had been parked nearby. They all looked to be somewhere in their twenties. Each wore a blue sash tied to their belt. The blue sash was the mark of a Davendry. I sent Lady into the air. It was time to put on my show-face. I waved and hollered to let them know we were coming. They all gathered around, watching us approach riding the slow-moving lizard.

"How's the water?" I asked, smiling.

"It's wet," one of the Davendries replied in a cross tone.

"Good," I said cheerfully. "This big lizard here needs a good waterin'."

"You best keep on goin', mister. This here spring is uh..." He smiled at a companion to his left before returning his gaze to me. "...down for maintenance. You'll just have to ride on to the next one."

I at least had the victory of getting them to dismiss us. The downside was that the tracks led to the waterhole. This meant that unless I could get a closer look, I'd not be able to tell where the tracks continued. There were only two options. We could continue on and circle back later hoping the Davendries had moved on. Or we could try to get them to talk and find out if they had seen anyone pass. I felt lucky.

I forced a confused expression. "But Lily and Pete were supposed to meet us here hours ago."

They perked up; the playful superiority faded from their eyes. They scowled. "A man and a woman you say?"

I didn't like the way they stared one bit. It told me more than I expected it to. They had seen the girl's parents all right. They looked like children who had been caught with their hands in the cookie jar–in a marauding bandit sort of way. There was something else in their eyes. Some piece of the story they didn't want to share. Did they kill Ryna's parents? Did they know what happened to them? I needed to know. But I also wanted to avoid a shoot-out as much as possible with Miri and Ryna so close. I figured I'd drop a little gunfighter lingo into my talk. Just enough to dissuade them from openly attacking. I smiled and nodded. "Yup, as sure as shootin'. Have you seen them around?"

The Davendry smirked. "Yeah, I guess you could say they're guests of the Davendries."

That much told me Ryna's parents were alive. But I still needed to know where they were being held. I smiled wide. "All righty! Bring 'em on out. I'll rustle us up some game to roast and we can all eat."

Another Davendry rolled his eyes. "They're in orbit, you ninny."

I suppressed my smile and forced another confused look. "Well, then how am I supposed to meet up with them?"

"You don't, old man!" the first Davendry said. "Now git out of here before we roast you!"

I put up my hands. "Okay, okay. We're goin'."

"Hey Pim," the second Davendry said, pointing to Ryna. "Ain't that the girl the Corp was askin' about?"

Pim, the Davendry I was just talking with, smiled and drew his blast pistol. "Come on down from the camcam, stranger. We're gonna want a closer look at that young'un you got there."

Blast! And here I was thinking I could avoid another shoot-out. If they were on the lookout for Ryna, then they had to have a photo or a description they could match her up with. I quickly scanned the scene. All five wore a blast pistol at their hip. And all five of them wore their blast belt low enough to allow for a quick draw. These men were trained gunfighters. If I had the drop on them, I'd have a good chance, but they already had a barrel trained on me. How could I protect Miri and Ryna? If I had to be judicious with my movements, I couldn't keep them from the line of fire. Maybe I needed to play the fool for a little longer.

"Hey, hey, hey! Put that thing away. If you want an introduction, I'll oblige you." I climbed down from the smelly lizard. Incidentally, the hot sun didn't help its smell any. I turned to Pim with my hands up. "C'mon, put that thing away; we're all friends here."

Pim looked at me suspiciously but he did holster his gun.

I relaxed my arms.

"What's that flashin' light on your wrist?" the short feller asked.

I looked at my wristband. Lady was signaling that she was in position. "Oh, that? That means it's time for me to take my medication. But I can get to that when we've all got acquainted." I walked to the other end of the camcam and looked up at Miri. "All right, Sue. These boys want to have a look at little Loretta."

Miri eyed me with a worried expression but started climbing down with Ryna. She was scared but she trusted me. I would do everything in my power to make sure her trust in me was well-founded. As Miri and Ryna descended the rope ladder, I glanced to either side as inconspicuously as I could. All eyes were on them. They would only be distracted until Miri and Ryna were on the ground. This was my only opportunity. I bent my special knees and jumped backward. I flew across the spring of water and landed on the other side. Both my pistols cleared leather as the Davendries turned around. My first two shots each dropped a Davendry before the return fire came. I dove behind a large rock, squeezing off a few more shots. The remaining three Davendries scattered for cover.

Pim ran behind the only standing tree. The short feller dove between the camcam's legs—only a desperate man runs between the legs of a giant lizard. The pale-faced feller ducked behind a large rock and started shooting back at me. I put on my mask. I would need the enhanced vision to pull off these tricky shots. Pim motioned to the pale-faced one who started moving from rock to rock, keeping low. He was going to try to circle around me. Any smart man would prioritize taking him out. But Korr trained me differently. Pim was the leader, giving instruction. I wanted to take him out first. That would mean the pale-faced one would get awful close for sure, but the rest would be easy to manipulate without their leader coordinating.

I tapped a few buttons on my wristband and my eyesight darkened. I saw green geometry lines and angles overlaying the scene. I was in luck. A small flat stone lay on the ground behind Pim. It was the correct angle to bounce my shot. But I had to hit the rock in the dead center if I wanted the shot to ricochet correctly. I fired a few haphazard shots in Pim's direction, discouraging him from taking a shot at me. Then I aimed and squeezed the trigger. My blast bolt nailed the rock and bounced, cutting into Pim's back. He jerked back and fell.

Immediately, I turned my attention back to the pale-faced one. I didn't see him anymore. My heart rate sped up. My breathing grew shallow. My old companion, adrenaline, coursed through my body. An enemy you couldn't see was a death sentence waiting to pounce. My instincts shouted at me to get away from my current position. I dove around another large rock just as a blast bolt crashed into the rock, leaving a small burn mark. Sparks flew out from where the bolt struck. I still could not see where he was shooting from. Wherever he was, he was in a good angle. It was time to flush him out. I holstered my guns and leaped high into the air toward where I figured he might be. I landed with a *thud.*

A scurry of motion from my peripheral vision caught my attention. A solid fist slammed into my face, sending me toppling backward to the ground. My mask cracked under the punch and my vision faded to black. I swatted my mask off in time to see the pale-faced Davendry lunge at me. I rolled to the side, letting him hit the dirt. I got onto my hands and knees, like a frog ready to leap. I jumped forward with added velocity, crashing into the brute with my head butting him in the stomach.

We both toppled to the ground and rolled over a few times. I had knocked the wind out of him, but he quickly recovered. This suggested he was a scrapper by nature, well versed in fistfights. When our rolling stopped, he was on top, strangling me. I slapped my hands against both of his ears, causing his ears to ring. He flinched but still clung to my neck. I considered striking his ears again, but I only had seconds before I passed out. I couldn't be sure a second hit to his eardrums would work. I needed to get the man off me quick. I reached back and felt the ground. My fingers found a sizable rock. I struck the pale-faced feller and he let go. I rolled over, toppling him over to my side. I drew my blast pistol and ended him. I rubbed my neck quickly and got to my feet.

"Hold it!" the short one shouted.

He held Ryna in an arm lock with his blast pistol to her head. Miri lay on the ground at his feet. The sight of Miri boiled my blood. I did have one of my blast pistols in hand, but it was pointed down while his was pointed at her head. I was fast enough on the draw to beat a man in clearing leather, but was I faster than a man's trigger pull? It wasn't worth the gamble. Especially if it meant losing someone else's life to find out. No, I couldn't do that to the young girl. If she died, I would be just as guilty as if I pulled the trigger myself.

I stared at the man, not moving.

"Drop the gun!" he ordered.

Yeah, right, like I was going to let my Starfield & Tanner blast pistol drop to the rocky ground and risk damaging it. Starfield & Tanner pistols were more than the upper end of quality and expense. They were custom-built and took years of patience on the waiting list. I hadn't handled anything before that had shot straighter or more reliably and felt so natural in my hand. "All right," I said, raising one hand in surrender while setting my pistol on the ground.

"Back away!"

I obeyed and took a few steps back, keeping my hands where they could be seen. "So what happens now?"

He swallowed, allowing a bead of sweat to run down his face.

This one was clearly not a senior member of the gang. That gave me an advantage. The only problem was I didn't have any clear way to exploit that advantage; not while he held his gun on her. "You know what I want," I said. "And I know what you want, too."

He nervously shifted his feet.

"You want to live," I continued. "And I want to go in peace with the woman and the girl."

"Don't try anything!" he shouted.

This man must have been greener than I had thought. He seemed too scared for his own good. His eyes showed only fear. No, more than fear. This man was terrified. Emotion and logic mix about as well as oil and water. The situation called for a compromise but he was in no shape to think logically. This was going to be tricky. I still had Lady in the air. But with both of my hands held up it would look too obvious if I reached over to my wristband to call her. I could only hope she would take the initiative to strike on her own or that I could somehow calm this feller down.

I was running out of options and the man's hand started to tremble. If I didn't do something quick, his nervousness alone would cause that blast pistol to fire. Now I had time working against me as well as this man. "Calm down, son. I ain't gonna try nothing. All I want is to leave here as I said."

It wasn't working. He was too scared to think straight. Did I dare look up into the sky to look for Lady? No. Even if I did see her, all it would do is make the man more nervous–if that was possible at this point. And I couldn't afford to spook him into pulling the trigger. "I ain't gonna hurt you, boy," I said, trying to calm him down.

He simply stared at me with crazed eyes.

I relaxed my posture and looked away from him. Maybe the lack of intense attention would ease things up a bit. I still watched him from my peripheral. Never take your eyes off an enemy. We would have to wait until his adrenaline ran out and his body's chemistry forced him to calm down. Except that we couldn't wait; his shaking hand might inadvertently fire his gun. I had to act. But what could I do?

Ryna strained her eyes to look at him. "It's okay," she said. "It will be okay."

The man's trembling hand steadied. The crazed look drained from his eyes. Was the man calming down? His intense stare softened, and his breathing slowed. Why was this man calming down? Could his adrenaline have run dry so quickly? No, not a man in the prime of his youth and in good health. It had to be something Ryna said to him. It couldn't have been her words; they were too simple. She didn't say anything much different than I did. Was it her child-like tone of voice? That couldn't be it either, the man had been calming down too quickly.

Something about her words was familiar. Ah, yes, the camcam. I hadn't given it much thought, but she did calm down the stampeding lizard after I shot its tail. I had just assumed some piece of Miri's charming had rubbed off on Ryna. But this was more than just being good with animals. This was something that directly pulled on the man's emotions. And suddenly it all started to make sense. Not just the man's calming, but this entire mission started to piece together. A girl with no name whom doctors called Subject 35, whose "parents" she met days ago, and who was interesting enough to hire gangs to find. Something was special about this girl. Special enough for powerful people to want her.

The man eased up his grip around her and stood up straight, lowering his gun. My first instinct was to draw and shoot the man down while his gun was lowered. But my boundless curiosity got the better of me. Just how far had she affected this man's emotions? How far from a man's right mind was he after Ryna's words?

"How you feelin'?" I asked.

"A little tired," he said. "Real sorry about all this, mister. Pim got the job from a company man. I don't want any more trouble."

I eyed him suspiciously. It wasn't normal for a man to spill his guts in confession during a gunfight. Then again, I had just seen a man go from crazy scared to comfortable and talkative in a matter of moments. Why should I expect anything right now to be normal?

"Mind if I collect my gun now?" I asked.

"There gonna be no more trouble between us?" he asked cautiously.

At least his brain still worked correctly; he was right to be wary of the man who dropped all his comrades. "No, I don't reckon there'll be any more trouble."

The man holstered his blast pistol, and I retrieved my Starfield & Tanner. I walked back around the spring over to them. He had dropped his arm from around Ryna. Miri was stirring on the ground. Her curly black hair moved about in the slight breeze. I turned my attention immediately to her, helping her up. She was understandably apprehensive about a Davendry standing behind Ryna. She took my lead all the same and kept her objections quiet. She rubbed the back of her head.

"I'm mighty sorry, ma'am," he said. "Is your head okay?"

She glared at him, nodding.

He slowly reached into his vest pocket and pulled out a small photo. "This is what we got from the company man. The one who hired Pim and us to find her."

It was a black and white photo of Ryna. She looked a little younger and all cleaned up. She wore loose clothing that one might expect to see in a hospital. The caption read: Project Osurious, Subject 35. Then I noticed the logo watermark on the lower right-hand corner. I felt like cursing but refrained, seeing I was with Miri and Ryna.

Miri noticed the look on my face. "What is it?"

I handed her the photo. "Check the logo."

She looked back up in surprise. "Westward Galactic? But..."

"But they're just a bank," I said, finishing her sentence. "What they really are is a powerful financial organization." I motioned toward the photo in her hand. "And they are apparently interested in more than just migration loans."

I turned back to the Davendry. "This company man, did he also give you a price for the man and woman who walked up this way?"

"Yessir. Not as much as the girl, but enough to set us to followin' them. We thought we lost the girl when we got that hoverwagon to crash."

I had to suppress a little anger at learning they caused the crash. He was talking and I wanted to get all the information I could. Besides, they already paid for it. Paid with their lives. I wished it hadn't ended that way. A man deserved a chance to change. "Where are they now?"

"Pim sent Mauv and Manny to take them to the *Death Hound.*"

"One of the two starcruisers in orbit?"

He nodded.

The hot sun was waning on the horizon. The cool sun would soon start its climb into the sky. I looked over at the bodies lying around the spring. It wasn't good to leave death near a pool of water. It wasn't like a stream or a river where the water was constantly moving. Water was scarce on this planet, and it needed to be kept clean.

I motioned toward the bodies. "I'll help with the buryin'."

He nodded appreciatively.

"What about the girl's parents?" Miri asked with worry in her voice.

"We'll get to that," I said turning to her. "You see, it was my gun that ended these men. That makes it my responsibility if the consequences infect this waterhole."

Miri rolled her eyes. "Wayfinders..."

I smiled. She knew what she was getting when she recruited me. Or rather, when she recruited this part of me. Being a Wayfinder was never only about the skills. It was also about the code. We had once had a great responsibility, and to guide it, we followed the rules of the code. Not everyone I met agreed with those rules. I had long ago come to accept that. And even with the Wayfinders gone, I still lived according to the code I swore to all those years ago.

Ryna glanced up at Miri. Then Miri's shoulders relaxed. I paused a moment, wondering. Was Ryna using her calming effect on Miri? She didn't speak to her. Did she have to? Had she ever used it on me? It was a disquieting feeling to think I could have been manipulated. No, I didn't like the thought one bit. I would not be content until I got a few more answers from her. We still had a long trip on camcam back to the *Astral*

Princess. Once aboard the *Princess,* we could get into orbit and see about rescuing Ryna's "parents". But for now, I had some men to bury.

EPISODE 2

My second dumbest idea

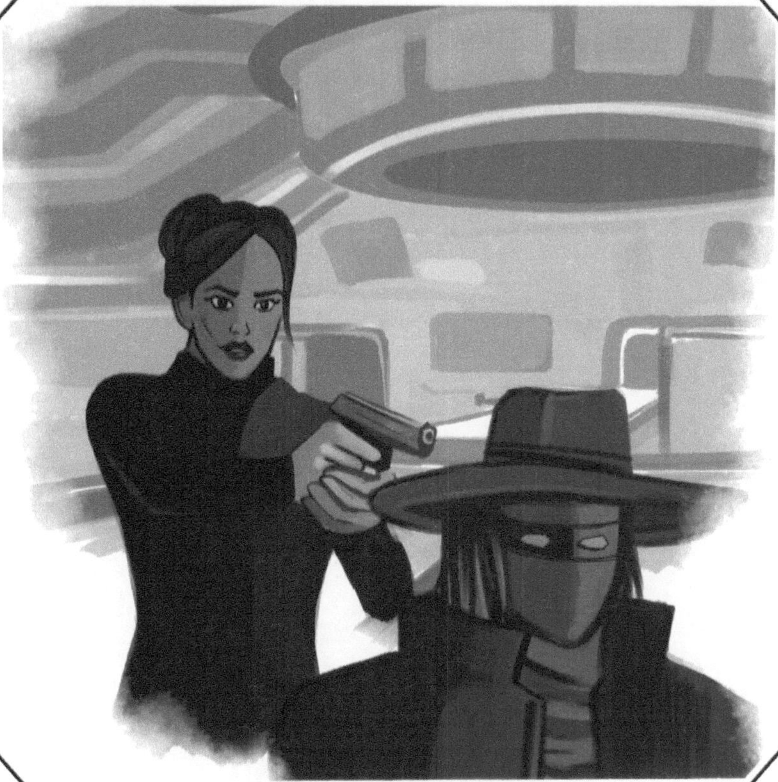

2

MY SECOND DUMBEST IDEA

I was happy to say goodbye to that smelly riding lizard Miri was so fond of. How could she stand riding camcams? They're smelly, slothful, and impossible to control. Well, except for Miri; she had always had a way with animals. Anything you saddle up and put a bridle on, she could get it to obey her. I swore she had some kind of superpower when it came to dealing with them.

I had always been the opposite. While I couldn't get a camcam to turn left to save my life, I could make any hunk of junk into a space-worthy craft in no time. I was a Wayfinder, at least I had been. And if it hadn't been for Miri's insistence that I help her, those skills would still have been rotting inside me. They'd have been wasting away while I played the role of a shuttle transport pilot. There was no shame in simple work, but there was no prestige in it either.

I slid off the back of the smelly camcam onto the dusty ground. Before me lay the *Astral Princess*. The *Princess* was a work of art, though nobody would know by looking at her aging frame and rusting hull. But she was fast, and in these parts that was what counted. I raised my arm and Lady, my enhanced falcon, landed. I stroked her feathered head. She and the *Princess* were the ladies in my life, well, until Miri came with that ten-year-old girl begging for me to help. And the job seemed so simple; deliver the girl to her parents. Why had things gotten so out of hand?

Then again, this planet was Cosstere, and Cosstere was anything but simple. I turned to Miri and Ryna. "Load up your things and let's get off this barren rock."

Miri shot me a disapproving look. She had told me it was the girl's home and wanted me to speak of it with more respect. Well, she wasn't paying me to be respectful about Cosstere. And a good thing she didn't try; she'd never be able to afford it. Cosstere had cost me an awful lot of annoyance and grief. The price I had set for speaking kindly of this desert rock was astronomical.

Miri and Ryna dismounted the smelly beast and began unencumbering it. I didn't offer to help with the unloading of the massive lizard because they each had two hands. Miri deliberately wore her hair down and dressed pretty. She knew I would be sweet on her—and it had worked.

But after assaulting that raider's compound to rescue her and burying four armed gunfighters, I figured I had done my fair share of the heavy lifting. Then again, she was quite attractive. *Focus, Rence,* I told myself. I needed to stop thinking about Miri, and about her kiss. They were seriously hampering my concentration on the mission. I climbed the ramp, into the *Princess*. I entered the cockpit and Lady flew over to her perch beside my chair.

Lady squawked.

"You think I should have helped unload the smelly lizard?" I asked.

She squawked again.

"Well, I disagree. Just because I'm sweet on her doesn't mean I gotta be always at her beck and call."

It was another fifteen minutes before Miri and Ryna had packed their belongings onto the *Princess*. Then they joined me in the cockpit. I pushed the ascent thrusters to maximum and the *Princess* shuddered as she lifted off. The rumbling was a sign of age but I called it a sign of class. Once we were in the air, soaring into the upper atmosphere, I remembered. Remembered the little trick I had played on the two Davendry starcruisers. I had played the part of the gullible and easily bullied pirate who had come to loot a lavish passenger liner. That was a lie, of course; there was no incoming passenger liner.

They wouldn't look back on that day with any degree of fondness. In truth, I had planned to run as fast as I could away from them. That would have been easy. Except it wasn't anymore. My luck had run out. Ryna's parents were aboard one of those starcruisers. I would have to find out which one was named *Death Hound* and figure out a way to steal aboard and mount a rescue. The Davendries were smalltime mercenaries and parttime pirates. Knowing that gave me an edge. But I needed more than just an edge; I needed luck now.

Miri and Ryna sat in chairs behind me. I could almost feel Miri's apprehension. I swiveled around in my chair. "Miri, I got an idea. Those Davendries tried to board me the other day when I arrived. I'm going to let them board us and take us as hostages. It will be the fastest way to get on board."

"I sure hope you know what you're doing," she said, not pleased at the news.

I didn't blame her; she had only recently been hostage to those raiding punks on the surface of Cosstere. And if I were in her shoes, I wouldn't be eager to get back into that position. As it was, *I* didn't even want to be in that situation. But it was either that or try to shoot our way on board.

I steered the *Princess* out of the atmosphere and into the starry black sky. I loved the stars. There was nothing so majestic and freeing as soaring amongst them. It was calming. If only rising starship fuel prices hadn't kept me returning to work just to keep the *Princess* starborne. A light blinked on my console followed by an alarm. The Davendry starcruisers had spotted us and were on an intercept course. I turned to Miri. "Just hold tight. I've talked with these guys before. Their greed will help us get aboard one of their starcruisers. From there, we should be able to rescue the girl's parents.

"How are you going to rescue them?" she asked.

It was a fair question. Unfortunately, I had to give her an honest answer. "I have no idea. First things first, we need to get aboard one of the starcruisers."

I flipped on the communication channel. "Hey–"

One of the starcruisers fired two bolts of green energy from its twin cannons. The bolts slammed into the *Princess.* I clenched the controls and veered the *Princess* away from them. Two more green bolts flew up and hit us hard in the rear. Sparks blew from the control panel as the whole ship shook from the impact. Why were they shooting? Either they were particularly cross about my lie, or they had learned about the four of them I gunned down in a fight. Either way, it was ruining my plan. There was no way I could get on board a ship that was trying to blast me into smithereens. Then again, my luck never had held out anyway.

"Are you sure this is a good idea?" Miri hollered over the blaring alarm and sparking electronics.

"Not anymore I'm not!"

It was time to hightail it. I didn't have any place in mind to head except away from those Davendries. In all the time I had visited Cosstere, the Davendries had always talked first and shot second. Something was amiss but I couldn't worry about it right then. I had to put as much distance between us and those starcruisers as possible. I steered for the closest moon. Since Cosstere had no moons I headed for her neighbor, a gas giant with large rings. She had twelve moons. One of them should be good enough to land on and make repairs.

Another volley of cannon bolts smashed into the rear of the Princess. The console in front of me exploded, showering my face in sparks. I yelled in pain and covered my eyes. They burned. My whole face burned. I forced one eye open, blinking in the light. My vision was blurry. I grabbed the controls anyway. We were starting to spin out of control. I engaged the maneuvering thrusters. Gradually, I regained control and leveled out of our spin just in time to see a big white blur in front of us.

I squeezed my eyes shut in desperation and reopened them. My eyes focused enough to see the rocky surface coming up fast. I pulled up and hit the descent thrusters. The *Princess* shuddered and quaked. I couldn't see well enough to know if our approach angle was correct. I could only hope.

Lady squawked.

I could usually guess what was bothering her but under those conditions, I had a lot of options to choose from. She had seen me do hundreds of landings, so I guessed it had to do with my landing angle. I pulled up a little more.

She squawked again.

I pulled up harder and hit the breaking thrusters. The *Princess* struck the ground, and I was thrown forward. My head hit the blast screen window. The irony was that those chairs came with seatbelts; I just had never needed them before. I heard Miri scream my name as I blacked out.

I heard laughter and the chirping of birds all around me. I opened my eyes and found myself dancing in a circle with several children. I was young. Not a scar on me. That couldn't have been right, could it? Wait, I knew those children. Bilby, Connor, and Samantha. I knew them so well. And they were beckoning me to follow them.

A faint voice called to me. "Rence, stay with me!"

"But I'm right here," I said to the children. They laughed and ran through the waist-high grass. A beautiful yellow sun shone in the blue sky. The wind ran its fingers through my hair as I ran with the children. But something was not right. The air smelled of sulfur and oil. Still, the children urged me onward. I smiled. I wanted to stay with them and run through the grassy fields.

The voice called again but was fainter. "Ryna, get me the other case!"

Ryna! I knew that name. I stopped running despite the urging of the children. One by one the children faded from view. The sun grew dim and blackness gathered around me. What was happening? I felt pain in my head. A sharp surging pain. Was I dying? No, I was gaining feeling. Granted, that feeling was pain, but I was feeling. Then I remembered the girl who belonged to the name Ryna. I remembered the gunfights and the smelly lizard. It all came back to me. We had crashed and I was injured.

I heard the sounds around me much clearer. I heard the hum of a laser calibrator and the occasional rustling of tools from my tool chest. I opened my eyes and squinted in the bright light over my head. My chest ached as I drew in a large breath.

"Rence!" Miri said with tear lines down her face.

With one finger, I wiped away a tear line from her cheek. "I owe you one, Miri."

She smiled through her last bout of pouting sobs as she got her breathing under control.

I turned to Ryna. She had tears in her eyes and a frightened look about her. I smiled. "Sorry for scaring you, little miss. I'm okay now."

She stayed kneeling, unmoving.

Miri helped me into a seated position. I was sitting in the center of the floor. Lady danced nervously on her perch. I looked back to Ryna and winked. "I'm all right. It'll all be okay."

She smiled timidly and pointed to my chest.

I looked down. My shirt was open and my wires and circuits were exposed. Yeah, that wasn't exactly a comforting sight for a young girl. I glanced at Miri, who pulled out another tool from my tool chest.

"Why didn't you tell me you were shot?" Miri asked.

"It was yesterday when those scavengers nabbed you. I went after them to rescue you. Then one thing led to another and I plum forgot."

She scowled in disbelief. "How do you forget being shot?"

I shrugged. "Sometimes I forget how much machinery is a part of me these days."

"Well, it's a good thing your skull was durotanium; it saved you from a massive head injury."

I smirked. "Too bad it didn't stop the migraine."

I was happy I got a laugh out of Miri. One thing was clear; I was darn lucky Miri knew her way around repairs. My lands! How differently this could have ended if I hadn't told Miri about my cybernetic implants? If I had told her to mind her own business, she would not have learned how to put this Humpty Dumpty back together again. Secrets kept a man alive, but trust, it had just proven, brought a man back from the abyss.

Miri closed my chest panel. "There you go," she said. "And the way I see it, I still owe *you* one."

I buttoned up my shirt and climbed to my feet. I felt dizzy and held my head. It had been wrapped in a make-shift bandage. Miri had torn a large piece off the hem of her long shirt to make my bandage. I loved that flowery shirt on her. She wore it hoping I would be sweet on her. Funny thing was, she didn't have to wear the shirt for me to be sweet on her. I fancied her anyhow. *How come we don't fly together more often?* I wondered.

"Too bad," I said to her.

"What?" she asked.

"Too bad you had to tear another piece of your shirt to bandage me. I'm still rather fond of how you look in that long shirt."

She blushed and turned away, putting my tools back in the tool chest.

Ryna walked up and handed me my hat.

I nodded. "Thank you, little miss."

I turned my attention to the *Princess.* Crashlanding, wherever we had, was surely not good for her. My pilot's console was smashed. The indent almost outlined the idiot who slammed into the console on account of not strapping in. I walked to the rear of the cockpit and turned on the secondary console. The Norgon transports always had a backup to every system. That was one of the many things I loved about the *Princess.* I ran a full diagnostic and hung my head.

Miri noticed. "What?"

I sighed. "We have about six hours of heat left before we all freeze."

"Okay, we'll just have to work quickly then," she suggested.

"...and we have about twenty minutes of air left."

She rolled her eyes.

My top priority had become the CO2 filtration system. I climbed down into the guts of the *Princess.* Her primary system maintenance hatch was big enough to fit a maintenance robot. That made for plenty of working space for several people at once. I pulled open the CO2 filter panel. A small pop of electricity shot out from the circuits. Ryna jumped back. I hadn't even noticed she had followed me down here. "It'll be okay, little miss. A simple short in the wiring, causing little sparks. No need to worry."

"Can you die?" she asked.

I looked at her. "You sure speak your mind, little miss."

She stared at me.

"Yes, I can die just like any other man."

She shook her head and pointed to my chest.

I rolled my eyes. "Okay, not *exactly* like any other man. I'll admit I have a few replacement parts that can get shot without too much worry.

But as sure as shootin' I still get nervous of my life every time I'm in a gunfight."

That answer seemed to satisfy her.

"Rence?" Miri called from above.

I glanced up. "Down here."

She descended the ladder, carrying a plastic container in her hand. It was the spare EPS Relay I asked her to fetch.

I looked at the debris on the floor. "Watch your step."

She took one step toward me and slipped; the spare relay container tumbled to the floor. I caught Miri around her waist, preventing her from falling. Her face was right up to mine. I hadn't before noticed the pretty blue specks in her eyes. Her breathing slowed and mine practically stopped. I didn't even notice my heart was beating faster. I gazed into her eyes.

She relaxed in my arms, staring back at me.

I didn't stare for very long. It couldn't have been very long. Either that or time had slowed down somehow. There was something comforting about having my arms around her. Something I couldn't put my finger on. But what was baffling to me was why Miri was looking right back at me. She knew me longer than most folks and probably better too. With all the things wrong with me there was no reason she should keep her eyes on me. Yet something about this felt right; it felt complete somehow.

"Are you two going to kiss?" Ryna asked.

Miri was at the far end of the room in a matter of seconds. *Not anymore,* I thought, pretending to cough while pulling the brim of my hat low. My cheeks felt hot and I could only guess how they looked. "Ryna," I asked. "Could you please bring me that container Miri brought?"

I hastily fumbled with the replacement part. For whatever reason, it was incredibly stubborn coming out of the package. I had opened boxes like these before, it should have been no problem. My floundering only heightened my tension. So much for looking nonchalant.

"It's okay," Ryna said. "She's gone now."

Miri must have escaped while I was wrestling with the container. I wasn't sure what was more annoying, the interruption or how keenly Ryna could read me. I took a deep breath and relaxed. My heart rate was still fast yet I felt comfortable. Why was I feeling comfortable? I had just been in a very embarrassing situation. I looked at Ryna. "You're calming me down, aren't you?"

"Is that bad?" she asked innocently.

"Well, I don't know," I answered honestly. "Calming that feller on Cosstere saved your life. So, I guess it can't be too bad. But all the same, I think you should ask before calming me."

She looked down. "Okay."

I lifted her chin. "Now don't fret, little miss. I got no hard feelings. I like you all the same."

She smiled brightly and gave me a quick hug.

"Now," I said, changing the topic. "Go grab that electromag doohickey over there...no, the other one. Yeah, now bring that here. I'll show you how to replace an EPS Relay."

The girl was a fast learner. Still weak in her hands but she was a fast learner. I only needed to help her with the tricky part of getting the darned thing to fit into the chamber properly. I let her make the electrical connections and configure the jumpers on the circuit. I grinned, seeing how she was catching on. Once she had completed the replacement, I threw the power switch. The CO2 filtration chamber hummed to life. That gave us enough air to breathe until our power ran out. The power generator was my next priority.

I climbed out of the maintenance hatch and made my way back to the cockpit. Miri was needle-welding at the machining desk. I wandered over to her side. "The filter is repaired. We have air for as long as we have power."

She lifted her welding goggles and looked at me. "Sometimes I wish I knew more than just small-scale electrical repairs. Then maybe I could be more useful."

"Miri, don't fret yourself. A man's usefulness–a woman's usefulness isn't measured by fastening pins and regulators. Nor, I reckon, by saddles and bridles. You found an orphaned girl who needed help and you knew how to get that help."

"You mean, dragging you into this mess?"

I smiled. "You know how to get the ball rolling, so to speak. Most folks would call that leadership."

She blushed, smiling. "So does this mean I should start bossing you around?" She mimicked an over-acted authoritative voice, "Perry! March your hide down to the engine room and get the *Princess* starborne again!"

We both laughed.

"Ma'am, yes ma'am," I replied, smiling.

She set down the needle-welder and the welding goggles. "Here," she said, handing me what she was working on. It was my tactical mask. She had spot-welded the crack and repaired the circuitry.

I held it reverently as a sense of gratitude washed over me. I had almost written it off as a total loss when that Davendry socked me in the face. Korr, my mentor, gave it to me when I became a Wayfinder. And needless to say, they didn't make them anymore once Wayfinders were outlawed. I looked into her gentle eyes. "This means worlds to me, thank you."

She grinned a moment, but then looked serious. "Rence, can we talk about what happened down the maintenance hatch?"

Oh no. Things had just started to mellow out and she wanted to bring up those awkward feelings again. My heart thumped faster, and my hands became jittery. I didn't much like that awkwardness and I wasn't sure where this conversation would lead. I still fancied Miri and didn't want to lose that. What if she decided we should keep our distance? What if she felt it was best never to get close? Something inside me felt scared, worried I would lose that opportunity. "Sorry about that," I said. "I should have taken the time to clear the floor."

She opened her mouth to speak.

"Not to worry," I continued. "I'll get right on that." I turned to leave but she caught my arm.

"Rence, what I wanted to talk about–"

"Shhh," I said, holding up one finger.

She pursed her lips in frustration. "Can't we have an adult conversation–"

I put my hand over her mouth, quieting her objection. Then she heard it, too. A low moaning sound from outside. She glanced over to the blast shield window, and I removed my hand.

"What was that?"

I shook my head. "Either something is out there, or the *Princess* is shifting position on the ground. Neither one is preferable."

"How fast can you restore main power?"

"I'm gonna find out," I said, rushing down the corridor.

I dashed down the stairwell to the lower deck. I stepped into a puddle of water. Not good. The freshwater tanks must have torn a leak when we hit the ground. It also made the electrical repair a lot riskier. The lower deck had flooded with half a foot of water.

Ryna descended the stairwell behind me. "Why did you put water on the floor?" she asked.

"For the same reason that I crashed," I said, not attempting to mask my annoyance at the question. I didn't normally mind questions, even questions like that. But I was in a hurry to find out what needed fixing before the *Princess* got into deeper trouble.

I splashed through the water over to the far wall. The reserve batteries were half gone and the main generator had shorted out. I turned back to Ryna. "Little miss, could you run and get me the flux ionometer?"

She raised her eyebrows.

"It's the long pole-shaped thingy that resembles a magwrench only it's open-ended."

She stared at me with a blank expression.

I sighed. "Let's go fetch it together."

I took one step toward Ryna but froze. The moaning sound returned. It sounded very near. The water on the floor rippled from vibration. I put a hand on the wall to steady myself. Ryna clung to the stairwell railing. "What's that?" she asked in alarm.

"The *Princess* is sliding."

"Into what?" she further asked.

I shrugged and splashed my way back to the stairwell. "Time to find out."

I climbed the stairwell, skipping steps. Ryna followed behind as best she could. Miri met me in the corridor.

"Did you find out how long it will take to get main power back?"

"Nope," I said quickly, climbing the ladder to the dorsal observation dome. "New problem!"

"What is it?"

I climbed to the chair in the middle of the transparent dome. The *Princess* lay on an icy shelf. Big white clouds billowed up from underneath the ship. She had run her belly across the frozen ground and had come to a stop. But there was a cliff behind her. And we were indeed slipping toward the edge. The *Princess* moaned again as we moved closer to the ledge.

I hopped down from the observation dome. "We're on an ice shelf of frozen gas. And the heat of the *Princess* is melting it."

"Can't you bring good news once in a while?"

I hurried past her. "Working on that..."

I flung open the weapon's cabinet. I was in here often, but mostly just to clean. I grabbed the mag-harpoon. I hadn't used it in at least a decade. Hopefully, the cable hadn't rusted too much. I cleaned the guns really well, but the odd tools didn't get the same level of pampering. I needed to get outside but the entry ramp was on the bottom of the ship, so the main entrance was not an option. I carried the mag-harpoon in my arms over to the side evacuation hatch.

Miri stood beside me. "You're not actually going out there, are you?"

"Don't worry," I said. "I can breathe with my mask, thanks to you."

Her eyes widened. "It's 2.7 degrees kelvin outside!"

"Is that cold?" I asked.

"The water in your skin will turn to ice and your blood will eventually freeze."

Well, I thought, *at least she told me now instead of waiting.* I nodded as the *Princess* started to slide again. This time the sliding was something to hold onto a railing for. I dropped the mag-harpoon and clung to the doorway. Miri grabbed my waist and we both fell to the floor, sliding down the corridor. Ryna screamed and held onto the stairwell railing. Miri and I stopped sliding at the other end of the corridor. She blushed, seeing she was on top of me. I'm certain my cheeks resembled hers. The mag-harpoon slid on down the corridor after us.

My hat had fallen off and Miri glanced at my head bandage. She reached out and stopped the sliding tool before it hit my head. I must have hit my head harder than I thought that first time. Because with all the chaos around us, the one thing I noticed was how sweet her hair smelled. It was the oddest thing.

"Mighty kind of you," I said.

She smiled, her face only a finger's length from mine. "I didn't want to redo my repair job on you."

She rolled off me, keeping her hand on the mag-harpoon. I sat up and took it from her. The floor was now slanted. The aft end of the ship was sinking and now all the previously flat floors were inclined. I found my hat and planted it firmly in place. I put one leg against the wall behind me and pushed off with my enhanced knees. I flew up the corridor and caught hold of the escape hatch door. *If we ever get off this icy rock,* I told myself. *I'll weld some handholds on the walls.*

The outer escape hatch door was on the other side of the airlock. I kicked open the inside door and climbed into the airlock. I turned back to Miri and shouted down the corridor. "See if you can get to the cockpit and grab a headset. We may need to talk."

"So *now* he wants to talk," she grumbled, climbing up the inclined corridor floor.

Closing the airlock inner door, I searched for an exosuit. I knew plenty about space travel, but not much about spacewalks. Miri had mentioned that it was cold. And after thinking it over, I remembered once being told something about air pressure too. I knew I had an exosuit somewhere for just such an emergency. I rummaged around the supply locker and found a sealed box. Never been opened. I hoped that meant it was still in good condition. Emptying its contents, I found a complete exosuit along with the accompanying helmet.

I sure was glad I hadn't put on too many pounds in the last twenty years; the suit fit. Unfortunately, I didn't have time to connect the helmet's radio to the ship's intercom. So, I took out my tactical mask and fastened it on. I had to take my hat off to clamp on the helmet. Then I turned the suit on. My left arm had a few gauges: oxygen, air pressure, and temperature. The little numbers around the outer edge of each circle were meaningless to me. But each gauge had a needle pointing in the green. That was enough for me. I pressed the big red button next to the outer door and a red light started flashing and a countdown began. A dial on the wall, labeled Atmosphere, had a needle that started dropping. The air had to be vented before the hatch would open. It was a sensible precaution; no sense in getting shot out into space with a sudden decompression.

"Rence?" Miri's voice called through my mask.

"I hear you loud and clear."

"Please be careful."

"Always," I promised.

The hatch opened as the *Princess* started sliding again. I clung to the hatch's safety handles. The ground started moving and white gas billowed out from beneath. I looped my arm through the safety handle so I could use both hands. I touched the back end of the mag-harpoon to the outside hull of the *Princess* and flipped the switch on. It magnetized and stuck to the hull. I pressed the launch button and the harpoon shot out, spearing the icy ground.

The *Princess* halted its slide, supported by the taut harpoon cable. "Bingo," I said. "That should buy us enough time to get the engines online."

"Thanks, Rence," Miri said. "I'll get your toolbox down to the engine room."

"I'll meet you there." I pulled myself back inside the hatch and eyed the controls. Then, I heard a loud *twang* just outside. I peeked my head out the open hatch. One of the cable braids had snapped right at a rusty spot. A second cable braid burst and coiled around the remaining braids of the cable line. The rusted cable was breaking, one braided layer at a time.

"Uh-oh," I said, reaching out and grabbing the cable on both ends of the rust spot.

"Rence, what's wrong?"

"Tell me again, how confident you are at fixing spaceships?"

"Very funny, Rence. Are you back inside yet?"

Another braid of the cable snapped and the entire cable line stretched. I pulled hard on both ends, hoping to take some strain off the line. "Nope...need you...fix...engine..." I grunted, tugging on the line.

"What are you talking about? I don't know the first thing about starship repair," she protested.

I was only able to speak between short breaths. "Cable breaking...tryin'...hold it together..."

"I don't know how to fix a ship," she said with panic in her voice. "Maybe we can trade places?"

I was concentrating too hard on pulling the cable, otherwise, I would have rolled my eyes. "No...kinda...man's job..." Another cable braid started peeling. I tugged at the cable line harder. There was no way I could stop that cable from breaking for very long. I hoped that Miri could follow directions.

"Rence! What am I supposed to do?" she asked, sounding frantic.

"Lady...get...Lady...Ryna knows." Despite my efforts, the other cable braid snapped, swatting my helmet in the process. The cable line stretched even more. At least I was slowing down how fast they broke. The downside was that I was getting mighty tired.

"Rence, I'm in the engine room. Ryna has Lady. What do I do now?"

I let go of the cable just long enough to press a button on my wristband. Immediately the fourth cable braid snapped. I quickly grabbed the cable again. It was more difficult now that my eyes were seeing what Lady saw. I could no longer see the cable line. If I had had half a second more, I could have switched Lady's sight to only one of my eyes. Oh well, it would have to do. I again tugged hard on the cable line, trying to relieve some of the strain.

Miri was at the main power generator.

"Front panel..." I said, clenching my teeth.

Miri fumbled with the front casing until she pulled the panel open.

"Closer," I said after a deep breath.

Ryna held Lady closer to the generator. I had to force my eyes open. It seemed natural to close my eyes as I strained, pulling on both ends of the cable. The generator's resistance coupler had burned out. I didn't have a spare. I *knew* there was something I had forgotten to get last week.

"Rence, what now?"

"...coupler...blown..."

"Okay where do I get another one?" she asked.

I shook my head. And a lot of good shaking my head did since she couldn't see me. "Scavenge...attitude thrusters...your left...other left..."

Miri pulled off the front panel to the attitude thrusters and located the coupler. She fiddled with it for what seemed like an eternity before she yanked it out. "Rence! It doesn't fit!"

The fifth cable braid snapped, scraping my helmet in the process. "Make it fit!"

Miri shoved the coupler into the slot and pounded on it with the handle of a wrench. On the tenth slam with the wrench handle, the generator sprang to life. It thrummed, dumping power into the *Princess's* electrical grid. My jaw dropped. "You didn't shut off the breaker before opening it up?"

"Somebody forgot to tell me that step!"

Well, no electrocution, no foul. The main thing was that power had been restored. The strength in my arms, however, quickly faded. "Cockpit..."

"I can't fly," Miri protested.

"Autopilot...third-row...switches." The last cable braid snapped. Both ends of the cable each went their separate way. One cable end yanked out of my hand while I held onto the other. Something hard slammed into my side. I reached over and pressed a button on my wristband, reverting my eyesight to normal. I was holding onto the wrong cable end. I sat up on the icy ground and saw the *Princess* sliding down the hill away from me. The ground was slick but somehow I got to my feet in record time and dashed toward the *Princess.*

The nose of the *Princess* tipped up into the air as she slid off the edge of the icy cliff. If I got stranded here, I was a dead man. So, I figured I didn't have much to lose in jumping after her. I dove over the cliff and fell after my falling ship. Something in the back of my mind asked me what in the sam hill I thought I was doing. As I plummeted after the *Princess,* her main engines crackled and roared to life. The bleak blue ambient light quickly turned yellow. The main thrusters propelled her upward. I fell into the outer hatch and slammed against the inner airlock door.

My helmet cracked and the wind got knocked out of me. I forced in a breath and then pushed up on the door, fighting gravity and inertia. I reached over and pressed the big red button on the wall. The outer hatch door closed and the pressurization cycle commenced. I dropped to the floor panting. My arms felt like jelly and stung with soreness when I flexed any muscle in the arms.

"Rence! Please tell me you're inside!" Miri's voice demanded.

"I'm on board, Miri. You did well."

"Thanks," she said. I could hear a smile in her shaky voice. "What do we do now?"

"I'm gonna take a little nap right here, I think."

And I would have if Miri's panicked complaints hadn't driven me to get out of my exosuit and get back to the cockpit. I stumbled into the cockpit with my tactical mask back in my coat pocket. Lady wasn't on her perch. Instead, she was still on Ryna's arm. I dropped to one knee, bringing myself close to eye-level with Lady. "Looks like you're takin' a liking to Miss Ryna here."

Lady squawked and flew over to her perch.

I grinned at Lady. "Liar."

Miri swiveled around in her chair at the backup control console. She crossed her arms. "Man's job?"

I rolled my eyes. "Not the best description, I'll admit. But it was easier than saying: lots of upper arm strength required."

Miri giggled, failing to keep a straight face.

I took my hat off and looked at her. "But I am real blessed you are handy with a wrench."

She smiled big. "Okay, so what now?"

"We are going to hold this course for at least two hours. I don't know about you, but I need a little shut-eye.

I spent the next two and a half hours sleeping with vibro-massagers strapped to my arms. I wasn't sure I'd be able to fall asleep with those things vibrating my arm muscles. But it turned out that fatigue works wonders on falling asleep. I awoke to tingling sensations on my arms from all the vibrating, but at least my muscles had been relaxed. That would keep them from getting stiff and sore, but I still needed to take it easy for a while.

In the cockpit, I found Miri and Ryna had helped themselves to some food rations and had taken naps on the floor. If I had been here, I would have suggested they lay down in some of the passenger cabins. This was, after all, a passenger transport ship. Lady squawked and turned about on her perch. Miri and Ryna had left some food for Lady but it didn't look like she had touched it.

I smirked. "It ain't polite to turn your beak up at an offering, even if they don't know your tastes."

Lady squawked again.

I quietly picked up Miri. She was lighter than she looked. She stirred a little as I took her to a passenger cabin and laid her on the cot. I drew the blanket over her before leaving. Ryna was awake and attending Lady when I stepped back into the cockpit. I sat down in my usual chair, in front of the smashed primary control panel. I gazed out the blast shield window at the stars and floating asteroids. The icy comet we recently left continued to drift away.

I needed to think up a plan to get on board those Davendry starcruisers. But, for whatever reason, my mind circled back to Miri. It was a little strange having a woman around. Strange, and yet wonderful at the same time. My former career hadn't left much room for settling down. But now that I had been reduced to a transport pilot, maybe it was an option now? I shook my head. Miri had hired me because of my past career, not my current occupation. No, she didn't need a companion; she needed a Wayfinder.

"Are you thinking of Miss Miri?" Ryna asked.

"You read minds, too?"

She shook her head. "You just feel excited and also sad."

"How do you know how I'm feeling?"

She gave me a confused look. "I know how everyone's feeling."

"I'm not sure if that sounds interesting or plain spooky."

I was sure, however, that I needed to figure out how to infiltrate a Davendry starcruiser and get back out alive. That was my most pressing concern. I knew the traditional approach wouldn't work; they shot me down quite literally. I needed a way to make them want us alive. The *Princess* also needed a lot of major work done. She was spaceworthy but that didn't mean she was up for atmospheric landings. She always had been rather rough on entry and exit, to begin with.

If I was going to pull off a tricky infiltration, I needed to be a little tricky myself. I turned to Ryna. "How are you at pretending?"

She narrowed her brow. "The doctors told me never to pretend."

"In other words," I surmised. "Not very good."

After a moment of silent reflection, Ryna stole my attention. "Are you going to kiss Miss Miri?"

My muscles tensed and my cheeks flushed. Despite my self-control, I couldn't restrain my smile. "Why don't we stick with *my* topic?"

"But you like her, don't you?" she persisted.

I felt like a cornered man in a gunfight, pinned down without much room to move. Only I couldn't shoot my way out of this situation. My fidgety hands threatened to press random buttons. So, I resorted to folding my arms. "Little miss, you sure are curious about my intentions, ain't you?"

She nodded.

"Well, for now, I *intend* to keep that a secret."

She grinned with a hopeful sparkle in her eyes.

If I didn't know any better, I'd have thought those doctors had been trying to create a matchmaker. A few minutes later, Miri walked in.

"Sorry," she said, taking a seat. "I didn't mean to sleep so long. Did I miss anything?"

Ryna shook her head. "Only talking."

"What were you two talking about?"

"About you and Mr. Rence kissing," Ryna said as if discussing the weather.

Miri shot me a horrified glance.

Ryna continued, "But he said his answer was a secret."

I pulled the brim of my hat low. If only I could have escaped that situation. I would have paid handsomely for the ability to have left that room and all the awkward feelings behind.

"Now I know why you wear a hat," Miri accused.

I wasn't sure if she could see my sheepish smile or not, but I sure was glad the proximity alarm went off right then. I spun back around in my chair only to see the damaged control console. I had forgotten I needed to use the backup controls. I jumped out of my seat and sprinted the few steps over to the backup console. I plopped into the chair and swiveled around to check the screen. The sensor screen showed the two Davendry starcruisers approaching on an intercept course.

"Davendries have seen us," I said.

Miri glanced heavenward and grumbled.

I spun around in my chair. "I have an idea!"

"You had one last time too," she reminded.

I cut power to the engines, then picked up a datapad from the machining desk. I hastily typed up a quick script. Turning to Ryna, I asked. "Can you read?"

She nodded with an air of pride.

"What do you have in mind," Miri asked.

"I think we can win by losing," I replied, ushering Ryna into the chair by the controls. "Ryna, I'm going to have you talk to the Davendries."

Miri gasped in alarm. "What!"

I ignored her protest. "They are going to ask you questions. I have written down the answers, and I'll point to the answer you should tell them."

"I don't think this is such a good idea," Miri said, walking over to us.

Ryna looked over to Miri. "It's okay."

I was willing to bet the little matchmaker was calming her. I glanced over to Miri, and she looked relaxed. *No wonder Westward Galactic wants her so bad,* I thought. I switched on the communication channel and pointed to the first line I had written on the datapad.

"...is anyone...out there," Ryna read, sounding like a robot.

Miri shot me an 'I told you so' glance. I looked heavenward, wondering why I hadn't thought to have her practice her lines. I guessed I had been in the business of subterfuge for too many years. It hadn't dawned on me that anyone would struggle with the skill.

Miri knelt beside Ryna and whispered in her ear.

"Hello," Ryna repeated. "Is anyone out there?"

A gruff voice responded. "Identify yourself."

Ryna wrinkled her nose. "What does that mean?"

My heart raced. If Ryna could run off-script this easily, this might not end very well.

"Who are you?" the voice demanded.

I pointed to another line on the datapad and Miri whispered in Ryna's ear.

"The doctors call me Subject 35," Ryna repeated.

"Really?" the voice said with renewed interest. "What are you doing on that ship?"

Ryna answered before I could point to the next line of the script. "Miss Miri and Mr. Rence are taking me to see my parents."

I silently wiped my hand down my face in frustration. The girl was either a born conversationalist or outright honest. Both were good qualities unless you were trying to lie. I noticed I was pacing and forced myself to stop.

"I see," the voice said with a thoughtful tone. "And where are they now?"

I frantically pointed to a line on the datapad but Miri was quicker, whispering into her ear.

"I think they are hurt," Ryna again repeated. "Can you help?"

The voice instantly softened to a sly tone. "Yes...we'll come right away."

Ryna turned to Miri. "I don't like him."

Miri quickly put her finger to her lips to hush the honest outburst. I had never considered myself a nervous man, but those intense seconds were enough to drive a man to drinking. I pointed to another line on the datapad and Miri whispered to Ryna.

"What do I do?" she repeated.

"Just sit tight, Subject 35. We'll latch on real soon. Then all you need to do is open the door."

Miri whispered again and Ryna answered, "Okay."

I switched off the communication channel and wiped the perspiration from my brow. Miri hugged Ryna, telling her how well she did. I stared at Miri, seeing her with Ryna's arms wrapped around her neck. If I didn't know better, I'd have assumed Miri was the girl's mother. The two of them seemed to fit together like pieces of a puzzle. But how much of that was the influence of Ryna's ability? I ended up second-guessing each of my observations anytime I remembered Ryna's ability. But even knowing that, it was real easy to love that girl.

Miri and Ryna glanced around when they heard clanking sounds. The Davendry starcruiser latched onto the *Princess*. They would be boarding us soon.

Miri looked at me. "Now what?"

"You two hide," I said. "I'm gonna steal onto their ship and take a look around."

Miri nodded and ushered Ryna out.

I drew my blast pistols and inspected their power cells. One was low. I set it into the charger and exchanged it with a fresh one. I clamped on my tactical mask and counted my detonators. It was showtime. I ran to the docking hatch and climbed up onto the ceiling pipes. They were strong enough to hold my weight and dull enough in color that they did not draw much attention. I heard muffled noises on the other side of the door. They were hacking into the door control.

Sparks blew from the circuit panel and the door parted. Six men cautiously walked inside with their guns drawn. I patiently waited for them to disappear down the corridor before dropping to the ground. I tapped a button on my wristband and my eyesight through my mask changed to infrared. I was now able to see heat sources. I tapped another button and my infrared sight switched from both eyes to just one eye. It was a little disorienting for the first few moments, but my years of practice quickly returned.

I walked briskly down the brightly lit, smooth hallways. These were night-and-day different than the corridors on the *Astral Princess*. She sported a rough steel and exposed cables look. I walked behind a counter with a computer terminal and started poking around. Computers were getting more and more complicated every year. It was hard to keep up with them. The Davendries were not government or military, so I had good odds they owned older hardware.

I heard footsteps and ducked behind the counter. I saw body heat through the wall. What I saw didn't make sense. The raiding party was returning from the *Princess*. Then my heart skipped a beat. One of the infrared silhouettes walked apprehensively alongside a much shorter infrared silhouette. They were returning because they found Miri and Ryna.

I was such an idiot. Why couldn't I have learned my lesson? If the Davendries were trained gunfighters, then it stood to reason they were also trained scavengers. They probably knew where to look to discover Miri and Ryna. My heart sunk into the pit of my stomach. My problems had just compounded. Not only did I need to find and rescue Ryna's parents, but now I needed to rescue Miri and Ryna.

I watched the procession pass by my counter before standing. They would probably be interrogated first before being locked up. Maybe they would get locked up close to Ryna's parents? Maybe there was a positive side to this blunder? I moved around the counter, and something on it caught my eye. It was a large black cylinder with circuitry on the back side. It looked interesting, so I took it with me. Perhaps it had computer data on it I could exploit.

The Davendries escorted Miri and Ryna into an elevator. After the doors closed, I dashed up to it. Prying my fingers between the doors, I forced them open. The elevator was moving upward swiftly. I jumped, nearly hitting my head on the bottom of the elevator as I caught hold of the bottom support beams. My arms were still a little weak and shook. I swung my leg over the support beam and crawled on top. That left only a small gap between my head and the floor of the elevator. It was cramped but at least I could rest my arms.

The elevator came to a stop and everyone exited. I swung my legs down and caught hold of the rungs of the maintenance ladder on the sidewall. I climbed the ladder and stepped on top of the elevator. Finding the emergency trap door, I climbed inside. I leaned my ear to the door.

"Well, Subject 35," the gruff voice said. "Where is Mr. Rence?"

"On your ship," she replied.

"I think you're lying to me."

"No," I said, stepping into the room. "She's tellin' the truth all right."

Four of the Davendries reached for their guns. My blast pistols each cleared leather and lit up the room. The four Davendries fell to the floor before they could get a shot off. The fifth Davendry dove for cover and the sixth grabbed Ryna and pointed his blast pistol at her head.

"Hold it!" the gruff man yelled, tightening his arm around Ryna's neck. "Drop your guns!"

"You think you can take me?" I asked.

The man glared at me. "You're fast, I'll give you that. But I'm bettin' you're not faster than my trigger pull. I'm gonna give you 'til the count of three before I turn this girl into a corpse."

"Not if the woman kills you first," I said.

His eyes darted over to Miri, and I pulled the trigger. My shot nailed him in the head and he tumbled backward, pulling Ryna on top of him. Miri screamed and ran to them. I took a few steps inside and pointed my gun at the last Davendry, cowering behind a pillar. "You packing?"

"Yes."

"Lose it," I commanded.

He slowly pulled out his blast pistol and slid it across the floor toward me.

"What's the name of this starcruiser?"

"*Death Hound*," he replied.

"Where is the man and woman that Mauv and Manny brought?"

"Tess sold them to the bounty hunter," he said in a shaky voice.

"What?" I said. This was *not* the answer I wanted. I felt annoyance building up inside me like a glass being poured. I was not about to go traipsing off across the known galaxy in search of those people. Starship fuel was expensive enough, and I had plenty of repairs I needed to make on the *Princess*. The costs were already adding up and I didn't expect Miri to be able to pay a whole lot. "When did this happen?"

I heard the high-pitched hum of a blast pistol activate close to my ear. "They were picked up this morning," a pleasant voice said.

I slowly turned my head and saw a woman dressed in a black uniform with her blast pistol inches from my head. Her perfectly set black hair was pulled up into a bun, which offset her bright red lips. She was a looker—no question about that—but it had been my fondest desire never to see that woman again. Unlike the men on the ship, she did not wear a blue sash to indicate she was a Davendry. She wasn't a Davendry by association, she was a Davendry by blood relation. "Tess Davendry," I said, lowering my blast pistol.

"I'm flattered you know me," she said. "But I have been known to a lot of Wayfinders over the years."

"What makes you think I'm a Wayfinder?" I asked, not caring for the answer. I mostly needed time to think of a way out of this situation.

"If the gun didn't give it away, the mask certainly did."

"Finders, keepers," I said.

She smirked. "You don't expect me to believe you found a Wayfinder's equipment and knew how to use it? No, it's simpler to postulate that you owned them already. Besides," she added. "The girl called you Rence. And one of the missing Wayfinders was named Rence Perry."

"Is that why you haven't shot me yet?"

She smirked, moving some hair away from her eyes with a gentle toss of her head. "There's a price on your head. But you don't have to be alive."

"Well, I hate to disappoint such a pretty woman, but I do believe you and I both won't be around to see that reward cashed in."

She laughed. "No point in flattering yourself. If you know me, then you also know my reputation with a gun."

"You apparently don't know mine. I *always* have a backup plan."

"Oh?"

I nodded. "I have something of yours." I slowly holstered one blast pistol. Then carefully, I pulled out the large black cylinder and showed it to her.

"A data drum?" she said with confusion. "You're a poor saboteur if you think one missing drum will hamper the main computer."

"You're missing the point," I insisted. "This is the real drum. Not to be confused with the explosive I switched it for."

The smile ran off her face.

"I know," I continued. "It's not much of a backup plan. But you see, I'm kinda prideful. I figure if I'm gonna bite the dust, I'm as sure as shootin' gonna take your starcruiser out with me."

"You're bluffing," she finally said.

"You have a clever mind, Tess. What do your instincts tell you? You figured out I was a Wayfinder. That much tells you I'm a professional. The fact that I was never caught tells you I'm resourceful. Then there's that data drum. It's the one piece that doesn't add up. You're thinking to yourself if the roles were reversed, where would you have planted a bomb? Would you have chosen the one place that can't be searched by the main computer?"

I slowly turned to face her. "Tell me truly—from one professional to another. If you were in my boots, would you have taken a chance on a bluff? Or would you have rather taken down the enemy with you?"

From her eyes, I could see the gears turning in her head. My chances were fifty-fifty that she'd shoot me. The only advantage I had was that she was a member of the Davendry family. I mostly knew them from reputation and I hoped it was enough. They were known to be cold, calculating, and careful.

"What do you want?" she asked.

"You already know what I want," I said.

"You came looking for information on those two the Corporation is after. That means you got what you came for."

I nodded.

"Then I want you off my ship after you tell me where the bomb is."

"First get the woman and the girl onto my ship, then I'll tell you."

She nodded. And without taking her eyes off me, she called over to the man behind the pillar. "Mauv, take them to his ship."

Mauv escorted Miri and Ryna past me toward the elevator.

"And uh," I added. "I would hurry if I were you."

Mauv nodded and ushered them into the elevator and descended.

"Now tell me where you planted the explosive?" Tess demanded, keeping her gun on me.

"To tell you the truth, I wasn't paying much attention to which drum I pulled. I picked it at random. But if you're quick enough, I'm sure you can match the serial number on this drum to find where it goes." I held it out to her.

She snatched it and backed away.

The elevator doors opened and Mauv stepped out. I nodded to Tess. "I'll leave you to your treasure hunt." Once inside, with the doors closed, I jumped up and hoisted myself up through the trap door in the ceiling. I wasn't sure if she was angry enough to waste a few seconds shooting through the elevator door. She might have wanted some revenge before scouring her main computer hardware. So, I wasn't taking any chances. I put my hands and feet on the side of the ladder and slid back down to the lower doorway. I ran through the hallway until I was safe aboard the *Princess.*

After I initiated the undocking sequence from the starcruiser, I headed up to the cockpit. I took the flight controls and headed away from Cosstere and the Davendries as quickly as I could. Miri and Ryna joined me in the cockpit. I turned to Miri, "Next time, let's steer clear of Cosstere."

She nodded emphatically, taking a seat beside me. "We'll need to stop for supplies."

I nodded, keeping my eyes ahead. "And repairs."

"How will you find the bounty hunter?"

I shook my head. "I don't need to. The bounty hunter was hired by Westward Galactic. Westward will know where they are."

"I'm sorry I dragged you into this. I never imagined this would get so out of hand," she said softly.

I took my mask off and put it away. "If I had known, I would have said no. So, for Ryna's sake, we're lucky I didn't know."

She looked down. "I promised nobody would find out about you being a Wayfinder. It looks like I wasn't able to keep that promise." She looked into my eyes. "I'm very sorry."

I took a deep breath. "Wasn't your fault. Not sure how it could have been. It was my mistake in how I tried to handle the Davendries. I was the one who crash-landed."

"I'm still sorry for roping you into helping," she said.

I looked into her eyes. She was sincere. Something in my stomach churned at the thought of her alone on Cosstere, dealing with all this. No, I couldn't have left her. My logical mind would never have withstood the whipping my heart would have lashed out had I said no. Deep down, I knew the truth of the matter better than I let on.

"Miri, I was a bit hasty in my reply. When I remember you standing there, asking for help, I know the truth as plain as day. If I could choose over again, I still would have said yes."

She smiled and ran a tender hand down my arm before leaving the cockpit. I stared after her for a while. That touch seemed more than usual. She had touched my arm on several occasions, but somehow this one was different. This one was special. I shook my head to clear my thoughts.

Ryna took Miri's seat beside me. "You are very smart," she declared.

I smiled. "Oh really? How so?"

"You know a lot about bombs."

"No, little miss. I'm really good at pretending."

EPISODE 3

The last thing I ever wanted

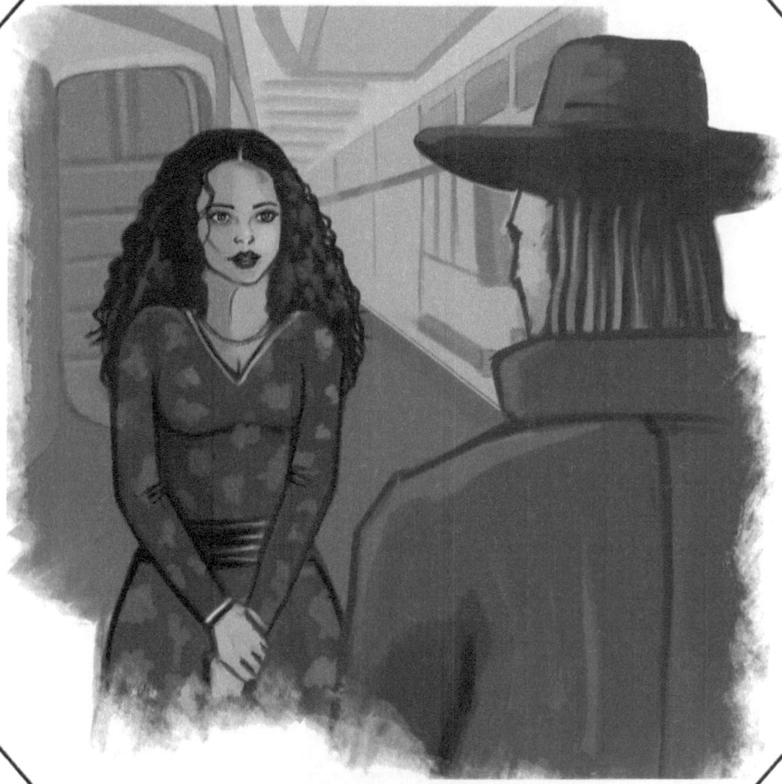

3
THE LAST THING I EVER WANTED

The Kuda were bad news. I could deal with the Davendries all day long. They were criminally trained gunfighters and scavengers. They were no walk in the park by any means, but they were a far cry from the Kuda. The Kuda were ex-military mercenaries. The cream of the crop, one might say. They knew combat better than most pilots knew their ship. They didn't know much about tracking, negotiating, repairing, or even how to drink right. But they knew warfare. That's why I didn't take the news very well.

"Rence!" Miri called from outside my cabin door. "You're being a baby about this."

"Then *you* deal with them!" I shouted.

"Maybe they're wrong. Maybe it's not them at all."

Yeah and maybe I'll be a sugarplum fairy tomorrow, I thought. The Kuda were easy to spot. They wore their blast armor everywhere. They painted a red skull on their pauldrons. Not easy to miss. If the word around town was true and the Corporation employed Kuda to guard their facility, breaking in was impossible. I got up off the cot and opened my cabin door. I needed to end this conversation. That was my first mistake. Miri wore her hair down like she had when I picked her up on Cosstere. She didn't normally wear her hair down but she knew I liked her with her hair down. To make matters worse, she had curled it.

I pointed a harsh finger in her direction, getting ready to verbally retaliate. But then I hesitated, pointing to her hair. "A new style?"

"I didn't have time to dry it," she explained.

That also was not the answer I wanted to hear. Either she was lying and she curled her hair on my account or her hair naturally displayed itself how I fancied her most. Neither one was going to help me win the argument. At least she had changed out of that pretty long shirt. That, combined with her hair and delicate eyes, had proven too much for me to reject. She knew I was sweet on her and had used her advantage to get me to help her.

I hadn't minded her using her advantage on me—and deep down, I still didn't. There was a part of me that would do anything for that woman. Yes, even gallivant across the cosmos in search of the girl's parents. Though even that mission had become complicated as of late. I reached over and touched Miri's curly hair. I'm not sure why I did. It was something I did without thinking. Immediately after, my mind replayed the events of the other day. When one of those scavengers on Cosstere had touched Miri's hair, it unnerved her. And I fancied Miri a lot. The last thing I wanted was to offend her in that way. For a lonely, rugged outcast, I still fancied myself a gentleman in that respect.

I pulled my hand back and glanced down apologetically. To my surprise, though, she didn't flinch. Either she was expecting me to touch her hair or she didn't mind. Ryna, who stood at her side, smiled.

"What are you smilin' at?" I asked. That was my second mistake.

"You like her hair," she stated in triumph.

I would have pulled the brim of my hat low to hide the color in my cheeks, but I had taken my hat off to lie down on the cot. I guess that was my third mistake. I turned to Miri. Her cheeks were burning the same color. Somehow, that disarmed my grim mood.

I smiled. "I'm still waiting on a few replacement parts. Perhaps you and the little matchmaker here could go into town and rustle up a few supplies?" We had landed at Jashur VII. It was a terrific place to repair the *Astral Princess.* Supposedly, it was an ideal place to infiltrate the Westward Galactic Financial Corporation. We needed to know where the Corporation had requested Ryna's parents to be brought by the bounty hunter. I also wouldn't mind a little more information on what those doctors were doing with Ryna and her special gift.

Ryna's eyes lit up in excitement. I reckoned the girl hadn't had much in the way of fun so it wasn't surprising that she wanted to go. Miri nodded. "I need to get her a change of clothes anyway."

I nodded, retrieving my hat.

"What are you going to do?" Miri asked.

"I need to figure out how to get past some Kuda. The solitude will do me some good."

"Or," Miri said with a slight smile and a twinkle in her eye. "You could come with us."

"Shopping?"

"It might be fun," she urged, smiling at me. She wasn't playing fair; I adored her when she smiled like that. "Who knows," she added. "A little distraction could be what you need."

I smiled, gazing at her. "Let's go."

Jashur was a planet by my standards. It no longer resorted to traveling by animal. It had hovermobiles and hoverbikes to get around with. Miri picked out a hovermobile to rent. It had red paint, four seats, and even a sunroof. With such fanciful features, I felt how I imagined wealthy people did. We stopped in front of a few shops Miri had pointed out. The buildings were not very tall, which wasn't surprising. Jashur was bustling but it was still a frontier world. Miri led us into a clothing shop. Ryna's eyes got real big rather quick. I reckoned she hadn't ever seen so many things to wear.

Miri went around holding up clothes to Ryna, gauging the sizes. The shop was the largest on Jashur but even with that, the selection was small. She had to hunt for the correct size. She seemed to like hunting in that respect. She looked to be in her element as much as when she was riding an animal.

Miri turned to her left and stopped beside a display with a red and white dress. She paused, gazing at it. Then she ran her fingers through the silky fabric as if in thought. I had known Miri for several years. I had learned what food she liked and even the smells she liked. But it wasn't until that moment that I realized how much she liked dresses. I looked down. I wanted her to be happy, but I also needed to keep us alive. Standing out in a crowd was the worst way to do so.

I touched her arm and whispered in her ear. "Sorry Miri, another time. We have to keep low, for Ryna's sake."

Her expression darkened and her eyes glanced to the floor. "I know...I just wish that..."

"Hey miss," a tall man from behind the counter called. "Is that feller botherin' you?"

I turned around expecting to see someone behind. Nobody was near Miri except me. My Lands! He was talking about me. I guessed what I said to Miri saddened her more than I thought. Enough for others to notice her demeanor. I didn't want to upset her. But how could that be helped? We were chasing the Corporation and dodging shots from pirates and mercenaries. It wasn't the life of silks and satins.

Miri glanced back at me and burst into giggles. She turned back to the man behind the counter. "Oh, Rence is okay. He's with me." She slid her arm around mine.

I liked her arm in mine. But I had no right to like it. Miri deserved more than the life I led. I was an outlaw of sorts, my career outlawed. All I had given her was blast fire to dodge and new worries. I was no good for her. Yet something about her smile when she asked me to join their shopping had me wondering. If I could go to town with them, could I fit in with her someday? Could I put this Wayfinder business behind me and settle down with her? Could I give her a life of silks and satins?

A man stepped through the open doorway, clad in blast armor and wearing a helmet. "That wouldn't be Rence Perry, would it?" He wore a skull painted on his pauldron.

"No," I said, careful not to give him any regard.

He stepped right up close to me. He was doing it on purpose. The Kuda didn't care much for propriety. Results were the only things they respected. And they counted on intimidation to do most of the heavy lifting for them.

"Then tell me, stranger. What's your name?"

Miri tensed up, clinging to my arm. Unfortunately, I needed my arm if this was going to decline into a fight. I pulled my arm out of Miri's white-knuckled clamp. "Alder," I said walking past him toward the door. "And I was just leavin'." The only names that came to my mind were Davendry—which was too conspicuous—and Miri's last name. I hoped it was enough. I reached for the door handle and heard the sound of him drawing his blast pistol.

I spun, clearing leather, and fired two shots. The barrel of his blast pistol had barely cleared leather when my two shots nailed him square in the chest. They glinted off his chest armor but knocked him to the ground.

He laughed, rising to his feet. "I don't know of any Rence Alder who can draw that fast. But a Wayfinder named Rence Perry is the fastest and straightest shooter in the colony worlds." He ran his finger across the burn mark in the center of his breastplate. "And I'd say you shoot mighty straight, Mr. Perry."

No. How could I think about settling down with Miri when I got a target on my back? How could she take on my last name when that very name draws mercenary scum like the Kuda into picking fights? Not only did I not deserve her, but I would never be able to give her a peaceful life. I was angry at life for the unfairness. Angry as a Valkyrian Hound before mealtime.

The Kuda's blast pistol lay on the floor and I was only a door away from escaping. The way I figured it; I could get beyond the door before he could retrieve his blast pistol. I went for the door but the Kuda tackled me to the ground. He must have suspected he didn't have enough time to pick up his gun. His armor added more weight to his tackle. Miri screamed my name. I jabbed my elbow hard into his side. That was a mistake. My elbow struck against his armor and sent a sting up my forearm.

He slammed his helmet against the back of my head. My vision started to blur and my head ached. How was I to fight someone I could not punch, shoot, or bluff? I let my head rest against the floor. It was throbbing and resting it on the floor seemed to ease the pain. Miri was shouting something at the Kuda but I couldn't hear. I felt tired and my muscles were relaxing.

I didn't have to try breaking into the Corporation building to get tangled up with the Kuda. This is what I got for believing I could settle down and offer Miri any kind of life. What would happen to Miri and Ryna? Miri couldn't fly and Ryna had a price on her head. If I fell to that Kuda, they wouldn't stand a chance. But my head was throbbing and my muscles wanted to give in. My heart started pumping faster and my breathing quickened. My thoughts fixated on that Kuda. My mind started dreaming up all kinds of terrible things he could do to her. That wasn't like me.

The Kuda pulled my arms behind my back. I winced in pain. Still, my mind lingered on those imagined images in my head. My muscles tensed and my nostrils flared. I scooted one leg underneath me. The Kuda slugged me in the ribs. I groaned and slid my other leg underneath me. He head-butted be again with his helmet. Even though my head was pounding, my blood boiled with anger. I threw my head back and slammed it into the Kuda's head, smashing into his helmet.

That dazed him long enough for me to get my feet under me. I pushed up with my special knees, jumping high into the air with the Kuda still on my back. We hit the ceiling of the shop, punching a hole in the shape of the Kuda's back and helmet. When I fell back to the floor, that Kuda was not on my back. He hung in the air, wedged into the ceiling hole for a few seconds before gravity pulled him back down.

That should have been where I ran. It made perfect sense to run now. But I didn't want to run. I felt mean enough to eat off the same plate as a Tolderian cobra. I sidestepped and let the brute hit the floor. I yanked a board off a shelf and slammed it into the back of the Kuda over and over again. What had gotten into me? The brute was on the ground and I was able to get away, that should have been enough. Why did I want so badly to pound him into the ground?

"Mr. Rence, I'm sorry!" Ryna called out.

Her voice sounded irritating, like an unwanted interruption. Something caught my attention–at least my mind was clear enough to notice. Why was she apologizing? She couldn't be thinking she was responsible for getting us into trouble. Sure, she was the spotlight on this entire mission—and every trouble associated with it. But she shouldn't have thought of herself as the cause of it. Or was she apologizing for another reason? I had asked her not to use her calming ability on me without asking. I supposed she could have tried to calm me without asking except I wasn't feeling calm. Far from it. I was feeling the exact opposite. I was as far from being calm as a drunken man is from being respectable.

Unless...unless there was more to Ryna than I had thought. I glanced at the girl and tried to ask her to calm me down. I wasn't sure how the words came out; my mind was still a bit muddled. I must have spoken well enough for Ryna to understand. Within moments, my mind cleared up. My hands stopped trembling. My breathing slowed, and my heart rate calmed. I was even calm enough to feel the throbbing inside my head.

I stumbled forward to the counter. The tall thin man behind the counter backed away with wide eyes. I pulled out some coins from my pocket and let them fall to the counter. I didn't bother counting how much I gave him; the pounding in my head was too distracting. "For the damages," I said.

I retrieved my blast pistol from where it had fallen when the Kuda tackled me and holstered it. I would need to check the alignment when I got back to the *Princess.* I picked up my hat and dusted it off before exiting the shop. I climbed into the hovermobile and sprawled out across the back seats, waiting for Miri and Ryna. They soon came out with a bundle of clothes. I wasn't an expert on how long it takes women to shop for clothes. But I reckoned it was mighty short compared to their intentions. That couldn't be helped. At least, I couldn't have helped it. If Miri was settled down with a man of little consequence to anybody else, she would have had the time she wanted.

Miri was kind enough to drive us back to the *Princess.* She had a long conversation with Ryna about what she had seen back there. I was glad she had the sense which I didn't in caring for Ryna's emotional state. She could have been a fine mother to Ryna if things were different. As for me, I took some head medicine and slept a couple of hours. When I emerged from my den like a bear in spring, my muscles were stiff but useful.

Miri found me in the main corridor. "Rence, how are you feeling?"

"I reckon I feel a little like the *Princess* after that crash landing."

She smiled. "I'm glad you're up. Ryna has been worried about you."

I had been wanting to talk with her anyhow so now was a good time. "Where is she?"

"She's in the cockpit, petting Lady."

The girl and my falcon had been growing fond of each other. That was nice at the moment, but it would make things hard when this mission was over and we would have to part ways. I strolled into the cockpit and found Ryna sitting in my chair with her attention on Lady.

She looked at me. "I'm sorry Mr. Rence."

"I ain't mad," I said. "But I am a little curious. You don't just calm people down, do you?"

She shook her head.

"You can make people feel emotions too."

She shook her head again. "I can't pick what they feel, I can only make it go up or down."

"So, instead of calming my anxiety, you heightened my sense of protection?"

She nodded, her eyes welling up with tears. "Only I did it too much."

I nodded to the side in contemplation. "Well, I can't argue with you on that. Even I was wondering what had come over me."

She let a tear fall. "I promise I won't do that to you again."

I stared straight ahead. "Ryna, I don't want you promising not to help me out. You might have overdone it, but you helped me out in that fight with the man in the armor suit."

"But it made you mad," she insisted.

One thing was clear, she was too young to understand the full consequences of her abilities. Here she sat, wanting to understand what had happened, and me, not knowing if I could explain it. "I wasn't mad at you, little miss; I was mad at that man. You see, a man's need to protect is often helped by anger. I reckon you could say it's like riding a camcam. I don't much like saddling up on those smelly lizards but it got us to where we needed to get."

Another tear fell from Ryna's eyes.

"I don't think you did nothin' wrong, little miss. The way I figure it, you were helpin' out in the only way you could. In a sense, you and I are a lot alike."

She looked at me with renewed interest.

"For me, I am quick on the draw and straight in my shot. A gun is a tool like most others; it can do a lot of good and it can do a lot of harm. I have a set of rules I follow to make sure I use them properly. Never draw lest to shoot, never shoot lest you have to, and always try to talk your way out first."

I wiped away one of the tear lines that ran down her face. "Your ability is like my gun. It can also be used for good things as well as bad things. I reckon you'll have to grow up sooner than you should have to. You'll have to know when to use it and when not to."

I wiped away her other tear line. "Don't let it fret you. If I turned out okay, you will too."

I smiled at her and she smiled in return, hugging me.

Some movement caught my attention from the corner of my eye. Miri moved away from the door and walked back the way she had come. How long had she been standing there? Why didn't she come in? Maybe she didn't want to interrupt? Or was she plain curious about how I would handle Ryna's concerns?

I turned back to Ryna, grinning. "And between you and me, we made a great team back there."

"Rence?" Miri called from down the corridor before poking her head through the door. "Some people are here with the new parts you ordered."

I passed Miri heading for the corridor when she caught my arm. "Rence," she whispered, nodding toward Ryna. "Thank you."

I looked back at Ryna who was happily stroking Lady's feathered head. "I meant every word."

It took a few hours to complete the repairs on the *Princess.* After completing it, I sat on the entry ramp, whittling a stick down to nothing. I had no ideas on how to break into the Corporation's building to get information; not with Kuda roaming around. Miri walked down the ramp of the *Princess* and sat down beside me.

"You look like a troubled man," she said, eyeing my whittling.

I sighed. "I got nothing, Miri. You saw my fight against that Kuda. That was just one. I can't think of a way to break into Westward Galactic with dozens of Kuda around."

"I'm sure it will come to you," she said, trying to sound reassuring.

I kept whittling.

"In the meantime," she said. "Could you teach me to shoot?"

I stopped my whittling and looked at her. Her expression suggested she was being serious. "You already know how to shoot a gun," I said.

"Yes, but not like you."

I dropped the whittled stick onto the pile of sawdust and woodchips beside my feet. "I don't know that you want that kind of life, Miri." I looked into her eyes. I had always found it dangerous to look into her eyes, my fancy for her had overridden my judgment many a time. "You heard that Kuda back in town. My reputation as a fast gun is what got us into that scrape in the first place."

"Rence, I want to help. Lately, it feels like you're doing all the heavy lifting. If we get into another fight, I want to be able to help."

I picked up another stick and started carving off the bark.

She touched my cheek and turned my head to face her. "Please, Rence? I'd like to help out."

"I'll be happy to show you what I know, Miri. But if you really want to help, figure out how to break into Westward Galactic."

"Well, actually, I've been thinking about that."

I raised an eyebrow. "Oh?"

She gave half a smile with a sparkle in her eyes. "The commandos, the Kuda, they're good in a fight, right?"

I nodded, not following where she was taking this conversation.

"Well, if they specialize in combat, then it would stand to reason they're not as well versed in intrigue."

I looked away and sighed. "I think I know where you're going with this and I don't like it."

"Rence, think about it. You said you couldn't think of a way in. Well, if they think as you do, then they also won't see a way someone can get in. They'll never see it coming."

I hated to admit it but she was right. I was so used to the direct approach, that I hadn't even considered the subtle, indirect method. Not only did it have merit, but as far as I could tell, it had the best chance of working.

I looked into her eyes. "You do realize if anything goes wrong, I won't be there to help you."

"That is a possibility, yes."

"And it's not a simple job either, this could take weeks to plan."

She nodded. "Look, you said I exhibited leadership. Well, how about letting me get the ball rolling on this one?"

I dropped my stick and folded up my pocketknife. "Get back into town. You're gonna need that dress."

She squealed in excitement and kissed me on the cheek. She bounded back into the *Princess* like a young fawn that found its footing. One thing was sure. They were not going to see this one coming. And I was as sure as shooting going to set her up for success. Why just fix something, when you can fix it and then some?

While Miri and Ryna headed back to town I sifted through my weapon's locker. I needed something suitable for Miri. One she could carry concealed yet operate without much fuss. Going through each sidearm was like a walk down memory lane. Each piece had a story. Each had a name. Even the two I carried, had a name and history. The first was Thunder and the second was Lightning. They were given as payment from Kray Shiltz, the man whose kidnapped daughter I brought back. He didn't have enough money to pay me so he bartered with his Starfield & Tanner set. They were worth more than money in my eyes.

I finally settled on Ivory, my short-barreled pearl-handled Reinhart 66. She was a holdout blast pistol. Easy to conceal but only had eleven shots. I picked up Ivory from a traveling dealer who needed coins more than he needed a gun. I had only used her once, and she had saved my life. She was perfect for Miri.

When I had put away the rest of the weapons, I heard Ryna's giggling voice down the corridor. She was in a happy mood. She walked up to me with a broad smile and triumph in her eyes. What was the little matchmaker up to? I heard Miri walking up the ramp. I collected the spare energy cell and charger and headed down the corridor to meet up with her.

When she walked around the corner, I stopped cold in my tracks. She smiled, wearing a red and white dress with a floral pattern. White lace lined all the edges and caressed the tops of her hands. A scarlet sash outlined her waist and gave her an hourglass shape. The dress billowed out at the bottom from many layers. But that was not all, she even painted her face with some makeup. Sparkling earrings hung from her ears, bouncing light around.

She smiled at me, cheeks flushing. "I...I figured if I wanted to be convincing, I ought to go all the way."

I stared at the magnificent sight.

The smile ran off her face. "What do you think?"

Most of what I had been carrying fell to the floor.

Ryna giggled from behind. "See, I told you."

Miri relaxed and grinned while I fumbled to pick up what I had dropped. I wasn't sure before, but I was sure then that we were going to succeed. She swayed the dress to and fro and even twirled around, demonstrating how well it fit.

"Well?" she asked. "Aren't you going to say something?"

"You give the stars something to envy, Miri. You really do."

I shook my head to clear my thoughts. It was gonna be tricky keepin' my head about me with her all dressed up and looking as she was. I couldn't get over it. It was like Miri had been touched by the wand of a fairy godmother. "I, uh, thought you should have Ivory."

She looked down at my offering. "Ivory?"

"It's a Reinhart 66 holdout blast pistol. I figured since I was going to teach you some shooting, you should have your own piece."

She smiled warmly and accepted the gun and accessories. "Can we start tomorrow?"

I nodded. "At sunup."

She practically danced down the corridor toward her cabin.

I watched her go out of sight, enjoying watching the breeze sway her dress as she walked.

Ryna giggled. "You like her, don't you?"

I wasn't about to gratify her prying. The little matchmaker had about sorted me out anyhow. I looked at her, unable to completely suppress my smile.

"I think I know what your answer will be," she said.

She was referring to her question from the other day. She had asked me if I was going to kiss Miri. "Got me figured out, do you? Well, it's a little more complicated than that."

"Don't you know how?" she asked innocently.

I squirmed where I stood. "It ain't about knowing how. Just because a man *can* do something, doesn't mean that he *should.* Everything I've done so far has had a consequence. Going shopping with you and Miri had the consequence of that Kuda attacking. I'm certain the actions I've done with the Davendries is gonna come 'round and bite me in the backside one of these days. So, you see, little miss, deciding if I *should* gets a little complicated."

"Oh," she said, not sounding convinced. "Well, you should."

I smiled, my cheeks burning. "I'll keep that in mind, little miss. Now you run along and get ready for bed."

There was a good chance the little matchmaker was right. The outlook of a child seemed so easy, so simple. I still had no right to hope for getting together with Miri; even my name was enough to attract trouble. Yet somehow, I found comfort in hoping for an impossible dream. A dream Ryna had instilled in me. Perhaps I needed that little girl as much as she needed me?

I got up early the next morning to give Lady some flight time. She didn't get much chance to stretch her wings yesterday and was acting a little restless. I had set up a small target on a tree about twelve paces away. It was close enough to practice fundamentals and yet far enough to challenge Miri. I had seen her shoot a rifle a few times, so I knew she could shoot. Pistol shooting from the hip, however, was an entirely different caliber of shooting.

I heard Miri's footsteps behind me. And by the smoothness of her stride, she was back in her normal clothes. I turned around just as the sun peeked over the horizon, silhouetting her with a golden halo. She walked up to me with her blast pistol in hand. Something had changed about her. I couldn't put my finger on exactly what it was, though. It was as if she had more curves and fewer stiff angles about her. It didn't make any sense. Without the dress, she was simply the Miri I knew—except I could still see her as if she had the dress on. I shook my head to clear my mind.

"Something wrong?" she asked.

"Nope." I lied, of course. What was wrong was my preoccupation with her. My thoughts, it seemed, were less obedient than a stray dog. "We're going to practice this every morning and every evening for a couple of hours each." I pointed to the target in the distance.

She held the blast pistol with both hands and at arm's length. She bent her knees slightly as she peered down the sights. She fired. The thin blue blast bolt sprang from her snub barrel and struck the center of the target. She glanced at me with a pleased smile.

"Bravo, Miri," I said. "You're a mighty fine shot."

"Now can you show me how to shoot like you?"

I nodded, taking her arm. I repositioned it to her side. "Now I want you to practice bringing your arm up from rest, all along the line of the tree trunk. And the moment your arm is high enough to shoot, take the shot. This exercise will be more about muscle memory than about eyesight."

She raised her arm slowly and then fired. The shot didn't even come close to hitting the tree. She was understandably disconcerted by the sudden change in performance. But she kept at it. For the next three days, she spent far longer than the few hours I had prescribed in practice. She spent nearly all day each day, taking time out only for meals and such. I had to admire that woman. When she got it into her head to learn something, she immersed herself completely. She went at learning a new skill as a Wayfinder would.

By the fourth day, I had her practicing shooting while in her dress. She needed to get used to the feel of the swaying fabric while lifting her arm and firing. She was getting better each day and I was growing restless. Each day we spent preparing was another day behind in pursuit of Ryna's parents. I knew only that they would be delivered to the Corporation, not much beyond that.

On the fifth day, when I had finished forging an identification card for Miri, she came to me wearing her dress. "Rence, what do you think?" she said as she turned herself about.

I had seen her in her dress quite a bit lately so I wasn't sure why she was showing it to me again. Did she want a little more encouragement? I tipped my hat. "You look mighty pretty, you do."

She dropped her hands to her side. "I meant; can you tell where I'm hiding my gun?"

I looked her over with my eyes. She had her hair pulled up into a braided bun and wore dangly earrings. She had added red gloves and matching shoes. I didn't see any bulges from her thin waist or a sagging hem. If I had to guess, she wore it under the dress and close to her hips. "I don't see anything that gives it away," I admitted.

She stepped closer to me. "Good, now I want to see if I can pass a search." She held her arms out and looked at me expectantly.

I looked at her, admiring the view, but was uncertain what she was asking.

She read my expression. "Rence, could you please search me? I want to make sure nobody can find it."

My cheeks flushed as I contemplated touching all around her. What she was asking was logical, but it was hard at the same time. I fancied Miri but I also didn't want to cross any boundaries into getting fresh. I hesitated.

She suppressed a giggle and took my hands, placing them on her waist. "Rence, thank you for being a gentleman, but I really need you to search me."

My heart pounded in my chest and I could feel my blood pumping. My breathing grew shallow. I took a deep breath. "All right," I said. "Please pardon me, I don't want to seem like I'm...like I'm..."

She smiled. "Believe me, I understand. It'll be okay."

I looked around to verify the little matchmaker was absent before proceeding. I ran my hands around her waist, across her back, and even down the center of her chest. Her upper half was clean. I patted down her hips and down the length of her legs. I pulled the brim of my hat low before patting down her inner thighs through the fabric of her dress. I felt instantly more comfortable once that job was over but it left me confused. I didn't find her gun anywhere. Then I lifted the hem of her dress and examined her shoes. I stood there, stumped.

She read my face and burst out laughing.

"You gonna tell me where you have it hid?"

She shook her head with a broad smile.

"But can you draw it without much fuss?" I asked.

"Rence," she asked, "What are you hiding back there?" She pointed behind me.

I turned to see the weapon's locker all locked up tight. I glanced back to Miri. "That's the weapon's—" I nearly dropped my jaw. She had her blast pistol in her hand. Wherever she was hiding it, was both hard to find and easily accessible. I smiled. "You amaze me, Miri."

She laughed.

"Here's your new identicard," I said, handing it to her.

She took it with delight in her eyes. "So what's my name?"

"Miri Alder."

She scowled. "Don't I get an undercover name?"

"You've been seen around town and people are bound to have heard your name. You answer to your name naturally, and they can run a background check on you all they want. The only change I made was that you now work for Westward Galactic. You're the new internal policy auditor."

She raised her eyebrows. "Sounds impressive."

"The title is vague enough to cover whatever job you end up needing it to be."

"What do I do once I'm inside?" she asked.

I handed her a tiny plastic disc that was small enough to fit on the tip of her little finger. "That should let me listen in on what's going on. And I'll have Lady nearby so I can keep an eye on you." I also handed her a data transmitter. "You'll need to place this somewhere on the mainframe server. An access terminal is not good enough. This means you'll have to get into the server room. I can take care of the rest remotely."

"You make it sound simple," she said.

"Straightforward, perhaps. But it won't be easy."

I handed her a small number three detonator. "This one is an explosive. Don't get it confused with the transmitter."

"What do I need this for?" she asked.

"You don't often need them, but they're real handy when you do."

"How long 'til it explodes?" she asked.

"Nine seconds. Once it is set, you only have until the count of nine until it blows."

She nodded. "When do we get started?"

I handed her a datapad. "Just as soon as you memorize this."

"What is it?"

"Names and faces of Corporation managers," I said. "Any executive should know them on sight."

"I'll get right on it," she said, heading toward her cabin.

It only took her forty-eight hours to memorize the datapad. That was about as impressive as how she looked in that dress. In total, our preparations set us back about a week, but I had high hopes. Miri was looking more and more confident in her dress. She had been getting rather good with her blast pistol too. I was confident that she could pull this off and get out alive.

On the following afternoon, we rented a hovermobile. She drove it past town and down to the Corporation facility. Westward Galactic Financial Corporation had a foothold on several planets. This one was the closest to Cosstere and the most likely place the bounty hunter would have brought them. That is unless there was a specific facility Ryna's parents were to be taken to. I didn't know if the bounty hunter's ship was faster than the *Princess* or not. It was best to just assume the bounty hunter had already come and gone.

We did have one advantage. All Westward Galactic facilities had a centralized computer database. So, tapping into one facility's computer system should get us the information we needed. This facility looked less of an office building and more like a government compound. Located several miles out of town, it had a few buildings sharing a parking lot. High fences encircled the perimeter with a checkpoint gate. Between the buildings lay two starship landing pads. The first was empty but the second had a landed corporate shuttle. The whole place looked like an asphalt island surrounded by wilderness.

I had asked Ryna to stay aboard the *Princess,* but she didn't want to be left alone. I took her with me earlier in the day and we nestled ourselves in a small grove of trees several hundred yards away. I opened my little suitcase and set up the small satellite dish. I needed to be ready to hack into the main computer once Miri planted the data transmitter. Then I pulled out my tactical mask and fastened it on.

"Ryna," I said, my voice slightly muffled behind my mask. "It's time to get Lady into the air."

Ryna pet Lady's feathered head. "Please watch Miss Miri," she said before thrusting her arm upward. Lady flew up and out of sight. It was showtime. I tapped a few buttons on my wristband, switching the eyesight in my mask to see through Lady's eyes. Lady landed on the roof of one of the buildings overlooking the gate Miri was stopped at.

The guard handed Miri back her identicard. "Please report to Director Scuzin," he said.

Miri smiled. "Will do." She drove up to the first building and a man and two armored Kuda met her at the door.

"Miss Alder, we were not expecting you," the man said, shaking her hand.

"Believe me, Ulric, it was not on my radar," she said with a warm smile. "But after hearing that your contracted security rooted out a known outlaw, I had to come. The board now feels there is much we can learn from your example. I'm here to take notes on how you run your facility so well and your clever use of contracted security."

"Allow me to give you a tour personally," he said with a grin.

"Thank you," she said, walking beside him. "By the way, how are your two boys doing?"

Lady flew down to a window ledge as they entered the building. Ryna rubbed my arm. I pressed a button on my wristband, returning my eyesight to normal. Ryna pointed to a small vehicle that was approaching our little grove of trees. I motioned for Ryna to lay low and I did the same. The hoverbike slowed as it passed by. The security guard glanced about the trees as he passed. When he was gone, I turned to Ryna. "It looks like a routine patrol. Let me know the next time it passes."

Ryna nodded.

I turned my attention back to Miri and switched my eyesight back to Lady's vision. Miri and Ulric passed by the window Lady was perched by and sauntered over to a door with a Kuda standing guard. "Through there is our server room," Ulric said, pointing to the door.

"You must have such good security in there," Miri said walking up to the Kuda. She held her arms out to her side and look at him.

He regarded her but did not move.

"Aren't you going to frisk me first?" she said playfully.

His dark helmet obscured his facial expressions, but his posture portrayed his annoyance. "Knock it off," he said, returning his gaze forward.

She turned to Ulric, "Your boys seem all business today."

Ulric opened the door and let her in. The door closed behind them and my view from Lady was blocked. I listened carefully.

"Wow, you have a clean server room," Miri said.

"State of the art quantum processing," he said proudly.

"I'd like to get a better look," she said.

"I'm afraid that won't be possible."

"I love computers," she insisted.

"Only authorized technicians beyond this point."

Come on, Miri, I thought. *Think of something.* This whole week would be for nothing if she couldn't get the data transmitter onto the server. Without that connection, I wouldn't be able to remotely connect to their system. I wouldn't be able to extract the information we needed.

"Oh Ulric, I have clearance. I'm sure it will be fine."

"...I'm afraid not, Miss Alder. You will find that the success of this facility is largely due to our strict obedience to protocol."

I pounded my fist against a small tree trunk. Leaves floated to the ground.

"...yes, of course," Miri said.

Ryna rubbed my arm again. I switched my eyesight back to normal. The patrol vehicle was approaching again. This time it was a hovermobile. Ryna and I again laid low.

"Ah, Captain Cretik," Ulric said. "I'm glad you're back. I'd like to introduce you to Miss Alder. She is a policy auditor from Corporate."

"Haven't I seen you in town?" a rough voice asked.

That didn't sound good. I switched one of my eyes to see with Lady's vision. Lady had already moved to another window sill. Miri and Ulric were standing in front of a Kuda with large dents in his armor. I knew there was something I had forgotten. The only hole in Miri's story was that she was with me in the dress shop. I hadn't even thought to come up with a cover story for that. I knew we were running behind but I should have been more careful. My brain was screaming at me that I had to get Miri out of there.

The patrol hovermobile came to a stop just outside our little grove of trees. Four armed guards hopped out. Ryna tensed up, frozen in place. One of the guards held a device in his hand that beeped. They were tracking some signal. I glanced over to my mobile receiver case with its satellite dish. I quietly reached over and switched it off.

The four men halted. "The signal has stopped," one of them announced.

"Fan out," another ordered. The four men drew their guns and cautiously advanced in a search pattern.

I heard Miri's voice in my ear. "Why yes, in the Blue Bonnet dress shop."

Miri was taking the safest course; she was telling as much of the truth as necessary. That was also the smartest choice. Neither of us knew how much Cretik remembered about that encounter. So, telling a lot of the truth would confirm his memory and allow a fertile place to plant a lie. The only catch was that her lie may or may not be one of the facts he remembered well. It was a gamble but it was the smarter gamble.

A twig snapped a few paces away from me. I slowly turned my head. One of the guards was creeping toward Ryna and me, one slow step at a time. He hadn't seen us yet, but if he got much closer, he would spot us. I quietly reached for my blast pistol.

Miri continued, "You must be that brave soldier that discovered the Wayfinder."

"Yes," Cretik said with suspicion in his tone. "And *you* called him by name."

"That's right, he introduced himself as Rence. Played the part of a real charmer that one did."

He took a step closer to Miri. "Acted real concerned about him, almost as if you knew him."

Miri turned to Ulric. "Are they always this paranoid?"

"Captain Cretik, is this *really* necessary?" Ulric protested.

"It is when I smell a rat."

A rustling of leaves to my left snatched my attention. Two other guards were approaching. All these men already had their weapons drawn. Once they saw us, I couldn't guarantee I'd be able to take them all down before they shot me or Ryna. I would have to shoot first. I slowly looked around, keeping my movements to as few as possible. Where was the fourth man? If I started shooting without knowing where the last man was, I could end up with a blast bolt to the back of my head. Could Ryna help? If she could feel people's emotions, was there a chance she could feel where those emotions were coming from? But did I dare whisper to her? That first guard was getting awfully close and might be able to hear.

It was too risky. Even if I could whisper quiet enough, I could not be sure Ryna would respond just as quietly. The smart thing to do would be to distract the guards long enough for me to get a good look around and find that fourth man. I slowly picked up a small stone and tossed it away with as little movement as I could. If it fell far enough away, it would make the perfect distraction. It struck a close branch instead and tumbled to the ground at my feet.

I hadn't considered myself a cursing man, but I cursed then. Each of the guards opened fire on our position. I grabbed Ryna and jumped. We sailed through the canopy of branches and leaves, arcing over toward the other side of the grove. I caught sight of a ship flying down from the sky toward the facility's empty landing pad. I didn't get a good look, falling through the air, but it wasn't a corporate shuttle. It looked more like an Isuza class, painted with desert camouflage. If I had to put money on it, I'd say my initial hunch was right; this was where the bounty hunter was bringing Ryna's parents. And that was the bounty hunter's ship.

I landed and set Ryna down and tapped a few buttons on my wristband. My eyesight switched to infrared. Four body heat signatures burned brightly in front of my eyes. They were running to our position, shooting as they came. Their shots were wild and without aim. They were trying to drive us out of hiding. That was a good sign; that meant they lost sight of us.

I heard Miri gasp. I quickly switched one of my eyes to see Lady's vision. Cretik had shoved Miri back against a wall. "This is outrageous," she said, feigning amazement. She looked at Ulric. "Director Scuzin, control your man!"

Ulric put his hand on Cretik's arm. "Honestly, you have gone too far, Captain."

Cretik backhanded Ulric and he collapsed to the floor hitting his head. He grabbed Miri by the throat. "I think you know where Rence Perry is. I want him."

I turned to Ryna. "I gotta go help Miri."

She grabbed my arm. "Please don't leave me."

I closed my eyes in exasperation. I had too many battles to fight all at once. I drew Thunder and Lightning and began shooting back. The men dove for cover. I leaped high into the air and landed between two of them. I shot them both before they knew what had happened. A blast bolt struck a tree trunk close to my head. I ducked and fired a shot back in the general direction it had come. Scanning the area, I saw the remaining two heat sources. One was crouching behind a bush and the other was running toward the hovermobile.

I heard Miri gasping for breath.

"If you don't tell me where he is, you will die," Cretik said with a sneer.

My blood boiled and all my instincts shouted at me to get to Miri. I fired two shots into the bush and dropped that man. Then I leaped toward the hovermobile. I landed on the hood of the vehicle as the man was climbing in. I struck him across the face with the barrel of my blast pistol and he sunk into his seat.

I glanced in Ryna's direction, holstering my pistols. "I'll be right back!" I hopped into the driver's seat, pushing the unconscious man into the passenger seat. I sped off toward the facility compound while switching one eye back to my regular vision.

I didn't drive toward the front gate. Instead, I headed straight for the tall fence. Far in front of me, I saw the bounty hunter's ship take off and streak across the sky. That meant he had finished delivering Ryna's parents. They must still be at the facility. I felt a surge of hope. This disastrous mission finally had an end in sight. Then the corporate shuttle lifted off into the sky. If Ryna's parents were going to be transferred elsewhere, they would go by shuttle. I pushed the vehicle's accelerator to the maximum, speeding toward the outer fence. I still had one eye seeing what Lady saw.

"Please," Miri said, gasping for air. She reached out and swatted Cretik on the back of his helmet. He head-butted her with his helmet and she collapsed to the floor.

He picked her up by the blouse of her dress and shook her. "Where is Rence Perry?"

She looked at him with a dazed look in her eyes. "...six," she said.

"What?"

"...seven..."

"Is that an address?" Cretic asked with annoyance in his voice.

"...eight..."

Lady turned her head just then. I caught sight of the flashing light of the detonator Miri slapped onto the back of Cretik's helmet.

"...nine," she said. The explosion startled Lady and she flew away. I grunted and turned off Lady's vision to my eye. The outer fence came up fast. I jumped before it crashed into the fence. My forward momentum carried me over the fence and onto the top of one of the buildings. My knees softened what would otherwise have been a painful landing.

I recognized the layout from what I saw through Lady's eyes and crashed through the second skylight. I landed beside Cretik's body. A large hole was in the back of his helmet. I looked over to Miri. She was curled up against the wall, crying. What had I done? I had introduced her to the horrors of combat. She should never have had to go through this. She had practiced her part so well. She did everything right. One maniac Kuda with a chip on his shoulder had turned this whole day sideways.

I picked up Miri, her dress draping over my arms. "I'm so sorry, Miri."

She smiled between her sobs and ran a finger down my tactical mask where my lips would be. "I knew you'd come for me."

"I'll always come for you, Miri. Always."

She smiled.

"We gotta go," I said. "The shuttle with Ryna's parents just took off. If we hurry we can catch them."

Five armed guards stormed into the room, pointing their blast pistols at me.

"Let the hostage go," one of them commanded.

I glanced at Miri and then back at them. I lowered Miri to her feet.

The guard beckoned to Miri and she walked over to his side. He looked back at me. "Hands in behind your head."

I obeyed.

Miri took a few discrete steps back behind the line of guards. In one swift motion, she slipped her fingers behind her braided bun and drew her small blast pistol. She pointed it at them. The pistol charged with a high-pitched hum. The guards glanced back at Miri with wide eyes.

"If you'll excuse us," she said. "We have a shuttle to catch."

We locked them in the server room and ran to her hovermobile. "Drive fast," I said, reloading my blast pistols. She drove for the front gate with the peddle to the floor. I tapped a button on my wristband to summon Lady. She would follow us home. I fired several shots at the gate guards as we passed. I didn't need to aim, I just needed them to scatter and deter them from shooting back. We stopped at the grove of trees and picked up Ryna before speeding back to the *Princess.* I had Miri drive around town instead of through it so we could avoid any delays. The rest of the Kuda on base would undoubtedly be on our tail in short order. We had a window of a few minutes to lift off once we reached the *Princess.*

Before Miri had even parked the vehicle, I jumped out and ran up the *Princess's* entry ramp. Dashing to the cockpit, I started the launch sequence. Ryna hurried into the cockpit with Lady on her arm. Miri soon followed. Ryna pointed out the blast shield window. Three hovermobiles with Kuda drove up fast. I hit the lift thrusters and the *Princess* rocketed into the air.

We soared into the sky and then into orbit. With both of their landing pads empty, we were beyond the reach of the Corporation, for now. I performed a sensor scan of the area but didn't find the shuttle. "They're gone."

Miri sighed and sunk into her chair. "We can't keep chasing them forever..."

I spun around in my chair, removing my tactical mask. "Miri, we didn't lose them. They passed this way within the hour. Their ion trails should still be detectable. I can track them."

She teared up. "We've been trying to track them for over a week."

I put my hand to her cheek. "Listen to me, Miri. We're on the home stretch. I am on their trail; they cannot get away now."

A tear rolled down her cheek. "Promise?"

I nodded, wiping away her tear line. "I promise. It won't be long now. The *Astral Princess* is fast for a reason. I have caught many a fleeing ship before. We're almost there."

She closed her eyes, pressing my hand to her cheek. She relaxed somewhat and basked in my touch. When she finally released my hand, she sniffled and smiled at me.

Ryna set Lady on her perch. Then she turned and looked at me. “You *really* should.”

EPISODE 4

The worst possible choice

4 THE WORST POSSIBLE CHOICE

Picking up their trail was easy. I had tracked for twenty years as a Wayfinder. That is, before the blasted Corporation convinced the government to outlaw us. Despite their efforts to eradicate Wayfinders, I was still a thorn in their side. That was the beautiful irony. Their shuttle had a head start on us, but we had speed.

I sat in the cockpit of the *Astral Princess* with Lady, on her perch to my right. Behind me sat Miri, the woman I'd known for years. She had always been spunky; an intelligent woman who dreamed of a life of silks and satins. If she had any flaws, she sure didn't let on. Either that or I'd been looking at her through filtered lenses. I was, after all, sweet on her. Sure, she could irritate me plenty. But there were times when I indulged in delusional thoughts about settling down with her.

Beside Miri sat Ryna, the ten-year-old girl who started this whole mess. Or rather, this whole mess was started because of what she is. We learned back on Cosstere about her 'parents'. They were actually scientists that she barely knew and they referred to her as the tall one. The Westward Galactic Financial Corporation, however, called her Subject 35.

But if that wasn't odd enough, Ryna had a gift. She could fiddle with people's emotions. She could suppress or flair what a person was feeling. And that, I suspect, is why they were willing to kill to get her back.

My console beeped twice. "I've got something on sensors," I announced, pressing more buttons. The shuttle was transporting Ryna's parents to another Corporation facility. If we could rescue them first, then this entire mission could come to a successful end. The computer hummed and displayed a wireframe diagram of what the sensors picked up. It was a corporate shuttle.

"We found them. They're dead ahead."

Miri sighed with relief.

Ryna, on the other hand, looked indifferent.

The sensor screen beeped again, this time showing a second sensor contact; a big one. "Oh no..."

"What's wrong?" Miri asked.

I must have said that last part aloud. "Looks like they've reached their destination."

Miri walked over and glanced over my shoulder. "That's a really big ship. How are we supposed to get on board?"

"Well, knowing nothing about them will make bluffing a little rocky," I said, leaning back in my chair. "Getting them to want to take us aboard and not blast us to smithereens will be the trickiest part."

"I thought the tricky part would be letting us stay on board until you rescue Ryna's parents."

"I stand corrected."

She was right. How would we get her parents aboard the *Princess?* She'd be watched like a Quellian Hawk. Too many problems to solve in a short time. We would have to go about this one step at a time and hope we wouldn't get ourselves cornered. "Let's first get ourselves on board," I suggested.

I left the cockpit and climbed down to the bottom deck. I had several shipping crates. They all had a little something inside them, but it would be easy to consolidate to make an empty one.

Miri descended the stairwell behind me. "I think you should take Ryna with you."

I shook my head. "That'll just slow me down."

"Do you remember what happened on the Davendry starcruiser?"

How could I forget? It was a great ruse to get on board their starcruiser, right up until the Davendries captured Miri and Ryna. I had asked myself why I was such an idiot for underestimating them.

"This won't be the same," I said, not sounding convincing. And truthfully, I wasn't so sure it wouldn't end up the same anyhow.

"Rence, please. The safest place for Ryna is beside a Wayfinder."

She had to keep bringing up my profession. I wasn't immortal by any stretch of the imagination. Nor was I infallible. Shucks, I'd had more than my fair share of failures. I sighed. She did have a point, though. Beside a Wayfinder was a pretty safe place to be.

"All right," I said. "Help me carry this over to the loading ramp."

"What's in it?" she asked.

"Me. In a few minutes."

"I'm going to deliver you as cargo?" she said, stunned.

"If you've got a better idea, I'm all ears."

She helped me slide it over to the loading ramp. I bumped against a stack of boxes and a small detonator tumbled to the ground. I picked it up with annoyance bubbling up inside. I had told Miri a thousand times not to leave her detonator lying about. She had used the last detonator against that Kuda and it saved her life.

"Miri," I said, holding the detonator out to her. "How are you going to have it when you need it if you keep leaving it lying around?"

She took it with a sharp motion. "Sorry, Rence. I wanted it with my dress but I haven't yet sown up the tear."

"It's an explosive, Miri."

"I know, Rence. I'll put it away when we're done with this crate," she said setting it back on the pile of boxes. We finished moving the crate into place. Once the *Princess* landed, a handling crew would be able to easily unload the crate. That was step one. Step two would be getting out of the crate and finding Ryna's parents.

"What if they search the crate?" she asked. "Then what?"

I shrugged. "Well, I guess I can fiddle with the lock so it can only be opened from the inside."

"Okay," she said. "That takes care of you and Ryna. What do I do?"

"You'll be the transport captain delivering a package for Project Osurious. Be bold and charismatic. Don't be a pushover but do follow their instructions."

"In other words, I pretend to be you," she concluded.

I smiled. "That's one way to put it."

We returned to the cockpit in time for the Corporation mega-ship to send a transmission. "Transport vessel, this is Corporate *Labship 7.* We have you on our screens, please identify yourself."

Miri grabbed my hat and put it on, sitting down in my chair next to Lady. Ryna and I stepped outside the cockpit door.

Miri leaned back in the chair, resting one leg on the control console. "*Labship 7,* this is transport Miribel. I've got that package ready to deliver."

"Transport Miribel, you are not on the schedule for today's deliveries."

"That ain't my fault," she said. "I just work here."

"Transport Miribel, you are not authorized to land outside your scheduled arrival window."

"Look, we're all tryin' to do our jobs here. All I was given was a destination, not an instruction manual."

"Listen, lady, I don't make the rules."

"Oh, please don't send me all the way back to WGFC for one measly crate. Can't you help out a damsel in distress?"

"...just one crate?" the voice asked.

"Just one crate," she promised.

After about a minute the voice finally responded. "You are cleared to land in bay two. A deboarding team will be standing by."

"Thank you so much, hun. I really appreciate this."

After she switched off the transmission, I sauntered back into the cockpit. "I don't really sound like that, do I?"

She giggled.

I took two spare power cells for my blast pistols and tucked them into my boot. I might not need them, but an ounce of preparation was worth more than a pound of luck. I picked up Lady from her perch and then turned to Ryna. "Wanna take a ride with me in a metal cargo crate?"

She stared at me blankly.

I shrugged, walking past her. "I don't blame you, little miss."

I walked back down to the shipping crate. Miri and Ryna followed.

Miri knelt and looked into Ryna's eyes. "Ryna, I want you to go with Mister Rence. He'll keep you safe."

"Who will keep you safe?" she asked.

Miri smiled. "Lady will watch over me."

"Technically, I'm Mister *Perry*," I said.

Miri rolled her eyes at me. "I know, but that's what she calls you."

I handed Lady over to Miri and stepped into the crate. After lifting Ryna inside, I turned to Miri. "How are you gonna get them to let you stay until we get back? Seems they might want you to leave immediately."

"On a ship this old," she said with a smile. "Something is bound to malfunction."

I winked at her. She was much quicker on her feet than I gave her credit for. If history had been different, she could have been an excellent Wayfinder. I pulled out one of the wires to the external lock keypad. That would prevent anyone from opening the crate from the outside. I put on my tactical mask and hunched down inside the large crate. While Miri closed and locked the lid, I switched my eyesight to see through Lady's eyes. It was showtime.

It didn't take the crewmen long to unload the crate. An anti-grav lifter made short work of it. Miri stood at the bottom of the ramp with Lady perched on her arm. That gave me a clear view through Lady's eyes of our surroundings. There were three men in the bay. Two unloaded while the third recorded inventory on a datapad. The landing bay had stacks of metal crates and metal barrels against a wall. It would be enough for Ryna and me to hide amongst if we could first get out of the crate.

Miri looked to be thinking the same thing. "Hey boys," she said playfully. "Any of you ever seen an Earth falcon before?"

"No ma'am," one of them said.

"Then this is your lucky day," Miri said, waving to them. "Why don't y'all come over and say hello to Lady here before we go."

The three men walked over to her.

I love her style, I thought, switching my vision to normal. Quietly opening the container, I got out and hoisted Ryna out as well. It was too easy. We kept low and amongst the barrels until we got close to the door. I tapped a few buttons on my wristband and changed my vision to infrared. Through the walls, I saw the heat signatures of people moving all about. Since we were the only shuttle in the bay, it was a good bet the corporate shuttle was in bay number one.

As soon as the hall was clear, I went through the door with Ryna on my tail. It felt a little weird not having my hat, but Miri needed it. We hustled down the smooth white hallway. In many ways, it reminded me of the Davendry starcruiser. But this ship smelled sterile, like a hospital or a laboratory. We ducked into a small room off the main hallway. There was a computer terminal that I could use to get the layout of the ship.

Hacking into their computer system was no small feat. They were well-financed and the hardware proved it. It took me a half-hour before I could access their system. The good news was that the other landing bay was on the other end of the same hallway. Once the coast was clear I led Ryna down to the landing bay one. We quietly entered and hid behind a wall of storage crates.

I turned my vision back to normal. Seven men and one woman were all talking in the center of the bay. I turned to Ryna. "Are any of those your parents?"

She nodded and pointed to the group of people.

"The man and woman in the center?"

She again nodded.

I tapped a button on my wristband and zoomed in my eyesight on those two people. They wore name tags. Dr. Carol H'Lar and Dr. Petre Xaan. I had suspected ever since I met Ryna that her 'parents' were just scientists who were assigned to Ryna. It seemed my suspicion was correct. Why was I even trying to reunite Ryna with them? If they weren't biological parents, what right did they have to the girl anyhow? Well, I wasn't about to turn back now—not when I was this close.

I drew my blast pistols and casually walked up to the group. I was almost an arm's length away before they took notice of me. "All right, everyone into the corporate shuttle except Petre and Carol."

They stood motionless, staring at me in shock.

"Come on," I said. "This ain't no request."

The six men shuffled over to the entry ramp to the corporate shuttle. And then I heard a pistol activate behind me with a high-pitched hum. I slowly turned to see Petre with a blast pistol aimed at me. "What?" I asked.

"Things are not what they might seem," he said.

"You can say that again," I replied.

One of the six men tapped his wristband and spoke into it. I was too far to hear what he said, but I was sure he was calling security. I turned back to Petre. "I came here to rescue you for the little girl's sake."

"She's alive?" Carol asked with surprise and guilt in her voice.

"It doesn't matter now," Petre said. "She's being tracked."

The doors to the landing bay opened and a dozen or so armed guards swarmed in, surrounding me. I was half tempted to shoot Petre. All this work for nothing–less than nothing, now I was caught. One of the guards took away my blast pistols. Another removed my tactical mask. A third guard searched my coat pockets and found my detonators.

Another guard walked into the circle dragging Ryna by the arm. That's when I *really* wanted to shoot Petre. They didn't take me anywhere; we just stood there. They were waiting for something. Another small group of people entered the landing bay. One prominent man with a long white lab coat and an expensive suit underneath stepped right up to me.

"Ah, Mr. Rence Perry I presume. My name is Dr. Vik Lenish. I would like to thank you for bringing back Subject 35 to me." His thick accent and perfect posture annoyed me.

"My pleasure," I said. "I'll be sure to send you the bill."

"Ah, the quick wit I have heard so much about. You have not disappointed me a single bit."

"Well, that makes one of us."

He looked over to one of the guards. "Bring him to observation room seven. He and I will have much to discuss."

As they hauled me out of the room, I glance at Ryna. She wore a sullen face, devoid of any hope in her eyes. The guard marched me halfway across the ship into a large glass room adjoining a laboratory. The windows were dark, most likely one-way glass. They sat me down and kept a few guns pointed at me. Dr. Lenish stepped into the room a few minutes later with an enthusiastic smile on his face.

He spoke into a microphone. "Bring in Subject 35."

I saw through the glass into the laboratory. The door opened and two doctors ushered Ryna in. They sat her down and connected electrodes to her head and turned on a monitoring machine. The second doctor held a clipboard and began talking to her.

Dr. Lenish turned to me. "Fascinating, isn't it? Twenty-three years of experimentation and we produce such a lovely accident."

"Accident?" I asked.

"Of course, Mr. Perry. I would love to claim scientific success. But the truth of the matter is that we were trying to produce something else completely. So, it was a happy accident that Subject 35 exhibited such astounding results. She has demonstrated the remarkable ability to suppress or inflame a person's emotions. The only drawback is that we have no idea how that happened."

"A shame," I said.

"A shame indeed. Instead of exploring her capabilities, we are trying to recreate this...happy accident."

"How is that coming?"

"We are not as close as I would like. I hope the new hyper-EEG and the KEGs will produce the data I need."

"And if it doesn't?"

"Then we will have to dissect the subject's brain. I would rather not have to spoil this specimen just to figure out how to recreate it. But either way, science will triumph in the end."

"I was getting rather fond of that girl."

He looked at me. "That is not a girl, Mr. Perry. That is the result of a genetically modified test tube insemination."

"You're kidding yourself," I said, with disdain in my voice.

"Who are you to judge me, Mr. Perry? I know who you are. We kept detailed records of the Wayfinders—especially the one that got away. And based on your record, you aren't even completely a man anymore."

I glared at him. "I'm more of a man than you'll ever be."

"You see, that's where you're wrong. I am one hundred percent flesh and blood. Whereas those with cybernetics give up their humanity for an extended lease on life. The one redeeming factor for you, Mr. Perry, is the amount of cybernetics you carry. You see, most people cannot handle more than eight or twelve percent replacement. The human brain can only handle so much. But you carry upwards of thirty percent replacement parts. This makes you a very fascinating specimen indeed."

"I'm sure a criminal psychologist would say the same about you."

Dr. Lenish smiled. "Such a quick wit. If only I didn't have to dismantle you for study. I would seriously enjoy our little prattle from day to day."

"I could always dismantle *you,*" I said.

He laughed out loud. "Such adorable bravado." He turned to the guards. "Please take him to a holding cell. And be sure to give him something to eat. We need to preserve the organic parts of him."

One thing was for sure. I wanted to rearrange his face. And if I was going to die, I was as sure as shooting gonna take him down with me. They led me to a small room with a sink, toilet, and sleeping cot. It was downright accurate to refer to it as a cell. Titanium bars separated me from the rest of the room. Is this what Ryna had been subjected to all her life? How much longer would they let her live? Then again, would it really be living at all? Life with two random scientists as 'parents' might not be ideal, but it would sure beat this place hands down. I may have judged Petre and Carol too quickly.

The Corporation had taken Thunder and Lightning, my blast pistols. They had taken my tactical mask and my detonators. But they couldn't take away my mind. And now I needed to use it to find a way out of here. I positioned myself on the cot facing the back wall. It would obscure what I was attempting and give the impression of despair. I unbuttoned my shirt and opened my chest panel. I didn't often tinker around in here. It wasn't smart to monkey with what kept my heart beating, but I needed to send a message to Miri.

A few minutes of tinkering allowed me to send a pulse signal to the *Princess.* It was meaningless as an actual message; I couldn't make a pattern or alternate frequency. It would be up to Miri to discern that I was calling for help. We hadn't established a code or signal of distress between us—which would be on my priority list if I ever got out of here. I hoped she'd get the message and use my signal to locate me.

I closed my chest panel and re-buttoned my shirt as Dr. Lenish and Petre stepped into the room. Dr. Lenish walked over to a storage locker on the far wall and unlocked it with a keycard. He pulled open a drawer.

"Dr. Xaan, you may stow the subject's exhibits in here. Ready access will allow me to quickly reference his psychological motives."

"Yes, Dr. Lenish," he said, carrying a bundle of my things. He delicately situated them inside the drawer and returned to Dr. Lenish's side.

Dr. Lenish turned his attention to me. "Well, well, well, Mr. Perry. My security staff was deeply curious about how you got aboard. It seems you had help from a lovely transport pilot. She will be joining us soon."

I gripped the iron bars, whitening my knuckles.

"She has no scientific interest for me but she might still prove useful. I need to understand your back history."

"Why do you do this?" I asked.

He raised an eyebrow. "Can you be more specific? I do a lot of things."

His accent got on my nerves almost as much as his methods. "Why do you torture and kill people under the guise of science?"

He glared at me, flaring his nostrils. "Our species would have become extinct thousands of years ago if not for science. Hydroponics saved us from starvation. Guns saved us from being victimized. Space travel saved us from overpopulation. But what will save us from the next calamity? The next course in our survival requires an evolutionary jump. And I am here to find that jump." He leaned in toward me—still too far for me to reach through the bars. "So you see, Mr. Perry. I am not a monster of humanity; I am their savior. Your sacrifice will save hundreds of thousands of lives to come."

"If you don't let the girl and the woman go free, I will bury you."

Dr. Lenish laughed. "Such dramatics. I really will miss our conversations." He turned to Petre. "Let me know when you have finished cataloging Mr. Perry. I want to get started with him as soon as possible."

"Of course, Dr. Lenish."

Dr. Lenish exited the room.

I stared at Petre. "You still haven't answered my question."

Petre lowered his clipboard and stepped closer. "You would not have gotten very far. They are tracking the girl somehow. Carol—Dr. H'Lar and I tried to free the tall girl but they tracked us all the way to Cosstere. We didn't see any sign of pursuit, yet they found us anyway."

"And yet you got back into Dr. Lenish's good graces somehow."

He looked down and swallowed. "It's not too unrealistic to suppose a pair of doctors were influenced by the tall girl's abilities. It's convincing enough even for myself."

I relaxed my grip on the bars. "You didn't think of saying, no-thank-you? You figured it was better that she and I be captured and dissected like lab rats?"

Petre's hands trembled. He kept his eyes lowered. "I...I thought to dispel any suspicion of our loyalties to Dr. Lenish. I...I'm sorry."

"What of your loyalties to decency and your fellow men?" I asked. "An innocent girl is going to die."

"Don't you think I know that?" he said, jaw trembling. "Carol and I risked everything! And we nearly got ourselves as well as the girl killed." He hung his head.

"Sounds like the two of you had a good plan. And all you were missing was a Wayfinder," I said.

He looked up, reading my eyes. "Why would you offer to help? There is nothing in it for you?"

"Setting things right is what Wayfinders do," I said, looking into his eyes.

The door opened and an armed guard stepped inside. Petre looked away and quietly excused himself, cheeks flushed. After Petre was gone, the guard stepped closer to the bars, staring at me. I didn't care to give him any regard, but he stood there, intently looking at me. I wasn't sure if it was curious or creepy. I stared back. Something was odd about him. His uniform hung a half-size too large. His helmet and visor were haphazardly positioned. And then there were his eyes behind the visor, the eyes of...

"Miri?" I asked.

She snickered, holding a silencing finger to her lips. She pulled out a keycard from a pocket and unlocked the cell door. I slid it open and promptly gathered my things from the drawer Petre had been good enough to abandon. Everything seemed to be here. But if my instincts about Dr. Lenish had merit, he would have been a careful man. I checked the power cells for my blast pistols. Sure enough, Dr. Lenish had them drained.

"An ounce of preparation is worth more than a pound of luck," I said, pulling out the two power cells from my boot.

Miri walked back to the outer door and glanced through the tiny window, peering down the hall. "I got your message; thanks for the heads-up about the guards."

"Actually," I explained. "It was an S.O.S. to come and rescue me. I didn't know you had been compromised yet."

She smiled at me. "I'm flattered you would ask."

"I'm lucky to have you, Miri," I said. "Awful lucky."

I snapped on my tactical mask and reloaded Thunder and Lightning. "Ryna is in one of these rooms down the hall. She'll have scientists in with her. Petre and Carol should be close by."

"Who are Petre and Carol?" she asked.

"The scientists we've been referring to as Ryna's parents."

She looked down in thought. "If they're not her real parents..."

"I know, I've had the same conversation in my head. We'll worry about what's proper once we're out of this mess."

Miri peered out the small window again. "By the way, I have Lady watching the landing bay from atop the ship. I figured that should let you see what we'll be up against on our way back."

"Good thinking," I said, joining her at the door.

"So where do we look first? Left or right?"

"Left," I said. "Let's get Ryna first."

She opened the door and walked out casually. I waited for her to round the corner before I slunk down the hallway after her. She rounded the corner and I peeked around it. Two guards approached from the opposite end of the hallway. They passed Miri and she glanced back at them. I waited for them behind the corner. Then I heard Miri whistle from down the hall. I peeked around the corner again and the two guards had turned down another passage instead.

I quickly joined Miri, looking through small door windows, hunting for Ryna. The fourth door I checked had Petre and Carol inside. And by the look of things, they were arguing. I could only hope they were discussing the virtues of helping Ryna again.

I tapped Miri on the shoulder. "Her parents are in here," I whispered. "We'll come back for them once we have Ryna."

She nodded, getting a look at them.

We continued checking the doors until Miri tugged on my sleeve and pointed at a door. I looked inside. Ryna was sitting on a chair with a scientist asking her questions, clipboard in hand. If this was the lab room, then the observation room I was recently in would be the very next door.

"Miri," I whispered. "I'll take care of whoever is in the observation room. Wait thirty seconds, and then dismiss the scientist and get Ryna."

I opened the observation door and stepped inside. Dr. Lenish and an assistant sat at a desk observing Ryna through the dark glass. The younger man assisting Dr. Lenish glanced at me and froze. Dr. Lenish took notice of me and his hand flew over to the intercom controls. My blast pistol flashed out of its holster and shot the intercom receiver in Dr. Lenish's hand. It sparked and blew a puff of gray smoke. He gasped, dropping the dead receiver. The assistant jumped back and tumbled over the back of his chair, hitting his head on the floor. Dr. Lenish stood and took a step back.

He eyed me nervously. "You have as fast a draw as your file indicates."

I holstered my blast pistol and picked up a clipboard. "Specimen: Subject V," I said, pretending to use the clipboard. "Reflexes appear average. Sense of imminent danger: significantly below that."

Dr. Lenish forced a smug smile. "I had your weapons disabled. Your ingenuity–"

"The specimen appears to be concerned with its life," I said. "Its reliance on civility, however, is a rather disappointing self-preservation tactic." I took slow steps toward him. "At present, the subject is lacking in judgment. Hypothesis: can the subject learn through osmosis?" I struck him across the face, sending him toppling backward.

I kicked his chair out of my way and took a step closer. Dr. Lenish got to his feet and threw a punch. I batted it away and swatted him across the face with the clipboard. He groaned and fell to his hands and knees.

"Wait!" he protested. "I'm sure there is an agreement that can be reached."

"Subject demonstrates a blatant disregard for human life."

"Stop talking like that!" he demanded.

"Ah," I said, feigning interest. "Subject responds favorably to audible stimuli."

Dr. Lenish's nostrils flared and he rushed at me, head butting me in the gut. We crashed against the desk, the clipboard clattering to the floor. I gave him an elbow to the back and then smacked him around until his will to fight ran out. I threw him back against the far wall and let him slide to the ground, blood running from his mouth.

I picked up the clipboard and stood over him. "Summary: this specimen has no redeeming qualities to contribute to the human race. Conclusion: the best way for Subject V to benefit the gene pool is by removing him from it."

Dropping the clipboard, I grabbed him by the collar and lifted him against the wall. I drew back my fist to strike. Terror filled his eyes.

"Mr. Rence, don't!" Ryna shouted in the small room. She and Miri had come in during the tail end business. I let Dr. Lenish slide back to the ground.

"Well, Dr. Lenish," I said. "It would seem the girl you wanted to butcher sees a reason you should live. You'd better ask yourself what kind of a society you want to create. One that looks at you like I have, or one that looks at you like she did?"

I left him lying there. Time would tell if he would take that lesson to heart or not. Men of power were often difficult to get to see reason. Miri, Ryna, and I hustled down the hall and burst into the room with Petre and Carol.

They jumped with a start and backed up. I may have made that entrance more dramatic than I needed to. I was still riding on adrenaline. "We're gettin' out. You two coming or staying?"

Miri closed the door behind us, keeping an eye out the small window.

"They'll just track her," Petre complained.

"I invite them to try," I said with defiance in my voice. "It ain't about what's easy. It's about what's right."

Carol looked at him and laid a hand on his arm.

He glanced at her a moment before sighing and looking at me. "Let's hurry."

All five of us headed down the hallway, walking swiftly but trying to look casual. We walked with Petre and Carol in front with Miri behind. Ryna and I were in the middle. We walked without a word toward the landing bays. Then the alarm sounded. Someone had found either Dr. Lenish or the guard Miri had taken the uniform from. Either way, it was inevitable. We raced through the halls, knocking down people as we passed. When we arrived just outside the landing bay the door didn't open.

I pounded the door. It was pretty solid. Miri reached over and ran her keycard across the sensor. It buzzed and displayed a red light. They must have locked out her keycard. I pulled out a detonator. Dr. Lenish had mentioned disabling my weapons. Could he have fiddled with my detonators, too? I pressed the center button. Nothing happened. I tried a few other detonators. All lifeless. I searched for a way to pry the door open but there wasn't any.

"Ventilation," Miri suggested.

"Maintenance hatch is one deck up," Carol said, pointing.

We ran back the way we had come toward the elevator. The doors refused to open here as well. They had this ship locked down pretty well. Miri again tried her keycard to no avail. I forced my fingers between the elevator door cracks and forced the doors open. We got inside just as blast bolts started flying down the hall at us. I fired a few shots in return and shut the elevator doors. Pressing buttons on the keypad did not move the elevator. I wasn't sure why I was surprised. I jumped, pushing open the trap door on the ceiling, and hoisted myself up.

I reached down. "Lift Ryna up."

Miri and Petre lifted Ryna to me and I pulled her onto the roof of the elevator. Next, I reached down and pulled Carol up, followed by Miri. Then I hopped down and hoisted Petre up through the trap door. I heard voices outside the elevator door. I jumped and hauled myself through the trap door. Miri had already started the others climbing the service ladder. I smiled. She had leadership inside her all right. Below me, I heard the elevator door open and chime. I climbed the ladder behind the others.

I kept peeking back at the elevator as I climbed. As soon as a guard poked his head out the trap door, I drew a blast pistol and dropped him. They shot back wildly through the trap door. I aimed my pistol and shot the stabilizer motor on the elevator car. It shook and slid down the elevator shaft, throwing sparks as it rubbed against the shaft wall.

"Bon voyage!" I called out after them.

"Rence!" Miri said, panic in her voice. "We need to open the elevator door up here."

I glanced up. She was trying to pry open the door with one hand holding onto the ladder. I holstered my blast pistol. I would have to get above them on the ladder to be of any good in helping with the door. A jump would get me high enough, but it would be an awkward angle. There'd be no guarantee I'd catch the ladder rungs on the way down. No, this would need some patience and tight quarters.

"Everyone move to one side of the ladder as best you can," I directed. I climbed up past them one by one, careful not to push them and equally careful not to slip on my footing. Once I was level with Miri, I turned to her. "I'm gonna need both hands. You think you can hold onto me as well as the ladder?"

"I've got you," she said putting her arm around my waist. Even through the helmet, I could have sworn I smelled the scent of her hair.

I reached up and forced my hands between the elevator doors and thrust them aside. I hoisted myself up and checked the hallway down both ends. It was clear, and I wasn't sure if that was a good sign or a bad one. I helped Miri and the others up and into the hallway. Petre looked particularly tired from that little adventure.

"Where's the maintenance hatch?" I asked.

"Down there on the left," Carol said, pointing.

We hurried down the hall and rounded the corner. Six armed guards came toward us, shooting. The blast bolts streaked past my head, illuminating my face. I ducked, drawing Thunder and Lightning, then shot back. One blast bolt hit me in the leg. I dropped to one knee but kept on shooting. Miri also returned fire, dropping two of them. Their helmets and blast vests protected them from a lot of our shots, but Miri was a good aim.

I took out one of my detonators and tossed it down the hall at the guards. It was useless, of course, but I was counting on them having some good combat training. They recognized what it was and scattered. Some threw themselves against the hallway wall, others dove to the ground away from it. I aimed and shot three more through their visor, while Miri dropped the last one.

"Nice shooting," I said to Miri.

"You've been hit," she said, sounding worried.

I climbed to my feet, my leg throbbing. I removed my bandana from around my neck and tied it around my leg. It was an insufficient field dressing, but it would have to do. I hobbled down the hallway a few steps before Miri put my arm around her neck. She helped me get to the maintenance hatch.

"Wait," Petre said, pulling out his keycard and moving to a door further down the hallway. He re-emerged quickly with an injection gun and a small glass bottle. He placed the bottle into a slot on the injection gun. "Here," he said, holding the gun to my neck. "This should dampen your pain receptors for a few hours. It should allow you to walk."

I nodded and he shot the drug into my neck. I flinched and then forgot all about my leg. Carol was already at the maintenance hatch and had opened it. I ushered them inside and closed the hatch behind me. The other side was dimly lit with unpainted metal walls. Gantry walkways with ladders and stairs lined every spare inch. It was a maze of sorts, but at least it increased our options instead of limiting them.

"Where to?" Miri asked.

"Well," I said. "We know we need to go down one deck, so we can ignore all the stairs going up."

I tapped a few buttons on my wristband, switching my eyesight to electromagnetic. I saw pulsing lines of electrical cables and plasma conduits. "I reckon if we follow the cabling, it will lead to the landing bays. I imagine it takes a lot of power to run those rooms."

I switched one of my eyes back to normal so I could see where I was going. We descended one staircase and walked along a narrow gantry that overlooked a long drop to the next deck. I heard the maintenance hatch swing open above us. By the sound of the feet pounding overhead, I reckoned there were ten or so men who had entered. If we were quiet enough, they would have to split up to find us.

As usual, though, my luck never did hold out for long. Multiple blast bolts streaked through the musty air. They struck metal posts, gantry flooring, stairs, and even the bulkhead wall. Ryna slipped and screamed. I drew one blast pistol and fired several shots back. Miri reached out and caught Ryna's hand, pulling her up. A stray blast bolt struck Miri in her blast helmet, dazing her for a moment. I took real offense at that and aimed between a pillar and the upper gantry floor and fired. My shot nailed the guards in the helmet, sending him tumbling over the ledge.

I aimed for the next guard and pulled the trigger. Nothing happened. I checked the power cell in my blast pistol. It was dry. I checked the power cell in my other pistol. I had four shots left. I needed a faster way to take out these guards. I aimed at the support strut that held up the gantry floor above us and fired. The shot struck the weld joint and bounced off. I cursed. It figured a ship this fancy would have reinforced struts.

I looked at Miri. She pulled the power cell of her blast pistol and examined it with an exasperated expression. She tossed the gun away and drew Ivory, her holdout blast pistol. We continued ducking blast bolts until we reached the ventilation chambers. We stepped off the gantry walkway and into the guts of the ventilation ductwork. The massive ducts also looked to be made of titanium.

We made our way swiftly down the ducts. We needed to make up time here. There was very little room to maneuver and no cover should blast bolts start flying. And come they would. Up ahead, I stopped. The ventilation duct had a chute going straight down. It was like a hole in the floor leading to who knows where. It would be tricky getting across it.

"Miri, you have the most shots left," I said. "Watch our rear while I get everyone else across."

She nodded, walking to the back.

I turned to Petre. "You're first."

He shook his head. "I can't jump that."

"I'm gonna give you a boost," I explained. I put my hands on his waist while he protested. I shoved him hard, pushing off a little with my knees. He flew across to the other side, tumbling to the floor. Next, I turned to Carol. She looked worried but didn't protest. I tossed her across with a little more finesse than my first attempt.

I looked at Ryna. "You ready?"

She nodded. "I really like you Mr. Rence."

I smiled. Over the years I had a lot of people tell me the opposite, so this was refreshing to hear. I lifted her and gently tossed her to the other side. She didn't weigh as much and I didn't have to use my enhanced knees.

"Miri," I said. "Time to go." She walked up to my side and I wrapped my arm around her. "Hold on."

She clung to me. I jumped, clearing the ventilation chasm and landing on the other side. She hugged me a moment before releasing her arms from around me.

I turned to Petre. "Are you okay?"

He nodded. "I'm regretting not spending more time at the gym."

Small vibrations rumbled through the ventilation shaft. I tapped a button on my wristband and switched my eyesight to infrared. I scanned our surroundings. There was lots of body heat above us, outside the ventilation shaft. They were generating intense heat concentrating on a single point. Small flares of bright heat emanated from that single point. I had seen that kind of heat signature many times before. And in our situation, this was very bad.

"They're cutting through one of the support beams," I said. "Hurry!"

We ran down the shaft. I tripped. I didn't feel any pain in my leg, but if I stepped on it wrong, it didn't work right. Petre helped me to my feet right as the support beam snapped. The ventilation shaft sagged, turning the smooth shaft into a slide. I heard Ryna scream amidst yells and groans. I thrashed around trying to stop myself but there was no use; we were gonna ride this one out.

When I finally stopped moving, I found myself lying on my back, still seeing infrared. I switched my eyesight back to normal and sat up. I was sitting in a foot of water. We were in the water treatment system of the ship.

"Miri!" I called out.

"Rence!"

I spun around, splashing. I dashed over to a wall of metal bars. Most likely to prevent large objects from reentering the filtration system. Miri and Ryna were on the other side. The ventilation shaft had crashed down, breaking through the ceiling. The fall had deposited us on either side. I grabbed the bars and shook them, hoping to find a weakness. They stood solid, mocking my attempt to free Miri.

Petre and Carol splashed up to my side, mumbling concerns about Miri and Ryna. I drew my blast pistol. "Stand back."

Miri and Ryna stood off to the side. I fired my last three shots. The blast bolts bounced off the bars. One of my bolts ricocheted and struck an overhead pipe. Steam burst from the hole. The floor started to rumble, sending ripples through the water.

Petre pointed to the opposite end of the room, where the water was flowing to. "The contamination door!" A large thick wall of metal was slowly lowering, threatening to trap us inside the water chamber. "It's losing the steam pressure that holds it up!"

I tugged furiously at the metal bars dividing us from Miri and Ryna. They would not budge.

"Mister, we have to find another way to save them," Carol said.

I looked up at the hole in the ceiling. The fallen ventilation shaft completely blocked off any retreat. And the shaft itself was too slippery to climb.

"Mr. Perry!" Petre urged. "If we don't go now, we'll all be trapped!"

My heart thundered in my chest. "No, no, no!" I kicked at the bars. Even with my special knees, the force of the kicks only pushed me backward.

"Rence," Miri said with tears in her eyes. "Promise me you'll come back for me."

My heart raced and my vision blurred. "I can't leave you."

"Mr. Perry, the door is closing!" Petre warned.

The guards clanked their boots against the gantry stairwells, climbing down after us. Miri took off her helmet and let it splash to the ground. Water dripped from her hair. She leaned forward letting her forehead rest between two of the bars. "You have to go now. Go and get some help. Then come back for me. Promise me please."

I yanked my mask off and looked into her eyes. That was, perhaps, a mistake. She was able to see a tear of mine lose its way and wander down my face. I hated this situation. I hated it more than anything I had before. She was right, as usual. The guards were coming, the door was closing, and I had no way to rescue her. My only choice was to come back for her.

She reached up and wiped away my tear. "It'll be okay, I've had a good teacher."

"If they lay a hand on you—"

"I'll let them know," she said.

"Mr. Perry! Come quickly!" Petre said as he ushered Carol toward the half-closed door.

I leaned in and kissed Miri through the bars. "I promise I will come back for you. And I'll bring Armageddon with me if I have to."

She sniffled, smiling. "I know you will. Now hurry."

I stroked her wet hair and then ran toward the closing containment door. Petre and Carol were already on the other side. I dove under the door, splashing. I pulled my legs out from under the door right before it rested on the ground, completely shutting us out. I felt a heavy weight in my chest. I knew I was doing the right thing, but I felt bad all the same. I knew what kind of people I was leaving them with. Hopefully, Dr. Lenish had learned something and would restrain himself around them. Of course, that would only hold as long as I was alive. If I were to die, my threat would be meaningless. I had to survive if they were going to.

I turned away from the contamination door, taking in my surroundings. Overhead, I saw pipes and conduits running in a line down the small metal corridor. I reckoned they led right to the landing bay. No normal room would need so many large pipes and cables this far from the engine room. We raced down the corridor until Petre begged for a break to rest. We stopped and he collapsed to the ground, Carol at his side.

"Thank you, Mr. Perry," he said, panting.

I looked at him. "What kind of research were you doing, if Ryna was an accident?"

"What is Ryna?" Carol asked.

He looked at Carol. "That's the name they gave the tall one." Turning to me, he said, "Exploratory research mostly."

"I'll need that answer translated for me," I said.

Petre pushed his glasses farther up the bridge of his nose. "Systematically tampering with the human genome in the hopes of discovering something amazing."

"If it was so systematic, how come you can't replicate it?"

"That, Mr. Perry, is the thing that frustrates Dr. Lenish so much. It seems the more we learn, the more there is to discover."

"It's more than that," Carol added. "He's a man who distinguishes himself as one who figures things out. And Ryna represents a stubborn mystery to him; a discovery he cannot reproduce."

"You ready to move?" I asked Petre.

He stood, nodding.

We continued down the corridor until we reached an access ladder and climbed. The ladder ended at an overspill drain grate. I pushed on the grate but it didn't budge. I couldn't see much through the grate except for the ceiling of the room above us. And since I didn't pay much attention to ceilings recently, that didn't help me figure out where we were.

"What is it?" Petre asked.

"Shhh!" I said.

I put my tactical mask back on and tapped a button on my wristband. I switched my eyesight to see through Lady's eyes. She was perched atop the *Princess,* as Miri had said. *Miri,* I thought. The pit of my stomach knotted up at the thought of leaving without her, even if I would be coming back. Now was not the time to be thinking of Miri, but how could I avoid it? I still felt her touch on my cheek. I shook my head to clear my thoughts. From Lady's vantage point, the room was clear of personnel. I stuck my fingers out through the drain grate. There, through Lady's eyes, I could see my fingers sticking out of a floor grate in the distance. We were at the right landing bay. That was the good news. The bad news was that this grate was bolted down very well.

I fumbled through my coat pockets for my detonators. There was always a chance Dr. Lenish had missed one. I tried each, one after another, all to no avail. They were all non-functional. It was partly a frustration and yet it was partly comforting. If I had found a working detonator, I wouldn't have been able to forgive myself for not using it to free Miri. I had to stop thinking about Miri and focus on getting out of here. Saving Miri now required that I leave this ship alive and return in force.

I stood there a moment, trying to think of something. Petre and Carol were good enough not to complain, but I could tell their arms were tiring. They were not used to a lot of physical stress. I thought about pushing up on the grate with my knees, but then I thought better of the idea. The ladder rungs looked weaker than the grate. Then my thoughts turned to

Lady. She was the only one who could save us now. The tricky question, however, was how.

I pressed a button on my wristband and Lady squawked, fluttering down into the *Princess.* On the floor to the left, I saw my toolbox. It was latched shut. *Good luck with that,* I thought. Lady was trained well, but she didn't have hands. I needed something she could simply fly out to me; something lying around. There, on a stack of boxes, I saw Miri's detonator. She apparently never did get a chance to put it away.

I wished I hadn't spoken to her as I had. She had saved me a second time now and I couldn't even thank her. *Thank you, Miri,* I thought. *Thank you for your little quirks.* I wasn't only going to miss her, I was also going to miss the little things she did.

I pressed a button on my wristband and Lady squawked. She flew over to the boxes, knocking one over, and snatched the detonator. She flew it over to me and dropped it. I switched my eyesight back to normal and grabbed the detonator.

"You two, get down and stand aside. We're going to blow the grate."

Petre and Carol climbed back down. I activated the detonator and set it atop the grate. I was careful to make sure it didn't fall down the grate on top of us. That would be bad. I climbed down the ladder and stood off to the side with Petre and Carol. The detonator exploded, shattering the grate and sending a warm gust of air down toward us. I felt part of the concussion wave slap against my back. I groaned. I should have stood a little further away. Well, live and learn.

Overhead a ringing bell sounded. The explosion set off the fire alarm. Personnel would soon flood into the landing bay; armed guards no less. We needed speed now.

"Climb! Move like your life depends on it," I told them. "I got nothin' to shoot back with."

I jumped up through the destroyed grate, landing close. Carol and Petre climbed the ladder while I dashed up the entry ramp of the *Princess.* Lady flew in after me. She landed on my arm and I took her into the cockpit, setting her on her perch. I started the launch sequence and then ran back down to the entrance ramp. Petre and Carol hurried up the ramp as the bay doors opened. Armed guards flooded in, shooting at us. I slammed my fist against the button on the sidewall. The ramp retracted and the door closed.

I bolted for the cockpit, leaving Petre and Carol behind. I would tend to their comforts later. Sitting in my chair, I ignited the vertical thrusters. Cargo canisters blew over and several guards fell on their backsides. The *Princess* lifted off the ground, hovering in place. I spun her around to face the landing bay space door.

Petre and Carol found their way to the cockpit and joined me.

"You two had better buckle up," I said, pointing to the other two chairs.

They took their seats and fastened the safety straps.

"How do you open the door?" Carol asked.

"Normally, I would contact the ship's flight control to request clearance to leave. Then they would open the space door."

Petre looked at me. "That doesn't sound like an available option at present."

"Nope," I said, pressing a few buttons on my control panel.

"What are you going to do then? Break into the door controls to open it yourself?"

"I guess you could say that," I replied.

I pressed another button and a missile fired from the *Princess*. It slammed into the space door, blasting a hole in it. The sudden depressurization ripped the space door apart like a popping balloon. The *Princess*, and everything else not bolted down, shot out into space as if fired from a cannon.

I reached forward and grabbed the controls again, steadying our course.

"A little warning would have been nice," Petre complained.

I swiveled my chair around, taking off my tactical mask. "I told you to strap in, didn't I?"

He pursed his lips and looked away.

I leaned over and picked up my hat. It was like greeting an old friend I hadn't seen for some time. When Miri had taken it to play the part of the ship captain, she'd worn it well. I put it on, feeling the familiar brim. At least the outside of me was whole again. My inside wasn't. And it wouldn't be until I got Miri and Ryna back. An alarm beeped on my console. Three patrol ships were chasing us.

"What's that?" Carol asked, startled.

"The Corporation doesn't give up easily," I said, slowing our thrusters down.

"Why are we slowing down?" Petre asked, eyes wide.

"If they wanna pick a fight," I said. "I'll give 'em one."

"But those are patrol vessels," he protested. "This is a transport ship."

"No, Doctor," I replied. "This is a Wayfinder's ship."

Carol shrugged. "That would explain the missile."

I flipped a switch, engaging the autopilot. I politely excused myself from the cockpit, climbing up into the observation dome. It was nice to see the black starry sky again. I had almost thought I was going to be seeing the inside of a laboratory for the rest of my life with Dr. Lenish gloating over me. I wasn't even sure I thanked Miri for getting me out. So many things today that I wished I could redo. I turned on the targeting scope. Three red circles lit up on the transparent dome. I needed them closer.

I pulled open the weapon's panel and flipped up all the red switches. The concussion mines were now all armed. I put on a neighboring headset and turned on the communication transmission. It was showtime.

"All pursuing craft, this is the *Astral Princess.* You are advised to stand down or face severe structural damage. I say again, you are advised to stand down or face severe structural damage."

I wasn't expecting a response so I was surprised that I got one. "Transport vessel, you are ordered to surrender your ship and prepare to be boarded."

This was an unexpected turn of events that could prove fruitful. I just needed to sell it properly. "Negative on that," I said. "We have uh...lots of big guns. Don't approach or you'll be destroyed in the blink of an eye. It's best if you turn back now."

The patrol ships pulled into weapon range and continued to close the distance. One fired warning shots across my bow. The green bolts of light streaked past the observation dome, illuminating it. I smiled. They had taken the bait.

"Wait, wait, wait!" I hollered through the transmission. "Hold your fire, hold your fire."

"Stand down and surrender your ship now," the voice demanded.

I watched the three red circles on my targeting scope move closer together. Still not close enough. I needed to stall just a bit more. "Look, you can have my cargo. You can have whatever you want, just please let me go!"

The lead ship fired a green bolt that struck my starboard thruster. The ship rattled and I fell to the floor. *That's right,* I thought. *These guys are government-trained.* With most outlaws and pirates I had a little more wiggle room to stall. And even though the Corporation was private, it employed government-trained personnel. Why had I forgotten that? I must be out of practice.

The *Princess* started to drift, red gas billowing from the starboard thruster. That was a problem. I needed both engines if I was going to outrun anything. I hopped down the ladder from the observation dome and scrambled to the engine room. I still needed to play my part so I kept the headset with me. "Mayday! Mayday! The starboard engine is hit, venting drive plasma!"

"Surrender now," the voice demanded.

"I surrender! I surrender!" I hollered into my headset as I pulled off the starboard thruster housing. I kicked open my toolbox and pulled out Old Faithful, the best tool I ever spent money on. "What do I do?" I asked as I worked on the thruster.

"Cut power to your engines and standby for docking connection," the voice directed.

"Please don't shoot! I'll do whatever you want!" I said, running a cable from the starboard thruster over to the port thruster.

"If you don't cut power to your engines now, you will be destroyed."

"Okay, okay. Cutting power to the engines." I ran up the stairwell and climbed the ladder to the observation dome. "Overload! We have an overload!" I yelled into the headset. "All hands, abandon ship! All hands abandon ship!"

I reached over to the red switches I had previously armed. *One-thousand-one, one-thousand-two, one-thousand-three,* I thought. *And...now.* I pressed two switches. A loud *clank* rang through the hull as the concussion mines released. They floated toward the three patrol ships. I hopped down the ladder and dashed over to the cockpit. I jumped into my chair and pushed the throttle to maximum. The *Princess* lurched forward, rocketing away from the patrol ships. The mines exploded, sending out a massive pulse wave, slamming into the three patrol ships. They listed and drifted.

I didn't always bluff my way out of situations. And the times I didn't were quite satisfying. I set a course for Bendune. It was an out-of-the-way trading post that had some very good repair facilities. That is, if you didn't mind the rough company and damp environment. I spun around in my chair. Petre and Carol finally looked relaxed.

"I'll freshen up two cabins," I said. "You both look like you could use some shut-eye."

"How can we ever thank you, Mr. Perry," Carol asked.

"Well, seeing as I need to go back for Miri and Ryna, I sure could use some help."

"We are not commandos," Petre explained. "We can give you information and even the occasional medical checkup, but that is about all we can offer."

"Information is what I need most," I explained. "Commandos I can get. Well, assuming I haven't burned that bridge down entirely."

"Sure," Carol said. "Whatever we can do to help."

"For starters, where is the Westward Galactic's data center?"

"It's on Dentum Prime. It has a lot of security. You would need an army to break in."

"Or," I said. "Or just a really good distraction."

I showed them to their rooms. It was late and everyone was tired. I stayed up, reconfiguring my communications transcoder. It was a real headache to send untraceable messages, but the situation warranted it. I typed up a brief message and sent it. It would take a few hours for the message to get where it needed to, so I took a short nap in my chair. I awoke to a beeping sound on my console; the reply transmission I was expecting.

I pressed a button on my little transmission screen. It flashed to life and displayed the image of the woman I had told myself I never wanted to see again.

"Rence Perry," she said, folding her arms. "I swore I would kill you the next time I saw you."

"Tess Davendry," I said. "I need your help."

EPISODE 5

Finally some payback

5

Finally Some Payback

Tess Davendry leaned her elbows on the table, glaring at me. Her dagger eyes told me she was still sore about our last encounter. Her crew had fired on my ship and took Miri and Ryna hostage. That part she didn't have an issue with. What she did take offense with was that had I shot several of her men. Also that I had bluffed her into thinking I was going to blow up her starcruiser if she didn't let us go. The way I figured it, we were even.

A young lady in her mid-twenties walked up to our table, her short skirt hugging her legs. She set down a cup for me and one for Tess. Unstopping a cork, she poured both our glasses. The drink wasn't the finest. But, then again, it was the best that this remote Bendune saloon could offer. The dim lighting and the muggy air allowed patrons to feel secluded. Bendune was a remote colony world with lots of moisture and not a lot of sunshine.

"You want me to leave the bottle?" she asked.

If this was going to be a fruitful conversation, quite a bit of lubrication would be needed. "Yes, please." I dropped a few coins on the table. She snatched up the coins before leaving.

Tess ignored her cup. "You have a lot of gall to come crawling back to me."

"How so?" I asked, not really wanting the answer.

"You deceived me!" she said, her face reddening.

I cocked my head to one side. "Well, you tried to sell me to Westward Galactic."

"You threatened my ship."

"You broke into mine."

"You shot my men."

"You kidnapped my passengers, intending to sell at least one of them."

She pursed her lips. "I didn't recognize it was you."

"But you suspected," I said.

"You never confirmed."

I nodded. "...you're right."

She picked up her glass and took a drink. "You left me."

I took a sip of mine. "That was a long time ago. Yan Davendry was going to sell me out to Westward Galactic."

"My father would not have dared. A little posturing never scared you before, why did it then?"

I took another drink. "I hadn't ever faced extermination before."

She gulped down the contents of her glass. "Rence, you didn't have to run. You could have worked the family business with me."

I refilled her glass. "I would have had to renounce the vow I had made."

She took another drink. "There wasn't much chance of that, was there?"

I shook my head and drained my cup.

She relaxed in her chair and took another drink. "Why couldn't things have been different between us?"

"I don't rightly know," I said, pouring myself another glass.

"Did you ever think about me?" she asked with sincerity in her voice.

My gaze dropped to the table. "I thought about you plenty. It haunted me enough to wish I would never see your face again."

"In all the time since, did you ever replace me?"

I took a long drink. That question was difficult to answer. I fancied Miri but I also didn't have any hopes of something more significant. Not while I was being hunted. The answer could go either way. But, then again, Tess may not have been asking a philosophical question. It was an indirect question that begged a direct answer.

She leaned forward with intense eyes. "You have!"

"Tess, I didn't come here to discuss—"

"Oh no," she said, leaning back in her chair. "If you want my help, then we are having this conversation."

I set my glass down. "There have always been two ladies in my life, Tess. There always will be."

"I'm not talking about your ship or your falcon, Rence, and you know it. Who is she?"

I couldn't continue reasoning that I had two ladies in my life, not after Miri and Ryna came into it. That meant I now had four ladies in my life. Two of which drove me out of my comfort zone. Especially Ryna. She asked blunt questions that got me evaluating my life. In a way, I needed her as much as she needed me. Would Tess understand all this? Did *I* even understand it? It was best to just avoid the topic entirely.

I poured myself another glass. "Maybe it would be best if—"

"The woman on my ship," she said triumphantly. "The one with the little girl."

I slammed the bottle down on the table. "What, did you take up mind-reading?"

She smiled, rocking back on the legs of her chair. "So, what's got you all sweet on *her?"*

And so the interrogation began. I sighed. Better to get it over with instead of wasting time fighting it. Tess had a way of getting what she wanted. I brought my glass to my lips but then set it back down. "I thought I knew," I said. "I've known her for a few years. She would pay me to run passengers to Corbet IV. Somehow, she found out I fancied her when she wore her hair down. She would wear her hair down whenever she really needed my help."

"Smart woman," Tess said, taking a drink.

"I thought that was why I was sweet on her. But when I lost her, I found myself missing the little things she did. The things that irritated me." I shook my head. "But that doesn't make much sense since a man shouldn't want what irritates him. I don't have the faintest idea why I fancy her. I have no reason to delude myself with thoughts about settling down with her."

"Since when are you willing to settle down with anyone?" she asked, draining her glass.

"Doesn't matter," I said sullenly, drinking my whole glass. "My life is no good for her. She needs someone who isn't hunted. Someone who can give her the life she deserves."

"You're more than sweet on her, are you?" she said, lowering the front legs of her chair to the floor. "You've fallen, haven't you?"

"I wouldn't jump to conclusions," I said. "If you'd been listening–"

"I have been listening," she said, setting her glass down. "You've fallen so far you can't get up."

She obviously hadn't been listening to me. I was no good for Miri, that was the problem. And what did falling for Miri have to do with anything? This conversation needed to end. Either that or I was going to need another bottle. I rolled my eyes and opened my mouth to reply but she was quicker.

"When you were on my ship," she asked. "Why didn't you tell me it was you? Why did you try to hide your identity?"

I shrugged. "There are a lot of people that want to shoot me because of my name. I reckon I wasn't sure if you had found yourself among them. We didn't part ways on the best of terms."

"I still might shoot you for that," she replied.

"I'm hoping that won't be necessary. You see, I didn't come here as a beggar, but as an employer."

She raised an eyebrow. "You have a job? I didn't think your Wayfinder ethics would stoop to my level."

"I never crossed the line, Tess. Westward Galactic had the line moved. I ain't an outlaw because of what I done, but because of what I *wouldn't* do."

"And so you figure as long as you're an outlaw, you might as well pull a job or two?"

I grimaced. "The job is yours. I got another goal while we're there."

"Which is?" she asked, refilling her glass.

I slid my glass over to Tess and she refilled it. "How much do you know about that little girl?"

"The Corporation has fifteen thousand on her head."

"A big enough price to catch any eye," I said.

"But it pales in comparison with yours," she said with a grin, taking a drink.

"It's only six thousand...unless it's been increased."

She took another gulp and set down her glass. "As of this morning, the price on your head is fifty-three thousand."

I sat back in my chair, stunned. I saved up a lot of money to buy the *Astral Princess* and she cost eighteen thousand back in the day. At today's price, I would have spent closer to twenty thousand. The price on my head was now large enough to buy the *Princess* two and a half times over and still have extra money. Someone wanted me real bad. And I had a pretty good idea of who. I had done a real number on Dr. Vik Lenish. The poor excuse for a human being wanted to dissect me because I was fascinating. He also expressed an interest in cutting open Ryna's brain. I had given him a good thrashing in the hopes of changing his mind. Knocking sense into people, it appeared, also had a few side effects. A massive bounty being one of them.

"I reckon I ought to be flattered," I finally said.

"And what's to stop me from turning you in and collecting the bounty?" she said, eyeing me carefully. "This time, I know you don't have a bomb on my starcruiser."

I didn't want to follow that line of conversation. Tess was more of a pragmatist than an idealist, so her motives would never be the same as mine. That was one reason why I hadn't gotten very close to her. Her life was one of business whereas mine was a life of trying to put things right.

"The bounty is a distraction, Tess," I announced, shifting topics. "Westward Galactic took something from me and they're scared I'll come for it. Scared enough, it seems, to want every bounty hunter after me. And that's why they'll never see this coming."

Tess stopped in the middle of taking a drink and instead put her glass back down. "What is it you're planning?"

"I'm gonna pay Dentum Prime a visit."

She stared at me, wide-eyed and mouth open. "You're going to rob the most powerful bank in the sector?"

That, of course, wasn't my main objective but that was an easy side-effect once I was inside. Besides financial records, the Corporation had a lot of other useful data. Ryna's lab records would be among them. I needed to find out how they were tracking her. It would have been far easier to break into a laboratory computer on their lab ship. But that avenue had been foreclosed. This approach, at least, had the benefit of nobody considering it an option. That made them complacent. It also put me in a position to transfer funds from Westward Galactic to the Davendries. That should pay for their services and be more enticing than collecting the bounty on my head.

"As I said, Tess. The bounty is a diversion. Help me get into Dentum Prime. Then I'll see to it the Corporation gives a generous donation to a Davendry hedge account. Fifty-three thousand ought to seem like beans in comparison."

She sat there in thought long enough for me to finish my glass twice more. "What if it doesn't work?" she finally asked.

"They mean business on Dentum. If it doesn't work, you won't have to worry about shooting me."

"How do I know I can trust you? You are a very good liar."

"You know you can trust me. If anything, I should be worried about you."

She smiled, pouring the last of the bottle into her glass. "When do we start?"

"I have some recon I need to do. I'll contact you tomorrow night."

It would have been nice to have left that conversation confident this would all work. As it was, I was lucky she decided to go along with it. Only time would tell if my luck would hold out. I made my way back to the *Princess.* I had already resupplied her and finally got around to fixing that squeaky hatch. Miri had mentioned that squeak a time or two. I hoped she would be happy it was fixed when I got her back.

I had deposited Petre and Carol, Ryna's 'parents', in a little village on Bendune. It was safe for them there and I needed them out of my hair while I was dealing with the Davendries. Petre and Carol were very smart but they asked a lot of questions. That curious nature may have made them smart, but it always kept me explaining why I do things the way I do them. This job would be a lot easier on my own. I would return for them once I had what I needed.

I flew the *Princess* to Velios Arcturos. Velios was a backwater data installation built on the surface of a dead rock hurdling around a cold star. The only amenities it had to offer was solid ground to stand on. Velios's true value was in its position in the galactic arm. Its location extended the Corporation's galactic network to the new frontier. That was good for them and excellent for me. It meant I had a miniature scale version of the computer systems I would encounter on Dentum Prime. Not to mention, the security systems and personnel training as well. It was ideal for a trial run.

It was too cold for Lady to be out in the low temperatures for long. I wouldn't have that obstacle on Dentum but it was a tribulation at the present. I got out of my chair and picked up Lady from her perch. I stroked her feathered head. "I guess we get to test out that vest I made for you last year."

Lady squawked.

I brought her over to the machining table and picked up a small bundle of cloth. It was made of Yatikan wool with a little poly-synth weave to make it stretchable. I fumbled with it for a few minutes until I successfully put it on Lady. She didn't care much for it, it cramped her style. She would have to tolerate it, though; I couldn't risk exposure. Not only did I need her, but with the loss of Miri and Ryna, she seemed like the last friend I had. It wasn't true, of course, but that is how it felt.

"Come, Lady. Let's see what we're up against."

Exiting the ship, I stepped into the still and frozen landscape. Lady took to the air and I snapped on my tactical mask. Lady loved reconnaissance. She seemed more at home during a recon flight than anywhere else. I pressed a button on my wristband, switching my eyesight to see Lady's vision. The data facility was just over the next ridge. It was a fairly small structure with many satellite dishes and rectennae. Seven guards actively patrolled the perimeter with another guarding the door. That was a good sign. If the ratio held, Dentum's perimeter guard force would outnumber their internal one. That made it tough to get inside, but it also meant, that once I was inside, I had less to deal with.

I hiked through the frozen rocky terrain, thankful for the lack of a chilly breeze. The icy blue rocks and the dull blue sun overhead gave the landscape a picturesque mystery about it. It was about as removed from Cosstere as could be and yet it held a few similarities. Both worlds denied you of water as best they could and both hid their flora and fauna very well. Velios was an icy desert and Cosstere was a blistering one.

I crested the second ridge and peered into the valley beyond. There would be several perimeter guards in overlapping patrols. To time the approach, I was going to need a little help from Lady. I descended the frigid ground, careful not to send bits of icy rock tumbling to the valley floor. Once at the bottom, I switched my vision to electromagnetic and scanned the scene. In most high-security facilities I would see perimeter electronic security. But this place had none. Either it was too new to warrant the extra expense or the chilly environment made it unnecessary. Either way, that was good news for me.

I switched my eyesight to one eye with Lady's vision and the other eye to my normal vision. With one eye in the sky, I could time my crossing. And that would be important here. The timing of their patrols made what I was attempting difficult without being seen. If they had doubled the number of guards, it might have been impossible. But, as with all budgeting decisions, it looked like they went with second-best.

Waiting for the opportune moment, I dashed across the perimeter and over to a nearby building. Pressing myself against the building, I peered around the corner. The lone guard stood by the outer door, shivering. I wouldn't want that guy's job. I tapped a button on my wristband and Lady swooped down to the ground, snatching up a rock in her talons. She flapped back up into the sky, soaring overhead. The chill of the rock in her talons would not be appreciated, so I intended to use it quickly.

I pressed a button on my wristband and Lady released the rock. It tumbled through the air and clattered against the frosty ground. The noise stole the guard's attention. The moment he started walking toward the fallen rock, I rounded the corner with a casual stride. It was perfectly timed. I reached the door as his back was turned, still scanning the ground in front of him for what had made that sound. I switched my vision to infrared to see if any body heat was behind the door. Seeing no body heat signatures on the other side, I opened the door and stepped through.

The brightly lit data center was mostly automated. There were only a few computer stations for the necessary human work that the facility needed. I would make good use of them. I walked over to the farthest computer station. I chose the farthest because I wanted some reaction time in case of interruption. The computer was the standard Ballkean model but the software was much newer. This I didn't like. It meant I would have a few surprises. And surprises were not the most helpful in this situation. I switched my eyesight back to normal; I would need all my concentration.

I cursed in my head as I fumbled around with the security login. My usual tricks didn't work. And I only had a few remaining attempts before I would trigger a lockout, denying anyone access. I pulled out my decryptor from my coat pocket. It was a clunky little gadget that sometimes came in handy when my usual tricks failed. I couldn't remember where I picked it up, but it cost me three months' wages to get it. I touched it to the terminal box and listened to it hum. I didn't like using it much because it involved a lot of waiting without much idea of what was happening. When the cycle was complete and it beeped, either you were in the system or you were again denied.

The decryptor beeped. I put it away, cursing. Their security was more than what I had prepared for. Needless to say, this was not a good sign. It meant Dentum would be anything but a walk in the park. All the hassle of getting inside the facility would be worthless if I couldn't access the system. Unfortunately, I would have to try again another day. I was out of resources and Lady's temperature would be dropping in the cold air.

I retreated to the door, switching my eyesight back to infrared. The guard had given up on Lady's rock and returned to guarding the door. The simplest method for my retreat would be to open the door and knock out the guard. But, if I wanted to try this again, it would be best if my presence here was unnoticed. I tapped a button on my wristband and Lady picked up another rock. This time she dropped it a little closer. The guard drew his blast pistol and carefully approached the fallen rock.

I slipped out the door and back to the outer wall of the building. After slipping past the perimeter patrols, I made my way back to the *Princess.* Lady seemed happy to be back in the warm cockpit. I sat back in my chair, wondering how to defeat such an advanced security system. While it was true that I was handy with a computer, I was by no means an experienced hacker. I needed to think up another angle. I remembered an old saying from Korr, my mentor: Sometimes the best way in is from the side. It was a phrase he used often when he needed to think outside the box.

I would have to think more on that later; I needed to get back to Bendune to meet up with Tess. I put the *Princess* on autopilot while I got myself some shut-eye. I wanted to be well-rested before meeting up with Tess. She had a clever mind but she was also prone to looking for ways to get more of what she wanted out of a situation. It was part of what made her an effective pirate but it also caused trouble for me. I needed to be alert. I landed the *Princess* and refueled her before sending a message to Tess. This time we were to meet aboard her starcruiser.

The rendezvous was uneventful, her crew had already been informed of our partnership. Though, some of the men still looked at me with wary eyes. I didn't blame them. Mauv gave me a wide berth. He was the one I didn't shoot last time. I was escorted up to the bridge of the starcruiser and then off to a ready room at the side. Mauv showed me to a chair and I sat down.

"Long time, no see," I said to him.

He looked at me nervously.

I chuckled. "You don't gotta worry about me. We're on the same side this time."

"You...you a Wayfinder, ain't you?"

"Well, what do you think?"

"You're awful fast on the draw, mister. But I don't know much else Wayfinder could do."

I nodded. "Fair enough."

"What did Wayfinders do?" he finally asked.

I smiled. "Well, there's an old saying; Where there's a will, there's a way. You familiar with it?"

He nodded. "Yeah."

"Well, I guess you could say that Wayfinders always have the will."

Tess stepped into the room dressed as a Corporation security guard. I must have been staring because she burst out in laughter. "Well?" she asked.

"It fits like you had it custom tailored," I replied. "The shoulder patch indicates you are from regional security. The collar pin suggests an investigational unit. And you cut your hair to chin length. I'm guessing there's a reason for that?"

"Very good," she appraised. "I would rather not have cut my hair. But this is what is allowed by the current regulations for the rank I'm posing as."

"Extremely attentive to detail, as always," I said, tipping my hat.

"What have you learned from your reconnaissance?" she asked.

I looked away from her. "...that their computer system is practically blast-proof."

She frowned. "Well getting us inside will do no good if you can't hack into the system."

"You would be correct," I said, leaning back in my chair.

"But you have a plan, right?"

I looked at her. "I have *half* a plan."

"Half a plan?" she said, eyeing me disapprovingly.

I nodded. "I have figured out a way to get past the security," I said.

Her eyes narrowed. "I hear a 'but' coming."

"But it will need a lot more creativity."

"We were only supposed to get you inside. Now you want us playing a much bigger role?" she complained.

"I admit it isn't my first choice. But beggars can't be choosers."

"I don't know," she said. "That bounty on your head is looking a lot more appealing than bluffing our way through this."

I forced a smile. "Now, now, Tess. There's no need to go throwing insults. With your attention to detail and my way with words, we'll have this job finished as quick as you can crack a whip."

She pursed her lips. "I don't like going off script."

"You're a careful one, I'll give you that. But I don't reckon you'll need much worry. People are much more predictable than computers."

"You had better be right about this," she warned. "'Cause if it backfires, I'm selling you out."

"I aim to make that threat obsolete."

Our discussion lasted a bit longer, discussing details of positioning and timing. Tess had a knack for precision. When she wanted something to go down a certain way, she made sure it only could go down that one way. That was her strength. Her weakness was in improvisation. Her perfectionism wasn't very flexible in evolving a story to suit the circumstances. That was my specialty. My Wayfinder mentor, Korr, had told me as much.

I stood to leave and Tess caught my arm. “We could have made such a great team, why couldn’t things have been different?”

I shrugged. “I reckon fate had other plans. Only time will tell if it was for the best or not.”

I left there wondering what my life would have been like had I never left. What if I hadn’t had to leave and had wanted to work alongside Tess? Several scenarios flashed across my mind. I could have been a robber baron and a powerful man within the Davendries. Or could I have been? That kind of life was not the way of a Wayfinder. The code I had sworn to didn’t allow much flexibility. And then my mind caught hold of Miri. I would never have met her. My heart grew heavy. I swallowed back a lump in my throat. My stomach felt empty. I would never have met Miri.

Miri was a good woman. Sure, she got us tangled up in this whole mess. But it was because her nurturing instincts were to help a lost, lonely ten-year-old girl. She had compassion and she wasn’t afraid to ask for help. My mind replayed the memory of her before we ran into that Kuda. She had flashed that playful smile of hers when she asked me if I wanted to come shopping with them. Everything about Miri was on the up and up. She was honest and playful without deceit. There was no question on whether I would have to lower my standards with her. If anything, I’d have to raise them. My mind could have played a thousand scenarios of what could have been with Tess. And they all would have paled in comparison to being with Miri.

I needed to get her back. I spent the rest of that night thinking up plans and counter-plans. Breaking into Dentum was the one way I had to get Miri back. And I was as sure as shooting going to do my very best.

We waited another three days to begin the job. Tess had said the timing would coincide with another reason for her to make their appearance. I didn’t pretend to understand what she was talking about. She was meticulous in everything she planned. So, I trusted her.

I arrived on Dentum Prime a day early. Lady needed the flight time to get used to the area and to get her jitters out. I didn't have to tell her we were doing a mission, she seemed to sense from me when we were beginning a mission. She would get a little jittery and hyper-focused. We sat in a large Gulgam tree overlooking the jungle ridge and the massive data facility in the valley. The darned thing was as large as a big city. It had sections for worker housing and a commercial district. At least a dozen landing pads were scattered throughout the compound. Large satellite dishes and transmission towers rose above the steel and concrete buildings. The gentle rain made a partial rainbow arc through the gray cloudy sky.

The hot muggy air collected moisture around everything, including me. It was like stepping into a room after someone had just taken a shower. I wasn't sure how people could stand the weather. I would much rather take the dry desert heat any day of the week. The humidity did make everything green but if I had to live on this planet, I'd be afraid of myself turning green.

I turned to Lady. "It's showtime."

She leaped from my arm like an arrow from a bow. She glided overhead and off into the distance. I fastened on my tactical mask and switched my eyesight to see what Lady saw. Hundreds of security personnel patrolled around the ten-foot-tall outer wall of the city. Four or five airships zoomed overhead, patrolling the air space. Carol was right about needing an army to break in. I hoped I was also right about only needing a really good diversion.

I didn't have to wait long before I saw two large shuttles on the horizon. Tess was punctual. The airships diverted from their search patterns and moved to intercept the shuttles. Many security personnel abandoned their patrol routes. They swarmed to the east side where Tess's shuttles were approaching. That thinned out the security line quite well.

I crept down close to the city wall, still a few paces from it. Hiding in all the thick foliage was probably the one redeeming factor to this damp planet. It sure offset my annoyance with those pesky insects buzzing around my ears. I should have brought my gloves. They would have kept me from needing to swat so many bugs that landed on my hands. Had I thought through a few more details, I might have looked into a local bug spray. The trouble with bug repellent was that you had to find some that were locally made. A spray might repel bugs on one planet but cause bugs on another planet to swarm. A part of me wished it would rain harder. Perhaps that would keep those insects at bay.

I waited for the next patrols to pass while also paying attention to what Lady could see on the other side of the wall. It was tricky timing it right to be clear on both sides. I had waited a good ten minutes before I found my window of opportunity. I jumped, soaring overhead the patrols, and clearing the wall. My aim was off a little. I landed on a tree on the other side. I had hoped to miss hitting that tree. The loud crack of the breaking branch echoed in the alley. I wasn't worse for wear, but I practically announced my entrance. I dashed over to a nearby building and leaped to the top.

I crouched low, keeping out of sight from the street. It also lowered the profile that could be seen from the airships above. Lady landed on the ledge beside me. "Good girl," I said, stroking her feathered head. "Now let's find the data center."

She flew off, soaring around overhead all the buildings. The data center stood tall in the center of the city-sized compound. Large transmission towers and power generators loomed high, casting shadows over smaller buildings. The sprawling population cluttered the streets and most alleys. It was difficult to find an opening to jump to the next rooftop without attracting attention. So, instead, I let myself down to the ground and made my way as close to the data center as I could. The guards around the data center were sparser than outside the city. They stood watch over all the entrances.

It was time to see if I could get in the same way I had on Velios. The trouble here was that there weren't a whole lot of rocks or debris. Mud and vegetation were the primary decorations nature had afforded it. On the bright side, this facility was like a large city, so it stood to reason that it had the same ailments as a major city. I pulled a coin from my pocket and tossed it to the ground. It clinked on the cobblestone street.

The guard turned his head toward the sound but did not move from his post. I shook my head. These guards were disciplined. I hadn't seen much of that in my time. Most guards were bored out of their minds and easily distracted. Which, admittedly, I was counting on. I couldn't risk them raising the alarm and locking down the data center. That would make things a whole lot more complicated. I needed an easy way in. The trouble was that I was running out of options. It looked like the only way to avoid making a scene was to create one deliberately. I took out another coin from my pocket and casually strolled out across the damp sidewalk. As I passed by, I threw the coin. It nailed him in the forehead.

He glared at me with a shocked expression.

I smiled wide and offered him a rude hand gesture in return.

His discipline kept him at his post despite my behavior.

Whatever training those guards received was pretty good. But at least I was pushing the man's buttons. He grew red in the face as I described to him what I thought of his mother, followed by another coin to the face. He bolted after me like a starved dog let off its chain. I ran back down the alley and around the first corner. I jumped, pulling myself up onto the roof. Dashing back across the roof, I headed toward the door the man was guarding. I dropped from the roof in front of the door and attempted to let myself in. The door was locked and required a keycard for the entrance. That was also something different from Velios.

I hadn't brought anything with me to override the electronic lock. What I brought was to hack into the computer system. I also didn't have time to go back to the *Princess* to get one. I never would have dived into something like this with so little preparation a few years ago. I must have been loosing my edge. I considered kicking in the door, but I decided against it. When the guard would return from chasing me he would notice a damaged door and raise the alarm. I needed a fast way inside. I jumped back onto the roof.

There was a roof access door that I could exploit. It had the telltale signs of being wired up to an alarm system, so I couldn't simply break in. This would need more precision. At least with the airships occupied by Tess's shuttles, I didn't have to worry about being seen just yet. I tapped a button on my wristband, switching my eyesight to electromagnetic. The wiring ran deep through the concrete but was exposed at one small discreet spot.

I pulled out my boot knife and stabbed the cable. The electrical signal still ran to the door alarm. *They must have a backup power line,* I thought. After examining the electromagnetic signal a moment or two, I saw it. A wireless electrical receiver was built into the door alarm. That would require a little more ingenuity. The good news was that they employed both a wired power connection as well as a wireless one. That meant I could send a power surge through the wired cable to short out the wireless power receiver.

I hated monkeying with what made my heart tick. But desperate times called for desperate measures. I unbuttoned my shirt and opened up my chest panel. I extended the red and white wire and touched it to the exposed alarm wire I had cut.

Every muscle in my chest instantly tensed up and I lost my breath. It was like I had the wind knocked out of me. I dropped to the ground, gasping for breath and feeling my pulse. My heart was beating quickly but at least it was still ticking. *Let's not try that again,* I thought. I was not much use to anyone dead. I closed my chest panel and buttoned up my shirt. Climbing to my feet I noticed the door alarm was dead. At least I succeeded in shorting it out. I switched my eyesight back to normal and proceeded to kick the door in.

Two solid kicks with my enhanced knees folded the door in on itself. I never did like metal doors. They didn't break, they only bent. I slid past the damaged door and descended the stairs into the server room. That room was an engineering marvel. Rows upon rows of server computer hardware created a maze of walkways. They were lined with running cables and flashing lights. The steady cool and dry atmosphere was carefully controlled. It maximized the lifespan of the equipment. Redundant power generators lined a wall with four small computer stations. The labyrinth of computer servers was intimidating, but it would serve my purposes. The larger the equipment footprint, the longer it would take them to find my tampering.

I picked a server rack at random and patched in the compu-transceiver I prepared for the mission. It was able to send and receive massive amounts of data in a short time. It had a limited range, so I would have to do the dirty work before I left Dentum. All that was left, was getting past the security system to gain access. Once I had access, I would be able to transmit Ryna's file to the *Princess.* I would also be able to transfer a lot of money to the Davenry's hedge account that Tess had given me.

I made my way to the workstations and sat down. I pulled out my decryptor and attached it to the computer. It ran a few cycles and then beeped at me. It wasn't a surprise that it had failed. It had failed back on Velios. My plan to beat the security system was a little juvenile but it was the only option I could think of.

The door to the back of the room burst open and seven armed guards swarmed in, surrounding me with guns drawn. One of the guards, who wore a gold rank pin, pointed his blast pistol in my direction. "Reach for the sky, Wayfinder scum."

How did he know I was a Wayfinder? That hadn't been common knowledge. As far as they should have known, I was just a common criminal that had come to steal data. Unless...unless Tess had told them. And if Tess told them, that would explain how they knew where I was. At least I could still keep my confidence in my alarm cutting skills. It would have been a real shame if I had almost electrocuted myself on the roof for nothing. I slowly raised my hands in the air.

Two guards confiscated my blast pistols and hauled me from the room. They wasted no time in dragging me to the security office. Once inside, they took my mask off. The security office had monitors along the walls and several computer stations. A blast rifle rack hung on the far wall. They sat me down at a circular table in the middle of the room.

Tess sat across the table from me. "Long time, no see, Rence," she said in a triumphant voice.

"Not long enough, apparently," I said.

She glanced over to the security guard with the gold pin. "Hanley, how far did he get into the system?"

Hanley gave a smug smile. "He was trying to cut into the system with this," he said, tossing my decryptor onto the table.

"Please be careful with that," I said. "It ain't cheap."

Hanley leaned in close to me. "You're in a lot of trouble, mister. Westward Galactic doesn't take kindly to people breaking and entering."

"I'll remember that next time," I said.

"What makes you think there will be a next time?"

I forced a smile. "Well, I'll tell you what," I said. "Since I already got what I came for, I'll give it back to you in exchange for letting me go."

"You don't have *anything!*"

"Are you *sure* he didn't get inside the system?" Tess said with concern in her voice.

He shot a glance at her. "Yes! He was sitting at a terminal and caught at the login screen."

"You idiot! He's a Wayfinder, he doesn't need to log in!"

Hanley rushed over to a computer screen and examined the statistics. "No suspicious transmission, no anomalous data processes. He didn't get anything."

He was right, of course. I hadn't been able to get inside the system yet. But that wasn't the point. The point was that he needed to believe that I had. So, I snickered. I snickered loud, hoping it would catch Hanley's attention.

Hanley glanced at me, worry in his eyes.

"Log into the system and make sure," Tess ordered.

Hanley punched his password into the computer and pulled up the database. He examined the screen a moment before sighing with relief and logging out. "No data has been extracted or modified to exceed normal baseline use."

He turned around and looked at me with contempt in his eyes. "You're a very good liar, but a poor hacker."

"There will be no more tomorrows for you, Rence," Tess said. She looked over to Hanley. "Assemble a firing squad."

My eyes lit up. "What?"

Had she gone crazy? Was this her idea of improvising? Or was this her plan all along? My breathing became shallow and my heart raced.

"I'll get one put together in twenty minutes," Hanley replied, leaving the room.

"You are too dangerous to keep alive," Tess explained. "Besides, the price on your head does not specify that you have to be alive."

I looked around the room. The guard to the left of me was the one who had taken my blast pistols. He held them in one hand. The one to my right held my mask. Getting my guns and mask back would be easy if they didn't have two more guards with blast pistols pointed at me. I would never be able to get out of my chair before they shot me, to say nothing about taking care of the guards. The timing wasn't yet right. I needed to wait a little longer.

"That's funny," I said. "Being a Wayfinder was what always kept me alive."

"Then it is a poetic irony that it should be the cause of your death," Tess said.

I really needed to stop getting captured. It seemed everyone wanted me dead one way or another.

Hanley stepped back into the room. "The firing squad is being assembled as we speak." He turned to me. "A fitting death for the last Wayfinder, don't you think?"

"Well, I don't know about that," I said honestly. "I kinda fancied old age myself."

"Second-rate filth such as yourself have no right to expect to live that long," Hanley said with a sneer.

I rolled my eyes at him. "You obviously don't know much about Wayfinders, do you?"

"I know all I need to know," he snapped.

"For example," I said. "A Wayfinder would never stoop to becoming rent-a-cop in a monkey suit."

Hanley's nostrils flared. He punched me square in the face. My head was thrown to the side and my cheek throbbed.

"We're also fast on the draw," I said, pretending to ignore his punch.

He punched me again. The force of the hit scooted my chair to the side. Blood ran down the corner of my mouth. My jaw throbbed as much as my cheek.

"Yeah, I've heard you guys are fast with a gun," Hanley declared. "Well, you ain't got your guns now, do you? So, you're gonna have to take every hit I give you."

"No, I don't, actually."

He feigned surprise. "Oh really? And why is that?"

"He's taunting you," Tess warned.

I shot a glance over to Tess. "I don't have to taunt him. He already knows he's chicken-hearted soldier-wanna-be playing dress-up."

Hanley pulled me out of the chair and held me against the nearby wall. "What makes you think you can sit there, throwing insults at me? Without your guns, you're just a measly punk."

I smiled at him. "It doesn't have to be *my* gun."

He glanced down as I grabbed his gun and shoved him back into a guard. The guard dropped my mask and fell backward also. I spun, dropping to one knee, and fired at the guard behind me. His shot knocked my hat off and mine tore into his stomach. I fired another shot into the guard next to him. I dove toward him and ripped my pistols from his hands before he fell to the floor.

Hanley rolled off the other guard and drew *his* blast pistol. They both opened fire on me. I dove to the ground like a baseball runner sliding into home plate; only I was sliding out the open door. As I slid out the doorway, I grabbed my hat and mask from off the floor. Once in the hallway, I glanced back through the door and saw Tess on the other end of the table. I took a shot at her but she ducked, letting my blast bolt sail over her head and blacken the wall behind her.

I scrambled to my feet and punched the button on the wall to close the door to the security office. After the door slid closed, I smashed the door controls with the butt of Hanley's blast pistol. I felt really good about shutting them up in that room. *There is one downside to locking them in the office,* I thought. The overhead lights turned red and an alarm blared. *And that would be the downside.* I planted my hat on my head and clamped my mask in place.

I took off running back down the hallway that they had dragged me, making my way back to the server room. I slid around the corner only to see guards coming out of the server room. I needed a new exit strategy. Unfortunately, I had run so fast that I couldn't stop myself in time. I slid toward the guards and landed on my backside as they started shooting. The blast bolts sailed over my head. I fired Thunder and Lightning, my twin blast pistols. I dropped three guards as the rest retreated down the hallway in panic. That wasn't the most elegant of shootouts but it worked.

I scrambled into the server room and shut the door. I slid a computer desk in front of the door to block it off. For good measure, I tipped a metal cabinet onto the desk. That would hold them for a while. But with the alarm going off, I would soon have to worry about the airships outside. They would be descending upon the building.

I sat down at a computer station and typed in the password I saw Hanley use. It worked. I was in. I pulled up all files on project Osurious and started the upload to the *Astral Princess*'s computer. I then spent the next five minutes moving money around in their system. It was tempting to take some money for myself, but that would be dirty money. If I needed money I would fly passenger transport again. It was slow but it was honest work. Though, one might say what I was just doing was the opposite of honest work. I figured I would have time to justify it later when I wasn't being shot at. Even though I didn't know where all my activities fit into my standards, I at least had standards.

I was about to leave when a thought crossed my mind. What good would it do me to learn how they are tracking Ryna if they were still able to track her? Was there anything I could do about it? I checked the upload with the *Princess.* The records had finished uploading. There was something I could do about it. I hit the delete key. A warning message flashed up on the screen asking me if I was sure I wanted to erase the files on project Osurious. I hit "yes". The computer system began purging the files from the database.

I ran up the stairs to the roof but stopped short of exiting the stairwell. An airship was hovering over the building and had extended a rope ladder. Armed guards were climbing down onto the roof. I pulled out a detonator from my coat pocket and pressed the center button. That gave me nine seconds before it blew. I waited five seconds before dashing out the door onto the roof. Guards from the hovering airship began shooting at me. I tossed the detonator into the air at them. It exploded in mid-air. The blast blew the ship back, causing several guards to fall off the rope ladder. I wasted no time diving off the edge of the building.

More airships descended on me like vultures, shooting their blast cannons at me. The blasts made potholes in the cobblestone streets. The explosions of the cannon fire into the street sent up dirt into the muggy humid air. Small pieces of rubble flew at me from behind, stinging my skin whenever I got struck. I dove for cover down an alley and the airships passed by overhead, turning around for another pass. I bolted back down the street toward the outer city wall.

People all around shouted and pointed at me and the ensuing ruckus. When I got near the city wall I jumped and cleared the wall, landing with a loud thud. My special knees absorbed much of the shock, for which, I was grateful. But, I was not grateful for the muddy splash of water that my landing sent up into my face. I tore my mask off, feeling the sandy grit in my teeth. I continued running into the dense bug-infested forest. The airships continued shooting wildly, blasting trees and foliage into the air.

I pressed a button on my wristband to call Lady, in case she wasn't already following me back to the *Princess.* It still took me a while to race back to the *Princess* even though I was sprinting most of the way. It wasn't 9exactly how I had planned to leave Dentum, but at least I was alive. Once aboard, I started the launch sequence and lifted off without losing a moment.

Lady squawked at me from her perch beside my chair.

"Yeah, you're tellin' me," I replied. "It hasn't been this crazy in years."

I flew up into the atmosphere with several airships in pursuit. The airships would follow as far as they could, but they couldn't leave the atmosphere. And, as it turned out, they didn't have to. Three starcruisers started shooting their blast cannons at me once I left orbit. I hadn't seen them when I arrived. They may have been patrolling on the other side of the planet.

I pushed the *Princess's* throttle to maximum, steering erratically to dodge their fire. I took a couple of hits to the aft quarter of the ship but thankfully nothing was hit that hindered my escape. The *Princess* was fast and she was fast for a reason. That was one of the many things I loved about the Norgon-class transports. They chased me halfway across the solar system before I outran them.

I set the *Princess* to autopilot and leaned back in my chair, breathing heavily. My lungs felt like they were on fire and my leg muscles were sore. I reached over and stroked Lady's feathered head. "I might be getting a bit old for this kind of thing."

I laid my head back and darn near fell asleep before my console beeped at me. It was an incoming transmission. I pressed the button on the little screen. It blinked and then showed a video image of Tess.

She smiled. "Well done, Rence. My father is going to be pleased with the size of the donation Westward Galactic just gave us."

I crossed my arms. "Firing squad?"

She gave me half a smile. "I had to make it convincing."

"Convincing?" I said with dismay. "You already got him to type in his password, why did you need to be more convincing?"

"Oh come on," she said winking. "You have to admit, it was convincing enough for you."

"It looked to me like you decided to collect on my bounty instead of our agreement!" I said.

"If you thought I was double-crossing you, then why did you transfer the money?"

I paused a moment. I knew why. And somehow, I thought she would have known as well. "Because I always keep my word, Tess. Don't you know that?"

She paused a moment. "Anyway, I'm glad I was right about you."

I rubbed my forehead. "And what exactly were you right about?"

"You were born to do this kind of work," she said with sincerity. "Come and work with me, Rence."

I couldn't think of a polite way to say that I'd sooner dance on my mother's grave. I instead resorted to a slight change of the subject. "Tess, I gave my word to Miri that I would go back for her. And I always keep my word. I got people counting on me and a score to settle. Until then, I can't set any other plans for the future."

Her face was calm and collected. The kind of face that could hide a dozen emotions. But her eyes betrayed her. Her eyes hinted at a sense of rejection. The same look was in her eyes the day I left her years ago. This time, however, I was not leaving because I had to. This time I was leaving because I chose to. Every time I thought about what kind of life I could have had with Tess, my mind kept circling back to Miri. I didn't know Miri as long as I had known Tess, but what I did know was that I wanted to be my best self when I was around Miri.

"Then I'll see you around," she said.

I tipped my hat. "See you around."

EPISODE 6

Calling in some favors

THE LAST WAYFINDER

6

Calling in Some Favors

I sat in the cockpit of the *Astral Princess*. The *Princess* was a fast ship with a few personal upgrades. To my right sat Lady on her perch. And not long ago two more ladies entered my life. I had known Miri Alder for a few years and had been aware of her generosity. And her request to help Ryna had seemed like such a simple task. But then again, Ryna wasn't so simple either.

We had gone through a lot rescuing Petre and Carol, the scientists we thought were Ryna's parents. But in the end, I had been forced to leave Miri and Ryna behind to go and get help. Leaving Miri had been the hardest thing I had ever done. And there was nothing else on my mind other than getting them back.

I spun around in my chair, picking up the datapad off the control console. Petre and Carol sat in the seats behind me. I handed the datapad to Petre. "I had a look but most of this is scientific gibberish."

Petre scrolled through a few pages. "You have the unabridged project files for Osurious," he said, surprised. "How did you get it?"

"I raided the Corporation's data center on Dentum Prime," I answered as if discussing the weather. "Just be careful with it, it's now the sole surviving copy."

His eyes grew wide.

"Listen," I said. "I can bore you with the details later, doc. But right now, I need your help."

"Sure, sure," he said. "Anything."

"Remember how you told me the Corporation was tracking Ryna?"

He nodded.

"Well, poke your nose into those files and see if you can find out how. If they can track her, so can I."

Petre spent a good half hour perusing the files until settling on a particular document. "Here it is," he declared. "All assets classified as essential to the success of the program," he read. "Must be tagged with radioisotope kaligeenium-62."

"Thanks for the narration, doc," I said. "But I was hoping you could translate that mumbo jumbo into something I could understand."

Carol answered for him. "They placed a chemical marker in her blood that can be tracked across long distances."

"How far?"

"Theoretically, across galactic quadrants. Though, its true range has never been successfully tested."

I sat back in my chair. "That would be a problem." I turned to Petre. "Any chance of that stuff wearing off someday?"

"Kaligeenium-62 has a half-life of 12.26 years."

I turned to Carol. "What did he say?"

"The signal will get weaker every decade. And we don't know how many decades until the signal is too weak to track."

I rubbed my hand across my face. That was not the answer I was hoping for. It made sense the Corporation wanted to keep tabs on what they spent money on. I was just hoping it would be easier to release Ryna from their grip. What I needed was a new angle to approach the problem. But what could it be? Then my mind settled on something Petre had read: *all* assets classified as essential.

"Doc, they must have hundreds of assets they tag with this...marker, right?"

Petre nodded. "Probably thousands."

"How do they know which signal belongs to which asset?" I asked, rubbing my chin.

"The decay rate alpha—"

"In English, doc," I said, pleading.

Carol turned to me. "They adjust the marker to read like a serial number."

"Would it then stand to reason that if they no longer know what serial number to look for, they won't know how to track Ryna?"

"Yes," Petre answered. "But you would have to erase the entire catalog."

I nodded. "Done."

"Okay, then if you have purged the database and deleted the backups, then they won't be able to track the girl anymore."

My eyes lit up. "Backups?"

"Yes," he explained. "In case of a catastrophic failure, the database can be restored from backup."

I hung my head. I should have known to check where the database was being backed up to. I was *really* off my game. "Drat," I said. "I forgot about looking for backups when I deleted the files from the database."

Carol sunk into her chair. "Then they can simply restore the database."

"But it will take them some time," Petre said. "They would have a lot of transactional data to account for before they restore the database. Or they risk losing financial data. So, you would still have some time before that happens."

That was good news. And I needed good news right now. It meant I had a small window of time where I had an advantage over Westward Galactic. Which meant my next goal was to figure out how to start tracking Ryna's marker signal. If I could do that, I would find her.

"Petre, do those records tell us what Ryna's serial number is?"

He looked at me. "The isotope decay frequency? Yes, it does."

"Good. Then we just need to build us a signal tracker."

Petre shook his head. "We're scientists, not engineers. We can give you the specifications but we don't know how to build equipment."

"That's good enough. I know a guy who owes me a favor."

The man's name was Mik Ag'nar. He was an engineer who I had helped out some years back. He said he owed me one. I never thought I'd be one to call in a favor but times were getting desperate. So desperate in fact, that I was heading back to one of my least favorite planets. Mik lived on Cosstere, the barren rock that somehow passed for a planet. I set my course for it and engaged the autopilot.

"I'm gonna get some shut-eye," I told them.

"There is one other matter, Mr. Perry," Petre said. "When we tried to rescue Ryna, we were trying to do the right thing. But we were unprepared for what we were getting ourselves into."

"That's understandable," I said, walking to the doorway.

"What he's trying to say," Carol said. "Is that we are not suitable to care for the girl."

I spun around. They were trying to back out of the deal. The deal was that I returned Ryna to her 'parents'. But if they didn't want that role, then what was I gonna do? I clenched my fists.

Carol held up a hand. "Mr. Perry, please don't mistake us. We understand what kind of burden we would be leaving you with. But with the Corporation hunting for her, the safest place for her is with you."

My blood boiled. If they were not going to care for Ryna, then what was this whole mission for? What did I lose Miri for? The whole situation smelled of camcam dung. I didn't like it. Not one bit. It was like being told that I didn't have to lose Miri. And that I lost her for no reason at all. That meant I was no better off than before I stepped foot on that no-good Corporation ship.

I stared into her eyes. "I did not lose Miri for no reason. Until I say otherwise, we're stickin' to the original arrangement." I didn't wait for a response. I stormed out of the cockpit and slammed my cabin door shut. How was I supposed to get any shut-eye now? Petre and Carol's words ran through my head like water over a log. Over and over, I heard their words. Over and over, I wanted to kick myself for leaving Miri.

I did eventually fall asleep. Only after my mind had worn itself out of grief and worry was I able to nod off. The autopilot alarm woke me up. We had arrived at Cosstere. I made my way up to the cockpit, still bitter over my conversation with Petre and Carol. They had retired to their cabins and I found myself alone with Lady.

Lady squawked.

I stroked her feathered head. "I'm upset too. But we gotta make the best of it."

I took the *Princess* off autopilot and took the controls. The Davendry starcruisers didn't bother me this time. I must have been added to their green list. Working with Tess Davendry to break into Westward Galactic had its perks. The *Princess* shuddered as I engaged the vertical descent thrusters. She was always a little shaky on takeoff and landing. Some might call it a sign of her age. I called it class.

We landed just outside Bithro'Shendale. A small mining camp with the makings of a town. It had grown since I saw it last. It now had a full hotel and saloon along with a machinist shop and several merchant stores. There was now even a small hospital. This mining town was the last place I saw Mik. And I hoped he was still here.

I strolled through the streets, looking for the machinist shop. Every time I passed by a camcam, those big smelly riding lizards, I thought about Miri. She had a way with animals. Any beast you could throw a saddle on, she could get it to obey her. Even though I never cared for camcams, somehow, I found them comforting.

The machinist shop was close to the center of town. I walked inside. It was run down, rusted metal floors and walls. Debris was scattered all about. And there was no one in sight. It looked abandoned. The machining equipment was gone. Patches of brighter colored floor were all that remained where they once stood.

"Mik?" I called out.

I didn't like this one bit. I had to find out what happened to Mik's shop. And unfortunately, my first clue was not what I wanted to find. On a rusty shelf, an armored helmet sat, collecting dust. I picked it up and brushed it off. Just looking at it brought back memories of Jashur VII. That was where Miri and I encountered Kuda mercenaries working for the Corporation. I stared into the dark face glass of the helmet, seeing my reflection. The sight of it reminded me when that Kuda walked up to me, looking for a fight.

This helmet did not belong to the same Kuda; Miri had blasted a hole in the back of the last one. This helmet belonged to a different Kuda. And, by the look of the dust collection, the owner was either dead or retired.

A man stepped out from the back room. His armored boots thumped on the hard floor and his body armor scraped against the door frame as he entered. His head was hidden within an armored helmet, his face obscured by the dark glass. I didn't much like Kuda. The ones I'd known were cocky, self-important, and selfish.

"You had better put that back where you found it, stranger," he said, the helmet slightly muffling his voice.

"The helmet can't be yours," I said. "You're already wearing one."

"It ain't a helmet anymore," the Kuda said. "It's a trophy. And I expect you to put it back before I make you a part of that collection."

I wasn't surprised to find this Kuda to be no exception to the stereotype. I would have liked to teach him a few manners, but my last fight with a Kuda hadn't ended well.

I set the helmet back down. "This is Mik Ag'nar's shop. Where is he?"

"This ain't his shop anymore. He uh...retired, you could say."

"Where is he?" I asked, feeling my blood start to boil.

"The old coot was run out of town last year. Couldn't pay his bills."

I had to consciously relax my hands. I didn't want to show this mercenary any clenched fists. I knew Mik. He was a talented engineer. He had been the lead engineer for Starfield & Tanner. They were the most reputable gun manufacturer in the colony worlds. He had left to go into business for himself. His shop had always been busy and turning a profit. If he was having financial trouble, it wasn't for the lack of customers or skill. If I had to guess, I'd say the Kuda had something to do with it.

"That's funny," I said, forcing a grin. "He was never in want for a customer. Just what kind of bills couldn't he pay?"

"This little town has had troubles with raiders. That is, until I came around. I ran them off and have kept this town safe ever since."

I glared at him. "A Kuda doesn't do anything out of the kindness of his heart."

"A man's got to make a living," he said, crossing his arms.

"So I reckon everyone pitches in to pay your fee."

He nodded. "Quite a bargain considering the cost."

"Some might call it a bargain," I said. "Others might call it extortion."

The Kuda took an angry step forward, his hands to his side in fists. "You making an accusation, stranger?"

"Who am I to accuse the savior of the town?" I said, turning to leave. "Oh, I didn't catch the name?"

"Surius. *Sheriff* Surius to you."

I tipped my hat and again turned to leave.

"What's your name, stranger?"

The last time a Kuda asked my name, he was looking to cash in on my bounty. I had lied and given him Miri's last name. It was the quickest name I could come up with at the time. This time, however, I deliberately use it. Partly because it was obscure enough to keep the anonymity and partly because I missed Miri.

"Rence," I replied. "Rence Alder."

I turned and left. I had dealt with such men in the past. Preying on the weak, demanding money from them, all under the guise of protection. Men like that usually fabricated the danger so they could set themselves up as a deliverer of sorts. Then they terrorize the citizens, squeezing them dry of money. All the while, spinning tales of worse dangers out there. It was a wicked kind of crime. Not a singular event like a robbery. It was imprisoning people within their own town while sucking them dry of any living.

I needed information, so I headed to the saloon. It was the usual place for gossip and local news. I walked in and froze in my tracks. Three other Kuda sat at a table with their helmets off, drinking. It was a good thing I hadn't picked a fight with Surius; the other three could have joined in. I appreciated Korr's advice about not rushing into a fight. It had just saved me from a big mistake. I walked over to the bar and set down a coin.

The portly man who tended the bar set down a shot glass in front of me and poured.

"Whatever happened to Mik Ag'nar?" I whispered to him.

He glanced nervously toward the Kuda. "When Mik refused to pay up, they run him out of town and sold off his equipment to Fin G'Dal."

"Which way did he go?"

"North," he said, motioning with his head. "Toward Saggetville."

I tipped my hat. "Much obliged."

After leaving the saloon, I returned to the *Princess* to fetch Lady. I needed to scour the landscape and she was the most effective way. I stroked her feathered head. "We need to find old Mik," I said, sending her into the sky northward. I returned to the *Princess* and sat down in my chair. I switched one of my console monitors to see through Lady's eyes. Watching through her eyes was like soaring through the sky myself. I could almost hear the wind in my ears and smell the clean air.

I leaned forward in my chair as Lady passed over a small settlement on the outskirts of Saggetville. What caught my interest was the large solar panels on the roof of the building. Whatever was used in that building needed a lot of power. If Mik was alive, he would be working. And if he was working he would need quite a bit of power. And Saggetville was supposedly where he was run off to. I pressed a button on my wristband and Lady circled the property.

I engaged the *Princess's* vertical thrusters and lifted off. The rumbly takeoff was typical even when I was not exiting the atmosphere. I flew the *Princess* over to the settlement and set down a little way off. Not far enough to make a long walk, but not too close either. I still could be wrong about who the settlement belonged to.

I exited the ramp and Lady flew to my arm. I walked with her toward the main building. It was a rugged and sloppy building, thrown together with scrap metal and wood. Large black exposed wires from the solar panels ran down the side of the building. It was as if decoration was an afterthought. A small shack stood close to the main building along with what appeared to be a large shed or workshop.

As I approached, a man dressed in Kuda armor stepped out from the main building. He was not wearing a helmet. He had a blast rifle in his hands and he stepped cautiously in my direction. If this was going to turn into a shootout, I would need Lady in the air. But having her on my arm made me look less threatening.

I kept my pace as casual as I could. When we were close enough to exchange words, he offered none. So, I called out to him, "I'm lookin' for an old friend."

"You ain't no friend of mine," he replied.

We stopped about fifty paces apart. "His name is Mik Ag'nar. He's the finest engineer this side of the frontier."

"Who's asking?"

"Rence Perry," I said, hoping it was safe to use my name. I tried to avoid it as much as I could but Mik would not know me by any other name.

"Rence Perry, the last Wayfinder?"

"I ain't lookin' for trouble," I said. "I need a favor from an old friend."

He motioned with the barrel of his blast rifle toward the main building. "You walk in front. And keep your hands where I can see them."

I held my hands up–well, one of them at least–and walked in front of the Kuda to the main building. I couldn't put my other hand up because lady was perched on that arm. I pulled open the rickety old door and stepped inside. The interior was nothing like the outside. The place was swept and organized. Bright light fixtures kept the room without shadows. Shelves of parts lay along the walls. Several machining tables were strewn about the center of the room.

An old man with a dark suntan across his face looked up from the workbench. His brow wrinkled with welding goggles on his head. His mouth pulled up into a smile. "Rence Perry. Boy, are you a sight for old eyes."

I smiled, lowering my hand. "Long time, no see, Mik."

The Kuda stepped into the room and closed the door. "You know this man?"

"It's okay, Anruk. Rence and I are old friends." He motioned for Anruk to join us. "I added weapons to his transport ship. It was in exchange for him helping me settle a dispute that threatened my business."

"I would have expected a Wayfinder to look a little more high-tech." Anruk said.

I raised an eyebrow at him.

Mik chuckled. "Technology isn't what makes a Wayfinder." He walked around the workbench and eagerly shook my hand. "The years have been good to you, I see."

I smiled again. "Still the firm handshake."

He stroked Lady's feathered head. "And Lady is looking as good as ever."

"I could say the same about you," I replied. "I'd say your misfortunes here have not diminished you a bit."

He frowned. "How much do you know about that?"

"Your shop is left to waste, occupied by a Kuda answering to the name of Sheriff Surius."

"Sheriff?" Anruk said, incredulous. "He ain't no sheriff."

"That much I figured," I said, turning to Anruk. "He's holding the town hostage, pretending to protect it." I turned back to Mik. "The bartender said you were run out when you refused to pay."

"That's putting it mildly," he said, taking a seat on a stool by the workbench.

I glanced at Anruk. "I'm guessing that's your helmet Surius has on display?"

He nodded gravely.

Mik motioned toward him. "You see, Anruk is the Alpha leader of those Kuda–"

"Was," Anruk said with disdain in his voice.

"Let me guess," I said. "One of your men saw an opportunity for profit that you didn't approve of and didn't take no for an answer."

He nodded again.

"But what brings you to Cosstere?" Mik asked, changing the subject.

"I need a way to track a signal from a rare isotope."

Mik shook his head. "I don't have any of my biotech engineering equipment. I can only guess Surius would have sold it."

I sighed. "Well, it seems the only way you can help me is if I first help you."

"I really do appreciate the gesture, Rence. But that equipment is very expensive–"

"I didn't say anything about *buying*. What was stolen from you will need to be returned."

"If you think Surius is a man who will relent, you've got another thing coming," Anruk stated.

"How loyal are your men to Surius?" I asked.

"They follow whoever leads," he replied.

"And how, exactly, is leadership transferred?"

Mik shot a glance at Anruk. "Would that work?"

Anruk shook his head. “I would have to fight him myself. There can’t be any help in a call-out.”

“What if Surius was run out of town?” I asked.

“Good luck with that,” he said. “He’s the strongest of my men. He wouldn’t have been able to beat me in a call-out otherwise.”

“What if he was made a fool?” I asked. “Surely your men would think twice before following a fool?”

“How do you intend to do that?” he asked skeptically.

“Never ask *how* until you have first answered *what.*”

Anruk paused a moment before responding. “Yeah, that’d do it. No self-respecting Kuda would follow a fool. But if you go picking a fight, you’ll be dealing with all four of ‘em.”

“I’ll find a way,” I said.

Anruk opened his mouth to speak but Mik answered his unspoken question. “Rence isn’t called a Wayfinder for nothing, Anruk.”

He looked over at Mik. “Is that why you’re so fascinated with Wayfinders?”

“Well,” he admitted. “It’s why I’m fascinated with this one.”

Mik was kind enough to offer me some supper. He didn’t have much in the way of square meals. Just some dried meat and boiled beans. A man could live off it for a while, but it wasn’t ideal. The whiskey was better. I had let Lady fly loose outside, stretching her wings. It would also allow her to catch a meal more to her liking.

I leaned back in my chair, relaxing. “Mik, you ever done much with explosives?”

He nodded. “Plenty. Why?”

“I think I’m gonna need some.”

Anruk set down his cup. “Don’t you go thinking you can win an outright battle with four Kuda. They’re trained soldiers.”

“That’s true,” I said. “I have had my fair share of encounters with Kuda. I can’t win an out-and-out fight with them. Not unless they don’t know it’s a fight.”

“How would they not know it’s a fight? Whether you reach for your guns or a detonator, they’ll know a fight is on.”

I held my hands up. “Now I don’t mean any disrespect, Anruk. I know these are your men we’re talking about. They know warfare. But Surius does not have them doing soldier work. He's got them playing posse in a mind game against the town. And mind games are what *I* know."

He took another sip of his drink.

Mik got up, wandering over to a shelf. He sat back down having retrieved a small device in his hands. "They ain't pretty. But they'll go boom when you need them to." He set it down on the table.

"I'm gonna need to look like I make and sell them," I said, picking up the detonator.

The crude device was perfect. It looked like it was slapped together with no regard to appearance. If I hadn't known better, I would have thought it was held together with tape and glue. It was absolutely perfect for what I had in mind.

Mik looked at me curiously. "I'll need a couple of days but that shouldn't be a problem."

Anruk eyed me suspiciously. "What are you planning?"

I admitted that I didn't have all the details ironed out yet, but I told them my plan. I didn't leave anything out. If there was some detail I didn't know about, I frankly told them. Mik sat back laughing while Anruk stroked his chin in thought. I admitted it wasn't an elegant plan but it did have merit; merit enough for Anruk to consider it.

"It's risky," Anruk said. "If Surius catches on, you're a dead man."

"It's a gamble," I admitted. "But I've always been a gambling man when it comes to people."

Mik leaned forward. "It's a deal then. Once I have my equipment back, I will build your tracking device. I'll start looking for where my machines went."

"You might want to try a man by the name of Fin G'Dal," I said.

"The craftsman?"

I nodded. "Bartender said he was who Surius had sold your stuff to."

"I reckon that makes things a bit easier. We can start tomorrow."

"No," Anruk said, holding one hand up. "I can't accept your help; I don't have anything to pay you with."

I shrugged. "Don't let it fret you. You can always owe me a favor. I try not to cash them in unless necessary." I didn't expect payment; I was helping out the friend of a friend. But the way of the Kuda was the way of a mercenary. Payment for services was a part of their culture. And I had no problem accepting payment, especially cash. As it was, my bank account was running low. But I learned something as a Wayfinder. Sometimes, helping somebody out of a tight situation was more of a reward than the coins they could give. Mik was proof of that.

Anruk relaxed. "Then I guess I have no more excuses."

"I guess not," I said.

We got to work the next day. Mik worked hard getting lots of explosives made while Anruk and I set out to find clothes and a big hoverwagon. The clothes were easy. I needed to look like a settler with plenty of time on his hands. What was more, I needed to look older and a little eccentric. Anruk joked that I didn't need any help on that last part. I had put some thinned-out snowweed sap in my hair. It smelled like the inside of my boot after a hot day, but it did put a lot of gray into my hair.

I changed into long brown britches and a yellow linen shirt. It was far removed from my long coat and hat. I felt downright naked without my blast belt around my hips. Going against Kuda without my guns was an invitation for disaster. Then again, my blast pistols didn't do much against the blast armor of the last Kuda I squared off with. But even so, I still felt vulnerable without them at my side.

Twin holsters would definitely look out of place, so I had to leave them on the *Princess.* I didn't go completely unarmed, though. I took my blast carbine with me. A rifle would not look questionable on the frontier. After all, a man had to eat and fend off the wildlife.

Finding ourselves a hoverwagon that was big enough was tricky. In the end, we had to build one. And it turned out better for my costume since I was trying to pass for a tinkering engineer trying to make a living. Mik took some time out to help with constructing the hoverwagon. We were in luck that Mik had a spare motor lying around. It had been part of a moisture condenser that he hadn't gotten around to fixing. We fitted it with a canopy tarp and loaded it up with lots of debris. I was amazed at how much junk he had collected in the year he had been here. Then we loaded up explosives carefully into the wagon.

I found more snowweed and painted a sign on the canopy tarp saying, Jetom's Mining Wares. I wasn't sure I liked the name Jetom. I knew a Jetom once, and as best I could recollect, he still owed me money. But Mik assured me the name was common enough to not be recognizable.

Lady didn't much like the smell of my hair so she kept her distance. I didn't blame her. I just hoped the smell would wash out. I drove the hoverwagon into town early the next morning. I parked the hoverwagon right across from Mik's old shop; right where Surius was sure to see. I set up the debris like it was on display. By the time the yellow sun started peeking over the far ridge, I looked like a street vendor.

About half an hour later the streets animated with people walking about. Most of the people were whispering to each other and pointing at me. A few even came to inspect my wares. The folks were cordial, but they also didn't dare say much. These were intimidated people trying to be neighborly.

I didn't get any time to strike up a conversation. All four Kuda descended upon me, scattering the citizens. Surius was in the lead.

"Get outta here, you ain't wanted."

"You're mistaken," I said with a warm smile, trying to sound old. "Everyone has been so warm and welcoming. I have had my first few customers already. Are you a miner? Does the shifting rock gum up your drills–"

"I said, get!" he demanded, picking up something from my display. "Or you'll end up with a lot of broken products."

I forced a nervous look, pointing to the scrap metal in his hand. "Uh, careful, explosives don't break, they go boom."

Surius glanced at what was in his hand and then back to me. "This ain't an explosive."

I gently took the scrap from his hand and reverently laid it back down. "If you be wanting a free sample, sonny," I said handing him one of Mik's explosives. "Try something a little less dramatic."

He stared at the offering a moment. "You're one crazy old man. This is scrap, not an explosive." He threw it to the ground by his feet. I dove for cover. The explosion knocked over all my displays, pushing my cart aside. It also launched Surius a foot into the air. The other three Kuda drew their blast pistols instinctively. Then they laughed, pointing to Surius. He groaned, picking himself up, blood trickling down his armored leg. Blast armor or no blast armor, that explosive did a real number on his leg. My compliments on Mik's handiwork.

I got up and started picking up my display shelves. Surius cursed, hobbling away. The other three Kuda followed him. It wasn't over yet, but I had successfully landed the first blow. I set my displays back up and cleaned up a bit. Surius would tend to his leg and then he would be back. And he would come back harder and more forcefully. This too, I was prepared for.

It took Surius three hours before he returned, hobbling. This time he stood several paces away and had one of the other Kuda walk up to me. "You need to leave," he said.

I looked at him with wide eyes. "I just got here!"

"The Sheriff says you gotta go."

"Oh, you have a sheriff in this town?" I asked.

The Kuda turned and pointed to Surius. "He's the sheriff."

"Oh," I said, lowering my voice. "He really should be more careful around explosives."

I couldn't see that Kuda's facial expression behind the dark glass of his helmet. But something in his gestures told me he was smiling with amusement. After he recomposed himself, he pointed at me. "Time to leave, now."

"A sheriff can't make me leave without a reason," I said.

"Disturbing the peace!" Surius called out.

"I wasn't the one who made that go boom," I said, shrugging. "Most of my customers know how to handle explosives. I naturally assumed you knew how to be careful. If you had told me that you didn't know—"

"Enough!" he shouted, taking a few painful steps toward me. "I want you out of here!"

By now a wary crowd had started to gather. I paused deliberately as if in thought. "Well, I like to think of myself as a law-abiding man. If the sheriff says I did something wrong, I'll be happy to accept his written warrant. And I'll abide by the precise language."

"No!" he shouted. "No written warrant, no delays. Now get!"

"But only criminals disobey the law," I said, sounding concerned. "A sheriff follows the law."

Surius looked around at the gathering crowd, clenching his fists. He pointed to the Kuda standing before me. "Pym, get him out of town."

Pym, the Kuda in front of me, took a step closer. He froze in his tracks, eyeing the explosives in my hands.

I had to force myself not to smile. "I'm just a law-abiding man, selling homemade 'splosives," I said holding them out toward Pym. Pym and Surius each took a quick step back. They stood there, staring at me. To maintain authority, they had to be able to push me around. The chance of getting blown up stopped them from throwing their weight around. And with the townsfolk watching, they feared I might give them some ideas. I now represented a threat to Surius's operation. He had two choices; attack me openly and risk the entire town fleeing for their lives, or kill me quietly.

He wasn't angry enough to risk the town fleeing and destroying his revenue. So, he would wait until dark to make his move. Pym glanced over to Surius who angrily spun around, grunting at the pain in his leg. He hobbled off and the rest of the Kuda followed. Then I smiled.

Several of the townsfolk swarmed me asking about all the fuss. Some complimented me and others warned me. One old lady even went as far as to tell me I was crazy for standing up to the sheriff. I smiled and told her that I had been crazy for quite some time now.

The yellow sun's light began to wane, making way for Cosstere's cool red sun to rise. I ate a quick supper of dried meat that Mik had sent with me. The night I had rescued Miri from those Cosstere raiders, I had thought myself unfortunate. Without darkness at night, I couldn't sneak up on their compound. Now I was feeling fortunate because it also meant the Kuda could not be concealed by darkness either. It was one of the many quirks of a planet in a binary star system.

When the dim red sun was in the sky, I put a bundle of cloth under a blanket. It wouldn't fool anyone up close, but from a distance, it looked like someone was asleep. I activated a few detonators and spread them around the perimeter of the hoverwagon. I just hoped none of the citizenry would go snooping late at night.

Then I stole quietly out from my hoverwagon, rifle in hand. I crossed to the other side of the street and tucked myself between two buildings. Using my enhanced knees, I jumped to the stone roof. I had an excellent view from here. And it didn't take the Kuda long before they snuck out of Mik's old shop, creeping along the street toward my hoverwagon. Surius looked downright silly trying to creep on his injured leg.

They crept close to the detonators I had set up around the perimeter, but they were not close enough to set one off. Surius drew his pistol and aimed at the bundle under the blanket. I hadn't figured him for a cold-blooded killer. Men of war usually followed codes of honor. Of course, it had been nearly two decades since the Kuda saw any war. Maybe some of them had turned nasty without the rigors of army structure to keep them in line.

It wouldn't take him long to figure out I was not beneath that blanket. If Surius wasn't going to set off a detonator, I was gonna help him out. I aimed my blast carbine at the closest detonator to him. As soon as I saw the flash from his blast pistol, I fired my carbine. The detonator exploded, throwing Surius back. The other three Kuda opened fire on the hoverwagon. This time I didn't need to help them set off the detonators. One by one, they exploded, sending debris flying.

Surius had just gotten back to his feet before another explosion sent him back to the ground. One Kuda got a piece of shrapnel embedded in his helmet. He angrily pulled off his helmet and tossed it away. A second Kuda lay on the ground knocked cold. Pym, the last Kuda picked himself off the ground, cursing.

Footsteps came rumbling down the wooden walk. Shop owners and hotel patrons came out to see what the ruckus was about. It was now time for my follow-up. I hopped down from the roof, my knees easily absorbing the shock. I emerged from between the buildings.

I rounded the corner and asked the first person I saw. "What's going on?"

A skinny man wearing a bed cap shook his head. "Beats me. Looks like the sheriff is fightin' someone."

I snickered. "Who, the old man with the cart?"

He looked back at the scene with a confused expression.

I made my way farther into the crowd and hollered. "Can't a man get some sleep!" The people around me looked at me strangely but a few men in the crowd echoed my sentiment. Several others shouted demands for peace and quiet. I smiled. The plan was working; the town's people were expressing dissatisfaction with the Kuda. If my luck held out, the pressure to appear civil would force them to restrain themselves. And a little restraint would be all I needed to push them into looking like fools.

Surius rose to his feet yet again. He staggered to keep his balance. He looked at the upset crowd a moment before picking up his blast pistol from the ground. He shot the closes man in the crowd, his limp body falling to the ground. The crowd screamed and yelled, scattering for cover.

My luck never did hold out very long. Surius no longer cared to keep up appearances. He was either too mad or too crazy to care. Now that he was openly gunning down the townspeople, I needed to act. The problem was that I could no longer play the part of the fool. And worse, the townsfolk were being killed. I needed to counterattack in earnest, now. This meant engaging the Kuda in the one thing they were exceptional at; warfare. So much for my advantage.

I raised my carbine and pointed it in the direction of Surius. Once the people dispersed enough for a clean shot, I took it. The carbine was a ruggedly-built blast rifle that shot high-powered blast bolts. I didn't usually have a need for it other than for long-distance big game hunting. But a crazed armored commando was proving to be a very real need. My shot nailed Surius in the helmet. It knocked him off his feet. His armored body hit the ground with a large *thud.* The shot cracked his helmet but didn't penetrate.

Pym and the other two Kuda took shots at me. I ducked and ran to the corner of a building, using it for cover. I took a shot at Pym. The blast cracked his breastplate and knocked him off his feet. I ducked around the corner, avoiding the incoming blast bolts. The Kuda were dazed enough from the explosions that their aim was off. That helped, but I hoped it would be enough.

I poked my head around the corner, aiming for one of the other Kuda. They had scattered, finding cover. I needed a new angle. I retreated down the alley and around to the back of the saloon. I crossed over to the back of Mik's old shop. I crossed over to the next alley and peeked around the corner. One of the Kuda rushed to the corner of the building where they had seen me last. I fired a shot into his back. The force of the blast bolt knocked him onto his face. His already damaged helmet cracked across the face glass. The Kuda who had previously discarded his damaged helmet saw my shot and fired a few blast bolts at me.

I pulled back around the corner to safety. I hadn't expected to have needed another firing angle so quickly. I jumped to the roof of the stone building. Moving to the ledge I peered down. The Kuda without his helmet moved cautiously toward where he had seen me. I aimed at his exposed head but then hesitated. These were Anruk's men. Sure, they were trying to kill me, but I couldn't restore Anruk to a dead squad. I sighed. I needed to take these guys out without killing them. And heavily armored commandos were going to make that a tall order. So, I stepped off the ledge. The butt of my carbine slammed onto the Kuda's head as I dropped to the ground. He collapsed on the spot.

Pym rose to his feet and rushed me. I swung the barrel around and fired another shot into his chest. His breastplate fractured and split open. He staggered back, dropping to one knee. His chest was exposed through the gap in his armor. I couldn't risk another shot to his torso. I aimed at his helmet instead. A quick movement caught my attention from the corner of my eye. I spun the barrel of my carbine around just in time to receive a blast bolt to my chest. I stumbled back, dropping my carbine. The Kuda I had shot in the back had discarded his cracked helmet and had turned around in time to shoot me. He shot me in the chest again and I fell flat on my back.

I had never taken two hits to my chest panel before. It was made of some solid material but it wasn't designed as armor. It was built to keep my heart ticking. What was worse was that my head had hit the ground hard. My vision was hazy and I felt tired. I shook my head to clear my mind. It didn't work very well. My head pounded. I blinked, trying to clear my vision.

Pym stood over me. "He's still breathing."

Surius picked me up and thrust me into the wall, holding me there. "Well, well, Mr. Jetom. You're just full of surprises aren't you."

I saw my reflection in his cracked helmet. "Too bad I can't say the same about you."

He angrily let go of me and swung his fist. I ducked, letting his fist strike the stone building. His armored glove snapped and broke open. Surius groaned, clutching his aching hand. Pym took a step forward, throwing a fist at my gut. I kicked his incoming fist, powered by my special knee. The force of the kick spun him halfway around. The Kuda who had shot me aimed at me again but hesitated, fearing he might hit his teammates. He lowered his blast pistol, running forward.

Surius tore off his smashed armored glove, alleviating his throbbing hand. I kicked off the wall, sending me flying forward toward the third Kuda. He halted and raised his blast pistol. I plowed into him, sending him crashing against the ground. I slugged him hard in the face. The force of my punch knocked him out cold but made my hand sting. Two were down, all that was left was Surius and Pym.

Pym ran up behind me. I spun around and kicked. He grabbed my leg and jabbed his elbow into my thigh. I groaned, dropping to the ground. My leg throbbed with massive pain. My muscles in that leg didn't respond. They were either numb from the blow or I was going into shock. He dropped my leg and kicked me in the ribs. Pym picked up the blast pistol the other Kuda had dropped and pointed it at my head.

"No!" Surius shouted. "He's mine!"

Pym lowered his gun.

I turned over and tried to crawl away as best I could. Pym laughed at my feeble progress. Slowly, I crawled toward my broken hoverwagon. Maybe were still a few more explosives. Hand over hand, I pulled my throbbing body closer.

Pym laughed again. "He thinks he can get a bomb."

Surius laughed with him. "Let him try. Let's see if it'll do him any good before I shoot him."

I pulled myself closer, stopping only a second to rest. I pulled myself closer still. Yet the hoverwagon still seemed so far away. It was only a couple dozen paces or so across the square, so quick and easy on foot. But inching across the dry dirt with a bum leg and so many muscles throbbing, it felt impossibly far. After a while, my arms tired. I was still several paces away but my arms felt so heavy that they wanted to stop. I reached my hand out toward the hoverwagon and laid there, staring at it. My eyes drifted closed and I blacked out.

I came to, feeling myself being dragged. Pym was dragging me toward Mik's old shop. He dragged me by my boots, letting my face scrape across the rough ground. The dirt smelled of old whiskey and I felt the sandy grit of dirt in my mouth, mixed with my blood. My body still ached and my leg continued to throb. At least my head had cleared up.

Pym hoisted me onto the counter near the back. "You're in luck, Surius. He's still alive."

"Impossible!" the second Kuda said, removing his hand from his black eye. "I shot him twice, square in the chest."

The third Kuda, the one I dropped on, held a bag of ice to his head. He must not have liked wasting precious ice on a massive headache. Refrigeration was costly on Cosstere. He didn't take an interest in me. By the look in his eyes, he was still delirious.

Surius hobbled over to me. "Still more surprises from you, Mr. Jetom." He put his hands around my neck. "Just couldn't leave town, could you? Just had to stay and challenge me, didn't you? What made you think you could stand up to me?"

There were lots of things I could have said. Many answers I could have given. The honest truth was that I didn't like him. I didn't like his kind. Ruthless men who lived off the backs of those weaker than themselves. In my book, they didn't deserve to live. They were a cancer on humanity. I had the code of the Wayfinders drilled into my head firmly. So firmly that if I hadn't needed help from Mik, I still would have fought Surius. I still would have done my best to take him down. Men without law who kill the innocent deserved some of their own medicine. The words I chose, however, I hadn't planned on. They just came out of my mouth.

I coughed, then swallowed. "Any man who preys on the weak and defenseless is not worthy to wear a uniform."

"Is that right," he said, squeezing my neck.

Pym put his hand on Surius's arm. "Hey, Surius."

He shrugged off Pym's hand and continued to strangle me.

"That'll be enough!" a voice shouted from behind.

Everyone turned and looked toward the entry door. Anruk stood there with fire in his eyes. Surius released my neck and turned to face him.

"I told you never to come back here," Surius said.

"What in the *blazes* do you think you're doing, Surius!" Anruk demanded, pointing toward the street. "Those are *civilians* lying dead!"

"Don't you *dare* raise your voice to me, you dog! You couldn't even find us sustained work. *I* am the one who found a way to get steady pay!"

"And how has your life of crime turned out for you?" Anruk looked all around the room at them. "Look at yourselves, beaten half to death in the process."

"Listen to you! Preaching to us about taking a beating. This is combat, Anruk. We *live* for combat!"

"Combat?" Anruk said, taking a step closer and crossing his arms. "And just who is the enemy?"

Surius opened his mouth to speak but Anruk cut him off.

"The mothers of children?" He pointed out to the street again. "The shopkeeper lying on the ground, bleeding out? Are these your enemies?"

Surius glared at him.

Anruk walked up to Surius. "We fought in a real war once. Our brothers bled and died to stop tyrants from killing civilians. We fought so that fathers and mothers could raise their children in peace. But if you're killing civilians just as those worthless tyrants had, then you're no Kuda."

"I warned you that going soft would kill you one day," Surius said. "Losing the Alphaship in this squad didn't wise you up any." Without taking his eyes off Anruk, he called over to Pym. "Anruk here, has worn out his welcome. Escort him outside."

Pym stared a moment in thought.

Surius shot him an impatient glance. "Pym! Now!"

Pym strolled over to the shelf along the wall.

"What are you doing?" Surius asked.

Pym brought Anruk's helmet over.

"I didn't say to–"

Pym handed it to Anruk.

Surius backhanded Pym, sending him to the ground. "Coward!"

Anruk kicked Surius's leg. It happened to be the same leg that had been injured. Surius dropped to his knee. Anruk pummeled him several times until he fell on his back. Surius staggered to get up but Anruk swung his helmet like a bat, striking Surius back to the ground. He laid on the floor, breathing heavily, but did not try to rise again. Anruk put his helmet on.

Pym rose to his feet and saluted Anruk.

The other two Kuda stood and saluted as well.

Anruk returned the salute.

"Not so fast, Anruk," Surius said, panting. He sat up. "The challenge is not valid. Pym betrayed the squad by disobeying the Alpha Leader. Kuda cannot take sides in a challenge."

"There was no challenge," Pym stated, walking up to Surius. "But only a Kuda can lead the squad. And as Anruk has pointed out, you're no Kuda." He ripped off Surius's helmet. Surius angrily grabbed for his helmet but Pym kicked him back down.

"Hold it a moment, Pym," Anruk said pointing to me on the counter. "Before we proceed with Kuda business, take that civilian outside."

Pym pointed to the other two Kuda. They each took one of my arms and helped me outside. I leaned on them each time I took a step, trying not to put any pressure on my leg. Once outside they set me down beside the door and then returned inside. I squeezed my eyes shut, enduring the throbbing in my leg, then I passed out again.

I didn't know how long I was out when I finally opened my eyes again. The bright yellow sun shined on my face. The smell of sterile air assaulted my nose. I didn't have to open my eyes to identify that smell. I was in a hospital. I opened my eyes, squinting at the sunlight pouring into the hospital room. I didn't like frontier hospitals. The small staff tried to be your best friend, waiting on your every whim. It was like they had nothing better to do than pay close attention to you. A man couldn't blend into obscurity in that kind of madness.

"Well, well Mr. Alder, I'm glad to see you are waking up," a nurse said as she disconnected an electronic cable from my arm.

I lifted my head and looked around. "Oh no, not this again," I grumbled.

"Oh, there's no need to be such a grump," she said with a friendly smile.

"Shoot me now," I said, laying my head back on my pillow.

The nurse giggled. "Mr. Alder, you're such a hoot. Your uncle must be so lucky to have you."

My ears perked up. "Uncle?"

"That's right, sonny," Mik said, stepping into the room. "Uncle Mik checked you into the hospital."

I looked at the nurse. "Mind if I speak with...Uncle Mik alone?"

"Why sure thing, sweet pea. I'll just finish your checkup when you're done." She opened the window, letting the cool morning breeze float in before leaving.

Mik walked up to my bedside. "One of the Kuda said your name was Rence Alder."

My cheeks flushed and I smiled, looking away. "I uh...found it a handy alias."

He smiled at me. "Right...and I was born yesterday. You ain't the blushing kind, Rence. But you did for that name.

I took a long breath. "Remember that biotech signal I need your help tracking?"

He nodded.

"Well, I need it to rescue a woman."

"And not just any woman, I trust."

"Your instincts are sharp," I said. "But your nose is getting pretty long."

He chuckled. "All right, if you don't wanna talk, I won't make you."

"Let's just say, I hadn't ever thought about settling down before."

"...until this woman?"

I nodded. "Miri Alder."

He grinned wide. "I never would have thought I'd see the day."

"Yeah, well you almost didn't. What took you and Anruk so long?"

"Hovermobile died. We had to walk the rest of the way."

I rubbed my head. "That would be my luck." I fingered my chest.

"Don't worry," he said. "I made sure they didn't snoop. I'm just glad you're finally awake."

I looked at him with renewed interest. "Finally? Mik, how long have I been out?"

"Three days."

My eyes widened.

"Good news is that the doctor repaired your fractured femur. You might need a little physical therapy, but you'll be walking again in a day or so."

"I think I'll start walking today," I declared.

Mik held out a hand. "Whoa there, take it easy for a while. You took quite a beating."

"Mik, I will go insane with this much attention on me."

He chuckled again. "All right, I'll see about checking you out." The playfulness drained out of his expression. "It's not just that, is it? You're worried about your woman, aren't you?"

I looked away, out the window. "Mik, I left her to go and get help. And every day that passes is one more day that I could be too late."

He sighed. "Well, Anruk rounded up all my old equipment. As soon as we get you out of here, we can start building your tracking device."

Mik couldn't get me out that day. I was forced to endure another night of attentive, overly-cheerful people. On the bright side, it wasn't as bad as my leg was. So I couldn't complain...much.

On the following day, Mik signed me out of there and we returned to his old shop. It still had rust everywhere, but with all the equipment back, the place seemed to come alive. It was almost like a living organism. It had a rhythm, a pulse to it. Many of the machines did not have any flashing lights on them, but they seemed to hum with electrical power. It reminded me of space travel on the *Astral Princess.*

I felt much better finally dressed in my normal clothes. My long coat draped around my dark trousers and a white button-down shirt. My red bandana hung around my neck with my hat securely on my head.

As Mik worked, designing and constructing a tracking device, I perused his shelves. He had gizmos of all kinds. On the third day, my attention was caught by a small blast pistol with a sleek black wooden handle. I picked it up and felt the weight. It was a little small for my hand but it was well balanced, making the barrel seem to float. The light shined off its silvery-metal barrel. It was a work of art.

I turned it over and over looking for the manufacturer's stamp. I didn't see any. I turned to Mik, showing him the blast pistol. "Mik? I don't seem to see the manufacturer's stamp anywhere."

He looked up from his workbench, eyeing the gun. "Oh, that's because I haven't made a stamp for it yet."

"*Made* a stamp?"

He nodded. "That's right. That's the first one I've designed and built."

I looked at him, marveling. "Can I see how it shoots?"

He smiled. "That's right, you are an enthusiast. Go ahead and take it into the back room. It's rather echoey back there so I recommend you take some ears with you."

I nodded appreciatively, picking up earmuffs from the counter. I walked into the back room. He had been using this room to dial in the accuracy of the blast pistol. He had a target set up. It had range indicators along with geometry formulas scribbled to the side. I put the earmuffs on and switched places in my holster with one of my blast pistols. I didn't only want to see how the gun would shoot, I also wanted to see how it drew.

My hand flashed to my side. The blast pistol was instantly in my hand, sending a blast bolt downrange. It hit just above the center of the target. The gun was lighter than my Starfield & Tanner blast pistols. I would have to adjust my draw for that. I re-holstered it and relaxed my arm.

Again, my hand flashed to my side and the little gun send another bolt to the target. This time it hit dead center. The short barrel profile made it much easier to clear leather, though it would be less powerful of a shot. It was perfect for a beginning gunfighter. Just for fun, I holstered it again and turned around. With my back to the target, I spun. The little gun was in my hand sending three shots into the target in an instant. The shots were not very straight. They were slightly off-center and a little high. Again, it just needed a little adjusting in the draw.

Mik wandered into the back room. "Sounds like you've been having fun in here."

I again examined the gun with admiration. "She clears leather with ease and shoots straight. A lightweight piece with beautiful craftsmanship."

Mik chuckled. "Then it's yours."

"Oh, no," I said holding it out to him. "I can't afford something this nice. Besides, I already got a pair of Starfield & Tanners that I am used to."

He pushed my hand back. "Now listen, Rence. Building your tracking device was a favor I owed you. Getting my shop and equipment back has meant a lot to me. Please accept this as payment."

I grinned wide. "Much appreciated, Mik."

"And if you won't be using it," he said. "You can always give it to the next Wayfinder."

I nodded appreciatively as he walked out the door into the main room. I didn't have the heart to tell him there weren't any other Wayfinders. I was the last. And if my luck held out, I wouldn't be a Wayfinder for long. If Miri would have me, I would be settling down with her. I'd be trading in my badge and guns to give her a life of silks and satins...

Then I had a thought. My breathing stopped and my heart began to beat loud. A deep breath forced its way into my lungs. There was one aspect of my future plans that I had not considered. It had always been in the back of my brain, but I had always shooed it away like a pesky fly. *Silks and satins,* I thought as I caressed the elegant blast pistol I held.

I walked back out to the main room and joined Mik. “Do you also make blast belts with holsters?”

“Shouldn’t be too difficult.”

“Could you make one for this gun with a thin profile?”

He grinned. “I think I know what you have in mind. I’ll have it ready before you leave.”

The front door opened and Anruk stepped inside, followed by Pym and two other Kuda. For a brief moment, my heart raced. Images of my first encounter with a Kuda flashed across my mind. I relaxed when I recognized Anruk in his armor. Mik had patched up their armor really well. All four Kuda looked as good as new.

He crossed the room over to me. “You still want to go through with this?”

“I have to,” I said. “I can’t leave her behind.”

He nodded. “When do we leave.”

I paused mid-breath, taken aback. “We?”

Pym walked up beside Anruk. “Every soldier understands the concept, never leave a man behind.”

Mik looked up from the workbench. “By the look of things, I’d say you boys might be able to head out tomorrow.” He walked over to a large assembly of cables, circuits, and odd-shaped parts. He flipped a switch and it hummed to life. Picking up a handheld device connected to it, he walked over to me. “It’s picking up one signal in the sector.”

I took the device and looked at the little screen. It was detecting Ryna’s radioisotope signal across the stars. I blinked away a little moisture that collected in my eyes. The air in the room grew thick enough to stir with a stick.

I smiled, glancing upward. “Hold tight, Miri. We’re coming.”

EPISODE 7

What I had been waiting for

7

What I Had Been Waiting For

There have been times in my life when I knew that everything I prepared for had led up to a single moment. And there were other times when I have had to question what in the sam hill I was thinking. This was a sam hill moment.

My wrists chafed in the metal cuffs that bound to the back wall. I used my upper arm to wipe away a bead of sweat that ran down my face. This ship was not well ventilated. It was efficient and it traveled places but it was nothing compared to the *Astral Princess.* During this trip, I was on a dimly-lit, poorly-ventilated, Kuda ship.

It wouldn't bother someone who wore a suit of blast armor all day long. But for everyone else, it was downright unpleasant. In front of me stood a Kuda, all dressed in his blast armor and helmet. The Kuda were formidable enemies. My first run-in hadn't gone very well. They were ex-military soldiers turned mercenaries. They hadn't been needed for two decades, since the last great war. They lived in a state of perpetual readiness, waiting for the call to arms for another war. Without steady pay, their culture had turned into soldiers for hire.

The Kuda pressed a few buttons on the control console in front of him. The large computer screen turned on, showing the handsome face of the man I detested. Dr. Vik Lenish was a scientist that worked for Westward Galactic Financial Corporation. Working for Westward Galactic was not his biggest crime. He was the head researcher experimenting on human beings. His tinkering is what gave Ryna her ability to fiddle with people's emotions.

Dr. Lenish, the sorry excuse for a member of humanity, wanted to remove Ryna's brain to study it. He was frustrated that he couldn't create any more like Ryna. I gave him a good thrashing, hoping to change his mind. Some men will take the hint and change their ways. Dr. Lenish instead put a price on my head large enough to make a man rich. At least the man knew value when he saw it.

"So, do I have the pleasure of addressing Captain Anruk?" Dr. Lenish said in his annoying accent. I couldn't put my foot on what it was about his accent that annoyed me so much. Maybe it was that air of foreign egotism.

Anruk, the Kuda that stood between me and the screen showing Dr. Lenish, nodded. "Dr. Vik Lenish, I presume."

Dr. Lenish raised an eyebrow. "Naturally. And I thank you for returning my property."

"I ain't a good Samaritan, doctor. I'm a businessman."

"You will, of course, be paid as per the contract of the bounty," Dr. Lenish said with a wave of his hand. "But first, can I please see Mr. Perry?"

Anruk stepped aside, revealing me to Dr. Lenish.

Dr. Lenish smiled. "Ah, the high and mighty Mr. Perry at last. Such good fortune I have to reacquire you. Our last meeting was...less than gentlemanly."

"Some men actually learn from the lessons they're given," I said, glaring at him.

"Oh, that is where you are wrong," he said with a chuckle. "You see, Mr. Perry. You showed me a great deal of security weaknesses that I have since remedied."

"Too bad you didn't learn any decency."

"You are hardly one to talk of decency, Mr. Perry. Were you demonstrating decency when you brutally attacked me?"

"The decency was that I gave you a chance to wise up instead of just shooting you on the spot," I said, tensing up my bound fists.

"Squeamishness, Mr. Perry. What you adorn with the title of decency is only squeamishness to do what is necessary for humanity. I have no such delusions." He looked at Anruk. "Captain Anruk, please kill Mr. Perry."

My heart pounded and my breathing stopped. Anruk needed to get me on board their ship. How could I rescue Miri if I had to be dead to get aboard? Anruk was also a mercenary, not a conman. He was more of a man of action than of words. How would he cope with this surprising change of events? Would he actually shoot me?

Anruk folded his arms. "Do I look like your maid?"

Dr. Lenish frowned. "You get the same amount of money whether he is dead or alive. He caused me a lot of trouble last time. I want him dead."

Anruk paused.

"Why the hesitation, Captain Anruk?"

I closed my eyes a moment, cringing inside. This whole operation was in jeopardy. If Anruk couldn't come up with a convincing excuse to deliver me alive, we would fail. They would know we were trying to bluff our way aboard. Not only would Miri's rescue be botched, but we would spend a lot of time running away from their attack fighters.

Anruk turned his head toward me.

What was he thinking? Could he be considering shooting me? His first loyalty was to his men. If he couldn't find a way to salvage our rescue plan, shooting me would guarantee his men would not be attacked. They would also be paid handsomely for the reward. Would he really do it? Could he afford not to?

He looked back at Dr. Lenish. "What you do with your lab rats is *your* business. Collecting the money you owe me is *mine*."

"Surely a man of your kind is no stranger to killing. Why should you hesitate?" Dr. Lenish smirked. "Mr. Perry is a very cunning man. Cunning enough, perhaps, to orchestrate a scheme to get on board."

"You ain't payin' me enough to listen to insults," Anruk said. "You will pay me what you owe and you will do your own dirty work."

Dr. Lenish laughed. "Such intrigue. I'm afraid you will have to satisfy the skeptic in me, by shooting Mr. Perry."

I hung my head. Dr. Lenish wasn't buying it. He saw right through Anruk's ruse. Was it all for nothing, then? The tracking device Mik built to find Ryna, and the recovery at the hospital, were they all for nothing? No, I still had Mik's tracking device. I could still track Ryna. We could still try again somehow.

Anruk drew his blast pistol.

I looked at him in alarm. My heart raced and my blood pumped. I could not run; I was chained to the back wall. I was a sitting duck. I had hoped he would have felt a sense of obligation. After all, I did help him regain the leadership of his squad. It seemed loyalty only lasted so far with the Kuda.

He instead turned to Dr. Lenish. "No deal," he said, shooting the control console. In a burst of sparks, the communication transmission instantly ended.

He walked over to me and unlocked the cuffs. "That cocky egghead is too smart for his own good."

I looked at Anruk. "You had me worried there a moment."

"Whatever you believe about Kuda, remember that above all, we live for the battle."

"What battle?" I asked. He had just spurned Dr. Lenish and cut off all communication with the Corporation ship. That effectively ended this mission before it began. The only battle there had been was with words—and we lost.

"This battle," he said, punching a red button on the console. An alarm sounded. Pym and the other two Kuda raced in and took their seats. He looked at Pym. "Thrusters ahead full." Then he turned to another Kuda. "Target their closest landing bay space door."

"You're going to attack a capital ship?" I asked. "In this thing?"

Anruk glanced at me. "I'll be sure to knock before barging in."

We raced toward the Corporate Labship. The massive behemoth dwarfed our little assault shuttle. We were like a hornet moving in to sting an elephant. There were practical reasons why I deemed this course of action foolhardy. The foremost was the size difference. The Kuda didn't seem to mind. They hurtled their little shuttle ever closer. Massive deck cannons on the Lab Ship blasted large green plasma bolts at us.

I clenched the closest handrailing.

Pym steered the shuttle with a calm smoothness as if he were on a casual Sunday drive. To say that Pym was cool under pressure was an understatement. We weaved in and around the incoming green bolts of cannon fire, approaching one of the landing bays.

Anruk pulled me away from the pole I was clinging to and sat me in a chair. "Buckle up, buckaroo," he directed, strapping himself in.

"Cute phrase," I said, letting my annoyance show. "Did you make that up yourself?"

He pointed out the blast shield window toward the quick-approaching landing bay. "Unless you want to scrape yourself off the window after landing."

The memory of my crash landing on that ice comet flooded my mind. I remembered the headache and Miri feverishly working in my chest panel to revive me. All my muscles stiffened, and my breathing stopped. I grabbed my safety straps with white knuckles and jammed my buckles into place. Just as I secured my safety straps, three rockets launched from our assault shuttle. They zoomed ahead and slammed into the closed landing bay space door.

The door exploded, tearing itself apart under the sudden release of air pressure from the bay. Massive pieces of the space door flew past us, nearly hitting us. Pym jerked the stick back and slammed his foot against a floor pedal. The braking thrusters fired, slowing our momentum. We crashed into the landing bay. I was thrown forward in my seat, held back by my safety straps. I was suddenly real happy Anruk had insisted on strapping in.

Sparks blew from a nearby console, starting a fire. Anruk reached under his seat and pulled out a small fire extinguisher. "Time to move out," he announced, putting out the fire.

I unbuckled and stood, with my nerves still shaky. Like it routinely had been, it was now showtime. The difference here was that I had no plan. We were going to be improvising at every step along the way. I clamped on my tactical mask. I was partly glad Anruk had also insisted I leave Lady behind on the *Princess.* A crash like this had been would not have been good for her.

Anruk dropped the fire extinguisher. "Tuke and Oss, find us a set of wings to get us out of here when we're done."

The two Kuda seated in front nodded, unbuckling their safety straps.

"Pym," Anruk said. "Stay and watch over the tracking system as long as you can. When they overrun your position, fall back and rejoin Tuke and Oss."

"Yes sir," Pym replied. He then motioned toward me with his head. "What's the rookie's callsign?"

"Romeo," Anruk said without hesitation.

"Now, wait a minute," I said, my mask hiding the color in my cheeks. "Just what are you trying to imply?" I hadn't given them any indication that I was sweet on Miri, and Mik would not have told them. There was no cause for innuendos of romance. Nor did I want there to be any. The less they knew the better.

Anruk slowly faced me, his men chuckling behind him. "Your name begins with the letter R."

He was referring to the military alphabet. Twenty-six words were assigned to each letter of the alphabet. They clearly defined letters being spoken over a comm transmission. The letter R happened to be Romeo. I wanted to shrink where I stood.

"Oh," I finally said.

"But thanks for the tip, Romeo," Anruk said. "Looks like the woman's callsign is going to be Juliet."

I closed my eyes, my fists clenched. It had been a while since I worked alongside soldiers. I had forgotten the unwritten rule never to let on that a nickname irritated you. It was the fastest way to permanently brand yourself with that name. It was a flavor of camaraderie that took some getting used to. What I hadn't counted on was Anruk reading between the lines. I probably should have just kept my mouth shut.

"Let's move out," Anruk said.

As they passed by me, Oss patted me on the shoulder twice. "Say hi to the missus for me."

I *definitely* should have kept my mouth shut.

I followed them over to the boarding hatch. The assault shuttle had a small airlock to allow troops to board other ships. Pym closed the inner door, sealing us inside the airlock.

Anruk turned to me. "You'll need to suit up. There ain't no air pressure in the bay."

I grabbed an exosuit and put it on.

"Comm check, go," he said.

I heard his voice through my tactical mask. Since I had already embarrassed myself once, I waited for the Kuda to respond first.

"Alpha, Tango, roger," Tuke replied.

"Alpha, Oscar, roger," Oss answered.

"Alpha, Papa, roger," Pym said.

It looked like everyone's callsign was the first letter of their name in the military alphabet. "Alpha, Romeo, roger," I said, looking to Anruk for approval.

He nodded, pulling the cord that started the depressurization cycle. The air hissed on its way out of the airlock. The inside of my exosuit helmet smelled of somebody's aftershave. At least it was clean. The Kuda each readied a blast rifle. I looked at the tracker receiver in my hand. It was a small receiver connected to the tracking device Mik had installed on the shuttle. It showed me which direction and how far away I was from Ryna. It was then that a troubling thought occurred to me. Miri was not guaranteed to be with Ryna. How would I find Miri on a ship this big? The light in the airlock turned red and the ramp lowered.

The Kuda swarmed out and I followed. We didn't have air pressure, but we still had gravity from the ship. We swiftly made our way to the wall where the bay door controls were. Anruk pressed the button to raise the forcefield around the space door. That forcefield kept air pressure inside the bay. It also allowed shuttles to leave through the open space door. A loud hissing sounded as the landing bay pressurized.

Anruk gave a hand gesture to Oss and Tuke. They moved to stand on either side of the door. They assumed the ship's security guards to be standing on the other side of the door, waiting for the door to open. Once the door opened, it would be a shootout. I joined Anruk to the left of the door. Anruk reached over and hit the door controls. The door slid open.

A hailstorm of green blast bolts sailed through the open door into the bay. Tuke pulled a detonator off his belt and tossed it through the open door. The detonator exploded, sending a gust of hot air and debris into the bay. I had to admit, a man felt pretty safe behind four Kuda. We stepped into the hall.

"Security cameras," Oss said, pointing to a camera hanging high from the wall.

"Scramble 'em," Anruk said.

Tuke slapped a small device on the camera. A small light blinked on the device. "Battery on the scrambler will give us four hours tops."

"The second landing bay is at the other end of the hall," I said to Tuke and Oss. "You might find a set of wings there."

Anruk nodded and sent them away with a hand motion. He turned to me. "Okay, Romeo. Where to?"

I rolled my eyes. When we weren't on the comm channel, he didn't have to call me by my callsign. He was just enjoying calling me that. I decided not to protest again. I glanced at the tracking receiver in my hand. "Two decks up, and a little to the north."

We jogged to the other end of the hall and Anruk pressed the button to call the elevator. Nothing happened. They had already locked down the elevators and doors. Dr. Lenish wasn't kidding when he said he had learned from his security holes. I forced the doors open and we entered. I looked up at the ceiling hatch in amazement. The hatch was welded shut.

I looked at Anruk. "I guess he decided to trade security over safety."

"Cute," he said, aiming his blast rifle at the hatch. He fired several shots, punching holes through the hatch door. The hinges snapped and the weld broke. I jumped, pushing open the hatch and catching the ledge. I pulled myself up and helped Anruk. The edges of the trap door hole tore open wider as Anruk's armor squeezed through. The bulk was one downside to their armor.

Anruk pointed to the wall. "More home improvements?"

I looked where he pointed. All the rungs on the maintenance ladder had been cut off. Dr. Lenish must have studied my escape in detail. He had tried to eliminate every advantage I had had last time. "Dr. Lenish is thorough, I'll give him that."

"That's the sign of a scared man," Anruk said. He looked at me. "What did you do to him?"

"I taught him a few manors."

He grunted in approval.

I looked around for anything that could be used as handholds. I didn't see anything.

Anruk aimed his rifle at the door two decks above us. At such an odd angle, I was surprised he was able to hit it. His green blast bolts tore holes through the door. Then he walked over to the thick elevator cables. "Grab on," he said.

My eyes lit up. "You can't be serious? That's a one-way trip."

"You got a better idea?" he asked.

The truth was that I didn't have a better idea. We would just have to find another way down once we freed Miri and Ryna. I grabbed hold of one of the cables. He held onto the cable with one hand and aimed his rifle with the other hand. He shot the stabilizer motor. The elevator slid down the shaft, grinding sparks as it scraped the wall on the way down. As it fell, the cable pulled us in the opposite direction. It yanked us up. I clung to the cable, watching for the doors Anruk had shot.

When we neared the door, I jumped off the cable and caught hold of the ledge. Anruk jumped but missed the ledge. He flailed his arms trying to grab ahold of anything. I caught hold of his arm. His heavy armor strained my grip on the ledge. I would only be able to hold onto him for a short time. I needed to get him up to the ledge somehow, and it needed to be quick. Grunting, I started swinging him.

During the swing, he kicked against the wall, increasing his swing. It wasn't every day you saw a Kuda swinging like a pendulum. When his swing was wide enough, his foot touched the left wall. With a little kick against that wall, Anruk was able to reach the ledge. It was a good thing too; my arm felt like jelly.

I pulled myself up to the door and forced it open. I helped Anruk up before a green blast bolt hit me in my exosuit helmet, shattering the glass. The shattering glass made me flinch, but I spun, clearing leather. I sent two red blast bolts down the hallway before I saw who was shooting at us. One of the armed guards dropped his blast pistol, clutching his stomach.

The other three guards backed off, shooting. Anruk reloaded his blast rifle power cell.

He stood and charged down the hallway, shooting. The security guards scattered, running down different hallways. I pulled out the tracking receiver. We were close.

"Other way down the hall," I shouted.

Anruk stopped his charge and jogged back to me. "Lead the way, Romeo."

"Can you stop calling me that?"

"Nope," he replied, motioning for me to take the lead.

It was a shame he couldn't even see me roll my eyes. But I made up my mind to search for the most embarrassing nickname I could to call him. I carefully pulled off what was left of my helmet and tossed it aside. I charged down to the other end of the hallway, blast pistol in hand. I glanced at the tracking receiver again. The signal was coming from the other side of the next room. I peeked into the small door window. The room looked empty. I checked the device again. Her signal was coming from that room.

I figured looks could be deceiving, so I grabbed the door knob. It didn't budge. Dr. Lenish had been busy. It looked like he now locked the doors. "I just wish he would learn the right lesson," I said under my breath.

I took a step back and kicked the door. The door caved in, breaking the locking bar from the door frame. Anruk helped me force the bent door open.

Anruk took a look around. "Nothing."

I showed him the device. "This is where the trail ends."

As he looked at it, we heard shouts from down the hall. Anruk crouched, aiming his blast rifle at the door. "What then?"

My blood boiled. "Ryna!" I kicked over the shelves and tipped the desk over. I had come too far only to lose the trail. It wasn't fair. I had so many things on my side this time. I needed to win this one. I needed to find Ryna and Miri.

"We can't stay here," Anruk said. "They'll pin us down. They'd only need to toss in one detonator to redecorate the place with our blood."

I kicked the nearby wall, denting it. "Where is Ryna?" I shouted, kicking it again and again. All I could see was red. I hated Dr. Lenish and

I hated myself. Why couldn't I find her? I had successfully tracked her across the sector. Finding her room should have been easy compared to that.

My breathing slowed and my mind cleared. I relaxed my fists. My heart was still racing but I felt at peace, somehow. Was I coming to grips with reality? Was I accepting my failure? No, that couldn't be it; I didn't feel sad. Come to think of it, I didn't feel regret either. Just calm.

"Rence, they'll be here any moment," Anruk warned.

"Ryna is here," I said. "She is calming my emotions."

I yanked off my exosuit glove and pressed a few buttons on my wristband. My vision shifted to infrared. I saw body heat through walls and floors. Glancing around the room, I saw a body heat signature directly behind the far wall. "Clever, but not clever enough."

I switched my eyesight to electromagnetic and examined the wall. I saw a power line leading from the wall to a desk lamp. I smirked, crossing over to the lamp and turning it on. A part of the wall moved aside, revealing a room beyond. I switched my eyesight back to normal and ran into the next room. Ryna stood on her cot, pounding against a transparent wall, unable to make an audible sound.

Dr. Lenish was smart enough not to operate on Ryna. The very existence of this secret room was proof that my threat was taken seriously. That meant I still had hope for Miri too. I ran over to the wall controls and pressed some buttons. Surely one of them would open her cell. The wall control blinked red and beeped at me. I looked closer at it. It had a thumbprint scanner. I didn't have time for such games. I placed a detonator on the transparent wall and motioned for Ryna to back away. She didn't back away far enough, so I moved the detonator further down the transparent wall. I activated the timer and jogged to the other end of the room.

Ryna covered her ears.

It exploded, blasting a huge hole. I ran through the hole and scooped up Ryna in my arms, hugging her. She clung to me, tears running down her face. "You came back."

"I promised I would."

She sniffled. "You came back."

"This time I won't leave you again." I blinked back some moisture that threatened to blur my vision. "I don't suppose you know where Miss Miri is, do you?"

She shook her head.

I heard the loud zapping sound of Anruk's blast rifle firing. It was time to go. At least, it was time to go and find Miri. I led Ryna back into the room with Anruk.

Ryna froze, clutching my arm.

"It's all right, little miss. Anruk here is a friend."

Anruk glanced at Ryna and then at me. "Where's Juliet?"

"Working on it."

"Well, you'll have to work on it somewhere else. I'll cover you." Anruk fired a few more green blast bolts down the hall as I led Ryna by the hand further down the hall. We stopped around the next corner, waiting for Anruk to join us.

"Mr. Rence, I'm scared," Ryna said.

How was I to comfort her in the middle of a shoot-out? I looked into her delicate eyes. She was searching for something to believe in. Her life must have been filled with disappointments. Living with a scientist who looked at her as a large Petri dish could not have helped. Looking back on it, the time that she really emerged from her secluded shell was when she was with Miri. If Ryna was going to survive emotionally, she needed Miri.

I knelt and looked at her at eye level. "I wish I could calm you the way you can calm me."

She stared at me.

I took off my tactical mask, letting her see my eyes. "Don't you fret, little miss, I won't let anything happen to you."

She hugged me tightly around the neck.

Maybe I didn't need the ability to fiddle with emotions to calm Ryna. Maybe she just needed me. I hugged her back.

Anruk rounded the corner. "Sorry to break up this little reunion, but you have work to do." Anruk kicked at a neighboring door. It didn't budge. It looked like my special knees were required for these doors. I stood and kicked it. The door jamb cracked and the door locking lever snapped. I was getting better at kicking in these doors. This time it didn't fold in on itself.

Anruk pushed the door open and motioned for us to enter. He closed it behind us, using his foot to keep it shut. I dashed over to the computer terminal. I punched away furiously at the keyboard. It was no use. Dr. Lenish had updated the computer security. And I had left behind my decryptor when I raided the Corporation's data center. I slammed my fist against the keyboard.

"Trouble?" Anruk asked.

"He upgraded the computer security as well."

"Do you have another idea or do we abort?"

My blood pumped and I clenched my fists. Fear washed over me. The fear of not finding Miri. I wanted to find her badly. Ryna needed her. I needed her too. I had to think of a way to locate Miri and I only had a little time to do so. The Kuda were impressive but they didn't have enough power cells to fire their weapons all day long. And the massive ship had enough manpower to overwhelm us.

I thought a moment about my mentor before I repeated Korr's favorite phrase. "Sometimes the best way in is from the side."

"Come again?" Anruk asked.

"The computer may be secure," I said. "But people's emotions are not."

"That egghead is smart, he saw through it last time."

"But you said it yourself, he is afraid of me."

Anruk nodded. "You have a plan then?"

"I have half a plan," I admitted, clamping my tactical mask back on.

I wasn't sure exactly how to do it, but I needed to try. I squatted next to Ryna. "Little miss, you had said once that you know how everyone feels."

She nodded, eyeing me curiously.

"Can you tell me how Dr. Lenish feels?"

"Only when I look at him."

"Okay. I'll see what I can do about that." I stood, turning to Anruk. "I've got some electrical to tamper with. I'll be back soon. Please guard Ryna with your life."

"What is she to me?" he asked.

That's right, I was talking to a mercenary. But Anruk was more than just a mercenary. He was willing to come with me to rescue Miri and Ryna. There was more than just a mercenary inside Anruk. I suspected that deep down, he had the heart of a hero. Was there anything I could say to touch that side of him? I had touched it when I said I couldn't leave Miri behind. Could I do it again about Ryna? Or did I have to? He had told me that above all, the Kuda live for the battle.

"This is Ryna," I said. "That egghead, Dr. Lenish, considers her his most prized possession. The greatest blow you can land is to deprive him of her."

He nodded. "Understood."

I glanced down both ends of the hallway. I waited for a team of four security guards to run past before slipping into the hall. I jogged down the hall after them, keeping my footsteps light. They approached an elevator at the end of the hall, walking past a circuit panel. If they were going to enter the elevator, they would see me when they turned around. I had to work fast.

I pulled the panel open. Tapping a button on my wristband, I switched my vision to electromagnetic. The visual band signals were easy to distinguish since they showed up in another color. I glanced at the wall, seeing which electrical signals led back to the room Anruk and Ryna were in. I pulled my knife from my boot and cut the visual feed wire and spliced it into the data cable running to that room. The elevator at the end of the hall chimed and the doors opened. I quickly closed the panel and dashed back to the room.

I tapped three times on the door and Anruk let me in. "That was fast," he said.

"Had to be," I admitted. "Security is scouring the ship looking for us."

I crossed over to the intercom controls and pried the casing off with my knife. In a matter of minutes, I had rigged up a tie-in to the observation cameras in the laboratory rooms.

"Alpha, Papa, falling back to Tango Oscar, over," Pym's voice said over the comm.

"Roger, Papa. Out," Anruk replied. Then he turned to me. "They've overrun the shuttle. Pym is joining up with the others. That means more security will now be available to search for us."

"So, no pressure," I said in conclusion. I pressed a button on the intercom controls over and over again, switching the video feed from one room to the next. There could be hundreds of such rooms. And we didn't have a whole lot of time. I wanted to flip through the camera feeds faster, but I couldn't clearly see who was in the room any faster.

"Oscar, Alpha," Anruk said over the comm. "How close are we to evac? Over."

Oss's voice replied. "Almost patched in. ETA in ten, over."

"How long to prep the wings once in? Over."

"Assume twenty, over."

"Roger, break." Anruk turned to me. "The boys found us a set of wings. How long is this going to take?"

"Depends on how lucky we are."

"Oscar, Alpha," he continued. "Hold position once in. Golf acquired but negative 10-20 on Juliet, over."

"WILCO, over." Oss's voice replied.

"Roger, out." Anruk turned back to me. "I'm giving you thirty minutes, Romeo. After that, we have to hightail it."

"No pressure," I said under my breath, still flipping between video feeds. Ryna clutched my arm. I stopped and glanced at her. "What is it, little miss?"

She stared at the monitor that displayed the video feed.

I flipped back a few and saw the back of someone's head. Ryna squeezed my arm.

"Is that him?" I asked.

She nodded.

"What's he feeling?" I asked.

"Worry."

I looked back at Ryna. "Okay, I want you to squeeze my arm if he starts feeling scared. But if he starts feeling safe or confident, squeeze my arm twice. Understand?"

She nodded.

I picked up the intercom receiver and pushed the button labeled broadcast. "Hello again, Dr. Lenish." My voice echoed through the hallways.

Dr. Lenish spun around and motioned to someone off-camera. Two security guards moved into view. He shouted something at them and pointed out the door. They dashed out of the room. Dr. Lenish picked up his intercom receiver and pushed the broadcast button. "Well, well, Mr. Perry. Turns out I was right about your apparent capture by Captain Anruk." His voice also echoed down all the hallways.

Ryna squeezed my arm twice.

He was playing the role of the superior detective, keeping the conversation light and in his favor. I needed to darken the conversation a bit. I needed him more than just worried. For this gamble to work, I needed him scared. It was time to dawn my bravado.

"You know why I'm here."

Dr. Lenish paused a moment. "You are trying to steal my property."

"Not just your property, doctor. I assume you got my message about project Osurious? I left you a little present."

He pursed his lips. "If you think a minor setback to the database will prevent my research, you are dead wrong."

"I don't think you really understand, doctor. Erasing the Osurious project files was the bait. The present is hidden in the database backups."

Ryna squeezed my arm.

"You see, doctor, it would be too easy to catch if I tried to inject the database directly. But if the Corporation restored the database from backup, it would be undetectable."

Ryna squeezed my arm again.

Dr. Lenish smiled. "You're a very cunning man, Mr. Perry. Isn't it more likely that you are lying about this danger? You expect me to believe—"

"Shut your yap, doctor. What you believe is of no consequence and this is not a negotiation. You have someone I want, and I am holding a sledgehammer over your precious data. How eager are you to start from scratch?"

Ryna squeezed my arm twice.

What I said had sounded good. Why was he feeling more confident? My mind raced, sifting through memories of the day. Dr. Lenish had exhibited signs of being afraid of me. He had welded the elevator escape hatch shut and cut off the elevator shaft ladder rungs. He updated the computer system and even installed security cameras. They all pointed to him being afraid of me. *Afraid of* ***me***, I thought.

I had it all backward. Dr. Lenish was a practical man. One might even say a businessman. Threats, negotiations, and even playful banter were all in his realm of comfort. He even referred to losing the project Osurious files as a minor setback. He wasn't afraid of starting over. Starting over for him was just a setback. It all made sense now. What he was scared of was *me*. That was why he wanted me dead before being transferred to his ship. What scared him was that I would come for him and finish the job I started.

Dr. Lenish smirked. "You are in no position to negotiate, Mr. Perry. I have everything I need to begin again. And this time, I will also have you to study."

"It ain't working," Anruk said.

I held up a finger to him. I needed to gather my thoughts. I needed to make it realistic.

"Are you still there, Mr. Perry?" Dr. Lenish's voice echoed down the halls.

"I am too late, then," I said. "You already killed her." I waited until the echo of my voice faded from the halls. "Then there is only one thing left to do... She warned you what would happen if you laid a hand on her!"

Ryna squeezed my arm.

Dr. Lenish moved away from the intercom. He shouted something, pointing an angry finger at someone off-camera. He paced in the room for a few minutes until a security guard escorted Miri into the room, holding her by the arm. Dr. Lenish pointed to the intercom controls and the guard moved Miri over to the intercom. Dr. Lenish noticeably gave her a wide berth.

She picked up the intercom receiver. "Rence?" Her voice echoed down the hallways. It was the sweetest sound. My eyes started to blur. I blinked back the tears. My heart pounded and my shoulders felt light. I took in a deep breath. "Is that you, Miri?"

She smiled, a tear running down her cheek. "When you left me at the front, I knew right then, you were right, when you left."

Her response was confusing. What had they done to her? I balled my hands into fists. My blood boiled and my muscles tensed up. "Did he lay a hand on you?" I demanded.

"No," she said instantly. "Listen to me, Rence. "Up front, he left me alone. He did right. He did right when he left me alone."

Dr. Lenish waved her away from the intercom and the guard pulled her away, the receiver dropping to the desk. Dr. Lenish picked it up. "There, you have proof the woman is still alive and unharmed. So, I propose a trade."

My ears perked up. This was certainly a change. How did he go from being super confident he would have me in his lab to wanting to trade? My gamble had paid off in that I now knew Miri was alive and that she was somewhere with Dr. Lenish. But could my gamble have worked so well that he was willing to negotiate?

Ryna squeezed my arm twice.

Dr. Lenish continued. "My security team reports that you have taken Subject 35. I will trade you the woman for the girl. What do you say, Mr. Perry? You return my property and I return yours?"

Ryna clenched my arm. I looked down at her and saw fear in her eyes. Even for her age, she knew what the bargain was that the doctor was making. And even with all my reassurances, she was still afraid I would leave her. She was scared I would trade her for Miri.

I could always lie and tell the doctor I would just so I could get close to Miri. I would understand the ruse, but would Ryna? What would she believe about me? For her whole life, adults treated her like a sack of beans; to be used and traded. Would she still consider me as an exception, or would I confirm her notion that adults are all the same? She didn't trust Dr. Lenish. And if I did anything similar to him, she would not trust me either. I could try explaining that I needed to lie to the doctor. But if I lied about one thing, she might suspect I would lie about another.

"I can't," I finally said to Dr. Lenish. "I made the girl a promise. But I would be willing to trade myself for the woman."

Dr. Lenish narrowed his eyes and tilted his head. "Interesting..." He stood with his hand to his chin for several minutes. "Something has just occurred to me, Mr. Perry. Your interest in the woman goes far deeper than I first had anticipated. You want her freedom in exchange for yours. This tells me I have been sitting on the perfect bargaining chip all along."

Ryna squeezed my arm twice. Yet, I didn't need her to squeeze my arm to know that he was gaining confidence. I saw it in his eyes. I heard it in his annoying voice. My heart sunk into the pit of my stomach. I could smell this conversation going rotten.

"So, I tell you what I'm going to do, Mr. Perry. I'm going to give you seventeen minutes to come out, unarmed, with Subject 35. And I do hope you ask me why such an odd number of minutes."

I breathed out hard and slow. Ryna squeezed my arm twice more. Dr. Lenish was telegraphing his emotions so well that I no longer needed Ryna. "Why the odd time limit, doctor?"

"Seventeen minutes is precisely how long it takes to depressurize an entire cargo bay. That is, before dumping its contents into space."

His last words echoed down the hallways, sending ripples through my heart. The weight pulled on my chest. My eyes blurred and I didn't even try to hold back the tears. I was grateful my mask hid them from view. How could things have gone so wrong so quickly? But what did it matter now? I had made a promise to Ryna that I would not leave her. I had also made a promise to Miri that I would come back for her. It seemed I had to break one of those promises. How could I choose? How could any man choose?

I dropped the intercom receiver on the desk and slid down the wall until I was seated on the floor. I looked at Anruk. "I've lost her again..."

"No, you haven't," he said confidently.

"Anruk, I can't search this ship in seventeen minutes!"

"You don't gotta search the whole ship."

I cocked my head in confusion. "What do you mean?"

"If you'll pull your head out of your hormones a few minutes, you'll see what I'm talking about."

Ryna placed a hand on my shoulder. She asked me with her eyes if she should calm me.

I nodded.

My heart rate slowed. My breathing calmed, and my head cleared. I relaxed my muscles. My heart was the only thing still aching. I did not want to lose Miri again. Her words ran through my head again. It was such an odd reply she gave.

I turned to Anruk. "She said I left her at the front and was right to leave her...I don't understand what she meant."

"That may have been what she spoke, but that ain't what she said," he replied.

"You've lost me..."

Anruk took a deep, annoyed breath. "She said when you *left* her up front, she knew you were *right*, you were *right* when you *left* her."

My mouth fell open but words did not come. He was correct. But that was not all she said. She asked me to listen to her. I tapped a few buttons on my wristband, rewinding the recording from my mask. I played the scene again. "Listen to me, Rence," I repeated. "Up front, he *left* me alone. He did *right*. He did *right* when he *left* me alone."

I turned off the video playback from the mask's eyes and looked at Anruk. "She's giving us directions."

He nodded. "And both times she said, up front or at the front."

The lightbulb in my head lit up. "At the front of the ship, turn left, then right, then right again, then left."

"Is Romeo ready to rescue Juliet?" he asked.

I climbed to my feet, taking in a deep breath. My shoulders felt light and my blood was pumping with excitement. "Start the countdown for evac."

Anruk nodded and spoke into the comm. "Oscar, Alpha. Are you in position? Over."

"Affirmative, over," Oss's voice replied.

"Begin prepping for evac. I say again, prep the wings for evac, over."

"WILCO, over."

"Roger, out." Anruk turned to me. "Our flight leaves in twenty minutes, let's move."

I stooped to be eye-level with Ryna. "We're gonna go rescue Miss Miri. Now there'll be lots of shooting. Just keep close to me, you hear?"

She nodded.

I took her by the hand and led her to the door. Anruk glanced out the small door window before exiting. Seven security guards rounded the corner and started shooting. The swarm of green blast bolts knocked him over, producing burn marks on his armor. Anruk fired a few shots in return, dropping three men. I drew Thunder and Lightning, my twin blast pistols, and peeked out the door. I fired four shots, sending red blast bolts into the guards. They each fell to the ground.

Holstering my blast pistols, I helped Anruk to his feet. "That armor has some impressive resistance."

"Against small arms fire," he said, reloading his blast rifle's power cell.

I took Ryna's hand and followed Anruk down the hall. We jogged at a moderate pace; Ryna couldn't run as fast.

The hallway echoed with Dr. Lenish's voice. "Mr. Perry, are you still there?"

Anruk glanced back at me. "I'm betting he'll start that seventeen minutes real soon."

We needed to hurry, but I couldn't drag Ryna any faster. My heart pounded as we jogged down one hallway after another. The one good thing about having the whole ship on alert was that it kept most people out of the halls. I didn't have to worry about someone getting hit in the crossfire.

Anruk pointed. "Here's our first left."

Ryna pulled her hand away and stopped, panting.

"Hold up," I said to Anruk.

He turned around. "We don't got time for this."

A caravan of security guards walked past the end of the hallway, escorting Miri to an airlock.

"Miri!" I shouted.

The guards all looked at us. Six of them stopped to shoot while the other three ran on ahead, dragging Miri along.

"Rence!" her voice echoed from around the far corner.

I pulled Ryna to the ground while drawing a blast pistol. Anruk spun to meet the oncoming shower of green blast bolts. He dropped to one knee, shooting back. I fired a few red blast bolts, and two guards fell. Anruk dropped another three until he jerked back and fell on his backside. I shot the last guard who fell on his face.

Anruk cursed, inspecting his rifle. A stray blast bolt hit the discharger coil. That rifle would never fire again. He cursed again and tossed it aside.

He drew a backup blast pistol from a holster on his belt. I scrambled to my feet, dashing down the hallway after Miri.

"Bring Ryna when you can!" I shouted back.

I drew my second blast pistol also as I ran down the hall. I rounded the corner and sprinted after them. One of the guards heard the stomping of my footsteps and turned around, shooting. I dove to the floor, firing both blast pistols. The guard dropped his blast pistol, clutching his chest. I stayed on the floor and aimed at the second guard. I fired. The red blast bolt whizzed through the air and struck the guard in the back. He tumbled forward to the floor. I aimed at the guard in the lead. He was too far for an accurate shot, and he was also pulling Miri along by her arm. I couldn't risk hitting Miri.

I again scrambled to my feet and dashed off down the hall after them. Miri glanced behind, seeing me in pursuit. She dropped to the ground, yanking the guard back from his run. He cursed and kicked her, ordering her to her feet while pulling her along the floor. Miri had not only slowed their pace, but she also left me with a wide-open shot. Only one blast bolt was enough to do the job. But after seeing him kick her, I peppered him with six bolts.

I skidded to a stop in front of Miri as the last guard fell. "Good thinking," I said.

She moaned, holding her side where the guard kicked her. Then she looked at me. "I knew you'd come back."

"I'll always come back for you, Miri."

"Where's Ryna?" she asked.

I glanced back down the hall. Anruk and Ryna jogged down after us. Ryna sprinted once she saw Miri. Miri kneeled up as Ryna flew into her arms. Miri held her tight, tears running down her face.

I turned to Anruk. "How much time?"

"About fifteen minutes."

I motioned behind me with my head. "There looks to be an elevator down there. It might take us that long to get these two down to the first deck. The boys will wait for us, right?"

"Of course, they'll wait. But let's not keep them waiting too long. Once that egghead realizes you have the woman, he'll send everyone he has to storm the landing bays."

I retrieved a fallen blast pistol from one of the guards and handed it to Miri. "Can you move?"

"Sure," she said, holding her breath against the pain.

"What about that?" Anruk said, pointing to a maintenance hatch.

I shook my head. "Absolutely not! Bad experience."

We hustled toward the elevator at the end of the hall with me in the lead. Anruk trailed behind Ryna, glancing over his shoulder now and again. Before we reached the elevator, its doors opened. Four security guards stepped out. I dashed forward, shooting my blast pistols. The surprised guards only got one shot off before I took them down. But that one shot struck me right below the collar bone.

I stumbled and fell to the floor.

"Rence!" Miri shouted.

She helped me to my feet. My right arm and shoulder ached. I holstered my blast pistols as Anruk and Ryna approached.

"Where'd you get hit?" Anruk asked.

I pulled my shirt open, showing him.

"It probably hurts like the dickens," he said. "But you'll be fine. Can you climb down with one hand?"

Before I could answer, Pym's voice called out over the comm. "Alpha, Papa. We are taking enemy fire. What's your ETA? Over."

"We're on our way. ETA ten minutes, over."

"Roger, out."

I pulled out a detonator and fastened it to the elevator wall.

"Wait," Miri said, placing her hand on my arm. "I've watched them use the elevators."

Miri pulled a keycard off one of the fallen guards. She tapped the card against the control panel and it beeped. Then she lifted the guard's hand and placed it against a black glass screen on the control panel. The panel beeped again and lit up. She pressed the button for the first deck and the doors closed. The elevator gently descended.

Anruk turned to me. "Kinda feel strange, taking the elevator in the middle of a skirmish."

"Yeah," I said, looking at him. "It's a little too peaceful."

The elevator chimed and the doors parted.

"There they are!" a guard shouted.

Keeping to the side of the elevator, we watched the hailstorm of green blast bolts spray the back wall.

"Me and my big mouth," I grumbled.

Off to my left, my detonator was still attached to the elevator wall. I pulled it off and activated it. I counted to five and then tossed it out the elevator door. Men shouted, diving for cover as the detonator exploded. Anruk dashed out of the elevator, shooting. I followed behind with Miri holding Ryna's hand.

My shoulder and arm ached with every stomp of my foot. I grunted with each step. That's probably why I didn't pay attention to where I was running. I tripped on the body of a guard and tumbled to the floor for the second time. Miri and Ryna stopped to help me up. I let out a terrible groan as my wound complained.

I looked ahead and saw Anruk charging down the hall, guards running from him. More security guards stormed in from a side hall. They were between us and the path to get to Anruk. They instantly noticed us and opened fire. We retreated back toward the elevator, shooting back. I reached into my coat pocket for a detonator. I cursed. They were all gone. We got back inside the elevator, breaking the line of sight.

"Romeo, Alpha," I said over the comm. "We've been cut off!"

"Roger," his voice replied. "I have to assist the boys, they're under heavy fire. I'll swing back around to you in a few minutes. Over."

This was not good news. They were being overwhelmed and Anruk was needed in several places. It would be a fight just for him to get back to us, let alone get back to the landing bay. There simply wasn't enough time. And I was not in much of a condition to fight off a large security force, not with Miri and Ryna in tow. I needed another option.

I could have tried the maintenance accessway again. But that was what got Miri and me separated in the first place. Besides, I didn't know what security improvements Dr. Lenish might have put in place down there. My best option was to find another way off the ship.

"Negative," I said. "Hold them off as long as you can and then evac. I'll go to their hanger and Juliet and...and...and whatever Ryna's name is, out in one of their attack fighters."

Anruk's voice came back. "You need to learn to say over at the end of a line, over."

I almost smiled. "Over."

"Roger, out."

I knelt and picked up the keycard Miri had used for the elevator and touched it to the sensor. It beeped. Then I put the hand of the dead guard on the sensor plate. The control panel beeped again and lit up. I pressed the button marked H. The elevator doors closed, blast bolts raining against the metal. The elevator descended, halting at the hangar deck. The elevator chimed and the doors parted. Pilots and flight personnel ran around fueling starfighters and prepping them to launch.

"Follow me," I told Miri.

I casually strolled across the hanger toward a couple of landed attack fighters. A man in coveralls disconnected a fuel hose. I walked up right behind him before he noticed anyone was there. "Sorry about this," I said, slamming his head against the metal frame of the fighter. It knocked him out cold. I didn't want to leave him lying on the floor. For one thing, I didn't want him to get run over. Secondly, I preferred he didn't get seen. There was no need to raise the alarm down here.

I directed Miri and Ryna to climb into the back seat of the attack fighter. Meanwhile, I hoisted the unconscious man into the cockpit of the neighboring one. I then climbed into the seat in front of Miri and Ryna. I looked over the various buttons and switches. It was a bit more advanced than a transport ship. On the bright side, most of the fundamentals were the same. Once I figured out how to start the engine, I closed the canopy and pressurized the cockpit. As I taxied the fighter down the runway, a flight deck crewman waved his hands angrily at me. I had no clue what his hand gestures were and I was tempted to show him a hand gesture of my own. I decided against it since ladies were present.

I rumbled down the hanger lane. I was close behind another starfighter that was taxiing into position. I pushed the throttle up and zoomed up behind him. I bumped the back of the starfighter, causing him to miss the turn and run into a wall. I turned onto the runway and noticed the space door at the far end was closing. Running a plane off the road and ignoring the flight director was probably suspicious.

I wasn't sure how to fire any weapons in this thing, so, I pushed the throttle up to full. We raced down the runway as the door continued to close. At the rate it was closing, we were not going to make it before the space door closed. There had to be a way to fire a missile or something at the door. I glanced around the controls and flipped a few rocker switches. An alarm sounded, so I flipped back the switches I could remember touching. It was much more straightforward on the *Princess.*

The space door was almost half-closed and I was not near enough to make it. I had to stop. Where were the brakes? I shifted around looking at some of the controls to my side. I accidentally knocked the throttle lever. I thought I broke it. I had knocked it past maximum thrust. The afterburner lit, throwing me back into my seat. The raw power of the afterburner lurched the fighter forward. We sped on toward the closing space door. I gripped the stick with white knuckles. It still didn't look like we were going to make it. My heart skipped a beat and my breathing stopped. We zoomed past the space door, scraping one of the fins against the closing door. We flew into the starry sky, leaving behind the Corporation ship.

I place a hand on my chest, feeling my heart pounding. I took some deep breaths, trying to slow my breathing. My chest was still pounding. Then I felt a wave of soothing calm wash over me. My pulse slowed and my breathing normalized.

"Thank you, Ryna," I said.

"You're welcome, Mr. Rence."

"Alpha, Romeo, over," I said into the comm.

Anruk's voice answered. "This is Alpha. Are you starborne yet? Over."

"Affirmative," I said. "How about you?...I mean, how about you, over?"

"Roger. Rendezvous at Mik's. And remember to conserve your fuel, over."

I glanced at my fuel gauge. My fuel was rapidly dropping. "Oh, dear." I fiddled with the throttle lever until I was able to pull it back into the normal thrust range. "Thanks for the tip, over," I said.

Anruk's voice replied. "Roger, out."

It took me a few minutes to find the navigation computer and plot a course for Cosstere.

"So," Miri said. "Romeo and Juliet?"

I was glad she couldn't see the color of my cheeks. "Long story," I said, hoping she would leave it at that.

"We seem to have plenty of time," she said.

I told her everything. It only seemed fair. At least I didn't have to look at her while I told the embarrassing parts. I don't know why I told her everything. Sure, I blushed plenty while telling it all. But somehow, it was like talking to an old friend that one hadn't seen in years. I enjoyed talking with her. In return, she told me all about being on the Corporation ship. She told me how she had threatened them with my wrath if they laid a hand on her. Dr. Lenish took her threat more seriously than anyone else.

I'm glad she had. It kept her from being harmed and it kept Ryna from being dissected. During the flight back to Cosstere, I reached my hand back and held Miri's. It was a simple gesture, but somehow, it meant a lot more.

Long trips aboard the *Princess* were a lot more comfortable; I wasn't cooped up in a small cockpit for hours on end. I was so glad when we landed on Cosstere. I was finally able to stretch my legs, and in doing so, rediscovered the sharp pain near my collar bone. It was only after Miri's insistence that I relented and went to the little hospital near Mik's place.

Thankfully the hospital simply patched me up and did not insist I stay the night. Miri and Ryna stayed with me while they patched me up.

"Ready to go?" Miri asked as the nurse left the room.

"To be honest, I was ready before I even set foot inside."

She gave a half-smile and handed me my hat.

Mik stepped into the room. Anruk was right behind him. "Well, well, well, Romeo. Congratulations on a successful mission."

My cheeks flushed. "You can call me Rence."

Mik looked at me. "I wanted to let you know that your ship has been refueled. You can leave whenever you're ready."

"Thanks, Mik. I owe you one."

He smiled. "Oh, speaking of favors. I neglected to give this to you before you left." He handed me the beautifully crafted blast pistol in a thin leather holster. It was connected to a small blast belt.

I took it reverently. "Thank you, Mik."

"A new blast pistol?" Miri asked.

I looked at her as Pym dashed into the room. "Anruk, there's a corporation ship in orbit. It looks like the same one."

I stood, pale-faced. "They restored their database and are tracking Ryna."

"You'd better hightail it," Anruk said. "They'll send search teams to the surface."

I nodded.

Mik looked worried. "If they are tracking the girl the same way you did, how will you ever get away?"

"One thing at a time, Mik. Right now, we gotta get moving. The *Princess* is fast enough, we'll be able to stay ahead of them. I'll just need to stay ahead of them long enough to figure out a way to stop them from tracking her."

"Take care of yourself, Rence. And come back to visit when this is all over."

I nodded. "You can count on it."

EPISODE 8

Something worth fighting for

Something Worth Fighting For

There are plenty of things in life that can get a man killed. Because of that, a man learns early on that there are things to run away from. Times when a man should back down, turn tail, and run. The concept of being a coward was invented just to stop a man from using his head and backing down when he should. And then there were also times when I found that the only right thing to do was to put my life on the line for another. That was where I found myself with Miri and Ryna.

The problem I now faced was that the Corporation could track Ryna once again. Some radioactive marker in her blood allowed her to be tracked across the entire sector of space. They were coming for her. And I could not fight them forever. Every gunfighter knows that sooner or later a blast bolt will have their name on it. And I couldn't go down like that. I was too well trained to think I could outrun them in the long term. What I needed was a way to stop them from tracking Ryna.

I sat in my chair in the cockpit of the *Princess.* Lady squawked, perched off to my side. I turned on the autopilot and spun around in my chair. Miri sat beside me with Ryna contentedly in her lap. On the other side of the cockpit sat Petre and Carol.

I stared at Petre. "Sounds to me like you're trying to renege on the original agreement."

"I understand the position you are in," Petre said. "But how can we realistically protect the girl from the Corporation?"

"Rence," Miri said, laying her hand on my arm. "They never had a chance."

"She's right," Carol said. "We did what we thought was right when we stole the girl from the lab. We didn't want to see her dissected. But we quickly found that we were in way over our heads."

"As I said before," Petre amended. "They tracked the girl and caught us, nearly killing us in the process."

"She's safer with us," Miri concluded.

Us. The only problem with that word was that it implied a permanent arrangement. I didn't have any qualms about being with Miri long-term. But I also didn't like being pushed into anything. Getting pushed into any situation, no matter how appealing, always got under my skin. But I also couldn't deny Miri's logic. Ryna certainly was safer at my side. And with Miri learning how to shoot fast, we were starting to become something to reckon with.

I sighed, glancing over to Petre. "I stand corrected."

Petre took a breath as the invisible wall of tension broke in the room. It was like an invisible person had just told everybody it was now okay to breathe and move. Ryna curled up in Miri's arms, closing her eyes with a relaxed smile on her face.

Carol leaned forward in her chair. "Mr. Perry, we would still like to offer any help we can from a medical and scientific standpoint."

Petre looked at her with a smile. "With the hope that it won't involve a lot of life-threatening excitement."

Even I had to smile at that remark. The poor scientists had been through a lot. Escaping from the Corporation's lab ship was the most excitement they ever wanted to see. I, on the other hand, had become used to it during the golden years of the Wayfinders.

"What I really need help on," I said, looking at Petre, "is a way to stop them from tracking Ryna. And before you get started on your sciencey mumbo-jumbo," I added, "I remember you saying it would take decades for the marker in her blood to run its course."

Petre nodded. "A 12.26-year half-life for the kaligeenium-62 isotope. We could run some tests to see if there are any materials that could dampen the signal," Petre offered.

Carol put her hand on his arm. "There is a certain signal degradation with polytitanium."

I didn't like where that line of thought was heading. I didn't know what polytitanium was, but it sounded a lot like titanium. And titanium was a metal. That meant encasing Ryna in metal to keep her from being tracked.

"Hold on," I said. "I appreciate the thought. But if we have to put Ryna in a cage to keep her from being tracked, aren't we back to square one? I didn't bust her out of a corporate cell just to put her into one of our own."

Carol nodded, looking down.

Petre glanced at me. "You erased their database once, couldn't you do it again?"

"They restored the database from backup, doc."

"Yes, but could you not do it again, and this time erase the backups too?"

I leaned back in my chair. "I suppose that's a possibility. A difficult possibility. You see, I had help on that one. And I had a devil of a time getting myself out in one piece. And if Dr. Lenish has anything to do with it, he'll have upgraded the database's security the way he did on the lab ship. Let's call that plan Z."

Miri lifted her head from Ryna's. "Can you recreate the marker signal that is in Ryna?"

"We would need some equipment, but that should be doable," Peter replied.

I turned to Miri. "You have an idea?"

"Well, if they are so keen on tracking that signal," she began. "Why not inject that marker into every bird, reptile, and snake among the colony worlds? Why not give them a haystack to hunt their needle in?"

I smiled at that notion. I felt a guilty pleasure in giving the corporation a wild goose chase. "I like the direction you're heading. However, there would still be one correct signal leading to Ryna. A stroke of luck on their part could still endanger her."

Petre shrugged. "Mathematically speaking, those chances would exponentially decrease with the more animals you inject. Though you would need to produce quite a lot of kaligeenium-62. And it is somewhat expensive."

"Maybe we don't have to," Carol said thoughtfully. "We may only have to inject Ryna."

"What do you mean?" he asked.

"If the marker is a specific frequency, maybe we can alter that frequency? Change the signal."

"Wouldn't they just follow the new signal?" Miri asked.

"Not if they don't know what that signal is," he explained. "They have thousands of assets tagged. Without the frequency, they cannot distinguish an asset on the loose from one they control. That is why Mr. Perry erased the project files from their database initially."

"And they wouldn't know her signal had been changed," Carol added. "To them, it would look like the signal simply stopped."

"Not quite as satisfying as the needle in the haystack idea," I said, glancing over to Miri. "But certainly less expensive." I turned back to Petre. "Is that something you could pull off, doc?"

He shook his head. "That would require a bio-radiologic chemist, which, neither of us is."

"What about colleagues?"

"All our colleagues work for the Corporation."

Annoyance built up inside me. "Give me something to work with, doc."

Carol turned to Petre. "What about Heinlin?"

He bobbed his head in consideration. "I suppose he might still be practicing. He retired a few years ago."

"Great, I'll take it," I said. "Where do we find him?"

"Ragshir's moon. He built a house there."

I spun my chair around and punched the new course into the autopilot.

"Is he loyal to Westward Galactic?" Miri asked.

"Well," Carol said. "His pension is paid by the Corporation."

"There's always something," I complained, getting out of my chair and heading for the door. "I hate to end this little powwow, but we have a 52-hour flight to Ragshir. You all best get something to eat from downstairs."

"Rence," Miri asked. "Help me with Ryna please?"

Ryna had fallen asleep snuggled up in Miri's lap. I gently picked her up, trying not to wake her. Miri followed me out into the corridor. I carried her over to Miri's cabin. Miri opened the door and I laid Ryna on the cot.

"You know, the two of you don't have to share a cabin," I explained to Miri. "There's plenty of rooms on the *Princess.*"

"Well, if you hadn't noticed," she said, covering Ryna with a blanket. "She's a little attached to me at the moment. We'll be all right for now."

I nodded and turned to leave.

Miri caught me by the arm. "Rence, thank you again for coming after us. It sounds like you went through an awful lot to do so."

I widened my eyes in recollection. Storming the data center, always wondering if Tess Davendry would double-cross me, was rough. Not to mention battling four Kuda just so I could help Mik build a device to track Ryna. Then, of course, raiding the Lab Ship to rescue them both. I had probably escaped death six times in all that.

I looked into her eyes. "If it meant getting you back, I would do it all over again."

She took in a sudden breath and her eyes watered. "Thank you," she whispered.

I tipped my hat and stepped out into the corridor. Miri hesitated to close the door. The air felt thick. If I had a stick in my hand, I could have stirred the air around. Part of me wanted to escape from the awkward feelings I felt. The other part of me wanted to stay with Miri. It was a strange contradiction inside of me. The second part of me won out.

"Miri."

"Yes?"

"Fancy a walk with me?"

She stepped out into the corridor and quietly closed the door behind her. She smiled as she slipped her arm around mine. We strolled down the metal corridor in silence. I wanted to say something, but I wasn't sure what it was that I wanted to say. And I could only guess what she was feeling. The corridor ended in front of the stairwell down to the bottom deck. To our left was the maintenance hatch that we were in when Ryna first asked if we were going to kiss. My cheeks flushed at the memory.

Miri smiled at me. "What is it?"

Miri had wanted to talk about what happened and I ran from that conversation faster than I could draw. She had been upset that I didn't want to have an 'adult conversation'. I was lucky that an impending crisis had put that talk on hold.

I nodded toward the hatch. "I reckon I still owe you a conversation."

She abruptly looked away. Either she didn't care to talk about it now or she was hiding the color in her cheeks. I didn't care to gamble on which one it was, so I held my peace. It was safer to wait for her to start talking first. If she changed the subject, I would know she didn't want to talk.

She giggled, looking back at me. "You have changed. A few weeks ago, you would have rather lived with a camcam than to talk about it."

Technically, that could be considered changing the subject. But it wasn't really a different subject, it was more or less a commentary around the subject. So, did this mean she wanted to talk about it? Or was this an invitation to talk about me instead? No, I knew Miri long enough to know better. When she wanted to talk, only imminent danger was a valid excuse not to talk.

I took a deep breath and opened my mouth. No words came. My mind wasn't exactly a blank, I did know I needed to talk with her, but how did one begin? "Well blast my boots, Miri," I finally said. "I can fight raiders, pirates, commandos, and the whole Corporation, but I have to pull teeth to talk about you and me."

She sweetly laughed. "Take your time."

"Miri, the whole time I was without you, you were always on my mind. I've had such conflicting thoughts ever since that first Kuda we bumped into on Jashur VII. I still remember that coy smile you gave me when you invited me to join you and Ryna to go shopping."

She blushed.

I continued. "I was real happy then. I even entertained the notion that I could settle down with you somewhere, give you a life of silks and satins." I glanced down. "That all changed when that Kuda heard my name. All my instincts tell me that I'm not good for you; that my very name attracts danger."

"Rence," she said with a shaky voice. "What does your heart tell you?"

I looked into her watery eyes. They looked delicate. As if they were on the razor's edge between either joy or sadness. My next words would dictate which direction they would fall. Since when did her heart lie in my hands? Who was I to be entrusted with such a treasure? Would it matter in the end? She asked me a question. And I aimed to shoot straight with her. She deserved as much.

"My heart tells me that I'm a mighty big fool for not doing it sooner."

A tear broke loose and rolled down her cheek. "Doing what?"

I stroked her cheek with the back of my fingers, leaned in, and kissed her. It only lasted a moment, but my heart pounded and I had to catch my breath. "That," I replied.

It looked like she needed a moment to catch her breath too. I waited until she looked at me again. "Miri, I may not be any good for you, and the sound of my name will likely stir up trouble. But if you have no objections, I will fight them all to be with you."

She stopped in the middle of taking a breath. I was about to ask if she was okay but then she finally breathed, placing her hand on her chest. She let go of my arm and walked back down the corridor a few steps before turning around. "You've given a girl a lot to think about," she declared, smiling. "I'll have to get back to you on that." She smiled again and floated back down the corridor.

I stood there dumbfounded. I could have conjured up a thousand ways that conversation could have gone. And never once would I have imagined this. What made matters worse was that I wasn't sure what to think. It wasn't a rejection nor was it an endorsement. Yet something about her smile seemed to convey a meaning. It wasn't a casual smile. It had hints of that coy smile she had given me back on Jashur VII, and there was something more. Part of her smile seemed to reflect her expression when she first eyed those fancy dresses. I had no idea what it all meant, yet somehow, I had the feeling that I was missing something obvious.

I retired to my cabin for some shut-eye. The trip to Ragshir was uneventful. I finally got some decent sleep and the ladies were able to unwind a bit. The only one that grew restless was Lady, squawking on her perch. She needed some flight time once we set down. Returning to the cockpit, I settled into my chair. Lady squawked and flapped her wings.

"Real soon, Lady. I promise." I stroked her feathered head.

The planet Ragshir was fast approaching. The pale blue gas giant had only one moon. The small moon had a cozy atmosphere with liquid water and plenty of vegetation. The *Princess* shuddered as she descended through the clouds. She softly touched down on the soft red ground. The small white sun in the sky was hot but the moon retreated behind the shadow of the planet every twelve hours. It provided a forested climate. Now, *this* was what I called a planet. Too bad it was officially called a moon. I picked up Lady from her perch and walked with her down the entry ramp and onto the soft dirt.

"Have fun," I said, tossing her into the sky.

She soared into the air, squawking an excited cry.

I watched her soar out of sight and then turned back to head up the ramp. I stopped short of bumping into Ryna. "Good morning, little miss."

She smiled at me. "Good morning Mr. Rence."

"Well you look happy today," I observed.

She nodded. "I'm glad you kissed Miss Miri."

There's no way she could have known that. The little matchmaker was on the warpath with cupid's arrow. That much was certain. What wasn't certain about was how she knew I kissed Miri. She was asleep in Miri's cabin. Though, she did see me kiss her back on the Corporation lab ship the first time when I was forced to leave them. Perhaps that was what she was referring to?

"Oh," I said, feigning wonder. "A few weeks back, when we were trying to leave the Corporation ship–"

"No, I mean last night," she corrected.

My heart started thumping in my chest. I felt like a child caught with my hand in the cookie jar. Could she see through walls now? I needed to entice her to tell me how she knew. "What makes you think I did anything last night?"

"Why else would Miss Miri be so happy today?" she said matter-of-factly.

Of course, I thought, glancing heavenward in exasperation. The secret to her uncanny powers was that she was growing into a woman. It was a wonder I even bothered trying to hide it from her. Something caught my eye when I looked up. It was a small piece of welding plate. Welding plates were used to patch up holes on the hull from weapons fire. The strange thing was that I didn't remember patching up that spot.

I did my own repairs on the *Princess.* And having done so for over a decade, I was on a first-name basis with every bolt and weld on that ship. I reached up and tugged on that welding plate. It pulled off into my hand. A welding plate would never be attached by a magnet. This was not a welding plate.

"What's that?" Ryna asked.

"Trouble."

I brought it inside and set it down on my machining table in the cockpit. It looked and felt like a welding plate. So where was its secret? I took out my tactical mast and clamped it on. I pressed a few buttons on my wristband. It changed my eyesight to see in the electromagnetic spectrum. Blue and purple lines ran all over the inside of that thing. It had complex circuitry inside.

"Morning, Rence. What are you working on?" Miri asked, having entered the cockpit.

"Mr. Rence says it's trouble," Ryna replied.

I switched my vision back to normal and held up the metal device. "I'd bet a week's earnings this is a homing beacon."

"Where'd you get it?" Miri asked.

"Found it attached to the *Princess's* hull."

"Somebody put it there?"

I nodded.

Miri wrinkled her brow. "But the Corporation can already track us through Ryna. Why would they need to tag the *Princess?*"

"You're right, they don't."

"Then...why do it?"

"My guess is that this was not put here by the Corporation. If they had gotten this close, they would have attacked, not tagged the ship. This is more likely the work of a bounty hunter—doubtless, Dr. Lenish doubled the price on my head. The only opportunity to tag the *Princess* was back on Cosstere, and Anruk and his Kuda were guarding us then."

Miri cursed under her breath. "So this bounty hunter needed to wait for us to be more vulnerable and tagged our ship."

Had I only imagined it, or had Miri said *our* ship? In the past, she had always referred to the *Princess* as *your* ship. I wasn't quite sure what that meant but I kind of liked the idea of sharing the *Princess* with her.

"Rence, I need another gun. Dr. Lenish took Ivory from me."

"Of course," I said. "Right this way." I led her out of the cockpit and down the corridor. I stopped short at the door to my cabin.

Miri looked confused. "Isn't your weapon's locker at the end of the hall?"

"Yes, but...I have something for you." I opened the door and went in. Miri waited for me outside. I returned and held out both hands. My right hand held the blast belt with the holstered blast pistol Mik designed and built. My left hand held her red dress all folded up neatly.

She eyed both hands inquisitively.

"I guess this was gonna be another conversation for us," I said. "I reckon now is as good a time as any. I had been assuming you wanted a life of silks and satins, seeing how you fancy these dresses so much. I stitched the tear for you."

She looked into my eyes with wonder. "You can sew?"

I shrugged. "*Sew* might be too strong a word for it. I'm handy enough with a needle to mend a tear but that's about it."

She smiled.

I continued. "Then, before I left to rescue you and Ryna, I saw Mik had designed a blast pistol and he let me shoot it. It sure is a beauty, and she shoots straight. He told me I could keep it and if I didn't want it, I should give it to another Wayfinder."

I felt adrenaline surging through my veins. My heart began thumping. Why was I nervous? I was only talking. Then again, I wasn't talking about the weather. "I didn't have the heart to tell him there weren't any other Wayfinders...then I had this crazy notion..."

She eyed both my hands once more before gazing into my eyes. "Am I supposed to choose?"

"Well...up until now I had been making my own assumptions. So, it would be real handy, you see...if I could know for sure."

"Look, Rence. I appreciate that you want to have this conversation, but don't you think this is a decision for after this is all over?"

I saw plenty of wisdom in her words. The problem was that I wanted to shrink and disappear. Even wearing my mask hadn't saved me from the awkwardness that crept into the air. At least I had bragging rights that I had the guts to say what I did.

"Uh...you're right," I said, tossing both items onto my cot. "Oh, wait." I went back inside and retrieved her dress. "This belongs to you."

"Thanks for mending it."

I tipped my hat and escorted her down to the weapons locker. I unlocked it and set before her my collection of blast pistols. "None of these are as small as Ivory was. You won't be able to conceal them. I would recommend–"

"What about this one?" Miri asked, fingering a blast pistol with a dark wooden handle.

I shook my head. "That's Prince Rupert. He sure is handsome to look at, but he bucks like a wild stallion. An hour of practice with him usually makes my arm numb."

I pulled out a long-barreled blast pistol with a silver handle and set it down in front of Miri. "Here, you should be able to handle Ol' Silver."

She picked it up and felt the weight.

Petre walked up the stairwell. "Mr. Perry, I hope we will be leaving soon."

I nodded, packing the rest of the guns into the weapons locker. "As soon as we take care of this," I said, showing him the metal homing beacon.

They followed me outside. I tapped a few buttons on my wristband. Lady squawked and swooped down. I held up the metal homing beacon. Lady snatched it from my hand.

"Take it someplace interesting," I called out to her as she flew off.

Petre and Carol led the way up the hill and down the valley to Heinlin's house. It was a single-story wide house with white brick and blue trims. Tall trees shaded the house and Steppingstones lined a path up to the front door. We all gathered on the front porch and Petre knocked. A woman in her late twenties answered the door.

"Can I help you?" she cautiously asked.

"We're looking to call upon Dr. Heinlin Veso. Carol and I are old associates of his."

Her countenance brightened up. “Please come in! Dad doesn’t get many visitors. My name is Bridgette.”

She showed us to the sitting room and bade us sit down.

Petre turned to Carol. “I knew Heinlin had a son, but I didn’t know he had a daughter.”

“There’s probably a lot we don’t know,” Carol said.

Bridgette soon returned with an old man in tow. Heinlin wore a brown sweater vest with large spectacles and suspenders. He displayed a confused look on his face until his eyes fell on Petre and Carol.

“What are you doing here?” he inquired.

“Oh, please, daddy. These people have come to visit you,” Bridgette said.

My muscles tensed up. My heart pounded and my breathing grew shallow into quick breaths. My blood pumped fast. All my senses were on edge. What was going on? My nerves felt like I was running headlong into a gunfight. I peeked a glance at Ryna. She stared back at me. She was inflaming my sense of danger. But why? True, we didn’t yet know if Heinlin would help us or be loyal to the Corporation, but that was hardly a cause for alarm. Or was it? Had Ryna sensed something and was trying to warn me?

“Heinlin,” Petre said. “It’s Petre and Carol. We worked on several projects together on *Labship 7*.”

Heinlin nodded. “I know who you are. And I’m not in the mood for guests.”

“You’ll have to excuse daddy,” Bridgette said. “He hasn’t had his tea yet.” She sat him down and took a seat next to him.

Petre continued. “Heinlin, remember the radioisotope bio-tags the Corporation uses to track inventory?”

He nodded. “I was the one who designed the frequency schema.”

“Oh yes, that’s right. Well, we have a particular asset that needs to be re-tagged with a different signal.”

“Why would you need to change the frequency?”

Petre thought for a moment. “I guess you could say we’re re-cataloging certain inventory.”

Heinlin stared at him a moment. “Don’t feed me that malarky! You finally saw enough of Dr. Lenish and wised up. Probably stole one of the girls and found out later they were all tagged." He turned to Ryna. "Which one are you? Number 28?"

Carol placed a reassuring hand on Petre's arm while addressing Heinlin. "We couldn't stand by any longer. What they do to those children..."

"Why do you think I retired?"

"Will you help us?" Petre pleaded.

"No can do. My, uh, daughter is visiting from off-world. Come back later."

"Oh, don't be silly, daddy," Bridgette said, smiling. "You can be a friend indeed to a friend in need."

A light blinked on my wristband. It was Lady, signaling me. *What have you spotted, old girl?* I wondered. I stood and walked over to the door.

"Leaving already?" Bridgette asked.

"Need to check something. I'll be right back," I replied.

I stepped out onto the porch and put on my tactical mask. I pressed a few buttons on my wristband to change my vision to see through Lady's eyes. Lady had perched atop a tall tree overlooking the rest of the valley. Three small shuttles crested the hill and flew into the valley. They were an unmistakable design: troop transports. How did the Corporation find us so quickly? And how did they know so precisely where we were? They were tracking Ryna, of course, but not even I was able to track down her exact location so fast. Unfortunately, those questions would have to wait. It was time to hightail it back to the *Princess.*

I switched my eyesight back to normal and went back inside the house.

"Rence, what's wrong?" Miri asked, noticing that I was wearing my mask.

"We got company. Armed troops heading this way."

Petre jumped to his feet in alarm. "Already? How?"

"No idea, doc. We'll have to figure that out later. Right now, it's time to skedaddle."

Petre turned to Heinlin. "Will you help us?"

"No time, doc. We gotta go now," I said.

Miri, Ryna, and Carol stood.

"Daddy, I think we should go with them," Bridgette said, pulling Heinlin to his feet. "We'll be safe and you can help them."

I glanced out the front window. Armed troops spilled out of the three landed shuttles. They charged up the gentle slope to the house. They wore visored helmets and blast vests, carrying blast rifles. We had a few minutes before they would break down the door.

"Out the back," I said, ushering them through the house. At least I was hoping the house had a back door. Most houses did. I wasn't worried though, I restocked my detonators. If worst came to worst, I could always create a back door.

Bridgette led us to the back door and helped Heinlin down the steps. A sound of breaking glass and splintering wood signaled that they had broken down the front door. I pulled out a detonator and placed it on the interior side of the back door before closing it. I jumped over the railing, skipping the back stairs.

"I hope your friend is insured," I said to Petre as I jogged past him.

"What do you mean?"

The back door exploded, sending men flying through the nearby windows. Troops flooded back out from the front door and soon spotted us. The hailstorm of gunfire began. Bright green blast bolts flew all around us. Our group couldn't move very fast with Ryna and Heinlin. I needed to buy us more time.

I caught up to Miri and Ryna. "Get them back to the *Princess.* I'll slow them down."

She nodded.

I turned around, dashing back toward the troops. I drew Thunder and Lightning, my twin blast pistols. I fired several wild shots in their direction. I wasn't trying to hit anything; I needed them to go on the defensive. They scattered, diving for cover. I took that opportunity to change course and head toward their shuttles.

I holstered one blast pistol and pulled out three detonators. I skidded to a stop at the first shuttle. I activated a detonator and tossed it inside. I ducked some green blast bolts from the troops who were hustling back to their shuttles. I ran to the second shuttle and again tossed in a detonator.

When I reached the third shuttle, a large muscular soldier stepped out. I skidded to a stop in front of him, firing my blast pistol. My red blast bolt ricocheted off his helmet visor. He swatted the gun out of my hand and threw a punch at my chest. I fell onto my back as the first shuttle exploded.

The muscular soldier looked at the explosion in alarm. I used that distraction to scramble to my feet. Before I could retrieve my blast pistol, he threw a punch. I hopped backward, narrowly evading the blow. I kicked him but he caught my leg. This guy was not only big, but he was also strong.

He brought up his arm, preparing to bring down his elbow into my leg. One of Anruk's Kuda had elbowed me in the thigh once. I hadn't been able to use my leg for a few days. I couldn't afford to lose my mobility now. Not while we were on the run. I was going to have to be a little more clever with this brute. I drew my other blast pistol and fired three times square in his chest. The blast vest absorbed the shots but he was still knocked back. He let go of my leg, dropping me to the ground, as the second shuttle exploded. The blast startled him, giving me time to get back to my feet.

He lunged and I leaped to the side, letting him stumble past me. I threw a punch at his lower back and struck his kidney. He grunted and spun around angrily. He put up his dukes and we circled each other. He was playing cautiously now and that suited his situation. But it was detrimental to mine. I had only a matter of minutes before his comrades joined him. I reached over to my wristband and pressed a button.

We circled once more before he broke the stalemate with a punch. I leaned out of the way and threw one of my own. He batted my arm aside and punched me in the gut. I doubled over; the wind knocked out of me. He kicked me before I could get a breath, but I caught his foot. I twisted it sideways, forcing him to fall to the ground. He yanked his foot out of my hands and I rolled away, gasping for breath.

I struggled to my feet in time to see him pick up my fallen blast pistol and point it at me. I froze. We stared at each other, panting. Why hadn't he shot yet?

"You disappoint me," he said jovially.

"How so?"

"You put up a good fight, I'll give you that. But I would have expected more from a Wayfinder. I guess those stories are just that: stories."

"What did we do in those stories? Breathe fire?" I asked.

He shook his head. "No, they talk about Wayfinders always having a trick up their sleeve. But when it comes down to it, you're just as vulnerable as the next man."

The light on my wristband flashed.

"It's a mighty shame you can't see the smile on my face," I said.

"Why is that?"

"Because your expectations have not been in vain."

Lady swooped down behind the muscular soldier and her talons struck him in the back of the helmet. The impact forced his head downward and pushed him forward. He stumbled toward me and I kicked him in the head utilizing the strength of my knees. The force of the blow whipped his head back and cracked his helmet. He fell on his back, out cold.

A swarm of green blast bolts sprayed in my direction from the incoming troops. I hastily picked up my fallen blast pistols and detonator. I tossed the detonator into the last shuttle as I dashed past. Nine seconds later, the shuttle exploded. Debris and flames scattered all around. The troops swarmed the site of the explosions. They seemed more interested in the destruction of their shuttles than in catching me. But I still spent a good deal of time dodging their retaliation fire.

I ran faster. I needed to catch up with Miri and the group. The pursuing troops would soon realize their only way off this moon was to commandeer our ship. That meant that while I slowed them down, they were still coming for us. Hopefully, I bought all the time I needed.

I came up to the group and stopped. They had all stopped to catch their breaths. Miri wisely had her gun out. "What kept you?"

"I guess you could say I ran into a huge fan," I said.

"Did you stop them?"

"I slowed them down. They're still on their way but they'll be on foot carrying all their gear."

"You disabled their shuttles, right? Once we take off in the *Princess*, they won't be able to follow, right?"

I nodded. "That about sums it up."

"Okay, then we need to get moving right away." She turned to the rest of the group. "All right, let's go, everyone. The ship is just at the top of this ridge." She ushered them onward.

Lady squawked from above.

I held my arm out and she landed. I stroked her feathered head. "Good girl. I owe you a Telurian mouse when we get back home."

A green blast bolt whizzed through the air and struck a nearby tree. I flinched, glancing back the way I had come. Some of the troops had come within firing range.

I tossed Lady back into the air. "Get back to the *Princess.*"

At the rate they were gaining, they would reach the *Princess* really soon after we did. That didn't give much time to prep the ship for takeoff. I needed a way to slow them down even more. I dropped to one knee and drew a blast pistol. With their helmets and blast vests, I would have to aim for their arms and legs. I aimed and squeezed off a couple of shots. One soldier dropped to the ground clutching his leg. A second dropped his rifle and grabbed his arm.

A green blast bolt struck the ground close to me, sending dirt into the air. I sent a few more of my red blast bolts downrange, dropping several more troops. The line of troops stopped their advance and crouched down to shoot. Another green blast bolt struck inches from my boot, kicking up dirt into my mask. Good thing the mask filtered the air I breathed. I backed off a few feet and fired off a few more shots.

Two more enemy shots hit the dirt in front of me and a third whizzed past my head. It was time to fall back. The enemy shots were getting too close for comfort. That was as long as I dared try to hold them off directly. I backed off wracking my brain for an alternative way to slow them down. Maybe blocking the path by shooting down a tree? No, it would take me longer to shoot down a tree than it would to shoot down the troops.

I pulled out a detonator and tossed it as far as I could toward the soldiers. I ran toward the *Princess,* hearing the explosion behind me. I stopped short, nearly bumping into Miri. "Why'd you stop?"

She pointed toward the *Princess* off in the distance. Seven soldiers stood around the *Princess,* inspecting it. A scout patrol had found the *Princess* but evidently didn't know it was my ship. I was certainly going to get my exercise for the week. "I'll draw them off," I told her. "Keep close to the *Princess* but stay out of sight."

She nodded and ushered the rest of the group into the thicket of trees.

I drew Thunder and Lightning, charging at the troops around the *Princess.* I fired several shots, nailing several in the chest. As soon as they started firing back, I bolted for the tree line opposite where Miri and the others were hiding. I holstered my blast pistols and ran faster. Green blast bolts flew past me, kicking up dirt and splintering tree bark.

It would do me no good to lead these men away if I still had all the rest of the troops advancing on the *Princess.* I needed to lead those men away also. I tapped a few buttons on my wristband, changing the vision in one of my eyes to infrared. I only changed one eye, because I still needed the other to watch where I was going. The last thing I needed was to run smack into a tree. Glancing around, I saw the heat signatures of the main body of troops. They looked to be really close to Miri's position.

I needed to get their attention. I couldn't shoot at them, there were too many trees between us. Maybe they would respond to a detonator blast? I dropped a detonator at my feet and kept on running. Nine seconds later, it exploded. The wave of heat licked my back.

I glanced over to the main body of troops. It worked; they were heading my way. Now to give them the slip somehow. And I needed to do it soon; I was getting tired. I ran around a large tree and skidded to a halt behind it. I jumped high into the air and caught a branch near the top. My legs were sore and my lungs felt like they were on fire. I wheezed, trying to catch my breath. It would be no use trying to hide here with all the noise I was making. I needed to jump one more time to another tree.

I sighed, climbing up on the tall branch. My body wanted desperately to rest. Then I thought of Miri and Ryna. They needed me and I was not going to let them down. I stood on the branch and jumped. I flew through the canopy of forest leaves and caught a large branch of another three. My grip slipped and fell to the branch below it. My heart raced as panic washed over me. I clung to the branch, safe for now. I waited until I got my breathing under control. Then I eased myself into a sitting position on the tall branch.

A short distance away, both groups of soldiers swarmed the scene, looking for where they had last seen me. I cursed under my breath. There was one flaw in my plan. The men that had come from the *Princess* would inevitably tell the others about my ship. When they gave up looking for me, they would return to the *Princess.* I had only bought a little time. Despite my aching muscles, I needed to get moving.

I dropped to the ground, my knees absorbing the shock. I made my way as quickly and quietly as I could back around toward the *Princess.* I needed all the time I could get for starting the engines and prepping for launch. Time which I may have just barely bought. When I arrived back at the *Princess*, Miri had already been guiding the others to the ship. Her face was flushed from the heat and the run.

"How is everyone?" I asked.

"Hanging in there," she replied. "Ryna has been a real trooper through it all; hasn't complained."

I knelt on one knee and looked straight into Ryna's face. "You've done good today, little miss."

She smiled.

Petre walked up, wheezing, with Carol supporting him. Heinlin wearily walked behind them, all red in the face from panting. Bridgette helped him along. She had the same rosy cheeks and bright disposition she had when we first met her.

Miri ushered them toward the boarding ramp. "Everyone inside."

"Everyone except for her," I said, pointing at Bridgette.

"Why?" Miri asked.

"Because she ain't the good doctor's daughter." I kept my eyes on Bridgette and called over my shoulder. "Isn't that right, Heinlin?"

"I don't know who she is," he explained. "She threatened to kill me if I didn't play along."

The innocent expression ran off Bridgette's face like a fast-moving stream. She gave a sinister smile along with a cold stare. "I didn't think I made any mistakes."

"To your credit," I said. "You gave a great performance."

"What gave me away?"

"Little things," I explained. "Things I wouldn't normally have noticed if Ryna hadn't tipped me off that something was wrong. First, the doc didn't remember Heinlin having a daughter. But that could have easily been just a lack of information on his part. Next, the Corporation troops came way too fast; they knew exactly where we were and came charging in. Someone had to have tipped them off precisely where we were. You also didn't seem very alarmed to hear that armed troops were raiding the house. Most folks first express disbelief. And last but not least, you are way too calm under fire for a rich doctor's daughter."

"I'll have to work on that."

"Wait a minute," Miri said. "She's the bounty hunter that's been tracking us?"

"She's the one that's been tracking us all right, but she ain't no bounty hunter," I explained. "Subterfuge is not in a bounty hunter's M.O. I'd bet coins to curses that she is a paid assassin."

"Very good, Mr. Perry," Bridgette said in a sly tone. "Only Dr. Lenish is not paying me. Killing you is just a personal favor to Vik."

"A mighty shame you won't be able to make good on that favor."

"Oh, we'll have to see about that," she said, reaching behind her back.

My blast pistol cleared leather in less than a heartbeat. She had barely pulled out her small blast pistol when my red blast bolt struck her in the chest. The force of the hit pushed her back against a tree trunk. She glanced down at the smoldering hole in her blouse. She had been wearing a blast vest under her shirt.

"You're the fastest I've ever seen," she said with amazement in her voice. "But I always keep my promises." She fired her blast pistol at Heinlin.

He collapsed to the ground as I fired several more shots at Bridgette. She dodged, shooting back at me. I jumped to the side, drawing my second blast pistol. I unloaded both pistols at her, sending a hailstorm of red blast bolts in her direction. One shot grazed her arm as she ran off into the thicket of trees.

Behind me, the muffled sounds of the approaching troops grew louder. I didn't have time to deal with Bridgette; we needed to leave. I pressed a button on my wristband to call Lady. I bolted up the ramp into the *Princess*, calling out behind me. "Ryna, get Lady!"

I plopped into my chair, flipping switches on my control panel. The engines whined and sputtered to life. Ryna walked in with Lady perched on her arm. She crossed over to me and transferred Lady to her perch at my right.

"Thanks, Ryna," I quickly said. "Is everyone on board?"

"Yes."

I pressed the button to close the entry ramp to the ship. Out the blast screen window, I saw the troops emerging from the thicket, firing at us. The gentle thumping of blast bolts against the hull sounded like muffled raindrops. I engaged the vertical ascent thrusters and the *Princess* shuddered as she rose into the air. The treetops faded below us, and the bright blue sky faded into black.

We crossed through the atmosphere into orbit. No sooner had we entered orbit than my sensor screen beeped, blinking a red light. We had a capital ship coming right for us. Most likely the ship that carried the troop transport shuttles to the planet. Its configuration was different than the lab ship. But it was broadcasting Westward Galactic's identification signal. Even though we left the forest behind, we were not out of the woods yet.

Large blue blast cannon bolts flew past, illuminating the cockpit. I bit my tongue, trying not to curse in front of Ryna. I accelerated the engines to full power. They revved up and then whined and revved down. That was not a good sound. I tried again. Still no luck. Either we picked up a lucky shot from the troops on the planet or Bridgette had another surprise for us. Either way, it was the worst outcome at the worst possible time.

I couldn't put the *Princess* on autopilot to check on the engines while we were being shot at. Just one hit from those blast cannons would become a really bad day. "Ryna, take Lady," I said, keeping my eyes ahead. "I need Miss Miri to help fix the engines."

She nodded and picked up Lady from her perch.

"And give her this," I said holding up a headset.

Ryna took it and left the cockpit.

I veered the *Princess* hard to one side, engaging the turning thrusters. Three large blue blast cannon bolts streaked past.

"Rence, we're in the engine room. What do you need?" came Miri's voice through my mask.

I pressed a few buttons on my wristband, switching the view of one of my eyes to see Lady's vision. It would be a struggle to pay attention to dodging the cannon shots while instructing Miri on engine repairs.

"Sorry for the inconvenience," I said. "I know how you love fixing starships."

"Very funny, Rence. Now, what am I looking for?"

"The turbo compressors aren't getting the influx of fuel as they should. Something's wrong. Check the large yellow drum-shaped compartment on the left."

She pulled open the curved panel door. Black liquid seeped out, dripping onto the metal floor. "Rence, it's leaking drive fuel!"

"Not good," I said, dodging another few blast cannon shots. "This is going to get a little messy."

I pulled the ship hard to the left, narrowly evading another blast cannon shot. Miri grabbed ahold of the panel door to keep her balance. Ryna clung to the stairwell railing.

"There's a crate of maintenance rags on the floor," I continued. "See if can use one to plug up the leak. Oh, and be careful what you touch once you get your hands dirty. That stuff doesn't wash out very well."

"Thanks for the warning." She pulled out a dingy red rag from a crate by her feet.

Another light blinked on my console. The sensors had picked up a second incoming ship. It was a small Correlline class ship. The Correllines were known for their sleek design and speedy engines. It was a good bet that was Bridgette's ship, joining the party. The Correllines didn't come from the factory with weapons since they were a civilian model. But if it was Bridgette's ship, she would have remedied that oversight. It would only take a few minutes for her to catch up to us and start dishing out some payback.

"Uh, Miri?"

"What is it?" she asked, her hands covered in thick black drive fuel.

"I hate to rush you—"

"Rence, I'm going as fast as I can!"

I had a few missiles on the *Princess*, but they were forward-facing. I would have to turn the ship around to use them. And with that Corporation cruiser on my tail, that wasn't an option. I had some concussion mines that I could release out the back, but I would have to leave the cockpit to get to them. That also wasn't an option with those blast cannons keeping me on my toes.

"Rence, I think I have the leak plugged. But I don't think it will hold for long."

"That's okay. It only needs to last until we find a place to land."

She shrugged. "Here's hoping."

"Good, now get another rag and clean up as much drive fuel as you can from the inside of that panel."

"Can't we clean up once we get away?"

"Uh, no," I said with wide eyes. "If that drive fuel ignites inside the maintenance panel..."

"...got it."

I veered out of the path of another few large blue blast cannon shots and glanced at my sensor screen. Bridgette was almost in range to shoot. And as sure as shooting, Bridgette would be a good shot. Once she started shooting, we were not going to last long. Maybe I could delay her with some adversarial banter? She seemed to enjoy it back on Ragshir's moon. Though, that was before I grazed her arm. It was worth a try.

I flipped a switch, turning on the communication transmission. I didn't know what channel she would be on, but if she was as good as I thought, she'd be monitoring most of them. "Nice of you to join the party, Bridgette, if that's even your real name."

Her ship entered weapons range.

"I'm betting it isn't. You look more like a Selma or a Naydine."

Her voice finally replied. "None of the above."

"Well, I see you just got close enough to shoot. So, before you end all this, aren't you at least going to tell me your name?"

"No," she said. "You just go on calling me Bridgette. I like the way it sounds when you say it."

"Then, I guess my last words will be to say goodbye."

"Goodbye, Mr. Perry."

"Rence," Miri called out. "That's the best I can do."

I punched some buttons on my console. The engines revved up faster and roared. The acceleration pushed me into my chair. "Goodbye Bridgette," I said with a smile as we pulled away.

She fired off a few shots and I dodged them as we quickly sped out of weapons range. The *Princess* was a Norgon class transport, and I loved Norgons. They were fast and easy to modify. I would have no trouble outrunning Westward Galactic's reach as long as I got her patched up. I turned off the communication transmission and set the *Princess's* course for Jashur VII. I wasn't too excited to return to Jashur, but it was the best place to repair. Once the autopilot was set, I took off my mask and sighed a breath of relief. We were safe now, but I had a strange feeling that I had not seen the last of Bridgette.

I leaned back into my chair to relax but my mind quickly turned to Heinlin. I dashed out the cockpit door and down the corridor to the loading ramp room. Heinlin lay on the floor, unresponsive. Carol and Petre had knelt beside him. Tears ran down Carol's face. Petre's bloody hands attested to his attempts to save Heinlin's life.

"Doc?" I asked.

Petre looked at me and shook his head.

My heart sunk into the pit of my stomach. I removed my hat. "Sorry for your loss, doc. I know he was a friend."

"I only ask, that you do not bury him in space."

"No worries there, doc. I believe every man has the right to rest under solid ground."

Miri walked in behind me and gasped. "Is he...?"

"Unfortunately," I said, answering her unfinished question.

"Rence," she asked. "Can I speak with you?"

I nodded, excusing myself from the room and following Miri into the corridor. She walked a little way down and turned to me. "Rence, I'm worried about Ryna. This has left her a bit shaken up. I've tried to talk to her, but I don't think I have gotten through. If you could talk to her, it might help."

What did I know about children? I was a rough man with an even rougher past. Dealing with feelings and such had always been the domain of mothers. At least that was the way I had always looked at it. But I trusted Miri's instincts. If she felt there was some good to be had by my talking with her, I was surely going to try.

"I'll do what I can, Miri. But I always thought she got on better with you."

"Believe it or not, Rence. But she has latched onto you. You are the closest thing to a father she has ever had."

I looked down. "I suppose she could have done worse in choosing a role model."

Miri kissed my cheek. "Thank you, Rence. She's in my cabin."

I put my hat back on and strolled down the corridor to Miri's cabin. I knocked on the door. "Mind if I come in?"

"Come in," Ryna said timidly.

I walked in and sat beside her on the cot. She held Lady perched on her hand, stroking her feathered head.

"It's been a crazy day, hasn't it?"

She nodded.

"You remember when I said I wanted you to ask me before fiddling with my emotions?"

She stopped stroking Lady's head and stared ahead. "I'm sorry Mr. Rence."

"Oh, no, I'm not angry. I wanted to thank you."

She looked at me with a puzzled expression.

"If you had to wait to ask me before flaring my uneasiness, I never would have picked up on that imposter lady. You saved my life."

Her eyes widened. "I did?"

I nodded. "And that's the second time your gift has saved me. So, thank you again."

She smiled and leaned into my chest. "You're welcome, Mr. Rence."

"I've also had a change of mind. From now on, if you see a need to fiddle with my emotions, you go right ahead."

She straightened up and looked into my eyes. "You mean it?"

"Absolutely. We're in this together, you and me. As far as I'm concerned, we're partners in this."

She beamed and hugged me tightly with her free arm.

Lady squawked.

"I ain't forgettin' you, Lady," I said with a wry smile. "I still owe you a Telurian mouse."

Ryna pulled away to look at me. "Is Mister Heinlin going to be okay?"

A deep breath invaded my lungs and I looked down. "I'm sorry Ryna. He died."

She shed a few tears and buried her face in my shirt. "He was a nice man. And he was going to change me so the doctors couldn't find me anymore."

I pulled her tight against me and rubbed her arm soothingly. "I'm sorry Ryna. I wish things had happened differently. But don't you worry about Westward Galactic finding you. We still have plan B, that Miss Miri thought up. We just need to rustle up some equipment and some money. It'll all be over soon enough."

Ryna again looked into my eyes. “Mr. Rence, when everything is all over, will you still want me?”

I knew what she was asking. She wanted to know just how long our relationship would last. Was it just temporary until all the smoke had cleared or would it last longer? The truth was that I hadn’t given it much thought. I started out on this mission figuring we would deliver Ryna to her parents. And it turned out she didn’t have any real parents. Now it was no longer a question of what *would* happen to her afterward, but what *should* happen?

“Little miss, I don’t leave my partners lest they want me to. So, if you don’t mind me asking, what would you prefer?”

She smiled again. “I would like us to be a real family. I can be the daughter, you can be the Pa, and Miss Miri can be the Ma.”

My cheeks flushed and my heart started thumping. I didn’t just walk into that trap, I practically asked for it. I stood and took Lady, walking to the door. “It’s probably about time you hung up your matchmaker hat for tonight and got yourself some shut-eye.”

“Please, Mr. Rence?”

I took a deep breath. “It ain’t entirely up to me, little miss. But you can bet your britches I’m working on it.”

She returned an excited smile.

EPISODE 9

The Final Showdown
Part 1

THE LAST
WAYFINDER

9

The Final Showdown - Part 1

I had often found some downtime between missions, allowing me to unwind, but not this time. We were on the run from the Westward Galactic Financial Corporation and an assassin. One that was personally sent from Dr. Vik Lenish. I had attempted to teach Dr. Lenish a few manners a while back. But I guess super smart people don't have much room left in their heads for some common wisdom. At any rate, my lesson gave him a chip on his shoulder large enough to land a starcruiser. It didn't entirely fall on deaf ears, though; he was wise enough to keep his hand off Miri.

Hiring an assassin, on the other hand, wasn't the doctor's style. He seemed practical and apathetic, that is, until you got him riled up. Hiring Bridgette to kill me was a sign that Dr. Lenish was taking things rather personally now. With Ryna's help, I had sniffed the assassin out and thwarted her last attempt. What would I ever do without that girl? Her special gift had saved my life twice. It helped me locate Miri on the Corporation lab ship, and even saved her own life when I couldn't draw fast enough.

There was no question that she was special. But she was also special in another way. Her childlike outlook on life had often got me thinking about mine. It hadn't taken me long to realize that I needed her. Maybe even more than I knew.

We had landed on Jashur VII. It was the best place to repair. We had repaired here once before when we first encountered the Kuda. I wasn't too sure about poking my face into town after our last exodus but Miri did have a good point. The only Kuda who could identify me was dead. Miri rented a hovermobile and all five of us crammed in. Petre and Carol took the back seats while Miri drove with Ryna between us.

Our first order of business was to repair the ship. I had ordered the parts and they would be delivered in the afternoon. That gave us time to go to town and see about equipment. We needed some for Miri's plan to work. The idea was to produce a large amount of the chemical marker that allowed the Corporation to track Ryna. We would then inject that marker into every creature that walked. It would give the Corporation years of wild goose chases. With any luck, we would buy enough time for the marker to work its way out of Ryna's blood. Or, at least, diminish enough so she couldn't be tracked.

Petre and Carol needed some equipment to pull that off. I doubted a quaint colony planet like Jashur would carry such expensive hardware. Sure, Jashur carried the lion's share of starship parts, but it didn't have much else to brag of. Still, it was worth a try and something to do while we waited for the new parts to be delivered. Petre and Carol headed off to the local medical clinic. They would inquire where they sourced their devices.

I stood on the boardwalk outside the Raging Comet restaurant and the Blue Bonnet dress shop. Ryna stood at Miri's side. I pulled out some coins from my pocket and counted them.

"Rence, I think I'll head over to the Union Bank," Miri said.

I looked up. "I ain't so sure taking out a loan is a good idea at this point. We have enough worries. I'll find a few jobs and we'll rustle up the cash sure enough."

"Rence, I have some money saved up that we can use."

"That's real kind of you, Miri. But this is going to cost us an awful lot."

"I have nearly thirty-eight thousand saved up."

My eyes widened as I stared at her.

"It's not fair," she continued, "that you should keep footing the bills. I can only imagine what you've already spent on fuel and repairs."

With how frugal she had been in spending money, I assumed she didn't have much. How had she managed to save up so much money? And why hadn't she told me until now? That kind of money could have come in really handy several times. Why had she held out on me?

I felt my heart rate slow down. My breathing relaxed. I glanced at Ryna. She was staring back at me. Why was she calming me? Was she afraid I would lose my temper? That hadn't ever happened. What other reason could she have to calm me? Was there something I was overlooking? Something I was missing? I studied Miri's face. She looked vulnerable, delicate. That's when things started making sense.

Miri hadn't wanted to part with her savings because she really wanted something. Something she had to scrimp and save for. Something so important to her that only now was she willing to give it up for Ryna's sake. My mood melted away and I brushed some of her wind-swept hair out of her face.

"Miri, you have a way with animals."

Tears welled up in her eyes. One broke loose and traced the contours of her face.

"If I had to guess, I'd say you were saving up to buy a ranch."

She nodded, looking down as two more tears lost their way.

"Tell you what," I said. "We'll try my way first. And if that doesn't work out, we'll consider your generous offer."

She wiped away her tear lines and sniffled. "Thank you, Rence." She excused herself and wandered into the restaurant to use the ladies' room.

I tipped my hat to Ryna. "Thanks, partner."

She returned a broad smile.

I knelt on one knee and looked at her. "Listen, little miss. I got a secret mission for you."

She nodded eagerly.

I pulled out some coins and dropped them into her hand. "You remember the last time we went shopping for clothes?"

"When the armored man attacked you?"

I rolled my eyes. "That was the time, all right. But you do remember she liked those dresses, right?"

"Yep. And I still know her size." She turned around and headed into the dress shop.

"Wait–" I hadn't finished giving her my instructions. Maybe it was best she didn't take my advice on which to buy. After all, it was Ryna who had been out shopping with Miri when she purchased her red dress. She would know better than I which one to get.

Miri stepped out of the restaurant door. I panicked. Ryna hadn't yet returned with the dress, and I wanted it to be a surprise. It didn't need to be a surprise. I could have told her I wanted to get her a dress. But somehow it felt like it should be a surprise. For whatever reason, I needed it to be a surprise.

I took Miri's arm and turned her to face the restaurant. "I had a great idea; why don't you go reserve us a table."

A confused expression spread across her face. "I thought we needed to find some work."

"I–well, yes–I just figured...in all our running around, we hadn't had time to sit down and get reacquainted."

She smiled warmly. "That's very thoughtful of you." She looked around. "Where's Ryna?"

"I, uh...she's running a small errand. We'll meet you inside."

For some reason, she looked at me suspiciously. She glanced at the dress shop and then back at me. She gave me an I-know-what-you're-up-to stare before walking back into the restaurant. My lands! I can outwit a Corporate scientist, bluff Tess Davendry, and fool Dentum's security force. But when it came to Miri and Ryna, those two could read me like a book. What was the galaxy coming to?

Ryna emerged from the dress shop as if she had struck gold and wanted everyone to know about it. She held out the dress, all neatly folded up and wrapped in brown paper and strings. She started rambling off every detail about the dress in one long unbroken sentence. She lost me in much of the terminology, so I politely nodded my head.

Once she exhausted her entire vocabulary, I suggested we enter the restaurant. I tucked the package beneath my long coat. We found the table Miri had reserved and sat down beside her. A man dressed in black clothes and a white apron walked up to our table and set down three glasses.

"What'll it be to drink?"

I glanced at Ryna. If Miri was right, and Ryna saw me as a father figure, then I needed to make some adjustments in my life. A man couldn't act himself under those conditions; he had to mind his p's and q's.

"Lemonade," I said.

"Lemonade?" he asked incredulously.

I felt my cheeks heat up and I wanted to crawl under the table and hide. I instead gave him an annoyed smile. "Yeah, it's made with fruit and sugar. Ever heard of it?"

He slowly nodded, looking at me with curious eyes. "Yeah, I heard of it. Just never heard anyone ask for it in these parts."

I didn't bother looking to see Miri's expression. I wasn't sure I wanted to know if she'd be displeased with how I was handling myself. I kept my eyes on the waiter. "Well, now you got somethin' to write home about."

"All right," he said, typing it onto a small datapad. "And for you, miss?"

"We'll all have the same," Miri replied.

The waiter smiled and left.

"So," Miri asked. "What would you like to talk about?"

Ryna piped up. "Miss Miri, Mr. Rence got you a surprise, and I picked it out!"

I pulled the brim of my hat low, hiding the color in my cheeks.

"Why, how lovely," Miri said in a practiced tone.

"It might be more of a surprise, little miss, if she didn't know she was getting it."

"Don't worry, Mr. Rence. She doesn't know what kind of dress it is."

I hung my head. There wasn't much use trying to control what came out of her mouth. The door to the restaurant opened, making the little bell chime. Petre and Carol walked in, scanning the room. I raised my hand and they spotted us.

"Mr. Perry," Petre said, taking a seat across from me. "I believe we are in business."

Carol sat next to him. "We have located some equipment we can use."

I looked up. "Do we have to buy it or can we rent it?"

"Neither," she replied. "I bumped into a former colleague of mine from Gale-tech University. She has set up a medical school in a neighboring town. She was quite shocked to find me on Jashur. She said I could come and use her laboratory equipment whenever I want."

"Splendid. Now we just need the chemical stuff, right?" I asked.

Petre looked down. "That's the not-so-good news."

"What?"

A stout middle-aged woman walked up to the table with a large pitcher. She poured lemonade into the three glasses on the table. Then she looked at me with judging eyes. "Want me to leave the bottle, hon?"

There was an edge of sarcasm in her tone. It wasn't much but it managed to rile me up on the inside. She deliberately referred to the pitcher of lemonade as a bottle. And she said it knowing that any other man would have ordered a drink that came in one.

I gritted my teeth and forced a smile. "Please do."

She set down the pitcher and then looked at Petre and Carol. "What'll the two of you have to drink?"

Petre smiled courteously. "Oh, I'll have whatever they are having—as long as it isn't too strong."

"Hon, you can't get anything milder than that. The next step down is cow's milk."

"Excellent. I'll have a double."

Carol smiled in silent amusement.

The waitress rolled her eyes, setting down two glasses in front of them. She poured their glasses and left as swiftly as she had come.

"You were about to tell me the bad news," I said, re-engaging the conversation.

Petre took a sip of his lemonade. "Ah, a pleasant lemony taste. You chose well, Mr. Perry."

"Focus, doc. What did you find out?"

"Forgive me, Mr. Perry. The only local supplier of kaligeenium-62 ran out last year. We will have to go to Pentarch III to get some."

"Pentarch isn't just a little hop, skip, and a jump away. It's near the core worlds. It could take us weeks to get there. There has to be something closer."

Petre shrugged and glanced at Carol. "Well, there is a Corporation facility just outside of town. We were transported there before we were shuttled to *Labship 7*. Surely, they should have some kaligeenium-62 on-hand for cataloging. But it would not be easy to get."

There was no possible way I could forget about that facility. That was the facility that Miri had infiltrated, dressed up all fancy. It was the facility that hired Kuda. Memories of that day swarmed my head. I remembered racing inside to rescue Miri and finding her curled up in a ball, weeping. I had enough of that facility to last me a lifetime.

I sighed. "It looks like we're goin' to Pentarch." I took a drink of my lemonade. The tangy-sweet sensation trickled down my throat. I licked my lips and stared at the glass. "This *is* good."

Ryna scooted her empty glass into the center of the table. "Can I please have some more?"

Miri poured her another glass.

"Mr. Perry," Carol said. "It would also help if we spent some time analyzing Ryna's blood. Perhaps you could leave us here with a blood sample while you go and get some kaligeenium-62. With any luck, we should have mapped out the frequency by then."

I nodded. "I'm all for using the time effectively, but do you have a place to stay?"

"We can stay at the local hotel for the next couple of weeks," Petre explained. "They're not—"

The front door chimed as an armored Kuda stepped in and walked to the front counter.

"That reminds me," I said, "of how much I love this town. The two of you can stick around, but the rest of us should get back to the *Princess*."

I exited the restaurant and waited for Miri and Ryna who followed behind. I was just starting to get comfortable on Jashur. Why did that Kuda have to walk in? It reminded me of everything about Jashur that I wanted to leave behind. Miri bought some supplies for our trip and even picked up another change of clothes for Ryna. I wasn't sure how she grew out of the last set of clothes so quickly. Miri assured me that was normal for children.

I spent the rest of the afternoon and the first of the early evening repairing the *Princess.* She was finally as good as new. After packing up the *Princess,* I called Lady back and we climbed on board. I sat down in the cockpit and started flipping switches. The twin engines revved up as I started up the rest of the launch sequence. Ryna brought Lady into the cockpit and set her down on her perch.

Lady squawked.

"What are you nervous about?" I asked.

She flapped her wings and squawked again, turning in place.

"With how jittery you are, you'd think we were heading into a mission."

A light blinked on my console, followed by a beep. The proximity sensors had picked up an approaching ship high in the sky. Probably a passing merchant ship, looking for a place to land. Why did I keep my sensor screens so sensitive? On such a busy planet, all these false alarms tended to make a man lax. I engaged the ascent thrusters and the *Princess* shuddered as she rose into the air.

Bright green bolts of energy streaked past the blast shield window. The *Princess* rumbled and lurched off to one side as a blast cannon bolt struck the hull. That passing ship was shooting at us. The damage alarm sounded, and I silenced it with the press of a button. I fired up the main engines and we barreled forward. Another cannon bolt struck the starboard engine. Fire danced around it despite the windy breeze of our forward momentum. Sparks blew from a panel over my head. I flinched but kept my hand clenched on the flight controls.

I bit my tongue, not wanting to curse in front of Ryna.

"Mr. Rence, I think you should put your buckle on!" Ryna declared over the sound of the waning starboard engine.

She had a point. The last time we crash landed, my body rearranged the front control panel. But her suggestion meant she was convinced we were going to crash. Well, I wasn't convinced. I may have lost an engine, but I still had altitude. I only needed to get high enough to leave orbit.

Miri raced into the cockpit. "Rence, what's going on?"

"Pretty sure somebody is shooting at us."

Another blast cannon shot struck the hull. The *Princess* rumbled and Miri was thrown backward into a chair. I clung to the steering controls. "Now I'm *confident* somebody is shooting at us."

"Rence, I think you should strap in!"

"We ain't gonna crash!" I said, flipping switches on my control panel. I diverted auxiliary power to the port engine. The *Princess* was nimble in space but she had a rough time taking off and landing. Whoever was shooting, knew when to hit us. We gradually climbed above the clouds, watching the sky grow ever closer. Then, another blast cannon shot struck the port engine. It shattered into flaming pieces, spraying large debris across the horizon.

Our altitude tapered off and for a brief moment, we were suspended in the air. Then the *Princess* plummeted toward the ground. I reached over and pulled my safety strap across my chest and snapped it into the buckle. I flipped switches on my control panel to reroute power around the damaged systems.

We passed through the clouds and rapidly approached the ground. The tiny terrain features grew large and distinctive at an alarming rate. I forced myself to take a deep breath to calm my nerves. It didn't help much. Every nerve in my body was bracing for massive pain. I closed my eyes momentarily and breathed out slowly. Then I continued rerouting power. The fastest way would have been to climb down to the engine room and stretch a cable. But we were falling too fast for me to climb down there, patch in, and then climb back up to the cockpit to steer. I had to do things the slow way.

A spark popped from my console. The lights on my control panel died. My entire panel had just shorted out. It looked like I couldn't do it the slow way either. At the rate we were falling, we would not survive. I needed another option. I unbuckled and put Lady into a small cage. She didn't like the crash cage, but it would save her life against the impact.

"Miri, stay strapped in but turn around to the backup control panel."

She swiveled her chair around.

"When I tell you to, flip the yellow switch labeled Ascent Thrusters."

"I don't know how to fly!"

"She ain't gonna fly anymore. Now it's all a matter of how gracefully we can fall."

She nodded, putting a headset on.

I dashed down the corridor and stumbled down the stairwell to the engine room. I ripped open the auxiliary guidance panel and pulled out one of the long cables. I yanked open the panel to the secondary thruster control and plugged in one end. I stretched the cable to the auxiliary power generator and plugged it in. As long as the cable held, the thrusters had power.

I put my tactical mask on. "Miri, hit the thrusters!"

The ascent thrusters fired, slowing the *Princess's* fall. The slight jolt from the thrusters knocked the cable loose. The thrusters died out and we started falling faster. I snatched the cable and jammed it back into the thruster control port. The thrusters again fired, slowing our descent. I kept my hands on the cable until we struck the ground. I was thrown against the back wall and I blacked out.

I awoke to Miri calling my name. I was ever so tired. I didn't want to open my eyes. I felt comfortable...or did I? No, my head was hurting and my leg felt twisted. But the pain felt dull somehow. The urge to sleep was stronger than the pain. And I was so weary.

"Mr. Rence?" Ryna's distant voice called to me. I wanted to answer, but I just needed some rest first.

I heard Miri's muffled, distant voice again. "Ryna, I need you to wake him up!"

There was more conversation, but I couldn't hear it. My muscles relaxed as I started to drift to sleep. The weariness ever pressing on me. Then all my muscles fiercely tensed up. My heart raced and my blood pumped. Where were Miri and Ryna? Were they okay? What if they were injured? They could be pinned under some fallen debris. They could be bleeding...dying.

My eyes shot open and I forced in a large breath. I scrambled to get to my feet but Miri held me down. Why was she holding me down? I needed to get up.

"Miri!" I shouted.

"Okay, Ryna. That's enough," she replied.

I again thrashed my arms around, trying to get up.

"Rence," Miri said. "It's okay. I'm here. I'm safe."

My mind held onto her voice. Her melodic voice. Something was soothing in her words...or was it something else? My body was relaxing and my breathing slowed. Once my breathing was under control, my mind cleared up. I was able to think reasonably again. My mask was lying on the floor at my side. Miri was crouched over me with my chest panel open. I glanced at Ryna. She intensely stared at me.

"You were helping me by fiddling with my emotions?"

She nodded.

"Thank you, little miss."

"You're welcome, partner," she replied.

I winked at her. "Partner."

Miri dropped a tool into my tool chest and closed up my chest panel. She had once again patched me up and Ryna had kept me from slipping away. Miri helped me sit up and a tear lost its way and ran down my cheek. What had come over me? I lost a few more tears. For whatever reason, I was really lucky to have both of them with me. Somehow, it meant more to me than anything I owned.

Miri hugged me, mingling her tears with mine.

I reached over and pulled Ryna in, making it a group hug.

After a short while, Miri helped me to my feet. My head ached, and again, I was mighty glad my skull was coated in durotanium. A normal head might have split open from an impact like that. But as before, it still didn't prevent the colossal headache.

I held my head. "How long was I out?"

"Just a few minutes, but it seemed like a long time."

"Whoever shot us down will be looking for the crash site. They'll most likely want to verify we're dead."

Miri mumbled a curse under her breath.

I bent down to retrieve my mask and my head suddenly started pounding as the blood ran to it. I quickly straightened up. "Ryna, would you fetch me my mask, please?"

She handed me the mask and I put it away.

Then she handed me my hat.

"Much obliged, little miss."

Miri helped me up the stairwell. The *Astral Princess* was level when she crashed. That might have been counted as a miracle in its own right. I stopped at my cabin and retrieved the small blast pistol Mik engineered. It was a beautiful gun holstered in a rough leather blast belt. Then we continued to the cockpit. I looked out the blast shield window. We had crashed into a thicket of tall forest trees. Great red dallifer trees, if I wasn't mistaken.

"We're in the middle of a bunch of trees," I explained. "That means there is no suitable place to land nearby. Whoever shot us down will have to land some ways away and hike in. That'll give us some time to gather together some supplies and head out."

"Where will we go?" Miri asked with concern in her voice.

I took Lady out of the crash cage and set her on her perch. She squawked but was unharmed.

I shrugged. "That all depends on where we are."

I picked up my two spare blast pistol power cells from their chargers.

I turned around. "Ryna, go fetch my blast carbine from the loading room."

She spun around and quickly left.

Miri saw the concern in my eyes. "Rence, what else is wrong?"

I sighed. "Without the *Princess*, we can't stay ahead of Westward Galactic. They'll be here soon enough. That means we're gonna have a fight on our hands and no way of retreating."

"How long will we last?"

I stared off into space, sorting out things in my head. "Probably ten hours, give or take."

"And then they'll capture us?"

I swallowed hard. "Well, they'll capture Ryna. They're definitely not going to give *me* another chance."

Her breathing nearly stopped. "Rence," she said in a panic. "We need to call for help."

"The closest help is Mik back on Cosstere," I said. "And with the *Princess* running on battery power, we can't send a transmission."

"We have to try something," she urged.

"We can send a hyperwave broadcast. There won't be any guarantee who will see it. But it's something."

"Something is better than nothing," she decided.

I flipped on the old hyperwave broadcaster and picked up a datapad. I typed out a simple message. I included the planetary coordinates along with an approximation of where we crashed. It wasn't much but it should allow a smart person to figure out where we were.

Miri picked up the small data storage device from the machining table. It was the one I used to download the Osurious project files. "Can you send this too?"

"You think it'll help?"

She shook her head. "I don't know, Rence. But it's the only leverage we have on Westward Galactic."

I took it and plugged it in. Then I hit the transmit button. It beeped as it encoded the message into the rudimentary hyperwave signals. It would take a few minutes to complete. And there was no guarantee of anyone answering either.

"Do you think Mik will get the message?" she asked.

"Well, if he doesn't..." *I won't have to worry if I bought the correct dress size.*

Silence loomed a moment. I held out Mik's blast pistol to Miri. "Probably no better time than now to start using it."

She glanced at my offering and then looked into my eyes. "I thought you were going to give me a choice."

True, I had offered her a dress or the gun. It was the only way I could think of to ask her what kind of life she wanted. Why couldn't I just ask the question like a normal person? Why did I get all gummed up in the mouth trying to talk to Miri about the two of us? What was it about my feelings that felt like an oil-starved engine coughing up rusty dust?

"I'm sorry about that," I said. "I guess I wanted to know what kind of future you wanted. If it was a future that I could provide you." I looked down. "But you were right, it is a conversation for after this is all over."

"Well, in case we don't get out of this," she said. "I would rather not miss my chance at choosing."

I pulled out the neatly packaged dress from my large inner coat pocket. I held it in my right hand with the blast pistol in my left. "Miri, at this point, I don't rightly care what danger comes. All I want is to have you by my side. And if you'll have me, I will be happy in whatever life you choose."

Her eyes watered and she gave a sly smile. "What if I want a camcam ranch on Cosstere?"

That thought hadn't occurred to me. But I had to admit that those smelly lumbering lizards did remind me an awful lot of Miri. When she was taken by the Corporation, just the sight of a camcam turned my thoughts to her. I had sworn off Cosstere and camcams, yet my desire to be with Miri threatened to make a steady diet of my own words.

"Miri, if you want to ranch camcams, I'll be wrangling them right beside you."

She smiled, letting tears caress her face. She leaned up to me and closed her eyes. I kissed her a long moment before reopening my eyes. She sniffled, spending a moment to catch her breath. Then she recomposed herself and glanced at both of my hands. She took the dress *and* the blast pistol.

She retreated down the corridor, passing Ryna who reentered the cockpit. She handed me the rifle and glanced back at the doorway Miri disappeared through. Then she looked at me with a confused expression. "She's happy, but she looks sad."

"Tears don't always mean sadness, little miss. Sometimes they make up for the words we don't have."

"Oh...what did her tears say?"

I turned my head before my cheeks could betray me. Ryna would figure me out anyhow, so I didn't feel bad changing the subject. I picked up Lady from her perch and handed her to Ryna. Lady hopped over to Ryna's hand. "We need to get moving mighty fast. Will you tend to Lady while I rustle up some supplies to take with us?"

"Sure thing, Mr. Rence."

I scrounged up two satchels, both in need of some mending but usable for our needs. I took them to the lower deck and stuffed them with food packets and water cans. I debated taking my toolbox. They were useful but would slow us down. I took a few choice tools from it and left the rest. I took the mess kit and the electric lighter. It didn't seem like this day would last long enough to warrant starting a fire. But my instincts told me to bring them anyhow.

Satisfied with my haul, I headed back up to the top deck to check on Miri. We only had a matter of minutes to leave the *Princess* if we wanted to stay ahead of danger. Our crash site would not be hard to find. As I walked down the corridor, Miri stepped out of her cabin. She wore her new dress. The snowy-white gown hung well and the many frilly layers swayed when she moved. My breathing stopped and my heart raced. That wasn't what I had in mind when I asked Ryna to buy a dress. That was more than just a dress, that was a statement. But what did I expect? I sent a matchmaker to buy a dress. My cheeks burned and I didn't even have the presence of mind to lower the brim of my hat to hide it. What was next on Ryna's list? A Parson?

She glanced at me and blushed. "I'm flattered...I guess I just didn't expect it would be so soon." She walked up to me, the bright white dress swaying with each step. "Yes," she said, caressing my cheek with her hand. "Yes," she repeated as she leaned up and kissed me.

I dropped the satchels.

I gently touched the soft fabric of her dress. "Not the most efficient for hiking through the forest, but you sure are a lovely sight."

She glanced at the floor. "Well...I didn't know when else I would get a chance to wear it."

I smiled. "You make me feel like I should get a shave and a haircut. Or at least be wearing a necktie or something."

She giggled and spoke in a playful tone. "Well, well, does this mean the handsome Mr. Perry is asking me out on a date?"

I smiled and matched her tone, offering her my arm. "Would you care for a brisk walk in the woods?"

She laughed and took my arm. "While dodging blast shots?"

I chuckled.

The lights dimmed and were replaced by red emergency lights. The last of the battery power had been spent. Now we were on emergency power.

"Time to go," I said, swinging both satchels over my shoulder. "We have ten minutes to open the outer door before we're all out of power."

"Did we ever get a response to our call for help?"

I shook my head. "No—"

I turned my head and angled my ear toward the cockpit. A series of beeps faintly echoed down the corridor. I raced into the cockpit. The hyperwave transmitter was receiving an incoming message. I picked up the datapad and started typing out the translation of the simple beeps.

Miri caught up to me. "What does it say?"

I shushed her with a raised finger. I needed to concentrate. The old hyperwave code was not something anybody regularly practiced. With live transmissions, most folks figured hyperwave was a thing of the past. Thankfully, somebody out there still knew the cipher.

I set the datapad down. "It reads: TRANSMISSION RECEIVED. HOLD OUT UNTIL ARRIVAL. ETA TWELVE HOURS."

"Does it say who it's from?"

"No, the message simply repeats."

I stuffed the datapad in my inside coat pocket. "Time to head out."

We descended the stairwell and entered the loading room where Ryna was waiting for us. I pushed the button on the wall and the loading ramp slowly lowered to the ground. It stopped short since the crash buried the base of the ship two feet in the dirt. We left the ship and Ryna tossed Lady into the air. She soared high and out of sight.

Miri strapped on her blast belt over her dress. The rough leather clashed with the fancy dress, but it would be practical enough for her to draw. I clamped on my tactical mask and picked a random direction. Until we got some aerial footage from Lady it wouldn't matter which direction we headed. We just needed to get some distance between us and the crash.

After a few minutes of walking, the light on my wristband flashed. Lady had found something. I pressed a few buttons, switching my vision to Lady's eyesight. Lady circled the crash site. A woman stepped into the clearing the *Princess* had carved into the landscape. She was dressed in a white blast vest and dark clothes. It was Bridgette. She carried a blast rifle in her hands and a blast pistol at her hip. Her tall burgundy boots carefully stepped over fallen branches. Her quiet approach meant she thought we were still on board.

I switched my eyesight back to normal. "It's Bridgette. It won't take her long to figure out we've moved on."

"Then we had better get as much distance as we can right now," Miri said, putting one of the satchels over her shoulder.

I picked up the second satchel and put my blast carbine over my shoulder. I pointed off into the distance. "Let's head for that ridge. It's the tallest point I can see and it looks defensible."

We hiked toward the ridge for a good half hour before Ryna needed a rest. I insisted we all drink some water. It kept us hydrated and lightened Miri's satchel a bit. We continued for another hour before the light on my wristband flashed again. I pressed a few buttons, switching my eyesight to Lady's vision. She was perched atop a tall red dallifer tree. Two assault shuttles streaked across the horizon. One hovered over our crash site, lowering ropes. Soldiers in blast vests slid down the ropes and swarmed the crash site. The second shuttle flew past Lady. I switched my eyesight back to normal when I heard the roaring of the distant engine. The shuttle flew overhead and over to the high ridge. Troops slid down ropes onto the top of the ridge.

"How did they know?" Miri asked in disbelief.

I sighed in exasperation. "They didn't. They just picked the tallest point so they could scout around."

"So now where do we go?"

"Well—" I spun around, hearing the snapping of a stick in the distance. Bridgette was gaining on us. She didn't have a ten-year-old girl slowing her down. She would soon overtake us.

"East," I finally said. It was the only direction that would take us directly away from the crash site and the ridge. Miri started walking but I held up my hand. "Wait."

She stopped and looked at me.

"That's the most logical place we would go. They'll be counting on it. We need to go someplace unexpected."

"The ridge?" Miri suggested.

"They have troops there," I said. "We would have to fight them."

"You said yourself, it's the most defensible position. If we can get there, we can hold out longer."

She was right. Heading for the ridge meant we would have to tangle with a few soldiers, but that was better than being driven into a trap. And, as she pointed out, we could defend ourselves better there. But then again, the ridge's defensible position would also be common knowledge.

Common enough that they could anticipate us heading there. I shook my head, clearing my thoughts. No use overthinking it.

"All right," I said. "To the ridge. Follow behind me and keep your head low." I stopped. "But first..." I pulled out one of my detonators and set it to proximity detonation. I placed it in some tall grass along our trail. A little surprise for Bridgette if she didn't pay enough attention.

We hiked up toward the ridge, keeping to the tree line and the shrubbery. I pressed a few buttons on my wristband and switched my vision to infrared. The body heat signatures up ahead gave me a good sense of their distance and where they were facing. We crept closer until they were all within rifle range. I switched one of my eyes to normal vision and zoomed in. I centered the scope of my carbine on one of the troops. He wore a blast vest and helmet, which made blast pistols less effective. But my blast carbine packed a wallop. I even proved it could crack Kuda armor.

I aimed for the center of mass and squeezed the trigger. My carbine barked like a mad dog, echoing through the trees. The soldier dropped his blast rifle and collapsed to the ground. The remaining five troops scattered behind tree trunks. I waited for them to peek around the trees. Curiosity would get the better of them eventually and they would want to scope me out.

My chance came quickly. One of the soldiers poked his head around the tree trunk and I fired. My red blast bolt struck him in the helmet. The helmet cracked and he fell backward. The blow knocked him unconscious.

I turned to Miri. "Time to move."

"Aren't you going to shoot some more?"

I shook my head. "Never take more than two shots from any location. Otherwise, they'll get a fix on our position."

We hiked around the left side, keeping to the denser part of the trees and foliage. Once we were a good distance from our last position, I aimed my carbine again. A green blast bolt flew through the trees behind me and stuck a tree inches from my head.

I ducked, cursing. That shot most likely came from Bridgette. The delay I took shooting some of the troops and her speed in tracking us allowed her to catch up. She was in rifle range. I scanned the scene with my infrared vision and picked out the red and white glow of her body heat signature. She was securely behind several large trees. She was very cautious aiming. I needed to get her off her rhythm; shake things up a bit. I aimed my carbine and squeezed off several shots in quick succession.

It wasn't enough to hit Bridgette, but it would tell her that her position was compromised. She would have to cautiously reposition herself. And, hopefully, that would buy us enough time to take out the rest of those soldiers on the ridge.

"I thought you said no more than two shots?" Miri said.

"Yeah, well—"

Several green rifle bolts sprayed through the trees and shrubs. The troops had zeroed in on our position. I had been too careless in trying to unnerve Bridgette. Miri and Ryna ducked behind a wide tree trunk. We were going to be pinned down really quick if I didn't do something fast. I needed to keep Bridgette at bay and also eliminate those troops on the ridge. I couldn't do both, which is why I was glad I had backup. I handed the blast carbine to Miri.

"Keep Bridgette at bay," I instructed. "And if you can, try to drive her close to that little patch of grass."

"What are you going to do?"

"Those troops on the ridge have invited me to dance," I explained, switching my vision back to normal. "So, I'm gonna go tango."

I ran a short distance toward the ridge and jumped. I soared through the treetops, skimming the canopy leaves. I landed in the center of the four soldiers. They swung their rifle barrels toward me. Thunder and Lightning each cleared leather and spit out red blast bolts. My shots nailed them square in the chest. Shooting them in the chest was not effective; their blast vests protected them. But my aim was muscle memory, so I didn't have much choice.

Two of the soldiers dropped their guns and stumbled backward. The third fell flat on his back, hitting the back of his head. His helmet covered most of his head, but he looked to have hit it in just the wrong way, knocking himself out. The fourth soldier managed to drop to one knee and keep his balance. He stood and swung the butt of his rifle at me like a club. It struck me on the side of the head. I dropped to my hands and knees, my guns falling to the ground amidst fallen leaves and blades of grass. My ear throbbed and rang. He swung again and I grabbed the butt of the rifle. I reached up and pulled the trigger. The shot threw the soldier to his back.

The first two scrambled to their feet and rushed me. One grabbed the rifle while the other one punched me in the gut. I let go of the rifle in exchange for clutching my stomach. They may not shoot so well but they sure could throw a punch. The blow winded me and I had to gasp for breath. The soldier with the rifle pointed the barrel at me. I grabbed the foot of the fellow in front of me and pulled it out from under him. He flailed as he fell, knocking down the barrel of the blast rifle. It fired and blew a puff of dirt into the air.

I scrambled to my feet and threw a punch at the man with the rifle. I cracked the glass on his helmet visor. The sting of the blow throbbed up my arm. That probably wasn't the smartest move. It practically made my hand useless for a few minutes. At least he dropped the rifle. The second soldier climbed back to his feet.

I had the choice to go for the dropped rifle or to slug the soldier. My aching hand preferred the milder of the two options. The only downside was that he might wrestle it away from me again. Could I use that to my advantage? I dropped to the ground and grabbed the rifle with one hand. My other hand pulled out a detonator from my pocket. The second soldier grabbed the rifle in my hand. We each tugged at it like two dogs fighting over a scrap of meat. The first soldier pulled off his helmet with the cracked visor so he could see straight.

The soldier wrestling with me for the rifle yanked hard and pulled me toward him. I pressed the detonator onto the gunstock and then let go. He stumbled backward with the rifle in hand. I had nine seconds to get a little distance. I ran past them, further up the ridge. One soldier ran after me while the one with the rifle took aim. The rifle exploded, ending the man who held it and knocking down the man behind me.

I skidded to a stop and glanced back to see if the soldier closest to me was out cold or still moving. Instead, a distant explosion caught my attention. Miri must have lured Bridgette over to my hidden detonator. A part of me hoped that would be the end of Bridgette, but my skeptical side wasn't ready to rule her out. She was a careful and deadly one. I wouldn't rule her out of the fight without visually seeing it for myself.

I glanced back at the soldier in front of me. He was out cold. It was time to get back to Miri. I switched my vision back to infrared and quickly spotted Miri and Ryna. I crept back toward them, not wanting to startle Miri into shooting me. When I was close, I softly spoke to her. "Miri, the ridge is clear, let's go."

Miri and Ryna skirted around the wide tree trunk and jogged up behind me. I scanned the distant scene looking for Bridgette's heat signature. I didn't see her. Even if she were killed, there'd still be residual body heat. She was hiding behind something that was either cold or very dense, masking her body heat. She probably caught on that I was using infrared. I didn't much like the idea of not knowing where she was. Especially when she was hunting us.

I led Miri and Ryna up to the top of the ridge. I retrieved my twin blast pistols from where they had fallen, and quickly checked their alignment. They were slightly off but not enough to worry about. I had Miri keep watch while I tied up the two surviving soldiers. No telling when they would come to. The sun was starting to wane on the far end of the sky. The evening was approaching.

I scoped out a few places to hide that we could still shoot back. The troops that scouted out the *Princess* would have heard the commotion and be heading up the ridge too. I pressed a button on my wristband, summoning Lady. I would need her to keep an eye on what was going on.

With no sign of Bridgette and the ridge secured, my second order of business was to find someplace to light a fire without being seen. The glow of a fire would too easily give away our position. I needed some way to obscure it from sight. It didn't need to be very big, just enough to keep Ryna and Miri warm through the night. In all my preparations, I had neglected to bring blankets. Somehow, I figured this whole thing would have been over hours ago. I sifted through my satchel and found the shovel–well, more like a folding trowel rather than a shovel. I set to work digging a hole. It needed to be deep enough that the fire's glow would be contained.

"Rence!" Miri said in a loud whisper.

I jogged over to her.

She pointed in the distance.

Several figures were lurking about in the shadows of the trees. The early evening light already obscured their movement. I switched my eyesight back to infrared. Six troops were cautiously making their way up the hill. Their movements were coordinated. They had finished scouting the *Princess* and followed our trail, staying in formation. We only needed to hold them off until nightfall. Night fighting was impractical for the attacker. Night vision equipment made short work of the cover of darkness. But the bright flashes of the blast bolts were enough to blind anyone using night vision.

Night time would protect us from a shootout but it would not protect us from a stealthy assassin. Bridgette would still be a concern. I took the carbine and aimed at the closest soldier. I squeezed off a shot. The carbine's bark echoed in the quiet woods. The red blast bolt illuminated brightly in the dimming daylight. It flew through the air and struck the soldier square in the chest. The force of the impact threw him backward and onto the ground. His blast vest smoked with a hole.

The remaining five soldiers scattered for cover. I wasn't concerned about shooting them, I only needed to hold them off until dark. But if one of them gave me a good shot, I would take it. The fewer of them there were, the better our chances of survival. Lady swooped down and landed on a low tree branch.

"Welcome back, girl," I said.

I handed Miri back the carbine. "That should keep them at bay for a while. If they try to advance, give them another shot."

"Rence, it's getting too dark."

I pulled off my tactical mask. "Here, you'll need this." I fastened it on Miri. She looked odd and a little eerie with it on. "Is that how I look?"

Her giggle was muffled from within the mask.

She pointed the barrel of the carbine downrange and watched the soldiers. I returned to building a fire. Once I had dug out the hole large enough, I stuffed it with some dry sticks and bark. Ryna found her way to my side and helped pack the pit with sticks.

"Are we going to sleep outside?" she asked, excitement brewing beneath her words.

"I reckon so, little miss. I hadn't planned on it, but we need to hold out for another eight and a half hours."

"What happens then?"

"Then we get some help."

"From who?"

I sighed and stopped what I was doing. "I hope from Mr. Ag'nar. He's the nice man who helped me find you and Miss Miri."

"What if he doesn't come?"

Then you alone will survive only to be dissected later, I thought. Ryna picked up on my hesitation and ventured a guess.

"They'll take me away again, won't they?"

I set down the sticks in my hand and pulled Ryna into a hug. "That is what they want. But I won't let that happen."

She was silent a moment. "What if they kill you?"

I looked into her eyes. They were delicate and moist. She was trying to fathom what could happen. And her realization was more sobering to me than to her. I didn't often think about my death. When it happened, I had always figured I wouldn't be around to care. Only now there was someone else who would care if I lived or died. If I counted Miri, there were now two.

I took a deep breath. "If they can pull that off, I will return as a specter and haunt them every moment of every day."

She didn't look comforted at all.

I brushed the side of her hair with my hand. "Don't fret, little miss. With you as my partner, we'll get through this. You just wait and see."

She hugged me and then wandered over to Miri's side. I wasn't sure if I gave her any measure of comfort. I certainly didn't give her any inspiration. Nothing about our current situation could be inspiring. Still, though, it got me thinking about my eventual death. I didn't rightly know if there was an afterlife. But if there was, I was as sure as shooting going to haunt Dr. Lenish.

I pulled out an electric lighter and started the fire. I had to lean down into the pit to light it. The smoke would not be visible at night and the glow of the fire should be contained. We had some heat. I sat back, admiring my work, and noticed the faint chirping of insects. The sun had dipped below the horizon and all the ambient light was departing. Night's dark veil had descended.

The loud shout from my carbine rang through the night air. I dashed over to Miri as she fired another shot. The troops were making a night raid, despite the darkness. They knew our blast bolts would give away our position. It was a clever tactic. But even with knowing our location, they would be hard pressed to fight an uphill battle in the dark. That didn't seem to stop them from trying. A retaliatory green blast bolt flew through the air and struck a nearby rock. Miri fired again, dropping a second man. Two more green bolts struck the rock nearby. Miri flinched and fired again. The four remaining soldiers once again scattered behind cover.

"Nice shootin'," I said.

"It helps when I can see them. Thanks for the mask."

"Mighty welcome. I'll sleep first, they'll most likely come in the early morning. Wake me up in five hours."

She sighed. "If I can stay awake that long."

I knelt on one knee in front of Ryna. "Little miss, I have a job for you."

Her eyes lit up. "A job?"

I nodded. "Yes, I need you to do two things. First, I need you to swell up Miss Miri's feelings of danger to help her stay awake and alert."

Miri glanced back at me before returning her eyes forward.

"Second, I need you to do the same with me when it's my turn to stand watch. If I wake you up, will you be able to do that?"

"I think so," she replied.

Ryna hit Miri with a blast of anxiety and then I ushered her over to the fire to keep warm. I lay down beside Ryna and kept one hand on a blast pistol. I wanted to protect Ryna, but the truth was that I didn't know just how I could do it. We had limited ammunition and nowhere to go. Westward Galactic was sending in more armored troops. And Dr. Lenish's assassin was still unaccounted for. Besides, the cover of night was only temporary. When the morning light came, so would another batch of troops.

A small light in the night sky drifted across the horizon and then descended to the ground, far away. Most likely a resupply shuttle carrying supplies the troops needed for the night as well as a fresh group of men. Today's conflict would be mild compared to what the morning would hold. Ryna's question was also resting heavily on my mind. What if help didn't arrive? Or what if we couldn't hold out long enough?

I knew that I would do everything within my power to protect her. I could only hope that it would be enough. And I had to hope—I had to trust—that help was on the way.

To be continued...

EPISODE 10

The Final Showdown
Part 2

THE LAST
WAYFINDER

THE FINAL SHOWDOWN – PART 2

I awoke with a start, hearing Miri's approaching footsteps. The night sky was still dark but it hinted at the approaching morning. The black sky was not black anymore. It was instead a dark blue. I stood and offered my spot to Miri with a gesture of my hand. She handed me my mask and blast carbine before settling down for some sleep.

I fastened on my mask and checked the energy level in the blast carbine's power cell. It wasn't good. It was more than 75% spent. I counted the notches along the power cell's energy meter. I had 13 shots remaining. After that, we would be down to blast pistols. And blast pistols were not very effective against the blast vests that the troops wore. The impending morning would make short work of us. What if I had been wrong? What if we should have spent the night running?

I shook my head. Second-guessing the past was pointless. For better or worse, I had committed us to holding the ridge. I quickly made my way over to the rock Miri had used to watch the enemy troops. My mask's vision was still set to infrared, and I could see the horizontal bodies of the sleeping troops. All except for the soldier on watch. The entire battle was on hold, like a recording that had been paused. The impracticality of nighttime combat provided the only respite we would have. And with the coming of dawn, came the full fury of the Westward Galactic Financial Corporation.

There was no way to hold them off for the long term. Their vast resources allotted them many legal and illegal means to get what they wanted. And in the outskirts of civilization that amounted to guns. The colonial marshals were spread thin across the colony worlds. So, the only law that was respected came out of the barrel of a gun.

Our only hope of survival was in getting help. Miri had requested that I send a hyperwave broadcast. Hyperwave was an outdated form of communication. It broadcasted a sequence of beeps that could be deciphered into a message. There were just two problems with it. Few people remembered the cipher these days and you could not guarantee who would hear the message.

But despite those deficiencies, someone had responded. Someone was coming and we needed to hold out long enough. I hoped it was Mik Ag'nar. Mik had proved an invaluable ally. At first, he was only paying back a favor I had come to collect. But now he had exceeded that initial favor. As I saw it, I now owed him. And if Mik was coming to help, I owed him big time. His Kuda friend, Anruk, would bring his squad with him. The Kuda, I had learned, lived for the battle.

But that was only if Mik was the one who had received my message. What if it was intercepted by a Westward Galactic ship? Well, aside from not getting any help, we wouldn't be any worse off than we already were. Things couldn't get much worse. I glanced at the battery meter for my tactical mask and then decided that things actually could.

The night sky kept getting brighter, turning the dark sky bluer and bluer. The distant landscape became more visible as the blanket of night lifted. Lady squawked and fluttered her wings in a tree behind me. I turned to her.

"You're up a little early. You must have the jitters too." I held out my arm and she hopped on. "How about a little early morning recon?"

Lady squawked, flapping her wings a few times.

I tossed her into the air and she soared out of sight.

I turned my attention back to the soldiers at the base of the ridge. They were stirring now. The early morning air beckoned me with its crisp cool touch. The smell of tree sap and limestone swirled in the morning air. I switched my vision back to normal as the first beam of sunlight peaked over the horizon.

At the bottom of the hill, twelve more soldiers emerged from the thicket of trees. They joined the four who had camped overnight. They organized into two ranks of eight men armed with blast rifles. They were preparing to charge up the hill. I searched my pocket for detonators and counted seven. I pulled one out and set it on the boulder in front of me for easy access.

I aimed my blast carbine at the troops. A part of me wanted to shoot one of them now to discourage their charge up the hill. But something didn't quite feel right about that. Sure, they were trying to kill us, but somehow, I needed to give them the chance to chicken out. I would wait until they started their charge before shooting any of them. I instead pulled out one of my blast pistols and fired a wild shot into the trees over their heads. If I was going to give them a chance to chicken out, I might as well remind them that they ought to. The men flinched and scattered for cover, firing a few green blast bolts in my direction. I holstered my blast pistol. It would have been easier to shoot the carbine as a warning shot. But with only thirteen shots remaining, I didn't want to waste any.

Miri awoke with a start at the sound of my shot. She woke Ryna and they joined me at the boulder overlooking the hill.

"Sorry to wake you," I said.

Miri shrugged. "Better to wake up at your shot than theirs." She brushed off some dried leaves and twigs from her white gown. She stopped abruptly and looked at me. "You probably shouldn't be watching *me.*"

I returned my focus to the troops at the bottom of the hill. "Sorry," I explained. "I figured it would be a real shame not to admire the scenery."

"Oh, now I'm scenery, am I?" she asked playfully.

I nodded. "The most exotic in these parts."

Ryna giggled from behind.

I winked at Ryna and then looked back at the troops. Here they came. The troops charged up the hill, sending a hailstorm of green blast bolts at me. I ducked behind the boulder, snatching the detonator I had set on top, and tossed it. The explosion sent two men heavenward several feet before dropping them. The transparent visor on the helmets of the rest of the troops kept the explosion's debris out of their eyes. They pressed on, shooting their way up the hill.

"Rence!" Miri shouted, pointing to the boulder I was using for cover. "Use that!"

I dropped to the ground, lying on my back, and pressed my feet against the boulder. Even with my enhanced knees, the boulder was heavy. It was like trying to coax a post out of concrete. The boulder shifted in the soil it had rested in for so long. With an extra push of exertion, I nudged the boulder a little closer to its tipping point. Miri ran over and threw her shoulder against the mighty rock, and it finally relented. Gravity pulled the boulder over the ledge and it crashed down upon the rocky surface of the hill. It splintered into three pieces and at least a dozen smaller rocks. The rocks tumbled down the hill, plowing through the men.

I drew Thunder and Lightning, squeezing off a few shots to add to the chaos. Miri drew her new blast pistol and fired off a few well-placed shots of her own. She took her time aiming and placed her shots well. Her light-blue blast bolts knocked down every man who evaded the tumbling rocks. Her draw still needed some practice, but her aim was good.

"Nice shooting," I said, smiling at her.

"Why thank you," she said, playfully.

The troops scampered back down the hill and took cover behind the trees once again. Their numbers had thinned to seven. Seven that could still walk, that is. I pulled Miri down into a crouch. With the absence of the boulder to hide behind, we needed to keep low. She holstered her blast pistol and picked up my carbine.

"Make each shot count," I cautioned. "She's only got a baker's dozen left."

She nodded. "What are you going to do?"

"I'm gonna check around back. Make sure they're not tryin' to flank us."

"Flank us?" she asked.

"I'm gonna make sure they don't try to get around to our rear."

I circled around the top of the ridge, inspecting the shear drop-off as well as the traversable sides. I wouldn't put it past Westward Galactic to try a sneak attack up the steep rockface. I didn't see any signs of troop movement. That meant they were concentrating all their forces on advancing up the hill. Militarily, that didn't make much sense. We had made it clear by now that we could hold the ridge. Finding an alternative method of attack was the most logical course of action. Why then would they be continuing a futile attempt?

Well, even though they did have access to weapons and men, these troops didn't have military training. That training was restricted to the military. These were hired guns. Mercenary-trained personal soldiers. That could explain their poor tactics, but I wasn't going to put money on that idea. Westward Galactic employed a lot of intelligent men. Even Dr. Lenish, inhumane as he was, was quite smart. The more reasonable explanation was that they wanted to keep our attention on the hill. So, I searched around a second time, looking for any signs of troop movement. Again, I found none.

Then I noticed the blinking light on my wristband. Lady was signaling. I tapped a few buttons on my wristband and changed my vision to see through Lady's eyes. She was perched atop a Jullian pine tree overlooking a small grassy field outside the tree line. Westward Galactic was using that small field as a forward operating post. A landed shuttle acted as a base of operations. Several men in security uniforms gave orders to troops and supply men.

One man stood in the tall wild grass of the field. He consulted a holographic map of the surrounding territory from a datapad. The man spoke to three others, intently watching the map. Then all four men abruptly looked skyward and watched a second shuttle land nearby. The cargo door opened, and a ramp extended. A large vehicle rolled out backward from the landed shuttle down the loading ramp. The large, tracked wheels made the vehicle look like a miniature tank. It turned around, revealing twin artillery cannon barrels.

Where were they getting these weapons? Those kinds of machines were not civilian issue, nor were they allowed for civilian use. Westward

Galactic had deep coffers, but they were still a private organization. Only military organizations were allowed the use of such machines. Westward Galactic was pulling out all the stops. And that thought amused me. But why all the heavy-handed tactics? They could easily wait a few days and starve us out. Or why not continue the little skirmishes until we deplete all the power cells in our guns? They acted almost like they were on a tight schedule. As if they needed to overrun our position in a timely fashion. But why would they be in a hurry? They knew something I didn't. Maybe they knew we had help on the way?

Several blast shots rang out from Miri's position on the other end of the ridge. The troops were making another push up the hill. I pressed a button on my wristband, switching my eyesight back to normal. The battery in my tactical mask was nearly spent. I had to hope our help would arrive soon. I hurried along the rocky ridge back toward Miri. I walked around the wide trunk of a great red dallifer tree and stopped cold in my tracks. I wasted all that time looking for signs of troop movement. I should have been looking for something more important.

I swallowed dryly as I stared into the barrel of Bridgette's blast pistol. Her once neatly-set blond hair had been disheveled. A shallow cut on her forehead looked to have stopped bleeding a few hours ago. The dried mud on the side of her face spoke of crawling along the bottom of a riverbed. That would explain why she disappeared from infrared. She did not carry her blast rifle and her blast vest was all torn up and charred. Those were likely a side-effect of the detonator I left for her along our trail. Her blast vest was too torn up to be of any use to her. She hadn't had time to discard it. By the look of her, she had been up all through the night.

"How's the shoulder?" I asked, referring to my shot on our first encounter.

She pulled the trigger.

Her green blast bolt struck me, causing me to stumble backward. A burning pain stung my side just below my ribs. I covered my side with one hand while grabbing onto some brush with the other, keeping me from falling over the ledge. I glanced down at the nasty drop. A few tree branches reached across the precipice, shading the dirt and rocks at the bottom. It looked like several small plants had tried to grow on the incline leading up the cliffside. But the continual sliding dirt and rocks prevented it.

I looked back at Bridgette.

She took a few casual steps closer. "When it comes to you, Rence, I've learned to shoot first and chat second."

Smart woman, I thought.

"Any last words?" she asked.

I guess I wasn't one for clever lines. The first thing that entered my mind involved bad language. The temptation to entertain those words vanished when I thought of Ryna. How would she react if she heard me say them? What if I didn't need to say anything clever? What if all I needed was a little bravado? If I could get her to roll her eyes, or anything to distract her, I would have a chance.

I smiled. "So...a first name basis. Does that mean we're courting now?"

Her eye twitched in exasperated annoyance. Not quite the eye-roll I wanted but it would have to do. I took that moment to let go of the shrub and draw my blast pistol. My hand grabbed a branch of the shrub along with my blast pistol. The tug of the shrub branch stopped my arm from raising my barrel to the proper height. My red blast bolt struck the dirt at Bridgette's feet a fraction of a second before she pulled her trigger again. Her green blast bolt struck me square in the chest, like a punch, pushing me backward over the ledge.

I fell for only a few seconds but it felt like minutes. I saw my entire life flash before my eyes. I saw memories I had forgotten along with ones I remembered quite well. I saw my Wayfinder mentor. Korr's wrinkled and wise eyes would stare at me as if to ask how many times he needed to reiterate his point. Then my mind rested on Miri. I was awful sorry I had let her down. She wouldn't get her camcam ranch now; Bridgette would see to that. Miri had such a great heart. She was willing to get tangled up in all this just to help a ten-year-old girl find her parents. There was no way she could have known what kind of infested waters she would be swimming in. But she knew enough to ask for the help of a Wayfinder. I felt sick inside, knowing I had let her down.

I felt the leaves and branches of the trees scrape and whip me as I passed through them on my way to the ground. The lovely smell of tree sap was spoiled by the smell of burning cloth where Bridgette had shot me. Branches cracked and broke beneath me, sending leaves flying all about. My arm was twisted and yanked hard. The wound in my side screamed at me with throbs. My vision blurred into blackness.

I awoke to a strong throbbing from my right arm. I couldn't move my right hand. I opened my eyes and saw the sun peeking through the leaves. My arm was caught between two limbs of the tree, suspending me in the air. My feet dangled in the morning breeze. I could only have been unconscious for a few minutes. The sun was still low in the morning sky.

I grabbed onto the tree trunk and wrapped my legs around it. I needed to get my arm free from the tree branches. With my free hand, I reached for my blast pistol and felt an empty holster. My blast pistol must have fallen out. It would be somewhere on the rocks below. If I ever found it, it would most likely be in several pieces. The Starfield & Tanners were great guns but a fall like that would irreparably damage them. My Starfield & Tanner set was no longer a set.

I glanced back up at my tangled arm. My second blast pistol was still in my hand. I didn't have any feeling in that hand, but the trigger guard still hugged my finger. Friction kept it in my loose hand. It wasn't a very secure hold. If my hand twitched, it would fall. I reached for it with my good hand, but it was too far away.

The throbbing of my arm intensified. I found a branch above my head and used it to pull myself up a little higher. I reached my good hand through the obstructing limbs and took the blast pistol from my bad hand and holstered it. Then I secured the safety strap. Losing one blast pistol was bad enough. Losing both would be appalling.

I pulled myself up a little higher in the tree, using my legs to support my weight. I still had some feeling in my upper arm and an insane throbbing in my elbow. I gingerly lifted my arm free from the limbs that had caught them and pulled my arm free. It stung as I moved it. The pain was so bad that I considered leaving my arm where it was. Thankfully, I rejected that idea in favor of getting down from this tree. I gradually relaxed my legs and my one good arm which were wrapped around the tree trunk. I slid down the trunk, scraping myself on the tree bark the whole way down. The bark scratched and ruffed up my hand and tore the front of my shirt. I didn't want to know what it did to my britches. That would be a worry for another day. At least my coat sleeves bore the burden gladly; they only showed light wear.

Bridgette's shot to my chest had hit my chest panel. There was no telling if anything was damaged without an inspection. But as long as my heart was still beating, I counted my blessings. My bleeding side, however, was a different matter. I pulled off my bandana and stuffed it into the hole in my shirt, pressing it into my wound. It would stifle the bleeding but not stop it entirely. I tore a piece of my shirt and put it around my waist. It came off easy after the shredding the tree bark gave it. Tying it with only one good hand was a challenge. In the end, I knelt and bent over, using my teeth to help my good hand tie the knot.

I looked back up at the intimidating steep ridge. Climbing up was not going to be easy in my condition. Then a thought crossed my mind. My heart raced and I felt the blood pumping through my neck. Bridgette was up there, and Miri had no idea. I had to warn her somehow. I knelt and rested my bad arm on my leg and pushed a few buttons on my wristband. If my wristband was free from damage, then Lady should get the instruction. Even if she did, how could she warn Miri? I had no choice but to hope Lady and Miri could understand one another. Or maybe I didn't. Ryna had been awful close to Lady recently. Maybe Ryna would be able to understand. Lady was a highly trained falcon, but she wasn't exactly a conversationalist.

Blast shots echoed from the ridge. My heart pounded. Bridgette was just one of Miri's concerns. There were still a bunch of troops and that artillery to worry about. There was no way she could hold out alone. She needed me now more than ever. And I was at the bottom of a cliff. I carefully stuffed my arm into what was left of my shirt. It was a poor excuse for a sling but it would have to do.

I needed to get up the cliff. The fastest way up would be to jump with my special knees. The danger would be in only having one hand to land with. And if I accidentally hit my wounded side, I could lose my grip and tumble back down. I thought of Miri and decided it was worth the risk.

I bent my knees and jumped. The ground fell away from beneath me as I rose into the air. The cliff ledge came up fast and I reached for it. My hand grazed the rocky surface and caught hold of a rock jutting out from the dry soil. My body thumped hard against the side of the cliff. My side throbbed in protest. I lay there a moment, waiting for the throbbing to subside. Instead, the rock I held onto pulled free from the dirt and I tumbled back down the side of the cliff. My injured arm banged against the rocky terrain and I flailed around with my good arm. I desperately grabbed at anything to stop my fall.

After a moment of tumbling and sliding, I found myself once again at the bottom of the ridge. My side pounded in pain and my arm shot waves of torture up my shoulder and into my neck. The pounding and throbbing were all I could think of. My vision blacked out again.

I opened my eyes to find myself lying on a bed. It was the bed I used to sleep on when I was in Wayfinder training, back on Onida Prime. This couldn't be right. How could I be here? I sat up and kicked the covers off. This must be a dream. I was alone in a dimly lit room. I recognized it. It served as my study and bedroom so many years ago. The sloppy décor and messy machine table were familiar. My Windancer Special blast pistol lay on the desk. It was my first blast pistol. I had lost it my second year as a Wayfinder.

The door opened and a tall thin man stepped into the room. His wide-brimmed hat and long gray coat looked just how I remembered. His seldom-shaved rugged face and aged eyes stared at me through the dim light. It was Korr, my mentor. He would often visit me within the late hours when he saw I had been struggling. His kind voice and wise words always comforted me and gave me new direction.

This night was different than the rest. This was the night after my fifth setback. I had been the most discouraged at that point in my life. I had been close to giving up on learning the ways of the Wayfinders. Even though I never mentioned it, Korr sensed it. He knew that at that time what I needed most of all was inspiration.

"Rence," he said in his old, scratchy voice.

"I am here," I answered.

"I brought someone I felt you should meet." He stepped inside my room and another man stepped inside behind him. My breathing halted and my heart raced, just as it had all those years ago. I knew the second man who entered my room. I knew him then and I knew him still. His black hat and long coat were not what identified him. His two pearl-handled blast pistols and the red sash around his waist were clues. But the real tip-off was his tactical mask. Every mask was hand-made by a master, and so each one looked unique.

I knew this man as Aundoon the Great. He had been a legend in his own time before he became a legend in my time. He was the first. All that I learned about the code and the principles to live by as a Wayfinder were founded by him.

Aundoon walked past Korr and strolled up beside my bed. I stood out of respect but he only motioned for me to sit back down. He sat beside me.

"What troubles you, young man?" he asked, his voice slightly muffled behind his mask.

I swallowed, unsure how to answer. "I failed," I finally said. "Miri needed me and I let my guard down. My broken body is now at the base of a cliff. I am unable to reach her." I felt moisture in my eyes. I sniffled. "And poor Ryna, she's only ten years old..."

Aundoon took off his mask.

There was understanding in his old eyes. He took my hand and held it close to my mouth. The faint breeze from my breath tickled the hairs on the back of my hand.

"What do you feel?" he asked.

"My breath?" I answered, unsure if I was giving the correct answer.

Then he moved my hand against my chest. "And now what do you feel?"

"...my heart?"

He nodded. "Wayfinders are not immortal. You cannot be everywhere and you cannot save everyone. But as long as you have breath, and as long as your heart beats, you have not yet failed."

My breathing intensified as I felt a warmth come over me. It was like his words infused meaning into my heart. I was a Wayfinder. I had not sworn to succeed; I had sworn to do my best.

Aundoon placed his tactical mask on my face. "You must see from a different angle," he said, clamping it in place.

A surge of confidence rushed through me, and I began to recite the Wayfinder Code from memory.

"With every breath I take, this vow I do make. My heart is clean and selfless, my gun defends the defenseless. My cunning defeats the strong, my deeds right what is wrong. My soul has the will and thus I pray, grant me the vision to find the way."

"You must hurry," Aundoon said. "Miri needs you."

The roar of a shuttle passing overhead startled me back to consciousness. I sat up, feeling the tactical mask on my face. *I have breath,* I said to myself. *And my heart does beat. I do not give in to defeat!*

I looked up. The sun was only a little higher in the sky. With any luck, I still had time to help Miri. The shuttle overhead flew past my field of vision from the base of the cliff. I couldn't see how many new troops were joining the fray. But I desperately needed to get back up there. I glanced at the ground where I sat. My hat lay there like an old friend encouraging me. I smiled, putting it on.

I used my bruised but still-good arm to gently place my bad arm back into my shirt. I rolled onto my knees and my arm fell out of my shirt. I groaned in pain as the flopping of my arm produced more throbs of torture.

I bit my fist, struggling to keep myself conscious. As soon as the throbbing subsided again, I put my arm back into my shirt. I shoved it in further this time. I looked up at the cliff high overhead and heard the sound of blast fire. I gritted my teeth and started the slow ascent up the shear rocky surface. I felt around the rocks above me with my good hand, searching for rocks solid enough to hold my weight. Little by little, I scooted up the side of the steep incline.

The muscles in my one good arm protested every step of the way. I pressed on, scaling the cliff face like a slow-moving insect. One carefully-placed hand at a time, I made my way up the steep rock. When I reached the top, I grabbed the shrub that had earlier both steadied me and betrayed me. I had returned to the very spot before I fell. I did not stop to tempt fate or gravity; I pulled myself the rest of the way to the top of the ridge.

I sat at the base of the great red dallifer tree, catching my breath. Some motion to my right caught my attention. Four soldiers crept over the ridge toward Miri's position, their blast rifles poised to shoot. From their angle, they would be able to shoot Miri from behind. That was the one thing I attempted to stop when I wandered away from her. I drew my blast pistol and aimed at the first soldier. It would do no good to aim for the center of mass or the head. Their blast vests and helmets were too strong for my blast pistol. So, I aimed for the shoulders. A solid hit to a shoulder would hurt enough. And it would render them unable to shoot their blast rifle with any degree of accuracy.

My red blast bolt shot through the shrubs and exploded into the shoulder of the closest soldier. He cried out in pain, dropping his rifle and clutching his shoulder. The other three shot wildly toward Miri's position, unaware of where the shot had come from.

I fired again, nailing the second soldier, taking him also out of the fight. The others were more observant the second time and fired in my general direction. I slouched a little more down the side of the tree trunk, obscuring my outline in the shade. I fired again. The third man fell to the side, dropping his blast rifle.

Once again, I had broken the cardinal rule of sniping. I had fired more than two shots from a single position. The last soldier knew where I was and fired a steady stream of green blast bolts at me, peppering the tree trunk. I poked my head around the trunk to fire a shot but was forced to retreat to safety. The soldier had me pinned down against the tree and he was circling for a better shot. Maybe I could toss a detonator at him? No, that soldier was too quick on the trigger for me to show my face. And the wound in my side warned me against risky moves. I couldn't afford to get shot again. What I needed was to follow the advice of Aundoon the Great and find a new angle.

My eyes lit up. My thoughts buzzed with excitement. *A new angle!*

I reached my hand into my shirt and gently pressed a few buttons on my wristband. My eyesight darkened. Green geometry lines and angles overlaid the scene. I didn't have the same luck I did on Cosstere. The first day I met Ryna I had to bounce a shot to strike a Davendry at a watering hole. I was lucky then that a nice flat rock was behind the man I shot at. This time I wasn't so lucky. The shot would be much harder.

The geometry lines calculated a moment. Then they showed me a complicated ricochet. It utilized the soldier's shiny helmet and the barrel of one of the fallen blast rifles. A shot like that would be a one-in-ten chance of success. I didn't accept those odds, so I decided to substitute my own.

I aimed at the approximate location the soldier would appear as he circled around to get an angle on me. I held my aim steady as the white helmet and visor stepped into view. I fired ten times. As soon as my first two blast bolts flew in his direction, he ducked to the side. I adjusted my aim, following the geometry lines as I squeezed off the last eight shots. One of my red blast bolts nailed him in the shoulder and he dropped to the ground groaning.

The battery light on my tactical mask flashed as my vision suddenly went black. My mask was all out of power. I took it off and tucked it away in my inner coat pocket. I forced myself to my feet in a single surge of exertion. I stood a moment, allowing for a dizzy spell to pass. Then I walked forward toward Miri's location. A light-blue blast bolt flew at me. I ducked, waving my hat in the air. Miri was probably expecting more troops and shot at me reflexively.

"Rence!" she called, rushing up to me with Ryna close behind her. Her white gown fluttered as she ran. She looked like an angel with a gun.

She ran into my open arm. I grunted at the pain when she collided with my arm slung in my shirt. She reeled back in fright, noticing my wound.

"What happened?" she frantically demanded. "I was afraid you weren't coming back."

"I'll always come back for you, Miri."

"Where did you go? Couldn't you hear me calling your name?"

"I hope you'll understand if I save this conversation for later," I said, putting my hat back on. "Let's get back into position."

A loud *boom* sounded in the distance. Seconds later, the spot Miri was guarding exploded. Rocks, dirt, and foliage flew into the air. We instinctively ducked as dirt and pebbles rained down upon us.

"On second thought," I said, suddenly remembering the artillery below.

I turned around. Another assault shuttle flew over the ridge. It dropped rope lines for troops to slide down.

I turned to Miri. "Where's the carbine?"

She shook her head. "I used it all up."

I bit my tongue, not wanting to curse around Ryna. "How's your blast pistol's power cell?"

"I'm almost out."

I looked back at the exploded ledge where the artillery shot had landed. "A different angle," I muttered. I motioned for Miri to crouch down. "Stay here, I'll be back." I held my bad arm against my body as I ran toward the half-destroyed ledge. I didn't trust my arm to stay slung in my shirt when I ran. And right now, I needed to run. The troops would start exiting the shuttle in moments.

I skidded to a stop overlooking trees at the bottom of the hill. The large artillery vehicle noticed me and turned, angling itself in my direction. I glanced back at the assault shuttle and quickly side-stepped a few paces. The artillery rotated, following me. I stepped up onto a large rock, completely exposing myself. The artillery hesitated. Why? Were they wising up to what I was planning? Or were they just suspicious? Well, I knew a remedy for both. I drew my blast pistol and aimed for the artillery's forward window.

I fired. My red blast bolt bounced off the shiny blast window but it left a nice black mark. I couldn't see too well at that distance but if my aim was right, it should have struck right in front of the gunner's face. The gunner knew he was safe behind the blast window. My blast pistol shots were not strong enough to punch through. It wasn't a threat; it was a blatant insult.

Less than a heartbeat later, the artillery cannon fired. Its large green blast cannon bolt flew straight at me. I jumped up with my knees, letting the cannon shot fly past and strike the assault shuttle. The troops had barely begun mounting the ropes when the cannon shot slammed into the side. The explosion threw the shuttle to the side. It smoked as it drifted over the side of the ridge and crashed into the trees below, erupting in a ball of flames.

I landed back onto the rocky ground with a *thud.* My knees absorbed the shock but the sharp jerk on my bad arm stung. I gasped in pain, clutching my bad arm. Then I heard the artillery fire again. Instinctively I jumped to the side and landed against a tree trunk. The wound in my side screamed at me in throbs. The ground I was previously standing on exploded from the artillery shot. Once again, dirt and pebbles rained down.

Miri ran to me. She tore off a long strip of the hem of her white gown and tied it around my bad arm. At my insistence, she tied it down tight so it would not move. Next, she opened my coat, searching for any more injuries.

She gasped in fright. "You're bleeding!"

"Most of me is still flesh and blood," I playfully chided.

She tore off another strip of her gown's hem and tied it around me just below my ribs. "Do me a favor and stop getting shot."

"You're preaching to the choir, Miri."

"Where's your mask?"

"Batteries," I complained, struggling to my feet.

My muscles felt comfortable while I sat. Now that I wanted to use them again, they complained with soreness. If I rested too long, I might not be able to get back to my feet. I holstered my blast pistol and reached into my coat pocket. I pulled out two detonators. They were cracked. A few pieces of the casing fell away in my hands. My fall must have been more brutal on my detonators. I dropped them and pulled out another two. One was smashed, and the other had a large crack but still looked intact. I needed two. I sifted for another in my coat. I had a few more broken detonators with only one more that looked promising.

"I really should have bought the better-quality casing."

"Are those big enough to blow up that large cannon down there?"

"No," I admitted. "But it'll discourage anyone from using it."

Another blast from the artillery echoed through the air. Another section of the ridge exploded. I ducked, lowering the brim of my hat against the raining dirt and pebbles.

"Please be safe," Miri said, holding onto my arm.

I chuckled despite myself. "Nothing about today has been even remotely safe."

She kissed me. "Promise me you'll be careful then?"

I nodded. "You can count on it."

I jumped over the destroyed ledge, and down the hill toward the artillery. I landed on the roof of the vehicle. My bad arm complained a bit from the landing but behaved itself. Miri's makeshift sling worked well. I dropped to one knee and reached down, placing one of the detonators on the artillery's blast window. The stunned driver and gunner glanced at my detonator through the window. Little lights blinked as the nine-second timer counted down.

They stared at the detonator, dumbfounded. I didn't put much stock in the theory of evolution, but I could have sworn those two were somehow related to possums. I leaned over and looked through the blast window at them. They regarded my upside-down head with startled confusion.

"Hey morons!" I shouted. "It's an explosive!"

In a wild panic, they opened the side doors and bailed out of the artillery vehicle. I tossed my second detonator through the open door and jumped away. I sailed high through the air and landed back on top of the ridge. The cab of the artillery exploded twice at the base of the hill, a fire burning inside.

I groaned as my arm once again complained about my rough landing. I dropped to my knees in exhaustion. Miri ran over and hugged me. "Is it over?"

I sighed and sank into her embrace, my tired muscles wanting desperately to rest. And I was thirsty. Ever so thirsty. I panted, trying to catch my breath. With my good hand, I brushed aside her curly locks and gazed into her eyes.

Lady screeched from high above.

I tensed up, my heart racing. I shoved Miri back as Bridgette's blast bolt struck me square in the chest for the second time. I fell on my back and Miri drew her blast pistol, shooting. Bridgette dove for cover, firing back.

I took shallow breaths. My heart thumped erratically. Something was wrong. The second shot to my chest panel damaged something inside. I put my good hand to my chest, trying to slow my heart rate. It beat in an unnatural rhythm. In front of me, I heard the exchange of blast shots. Miri was pretty good for one so new to gunfights. Her advantage was that she already knew how to shoot straight. That alone put Bridgette on the defensive.

I reached out and found a pine sapling near me. I grabbed it and pulled myself into a sitting position. I was fast losing the feeling in my legs. My blood wasn't circulating as it needed to. My breaths grew longer and slower. I did bring a couple of tools with me. I reached for my coat pocket to retrieve them. I couldn't reach far enough. My arm was slowly losing range of motion.

I suddenly heard a clicking sound up ahead. I glanced up. Miri's blast pistol was empty. Bridgette slowly rose from her prone position in the tall weeds with a wicked smile across her face. She dropped her blast pistol's power cell and slapped in a new one.

Miri didn't have that luxury. In our haste, we hadn't had time to fashion a replacement power cell for her new gun. That was the unfortunate downside to custom weapons. Their accessories were not standardized. Bridgette took a few confident steps forward. Her smile reflected inward gloating over the look of horror in Miri's eyes.

She raised her gun, aiming at Miri's head.

"Freeze!" I yelled.

Bridgette glanced over at me.

"You might not like talking much, but I sure do. And quite frankly, I am appalled at your manners."

"How are you still alive?" she asked in wonder.

"That's the wrong question, Bridgette. The question you should be asking is how much do you want to live?"

She looked at me with a critical eye and then burst into laughter. "You're in no shape for a gunfight. Look at you. You're pale from blood loss and you can hardly move. You're practically dead already."

"I'm only going to give you this one chance to walk away breathing. Don't waste it."

She smiled, "I fell for your bluff once, Rence. I won't fall for it again. False bravado can't save you this time. But don't you fret, I'll finish you in a moment."

She turned her attention back to Miri and aimed for her head.

My hand jerked in a reflex action, my blast pistol clearing leather and firing. My red blast bolt punched into Bridgette's chest, ignoring the shredded remains of her blast vest. She stumbled backward with a surprised look on her face. I fired again. She dropped to her knees and fell backward.

My mind started to cloud over, my thoughts getting muggy. I gasped for a breath and fell again on my back. Miri rushed to my side and cradled my head.

"Pocket..." I hissed the words out with what little air was left in my lungs.

Tears rolled down her face as she searched my coat pockets. She pulled out the tools I had brought and knew what to do. She dropped my head to the ground and then quickly apologized.

I tried to roll my eyes but was unsure of my results. Miri opened my chest panel and went to work trying to patch me back together for the third time. A spark popped from my chest panel, startling her. She glanced at Ryna. "Please calm me," she pleaded.

I laid my head back against the ground, the little weeds tickling my ears and neck. I didn't know how bad it was. I had usually been unconscious when she worked on me. I could only hope there was something she could do. She had patched me up twice before. Maybe this would be no exception. Then again, I had dodged fate twice before. What were the odds I'd cheat death a third time? I rolled my head to the side and looked at Ryna. She stared at me with tears in her eyes. Her question came back to my mind. The question of my death. I still didn't have any idea if there was a life afterward and I didn't care. All I cared about was who I would be leaving behind. Miri and Ryna were closer than friends to me. They were the closest thing to family that I had.

I reached out my good hand toward Ryna. She cautiously approached and took my hand. I stared into her eyes. "Don't fret, little miss," I said, my voice barely above a whisper.

"I don't want you to go," she said sullenly. "You are going to be the pa."

Tears fell from Miri's eyes as she frantically worked. There were more than tears in her eyes, there was frustration also. Bridgette must have made a real mess inside. Miri put a tool between her teeth as she reached inside with both hands. My eyes drifted heavenward. Another two shuttles approached. They swung wide around both ends of the ridge, dropping ropes.

I felt a sharp electric jolt in my chest. It felt like someone stabbing me with a sharp needle. I tensed up, arching my back.

"Sorry, Rence."

I struggled to keep my eyes open. "No worries, with all I'm putting you through, I probably had it coming."

A quick smile burst through her worried expression. It was almost a laugh, but not quite. She glanced into my eyes only briefly before refocusing on her work.

The troops were cautiously closing in, blast rifles poised. Ryna glanced to the side, noticing the advancing troops. Three more shuttles roared overhead. They lowered to the ground and opened the side doors. Men poured out with blast pistols and rifles.

Another spark popped in my chest panel, startling Miri. I flinched, taking in a deep breath. My heart started again to beat in rhythm. Miri looked at me with wide eyes. Her eyes searched my expression, wanting an answer.

"You did it, Miri."

She breathed out in relief, letting new tears run down her face.

"Reach for the sky," a gruff soldier's voice ordered.

Miri raised her arms and turned around. A dozen soldiers stood with their blast rifles ready to shoot. Behind them, a larger mass of men with weapons swarmed in. There were too many to continue fighting.

"Reach for the sky, you rats," another voice sneered.

"I can't," I protested, pushing myself into a seated position.

"He ain't talkin' to you," said a slightly muffled but familiar voice.

I hadn't noticed it before, but the men standing behind the front row of troops didn't wear blast vests and helmets. They looked more like a motley band than an organized militia. Blue sashes around their waists waved in the afternoon breeze. They each wore blast belts low for a quick draw. Several faces looked familiar.

My eyes scanned the group looking for the familiar muffled voice. I didn't have to search hard. The bulk from his full set of blast armor stood out, a faint ray of sunlight reflecting off the dark glass of his helmet. After spending an entire evening shooting up the inside of a Corporation starcruiser, I would recognize Anruk anywhere.

"You can lower your hands, Miri. That last order was directed at the Westward Galactic troops."

The soldiers looked behind, noticing they were the ones being addressed. The leader of the squad of Corporate troops shot an annoyed glare at them. "Aren't you Davendries a little far from Cosstere?"

One Davendry glanced at his band of men. "Well, well, the company man knows his geography."

The rest of the Davendries laughed.

The squad leader scowled. "That's stellar cartography, hog-brain. Now you and your boys had better get. This is an internal affair."

The Davendry chuckled to himself. "I guess you didn't see the badge, company man." He gestured to a shiny metal six-pointed star pinned to his red silk shirt.

The squad leader snorted. "You expect me to believe that a bunch of hooligans have been deputized by a colonial marshal?"

The Davendry chuckled again, addressing his band. "Oh, that's real cute. The company man knows his celestial stars but can't tell his legal stars apart." His men all laughed again.

"That ain't a colonial star," I said, stealing everyone's attention. "Colonial marshals have a five-point star. The six-point star is a federal marshal."

"That's right, company man. My boys here are officially a federal posse."

The squad leader motioned with his head and his troops turned around to face the crowd of Davendries. "Posse or no posse. Everyone knows the marshals are spread thin. We have another fifty troops on their way here in a few minutes. Now, if you don't stand down, we'll waste you and have it all cleaned up before supper."

"Not anymore, you don't," Anruk calmly replied.

"Don't what?"

He took a few nonchalant steps forward. "The reinforcements you speak of. They ain't coming."

The squad leader tapped his wristband. "Hawk 7, Hawk 6. What is your status? Over." He paused waiting for a reply.

I shewed away a fly that buzzed about my face.

A worried look escaped his controlled expression. "Hawk 6, come in!"

A slightly garbled voice finally responded. "Negative. Your six is uh...*occupied* at the moment. But please give my regards to Anruk when you see him. Out."

The other soldiers looked at the squad leader nervously.

"Well?" Anruk asked. "Are you gonna comply...or resist?"

The squad leader gritted his teeth and stared at Anruk, considering.

Three men crested the ridge from the hill just behind Miri and me. It was Mik walking behind two other men. The first was familiar: a tall man that was past his prime with a bushy mustache. He wore a metal five-point star badge. He was Marshal Corval, the colonial marshal assigned to the westward colony worlds of this region. Due to the vast territory he covered, it was rare to see him. The other man, I didn't know. He was young, wearing a blue uniform with a six-point star badge.

"Anruk?" Marshal Corval asked.

Anruk walked over to him. "Sir?"

He pointed to the blue-uniformed man beside him. "This is Federal Marshal Dane. I believe you spoke over transmission."

Anruk nodded. "Marshal."

"Why haven't you arrested these men yet?" Marshal Dane casually asked.

"I was giving them a chance to resist."

"Very funny," he said, motioning to the Davendries. "Take them into custody."

The troops set their rifles down and the Davendries surrounded them. Mik rushed over to me. "Rence, I had a feeling you were involved in this."

I smiled. "Thanks for responding so quickly to my message."

"Message?"

"Yeah, the message I sent by hyperwave broadcast. You had to have seen it, how else did you bring the cavalry?"

Mik scratched his chin. "My hyperwave receiver has been broken the last few days. I haven't gotten around to fixing it yet."

I motioned toward the Davendries. "Then what's all this?"

"Anruk heard that Marshal Corval was organizing a posse to arrest a private militia. When I heard it was Westward Galactic, I was afraid for you."

"Thanks, Mik."

"Rence Perry," an authoritative voice called from behind Mik.

Marshal Dane walked up.

I glanced at Mik and Miri. "Help me up?"

"Not the shoulder," Miri cautioned Mik.

They hoisted me to my feet. The wound in my side throbbed and my shoulder was equally vying for my attention. Miri held onto my good arm, steadying me. "Marshal Dane," I replied.

"You're a very wanted man."

"Well–"

"And I'm not just talking about being the last Wayfinder still at large," He explained. "In one month, the price on your head has increased six times. Three Westward Galactic starcruisers canvased the outer region colonies looking for you. And the illegal militia activity surged."

"I guess I should be flattered."

"When this came across my desk, I knew whatever you had stolen was something big. Westward Galactic doesn't commit that many resources to anything trivial."

"What is it you think I stole?"

"It could have been anything. Your record is clean aside from not turning in your badge and seal. And normally one man is not worth the time or the federal resources. It's more efficient to let the bounty hunters take care of it."

"Then what got you interested enough to stop by?"

He smiled. "I was out in this region investigating another matter when we picked up on an anonymous signal. A data leak sent over hyperwave. It contained a large collection of files on a covert project involving children. It detailed violations of four federal laws and two sanctions."

I glanced over to Miri. It was her idea to transmit the Osurious project files along with our call for help. Listening to her had just saved our lives. I turned back to Marshal Dane. "Pretty lucky break for you then."

"You don't happen to own a hyperwave transmitter, do you?"

I smiled. "Something tells me you don't ask questions you don't already know the answers to."

He smiled.

I glanced down the hill at the burning artillery. "If Westward Galactic got wind of your arrival, that would explain why they were in such a hurry to flush us out."

"As I said, you're a very wanted man."

I decided to change the subject. "So, how did you get the Davendries to join your posse?"

"I didn't. They volunteered."

I wrinkled my brow in confusion. I didn't remember the Davendries doing anything for free. I had to bribe Tess to get her help. Either they were getting something out of it, or something had changed in Tess.

He read the confusion on my face and continued. "I'll need your testimony in court."

I blinked. Was he crazy? I've been on the run from Westward Galactic because I stole Ryna. It was no walk in the park by any stretch. But if Westward Galactic found out I was going to testify against them in a federal trial that could shut down the entire corporation...

I took a deep breath. "You want me to testify against the largest financial corporation this side of the core worlds?"

"Yes," he said, sounding as if he expected my reply. "And I'm authorized to offer you a full pardon for not turning in your badge and seal. We can also send out a public statement that Westward Galactic can no longer pay the bounty on your head. That should keep the bounty hunters off your back."

I shook my head. "Not good enough. I can't continue to keep us alive without being a Wayfinder."

He took a breath and stared into my eyes, contemplating.

Behind him, another shuttle approached the top of the ridge. It turned to the side and opened the large side door. Two men and one woman hopped out onto the rocky weeds. Tess Davendry started walking toward us with two of her men. I turned my eyes back to Marshal Dane.

He shrugged and pulled off his six-point star badge. "Then I guess I'll just have to deputize you." He pinned the badge on my coat.

"Deputizing an outlaw?" I asked in confusion.

"Deputizing a Wayfinder," he replied. "The courts can dispute the ramifications at their leisure."

I smiled. "And I thought you said I was the clever one."

"Well, I didn't say you were the *only* clever one." He tipped his hat. "Good day, Mr. Perry—and don't disappear."

I nodded. "You have my word."

Marshal Dane walked off to talk with Marshal Corval. Tess and her two men walked up. She looked me up and down. "I knew you could take care of yourself, Rence, but if I knew you were trying to prove me wrong, I would have come quicker."

I smiled. "What kept you?"

"Corporate starcruiser didn't think we were serious."

I smiled. "I'm sure you cured them of that ailment."

She smiled.

"I hear you volunteered," I said. "Was it a change of heart or do you simply have a soft spot for me?"

"I guess you could say it was the *hope* of a change of heart."

I glanced down.

She gave an uncomfortable smile, eyeing Miri and her dress. "This must be the lucky one. And by the look of it, I'd say congratulations are in order?"

Miri smiled warmly. "Thank you. You will come, won't you?"

"You're already dressed for it," she observed. "Looks like all you need is the parson."

"They probably will want to wait a few weeks for Rence to heal first," Mik said.

"No," I said, suddenly aware that Miri had objected at the same moment.

We exchanged a glance before she replied. "With how many times we almost lost the opportunity these last few weeks; we'd rather not tempt fate by waiting."

Tess turned to the man at her right. "Manny, take the shuttle into town and bring the local pastor. Pay him whatever it takes."

He nodded and left.

I turned to Miri. "It's probably a bit last-minute, but is there someone I should ask permission from?"

She pursed her lips and shook her head.

I had always considered myself the old-fashioned type. Somehow it didn't seem right to marry her without asking permission first. I looked around and spotted Ryna. I gently dropped to one knee and beckoned to her. She ran to my side.

I took my hat off. "Little miss, seein' as you know how I fancy Miss Miri and all, what would you say to me marrying her?"

She hesitated a moment. "Will I get to be the daughter?"

I smiled and brushed her cheek with my hand. "You can bet your britches on that."

She beamed. "Then yes, you can marry Miss Miri."

I winked at her. "Thanks, partner."

I stood and turned to Mik. "Now we just need someone to fetch Petre and Carol."

I had heard of fast weddings before. And I had heard about short engagements too. If anyone was keeping track, I reckon Miri and I broke all the records. Somehow the setup was perfect. Anruk removed his helmet while serving as my best man. Tess, Carol, and Ryna were Miri's bride's maids. And Mik gave Miri away. Marshal Corval and Marshal Dane even offered to certify the event. And despite the damage caused by the artillery, Ryna was still able to find enough wildflowers to make Miri a bouquet.

After the preacher concluded the pronouncement, the Davendries and Anruk's Kuda all fired their blast pistols in the air. Then I gave Miri the kind of kiss I had longed to give her. The kind that promised her my heart and mind. I still didn't think I deserved Miri. But that didn't matter anymore. She was mine and I was hers. And both of us had Ryna.

The only downside was spending the wedding night in a hospital room. The pain medication kept me only half aware of my surroundings. It wasn't ideal but with the amount of blood I had lost, it sure was a good idea. The good news was that I hadn't broken any bones. My arm had been badly twisted, but it turned out all right in a few weeks.

Our first destination after leaving the hospital was Cosstere. Miri truly did want to ranch camcams though she was hesitant to ask me about settling down on Cosstere. She didn't need to worry, I meant what I said when I told her I would wrangle camcams alongside her. When I told her that, she looked into my eyes and announced how she was the luckiest person alive. I didn't argue with her aloud, but I knew for certain every time I laid eyes on Miri that I was the lucky one.

Epilogue

I pulled the reins hard left. The smelly riding lizard snorted and ignored me. I tugged left again and kicked my heels. The camcam snorted again and plucked a mouthful of wild brush from the rocky ground. I swear, these dumb brutes were smarter than they let on. This one was particularly aware when I was trying to get him moving. It was like the dull beast could sense my inexperience. It acted like the schoolboy that knew how to exploit the substitute teacher.

"Now you listen here, Oli. Miri made me promise to stop shooting your tail. But she didn't say anything about not using detonators."

The camcam stopped chewing and raised its head.

"That's right, I'm talkin' to you."

"Rence!" a voice called out behind me.

It was Miri, riding in on a camcam. She was probably coming to find out what was taking me so long. The yellow sun was starting to set, giving way for the cool red sun to rise in its place. That meant I was late for supper again.

I leaned over and whispered to Oli. "This ain't over yet." I slid off the back of the camcam and landed on the dusty ground, walking over to Miri. "Yes, my daisy?"

She smiled. "What's taking you so long? I would have thought you'd have the studs in the barn by now."

"Well, you asked me to stop shooting them."

She gave me a playful scowl. "Thanks for not shooting them."

A low moan from a distant camcam caught my attention. Ryna rode in quickly on a camcam–which was saying a lot for those lumbering lizards. She had five other camcams following beside her. Her hair was now down past her shoulders and waved in the breeze. Her blue dress fluttered.

I had told her at least a dozen times not to work in a dress. She loved wearing dresses and there wasn't much I could do to dissuade her. When I pointed out that the dress might tear, she told me she knew how to mend it. My son, Alder, sat on the camcam behind her, waving his hat around in excitement. He and his sister were inseparable.

As the camcams drew near, I cupped my hands around my mouth and shouted. "Ryna, take Oli with you!"

She nodded and veered toward us. Miri dismounted and walked up beside me, putting her arm around mine. "What's on your mind?"

I hadn't noticed I was staring at Ryna. I turned to Miri. "If only she could stop growing up so fast."

She tensed up. "Speaking of which..."

I rolled my eyes. "Don't tell me farmer Yewing's boy has been calling on her again."

"Rence–"

"I said no, and I mean no. She won't be sixteen for another three months. Surely the boy can wait another ninety days."

Ryna rode up alongside us and stopped. "Hey, Pa. That new foreman of yours accidentally let out your gerbils."

I glanced heavenward. I had been meaning to fix that door but hadn't yet gotten around to it. With the well pump going out and the northern condensators on the fritz, I hadn't given much attention to the mice. "They're not gerbils, they're Telurian mice. They're Lady's favorite."

Ryna shrugged. "Maybe it's better to have them on the loose. Maybe Lady might like catching them herself."

"I know, but your Ma and I already discussed it and she doesn't want any rodents in the garden."

"Oh," Ryna said as if remembering something important. She handed down a datapad. "Kipp said you would want to see this morning's paper."

I took the datapad. The headline read, WESTWARD GALACTIC FINANCIAL CORPORATION PRESIDENT CHIP HOSSK AND LEAD SCIENTIST DR. VIK LENISH INDICTED IN LANDMARK RULING AGAINST THE CORPORATION.

I smiled real wide. "Then it's finally over."

"Be sure to read page sixteen too."

I glanced up with a curious expression.

"I think that reporter that was snooping around here last week had something to do with it."

"The one I run off?"

"No, the lady Ma let in."

"I wonder what she said about me," I grumbled, scrolling down to page sixteen. The headline read, SENATE TO CONVENE OVER DISCUSSIONS TO REVERSE WAYFINDER BAN IN THE WAKE OF WESTWARD GALACTIC RULING.

I smiled.

"It's a good thing you listened to Ma and didn't run her off too."

I blushed. "Listening to your Ma has been some of the smartest things I've done."

A small shuttle flew overhead and landed a short distance away. The shuttle was a civilian model. Probably one of the newer Shelby classes. They were built for comfort and style. That put them on the more expensive side of the market.

A middle-aged man and woman stepped out and walked across the dusty field to us. He wore a dark suit and tall boots. His hat was fancy with brass buttons around the band. The woman at his side looked like his wife, wearing a fancy green dress and a feathered hat.

"Mr. and Mrs. Perry, I presume?"

"That all depends on who's asking," I replied.

"The name's Pennington. I hope you don't mind, a mutual friend told me where I could find you. My wife and I are in real need of help."

"What kind of help?"

"The kind of help that requires the last Wayfinder."

"It's about our daughter," the woman added in a mournful voice.

"When do we leave?" Miri asked.

Of course, Miri wasn't asking, she was telling me she was on board with helping these folks out. Since she had kept up with her practice, she wasn't far behind me.

I turned to Ryna. "Tell Vix and the rest of the ranch hands—along with that new foreman—that we'll be gone a few days."

"Sure thing, Pa."

"We?" Mr. Pennington asked. "It was my understanding that you were the last Wayfinder."

"You're in luck, Mr. Pennington. Now there are two."

About the Author

Benjamin Boekweg

Some men see things as they are, and say why. I dream of things that never were, and say why not. – Robert Kennedy

I was born a long time ago, in a galaxy far, far away...okay maybe not—but you've got to admit it would be pretty sweet to claim that! It would certainly make for a more interesting introduction. My name is Benjamin, and I love to tell stories of far away and the impossible. I enjoy a good sci-fi space opera or time travel story. My first introduction to fantasy was Brandon Sanderson, and I fell in love with his books. I simply love Sanderson's Rules of Magic.

Clean language? Why not? This is science fiction and fantasy; I can make up whatever words the characters use for "harsh language" and it doesn't have to offend me or my readers.

Buckle up; there's no Walmart where we're headed... My stories reside far outside the realm of normal modern life. They don't explore what we know, but what could be out there.

I believe the best stories are the ones that can send your emotions on a roller coaster and provide some humor as well.

Website: https://benjaminboekweg.com

You may also enjoy my other book:
Aberrant Star: Knights of the Solar Winds, Book One

www.ingramcontent.com/pod-product-compliance
Lightning Source LLC
Chambersburg PA
CBHW020459310726
48979CB00016B/2718/J
* 9 7 9 8 9 8 6 1 4 4 2 2 1 *